THE WRONG MAN

OTHER TITLES BY NATASHA ANDERS

The Unwanted Wife

A Husband's Regret

His Unlikely Lover

A Ruthless Proposition

The Wingman

The Best Man

This is a work of fiction. Names, characters, organizations
incidents are either products of the author's imagination

Published by Montlake Romance, Seattle

www.apub.com

ISBN-13: 9781503901773
ISBN-10: 1503901777

Cover design by Eileen Carey

Printed in the United States of America

I dedicate this book to my father, David Anders. Dude, seriously, you don't have to read all my books. Just keep them on a shelf and show them to your friends occasionally. Thanks for supporting my writing "hobby" when I was growing up. Love you.

PROLOGUE

Dahlia McGregor was trying to avoid a guy. Not just any guy, but the sinfully sexy man she'd stupidly fallen into bed with a week ago. He definitely wasn't her type; she wasn't sure why she'd done it. He was way too . . . *everything*. Too sexy, too arrogant, too male, and *way* too alpha. Lia liked nice guys, the quiet types who shied away from confrontation. After being engaged to a pompous, selfish, vain peacock of a man, Lia was looking for someone sweet and pleasant and comfortable.

But there was no avoiding someone when you were in the same bridal party. When he was head groomsman to your head bridesmaid. He stood opposite her in the church, beside her in every picture, and would soon be sitting next to her at the wedding reception.

"So last week was fun," Sam Brand, the guy in question, murmured into her ear, his gravelly voice more than a little smug. Lia shot him an appalled look. How could he be bringing that up *here* while they were posing for the group picture? Where anybody could hear him?

The ceremony had been beautiful, of course. Perfect and romantic, everything that Lia had once hoped hers would be. Lia's youngest sister, Daisy, and her new husband Mason's vows—which they had written themselves—hadn't left a dry eye in the crowd. Lia was happy for Daisy, yet she couldn't help but feel a stab of envy as well. If Clayton had been a better man—the *right* man—Lia could have been the one exchanging vows with someone who treasured her and loved her above all else. Instead, this was her sister's wedding and Lia was saddled next to *this* man—who was interested in nothing but bedding her—for the duration. And he kept making excuses to touch her and *breathe* on her and rub against her, and now he was speaking to her.

About something that he'd promised never to talk about again. The biggest—okay, maybe second-biggest—mistake of Lia's life.

"We're not discussing that here," she whispered, keeping her eyes straight ahead. "Or ever again."

"C'mon, Dahlia. I'm leaving tomorrow, and since Daisy and Mason are moving, it's not likely you'll ever see me again. I'm single, you're single—"

"So help me, if you say 'Let's mingle'—"

"Let me make you tingle," he finished, ignoring her interruption. She gasped, fighting back unwanted images of her stupid, drunken mistake last week. It was completely uncharacteristic, and she was not going to repeat it. No matter how great he smelled right now, how enticing that roguish grin was, or how mind-blowingly fantastic his body was beneath that tuxedo.

None of that mattered. Lia learned from her mistakes, and there were a lot of truly nice men here today. She glanced over at Sam Brand and caught him staring at her breasts and fought the urge to cover herself up with her hands. Lots of nice men here who were interested in more than just her boobies.

The photographer now wanted shots of just the bridal couple, and as the rest of them heaved relieved sighs and turned to walk away, Sam placed his palm in the small of her back, ostensibly to lead her through the departing group. She shivered at the intimate warmth of his hand resting so close to her butt and tried to glare at him, but it was a bit demoralizing when you were trying to freeze a guy with a glare and he reacted by smiling. Thankfully, he dropped his hand and turned to face her.

"You're so cute when you try to look stern, princess. You should get a pair of those half-rim glasses just so that you can glower at me over the tops. God, this is becoming a fully realized fetish," he groaned in dawning self-recognition. "But I don't even care. It's hot. *You're* hot. Let's go somewhere and fuck."

"You're just so . . . *ugh*. The other night shouldn't have happened," she snapped, her voice low.

"The other night was awesome," Sam recalled with a nostalgic smile. "I lost track—how many times did you come? Four times? Five? We could try for seven tonight. After all, I have to give you something to remember me by."

"Mr. Brand . . ." He sighed, the first sign of annoyance he'd shown her.

"Sam. Or Brand. Drop the 'mister.' It's weird since you've had my cock in your—"

"Oh, *please* stop." She held up both hands and his mouth snapped shut. "I don't usually sleep with strangers. It's not who I am. I'm Dahlia McGregor. I teach Sunday school, volunteer at animal shelters, I want to be a kindergarten teacher, for crumbs' sake. I don't *have* these kinds of conversations with men."

"I get it," he said, his voice placating. "You wanted to break out of your shell for a night. Be a bad girl. But here's the deal, princess, I'm not a stranger anymore. So it's okay for us to have one more night. And tomorrow I'm out of your life for good. And you can go back to being Miss Priss and teaching the homeless to play harpsichord or whatever the fuck it is you usually do in your boring suburban daily life. But why not take this one moment out of time and walk on the wild side? With me."

She stared at him mutely. She shouldn't be tempted, but she was—and she knew he knew it.

"I have to help Daff prepare something for the reception," she said, her voice far from convincing, even to her own ears. "Excuse me."

She brushed by him and hurried to catch up with Daffodil, her oldest sister, who was walking a few paces ahead of Lia. Sam Brand's teasing voice drifted from behind her.

"That's not a no, princess."

~

Lia spent the next few hours trying her utmost to avoid the man. Because she really didn't think she had it in her to say no if he was to proposition her again. Add a few drinks into the mix and she could feel her resolve weakening with every passing moment. After the toasts were made and the food was eaten and the dancing started, Lia began to think that she might have successfully avoided him. But then while she was watching the happily swaying couples on the dance floor, she looked up and saw him purposefully striding her way.

"Crumbs!" she muttered beneath her breath and ducked behind a waiter before inconspicuously slipping behind a huge floral arrangement in the corner of the grand tent. She stood still for a moment before realizing how ridiculous she must look, hiding behind the flowers in her poofy lilac bridesmaid dress.

She risked a quick self-conscious glance around the gigantic pale-pink-and-white peony arrangement and sucked in a horrified breath when she caught Sam's gaze. Disgustingly bad timing, that. His eyes creased at the corners, and he adjusted his course and headed toward her no-longer-so-secret hiding place.

He was there before she could leave, and he angled himself directly in front of her.

"What you doing over here, princess?" He leaned forward to murmur the words in her ear. "Are you anti-socializing? Nice. I like it. I think I'll anti-socialize with you. In our own private little nook."

Not her intention at all!

"I was just taking a quick break—" *From you.* "Time to head back into the fray, I think."

"But it's so cozy here," he said, running a finger up her bare arm and raising gooseflesh in the process. Lia fought to keep her breath even and clamped her thighs together when her lady parts responded with Pavlovian inevitability. ". . . and so *intimate*."

He now had his forearm braced against the support post above the flowers and was leaning into her, his breath warm on her face as he spoke into her ear, his lips brushing against her temple with each word. His other hand continued to trace lazy circles over her responsive flesh, and Lia bit back a groan. She was hanging onto the post herself; her legs had as much strength as a pair of overcooked noodles, and the post was the only thing keeping her upright at the moment.

"The party's winding down," he noted, making her moan when he caught her naked earlobe gently between his teeth.

"Stop it," she whispered, her voice lacking any semblance of authority. But he obliged her by releasing her earlobe, even though he maintained the intimate closeness between them.

"Wanna head back to my room?" he invited.

"I don't think so." Was it her imagination or were his light movements on her arm becoming a little more purposeful? Yes, in one smooth movement, his large hand dropped to gently cup the indentation of her waist, just above her hip bone.

"Your place?" *My place.* Please, she lived with her parents, like a lame duck incapable of leaving the nest.

"Definitely not."

"Quickie in a closet?" What did it say about her that she paused for a beat before once again issuing a curt negative in response to his almost-playful suggestion?

"You're making this difficult, Dahlia."

She winced. She wished he would stop using her given name. It was positively cringeworthy.

"The other night was a one-off, you know that. We agreed to it."

"I don't recall us doing very much talking. Just a lot of heavy breathing and moaning. And I remember you taking the Lord's name in vain very *many* times. Come on, Dahlia. How about a farewell fuck? A shag for the road? One last, glorious spin around my cock?"

Oh God. He was so vulgar. Lia found him disgusting and disturbingly attractive in equal measure. But he *did* know his way around a woman's body. He wasn't a selfish lover like her fiancé had been—instead he'd placed her wants and needs front and center, seeming to find gratification in her pleasure.

"I don't think it would be advisable at all."

"Why not? What's another night in the grand scheme of things? You have other plans tonight? You've already been introduced to my pointy end, so you know exactly what you're getting yourself into, yeah? I'm leaving first thing in the morning. You won't ever see me again, so why deprive yourself of the joy my cock and I could give you?"

God, the arrogance of the man.

"The other night was a mistake that I don't want to compound by repeating."

He sighed, his chest heaving with the exhalation of his breath.

"Do you mean that?" he asked, his voice light but his eyes serious.

"I do." Did she? She knew she didn't sound very certain.

"Do you?" He arched an eyebrow as he unwittingly repeated her own doubtful question. His hand, which had been a stationary, warm weight at her waist, shifted with whiplike speed to cup a breast. She wasn't wearing a bra—the dress had its own corset sewn into the bodice—but that meant that he could feel the immediate tightening of her nipple in response to his touch. He smiled appreciatively, and they both watched his thumb lazily circling the hard peak of her breast before deliberately brushing against the eager nub. She angled her eyes up to his face, but he was wholly focused on what he was doing, his eyelids at half-mast, his mouth slightly open as his uneven breath sawed in and out of his chest.

She lifted her hand and pressed it against his, flattening it against her chest.

"Stop it. We can't do that here," she said, her voice thick with desire.

"My room?"

She hesitated for a split second longer before nodding recklessly.

"But we can't leave together." He was staying in the only hotel in town, and she was already picturing everybody in town seeing her follow him in there. The rumor mill would start working before they even got their clothes off.

"You think I'm going to let you leave here without me? And have you change your mind again? My balls get any bluer and they'll freeze the fuck off."

She couldn't take him to her room. Not with her entire family in the yard for the wedding. Besides, it seemed wrong to do what they wanted to do in her childhood room. The thought gave her the heebie-jeebies.

That left . . .

"I know a place. Follow me," she whispered. *"Discreetly."*

"Oh God, Lia, what are you doing?" she whispered to herself five minutes later as she stood waiting for Sam to make his appearance. She was on the verge of changing her mind when the door creaked open and the distant lights of the marquee dimly lit the dark, stuffy interior of the quiet barn.

"Dahlia?"

"Here," she called quietly. A cell phone light flickered on and swept around the area.

"Is this a barn?" he asked incredulously. A quiet whicker from the corner stall answered his question. "Are there actually horses in here?"

"Only one. That's Kiki."

"Kiki sounds like a bird's name. A bizarre choice for a horse." He sounded fascinated. He aimed the light directly in Lia's face and then switched it off. Leaving her disoriented in the dark.

"My father named her, and he's not great with names. How do you think my sisters and I got our names?"

"Dahlia's a great name," he said. His voice sounded much closer than before. She couldn't see his face, but he sounded sincere.

"Said nobody ever," she quipped and gasped when his arm snaked around her waist and he dragged her up against his hard body.

"This is so fucking clandestine and hot. I like it."

Of course he would. She didn't have time to respond because his mouth was on hers, blistering and eager and sinfully delicious. His spicy tongue forged its way into her mouth, and she was alarmed by the instant sense of familiarity she felt in response to it. Her own tongue welcomed the invading presence with appreciative strokes and he groaned, practically eating her alive. He backed her against the wooden fence of an empty stall, and his hands fumbled with the layers of silk and tulle in her skirt before they found the bare skin beneath. He cupped her bottom and squeezed, lifting her against his rock-hard erection. He ground against her mound, and she moaned in frustration because she couldn't get close enough.

Her arms wrapped around his neck, and he hoisted her up until she took the hint and crossed her ankles behind his taut butt. When she was comfortably situated, his hands stopped kneading her behind and roamed up her slender back until they found the hook-and-eye fastening above the zipper. He fumbled with it ineptly, seeming clumsy for the first time since they met. She heard something tear and he swore viciously before burying his mouth in her neck and drawing her skin into his mouth.

"Oh." Why was that sensation so unbearably pleasurable? His fingers finally drew the zipper of her dress halfway down her back and his

hands flattened against the exposed skin he found there. Her bodice went slack and gaped in the front. He took full advantage of that fact, his mouth tracing kisses down to the mound of one breast before latching onto her nipple hungrily.

Lia keened, her fingers burying themselves in his short, thick hair and tugging on it almost viciously. Brand refused to relinquish his relentless, suctioning hold on her sensitive nipple, though, and Lia was practically giddy as the combination of pleasure and pain escalated almost unbearably. He was fumbling with the front of his trousers, and she felt the thick heat of his penis against the lace of her panties seconds later. He sawed up against her and the friction sent her sighing into her first orgasm of the night.

His hand moved between their bodies and tugged her soaked panties aside before he pushed into her with a grunt. His mouth was on hers again and his other hand at her breasts, devoting equal time to each aching peak. He was thrusting urgently, and Lia sighed with each powerful retreat and advance of his shaft.

"Fuck!" he swore and quite abruptly dragged himself all the way out of her clutching channel. She cried out in protest. "Sorry. *Fuck.* No condom."

He tugged at one of her ankles, and she reluctantly loosened her grip on his butt and allowed her legs to slide down to the ground until she stood wobbling in front of him. She couldn't see him at all in the dark barn, but she heard the fabric of his tuxedo rustling as he fumbled around, searching for a condom. He made a satisfied sound and she heard the crinkle of the little foil package being ripped open.

"Turn around, princess," he instructed her, and she turned blindly. He ran his hands down her arms until he found her wrists. He took gentle hold of them and lifted her hands until she felt the rough wood of the fence under her fingertips. "Hold on."

Once again she did as he instructed, folding her fingers over the top of the fence, her breasts spilling over the top of the gaping dress, and Lia was grateful for the dark that hid her brazen display from his greedy gaze.

His hands trailed down her naked back and over her rump, curling into the material of her skirt, which he dragged up until she could feel only air on her exposed behind, cooling the wet heat between her thighs. His fingers found her, once again moving the lacy scrap of underwear aside, and tested her receptiveness, easing gently in and out, getting her back into the swing of things. Lia gasped when his thumb came into play, teasing her clitoris with sure strokes. She was on the verge of another orgasm when he replaced his fingers with something much bigger and harder and she cried out helplessly, her legs nearly giving way and forcing her to hang onto the fence for dear life.

His large hands were at her hips, holding her steady while he continued to plunder her most tender flesh. When she pushed into his thrusts, he released her hips and his hands found her naked breasts, plucking at the tender nipples.

Lia groaned helplessly as her orgasm built until she came with a high-pitched cry. He continued to thrust into her, forcing another, gentler climax fast on the heels of the first, and still he continued. Lia was so unbearably sensitive by now that she almost begged him to stop, but when he lowered his hand down her to clitoris again, and buried his face in her neck to suck on the highly sensitive skin beneath her ear, she came again. Even harder and longer than the first time.

This time he groaned as she clenched tightly around him. When she loosened her death grip on the fence, lifting a trembling hand to cup his stubbled jaw, he made a surprised sound and slammed into her so hard she almost crashed into the fence. Luckily she braced before that happened, but he pushed her up against the wood anyway, until she could feel each individual slat grinding up against her torso and abdomen. He had his arm wrapped around her breasts, to protect her tender, naked skin from the wood, and she went up on tiptoes and then left the ground completely as his next couple of powerful thrusts completely overwhelmed her.

She felt him shudder, then sob and finally groan, the sound almost anguished as he held her suspended between the fence and his hard body for what felt like eons, her feet not touching the ground at all anymore. Eventually she felt the tension leave his body, while the shudders and hoarse breathing continued unabated for much longer. He eased her down until her toes and then the soles of her feet were back on the ground. He scrupulously adjusted her skirt, not saying a word, just dusting her off and zipping her up. He couldn't refasten the broken hook and eye, but her hair—which had been up in a chignon before this—had come completely undone and spilled halfway down her back, effectively shielding the broken clasp from view.

She ran her shaking hands through the tangled mess of her hair and then dabbed self-consciously at her damp cheeks. The first release had been so intense it had brought tears to her eyes, despite there being no actual emotional connection between them. Luckily the floodgates had closed almost as soon as the orgasm had waned, but she was almost certain she had raccoon eyes. She would have to make a quick detour back to the house and to her room to fix the damage as much as she could. She only hoped nobody else was in the house.

She heard Brand fumbling with his own clothes, heard the elasticized snap as he pulled the condom off, and she wondered what he would do with it. He couldn't leave it in here for some poor unsuspecting farmworker to find. But where would he put it in the meantime?

All the possibilities grossed her out a bit, and she shoved it to the back of her mind. That was his concern—she had other stuff to worry about right now. She sniffed and winced at the wet sound. She would kill for a tissue.

"You okay, princess?" he asked, his dark voice sounding almost genuinely concerned.

"F-fine." Well, she would be if she could stop shaking. She distractedly wondered if she were in shock, because she was trembling so badly despite the pleasantly balmy spring evening. He pressed something into her hand and, for a split second, she irrationally thought it was the condom and her reflex was to drop it. Luckily she didn't, because she soon recognized the soft, folded linen square in her hand as a handkerchief, and she gratefully lifted it to her face to pat at her wet cheeks and then blow her nose noisily into it.

"I don't want to do this again," she said in a high, shaken, and almost hysterical voice. She sounded terrified and shocked, even to her own ears.

"Well, it was fun while it lasted," he quipped, but his own voice had a tremor to it and she wished she could see his face.

"I don't usually . . ."

"No need to explain yourself to me, princess. I'm all for meaningless hookups. It doesn't make me respect you less. Besides, it would be hypocritical for me to judge you based on something that I enjoy doing so much myself."

His words made her feel a little sick and made the entire encounter seem even more sordid.

"Have a nice life, Sam Brand. I look forward to never seeing you again."

Her eyes had adjusted to the gloomy interior of the barn, and she knew from his dark silhouette on a slightly less dark background that he was standing directly in front of her. But even so, it surprised her when he cupped her face and graced her with the sweetest of kisses.

"You take care of yourself, princess," he said after lifting his lips from hers.

Lia didn't respond and turned to gingerly make her way, in the dark, back to the barn door. He didn't follow her.

CHAPTER ONE

Four months later

God, this hurt! Sam pushed the button on the morphine dispenser and lay back with a groan. He wasn't going to be macho about this shit. First time he'd ever been stabbed, and it sucked balls. How humiliating to have some scrawny fucker use him as a pincushion. While Sam had taken him down and beaten the guy to a pulp, he was still pissed off as hell that the asshole had managed to inflict five stab wounds in the process.

Five stab wounds! What the fuck? Three tours to Afghanistan plus numerous special ops missions without a scratch and Sam got himself wounded by some psycho stalker with a knife. Worse, the guy looked like a stiff breeze could knock him on his ass.

One of the penetrating wounds had missed his femoral artery by a quarter of an inch; another—the most severe—had punctured a lung. But the worst injuries—in Sam's opinion—were the double fractures of his ulna and radius thanks to his takedown of the attacker. He had miscalculated the landing and had wound up with the perpetrator landing on top of him. Sam's arm had broken the fall. That injury had required surgery as well, and Sam was now the reluctant owner of a couple of metal plates and screws in his arm. He would be setting off metal detectors in airports for the rest of his life. Wonderful. And of course, it hurt like a son of a bitch and would require lengthy rehabilitation.

He sighed when the morphine started to kick in and allowed himself to relax. He contemplated the plethora of flowers and cards scattered throughout his expensive, private hospital room. There were more than he'd anticipated. Turned out that saving everybody's favorite pop princess from certain death earned you more than a few fans. Five days since the dramatic attack had taken place at a celebrity/paparazzi–heavy charity gala and he already had three huge bags of fan mail cluttering up a corner of the hospital room. His employees thought it was fucking hilarious to leave them here, and none of his grousing had scared them into removing the bags yet.

He rarely did fieldwork anymore, usually operating behind the scenes, running the business. But Laura Prentiss—the aforementioned pop princess—while a pain in the arse, was a top-tier client, and what she asked for she usually got. After receiving a series of threatening letters that had escalated into full-on stalking, Laura had demanded Sam as her close protection officer, or CPO. The paparazzi had had a field day with that—thus, many "confirmed" accounts from "reliable sources" about Sam being her lover had surfaced. They had both shrugged the stories off, hazards of the job, so to speak, but every picture of them together had apparently enraged psycho stalker boy even more. The guy had somehow managed to finagle a job on the event caterers' waitstaff and had intercepted their path almost immediately after they'd stepped off the red carpet and into the actual building.

Sam was furious with himself for allowing the fucker to get so close to Laura Prentiss. It was inexcusable even though, according to his PR team, the rescue had resulted in more than a few new clients. People didn't get that it had been a fuckup of gargantuan proportions. All they'd seen was the bloodied and battered Sam Brand, heroically beating the snot out of a sniveling, rat-faced, hunting knife–wielding bad guy.

And how the fuck did he get a hunting knife past security in the first place? There was so much explaining to be done after Sam got out of this hospital. But that was for a different day. In the meantime he had some of his best men working with the police to get answers to these questions. Right now all he wanted to do was sleep and wake up without pain.

~

Three days later he felt ready to full-on murder someone. Maybe one of the relentlessly cheerful nurses with their singsong voices and bright smiles. Or Dour Dr. Doom the Evil Deliverer of Bad News—bed rest for four weeks, no strenuous activity for three months, six to eight weeks with a cast on his arm, followed by weeks of rehabilitation to get it back in working order. It was a never-ending catalog of bad news.

Worse, the fucking press wouldn't leave him alone. He now had a man assigned to the door because some sleazy bastard had donned a white coat and wiseassed his way right into Sam's room before anybody had been the wiser. They had gone into a feeding frenzy after Laura Prentiss had dropped by to visit him. Sam had been tempted to fire Tyler Chambers—her new CPO—on the spot. He should have talked her out of visiting. Only the fact that Sam had himself been Laura—Lally to those closest to her—Prentiss's CPO and knew how stubborn she could be had saved Chambers. Well, that and the fact that Chambers was a solid guy and a good friend.

Everything was shitty as hell at the moment and Sam was wondering what the fuck else could go wrong when he heard an unmistakable female voice just outside his room door. He groaned. This was the last thing he needed. He should have known she'd show up eventually. But he had hoped that the one phone call and three text messages they had shared since the incident would be enough.

She breezed into the room on a cloud of expensive perfume, with her current lapdog—carrying her fake (Sam hoped) fur stole—trailing adoringly in her wake.

"Oh, my poor baby," she lamented, coming over to plant a huge kiss on Sam's cheek. Say what you wanted about Catherine Lockerby-Brand-Hammersmith-Petriades-Christianson-Everett, she didn't believe in air kisses. Sam always received full-on hugs and kisses from his mother. "I've been so worried about you."

"Hi, Mum," he greeted, scrubbing at his cheek because experience told him he'd have a Scarlet Temptation lipstick smudge imprinted there. His mother winced theatrically.

"Samuel Noah Brand, how many times have I told you *not* to call me that? So crass. Mother or Mimsy, please."

"Mum, I have never and *will* never call you Mimsy. I don't get why you keep asking me to."

"I just like the sound of it," she said, before looking at the strapping young man—at least thirty years younger than her fifty-five—still standing at the door clutching her fur stole. "Craig, darling, do you mind?" She glanced down at the visitor's chair, and Craig rushed to dust it off before holding it while she gingerly situated herself on the cushioned seat. "Thank you, lovely. Samuel, have you met Craig?"

Sam sized up his mother's latest plaything. The guy was about ten years his junior and had that dumb, vacant look in his eyes that she seemed to like in her toy boys. After her five failed marriages, Sam couldn't blame his mother for giving up on that esteemed institution and opting instead to have fun. He'd worry if she ever got serious about her playthings, but she knew exactly what she wanted from them. And as much as the thought made him uncomfortable, Sam couldn't begrudge her a bit of fun and companionship.

He nodded at Craig, who smiled back enthusiastically.

"I saw the news footage of you taking down that guy, man," Craig said with the eagerness of a puppy. "It was awesome. Maybe you could teach me some of those moves?"

"Little laid up at the moment, mate," Sam pointed out.

"After you recover, of course." Poor guy actually thought he'd be around that long.

"Of course."

"Craig, do you mind getting me some coffee, please? And none of the stuff they have at this hospital. You know what I like."

"Sure do." *God,* was it his imagination or was the guy eye-fucking his mother? Oh damn! That was out of bounds, man!

"Craig!" he yelled, breaking the uncomfortably long eye contact between his mother and the man. *Boy.* Whatever the fuck he was. Craig diverted his gaze to Sam. "Be a good chap and go get her that coffee."

Craig nodded and strode off purposefully, a man on a mission, and Sam diverted his attention back to his mother.

"How old is this one, Mum?"

"He's twenty-seven." Seven years younger than Sam, then. "Not very clever, but I don't keep him around for his scintillating conversation."

"Ugh. I don't need to hear more."

"Yes, enough about Craig. Tell me how long you'll be in this hospital. Afterward, I insist you stay with me. In Milan. I can't stand London in spring. So *damp*."

God, no. The notion was horrifying beyond reason. He'd have to witness her affair with Craig fizzle out, then watch her go on the prowl for a replacement and listen to her nag on about her "stingy" ex-husbands and, worst of all, endure her inevitable *smothering* attention. He'd go crazy in a day.

"No, Mum. I have other plans."

"You do? Please don't tell me you're staying with your father—you know how *that* woman's smoking affects your asthma."

"Her name is Rita," Sam said wryly, referring to his father's lovely wife of twenty-seven years. "And she stopped smoking about a decade ago. And I never had asthma, remember? Just allergies . . . which I outgrew round about the same time I hit puberty."

"So you *are* staying with them?" His mother seemed affronted, and Sam huffed in exasperation. His mother, the consummate drama queen, always treated Rita like some home-wrecking other woman, when in fact his father had met and married the woman years after their divorce. Sam would never stay with the Brands, though—his father had always been kind but distant. The obligatory holidays Sam had spent with the man and his other family had been strained. And Sam definitely didn't get along with his three half brothers. They were so respectable. And boring. They were uptight, tightly wound arseholes.

Maybe he was being a bit harsh. They weren't bad guys, they were just . . . a unit. And Sam, being a number of years older, had never been a part of that unit. He didn't know or understand them and had always regarded them as little nuisances whenever he had stayed with his father during seemingly endless summer vacations. Sam recalled the way the boys had whispered to each other behind their chubby little fingers and stared at him when they were old enough to recognize that he was a stranger in their midst. It had gotten progressively worse with each holiday. They'd started trailing after him, hiding behind furniture and walls to spy on him. And whenever he spotted them, they had scattered like frightened mice. Sam had always felt like an interloper and a freak during those vacations and had been supremely grateful when they ended after his seventeenth birthday.

His half brothers had sent him a nicely worded get-well-soon card. Just one card from all three of them and their wives. His father and Rita had called. His father had suggested it was time he grew up and got a real job. The man didn't really know Sam well enough to comment on his work ethic, or lack thereof—he simply assumed that Sam enjoyed the same freewheeling lifestyle as his mother. Sam didn't care enough to correct the man's misconceptions about him. They casually observed the familial relationship, but there was no real depth to said relationship.

"No, Mum. I'm not staying with them. After I get out of here, I'll need extensive rehab and time away from the job." True enough, even though he really had no intention of *not* working. The place would fall to ruin without him to keep an eye on things. If his former business partner, Mason Carlisle, was still around, Sam would be a hundred percent more confident about taking the time off. But as it stood, Carlisle had sold his shares of the company to Sam nearly three years ago and was recently wed and now studying architecture.

Sam trusted his guys, but none of them were the type to sit in an office and crunch numbers or schmooze potential clients. Which meant he would have to run things remotely. Not ideal. Well, that taught him to go out into the field. Never again, no matter the client.

"So where will you stay and who will take care of you?" his mother asked.

"What's wrong with staying at my apartment in Chiswick? I could hire a nurse or something." His mother cast him a jaundiced look, clearly not thrilled with his answer.

"I know you better than you think I do, Samuel. You won't be able to resist going to the office. If you insist on staying, then I'll have to stay with you."

Dear God, no!

"I didn't say I was staying here; I just asked what was wrong with it," he backtracked quickly. His phone buzzed, and, grateful for the distraction, he yanked it up and stared at the name on the screen with wide eyes. Think of the devil.

"Sorry, Mum. I've got to take this," he said apologetically and fumbled to swipe at his phone screen, his left hand making him clumsy.

"Mase, hey!"

"Brand, what the fuck, man? You let a ninety-pound weakling stab the shit out of you?"

"Last week's news, mate," Sam said pointedly, and Mason chuckled.

"I've been keeping tabs. Colby has been sending me regular updates." Colby Campbell, who managed the company accounts, had been with them since the beginning, and Sam was toying with the idea of offering her a stake in Brand Executive Protection Services.

"Why didn't you just contact me personally?"

"Because I'm pretty sure you would have downplayed the seriousness of your injuries."

"It's nothing," Sam said automatically, and Mason laughed, the sound containing little humor.

"Yeah, a punctured lung and three days in the ICU is nothing."

"I'm fine."

"Sure you are. Do you need me to help out with the business for a while till you find your feet?" The offer was tempting, but Mason had started his studies just weeks ago, and taking him away from that would hardly be fair.

"I'll manage."

"Colby is willing to step up, you know? You just have to trust her."

"I *do* trust her."

"Not enough. Give her a little more responsibility. She'll keep the guys in line."

"The woman hides in her office all day long and looks terrified of most of the guys. I was considering making her a partner, but I would never expect her to deal with the CPOs."

"She'll step up because she has to. She just needs the opportunity to prove herself and she'll handle the guys just fine. Stop underestimating her."

The door opened and Craig reentered, gingerly clutching a Starbucks cup. His hair and shoulders were wet. Poor guy. While Mason was still talking, Craig spilled a bit of the coffee, and Sam's mother berated the man like he was a preschooler. Abruptly exhausted, Sam felt his head start to spin. He lay back and shut his eyes. Mason was still yammering on about something, his mother's high, sharp voice sent spikes of pain piercing into Sam's brain, while Craig's whine irritated the hell out of him. He just wished everybody would leave him alone to recover.

He needed to get away from all this. Find someplace quiet and peaceful to lick his wounds in private. And as he listened to Mason continue to laud Colby's abilities, the solution simply came to him.

"Mase, your cabin's empty now, right?" he asked, his eyes still shut.

Mason stopped talking in midsentence, and Sam could almost picture his friend's puzzled frown.

"Yeah, why?"

"Think I could stay there for a few months?"

"You'll let Colby handle the business?"

"I will, to a certain extent." He'd definitely want to be privy to her every decision, but that was what phones and computers and Wi-Fi were for.

"Then sure, I think it'll do you good to get away from everything. Let me know when you want to go, and I'll make sure it's fully stocked and ready for you."

"Thanks, mate, I'll owe you one. Give Daisy a huge smacking kiss from me."

"Take care, bru," Mason said in farewell, and Sam disconnected the call with a tired sigh. He cracked open an eyelid when he realized that the room was unnaturally silent. He really hoped that he wouldn't find his mother in a lip-lock with Craig, but the other man was gone and his mother was sipping her coffee and watching him speculatively.

"So *where* is your friend's cabin situated?" she asked calmly, and Sam suppressed a grimace, annoyed to have been caught in a lie.

"The western Cape in South Africa."

His mother gasped. "You're in no shape to make that trip."

"I can't go anywhere for three weeks, Mum. So it's not like I'll be leaving now. And I'll take the company jet, cushiest mode of transportation imaginable. It's an idyllic place with beautiful oceans and mountains, lots of fresh air. Mason's cabin is tucked away in a sleepy little town. No press to hound me. I wish I could leave today."

"Who will take care of you? And what about your rehabilitation?"

"Everything will be taken care of, Mum. Don't worry."

"I have to worry, you're my only child," she said, and he cracked a smile. She was a prima donna, but he adored her.

"I'm thirty-four years old, *Mimsy*," he teased weakly.

"Still my child," she said resolutely. "And I'd thank you to lie about your age from now on, please. I'm much too young to have a thirty-four-year-old son."

He chuckled, and she took his hand. Feeling comforted, Sam drifted off to sleep.

CHAPTER TWO

"Does everybody know what time it is?" Lia asked brightly. The group of adorable three- and four-year-olds bounced eagerly in response.

"Story time!" they yelled collectively. One precocious boy jumped up and did a little dance of excitement.

"Okay, settle down." She lifted the book from her lap so that they could all see the cover, and everybody squealed like giddy teens at a pop concert.

A little girl lifted her hands to her mouth, her eyes brightening with excited tears. "Hungwy Capilla." Her breathless voice was filled with reverence.

"That's right, Bongi, it's *The Very Hungry Caterpillar*! Poor Caterpillar is so, so, so, sooo hungry." The little ones settled back down and waited in anticipation as she cracked open the book. Lia started reading, using everything in her bag of tricks to keep the kids hooked and engaged by inviting them to count along with her. They all knew the story but gasped with every page turn as if it was their first time hearing it.

Lia loved this. She wished that she hadn't stupidly listened to her ex-fiancé and given up her job as a teacher's assistant at the preschool before her nonevent of a wedding. She should have known when he told her to quit—*told*, not asked, mind you—that their union would never work. But she'd been so stupidly keen to marry and start a family that she'd ignored all the warning bells going off in her head.

Her position had been filled at the school, but she happily substituted when she could. Today this group's teacher had to pop out for a doctor's appointment and Lia had been keen to step in for an hour or so. She wasn't yet properly qualified, but it had always been her dream to obtain her bachelor of education degree and become a foundation phase educator. She'd kept delaying, thinking that if she married and had her own children, this need to work with kids would go away. So stupid. She loved working with children—it had little to do with her maternal instincts, she just enjoyed watching them grow and learn. The ridiculous sense of achievement she felt when she taught a little one something new was a fix she'd need long after she'd birthed and raised her own children.

After breaking it off with Clayton, she had looked into obtaining an online degree and unbeknownst to her family and friends was now just starting her second year of the four-year BEd degree. Once she graduated she would be qualified to work with newborns to nine-year-olds. She wasn't sure why she hadn't told her family yet—fear of failure, perhaps. They would be nothing but encouraging, she knew that, but she wanted to do this on her own. To prove to herself that she could.

She finished the story just in time, because some of the kids were looking drowsy. Definitely nap time. Lia got them all settled down and was busy neatening up the kitchen area when Aisha Yusuf, their teacher, returned from her doctor's appointment.

"Hey," Lia greeted her longtime friend and colleague. "How did it go?"

"All good, baby's doing well, I'm doing well." Aisha's hand went to the slight swell of her tummy, and Lia suppressed a small surge of longing. It was Aisha's first pregnancy, and the woman was positively beaming with joy and good health.

"I could have told you that," Lia teased. "You look amazing." She gathered up her purse, and Aisha frowned.

"Leaving so soon? I thought we could have a cup of tea and chat."

"I'd love to, but I'm meeting Daff for a late lunch."

"Why don't you pop around for story time again tomorrow? This lot complains when I do story time—they say my voices aren't as good as yours." Lia laughed at that bit of nonsense.

"Liar. They pretty much adore anyone who reads to them."

"Well, *I* don't think my voices are as good as yours," Aisha said, and Lia gave her a hug.

"Thanks, Aisha. I'll make time to come around tomorrow morning." Lia literally had nothing but time at the moment. She tried to keep busy with her numerous charity projects, but her schedule was definitely flexible. Even though they would never say it, she was sure her parents were probably sick of her lounging around without any true purpose. Luckily she had some savings and a generous trust fund that their maternal grandparents had set up for all three sisters, which was paying for her degree and some measure of independence at the moment.

Lia had dreamed of perhaps renting her youngest sister Daisy's house, but, even with the trust fund, it would strain her budget. She needed a job. Their town of Riversend was small and offered few employment opportunities. She would have to venture out to Knysna or farther for a decent job, but she'd been in a complete funk since her failed wedding nearly two years ago and couldn't seem to find any focus.

God, she felt completely useless at the moment. Maybe that was why she had fallen into bed with Sam Brand so easily. Such behavior was completely uncharacteristic for Lia. She didn't sleep with strange men. In fact, nobody knew it, but Clayton had been her first lover. Lia had been all for saving herself for marriage—or engagement, as it were. She'd never dreamed that her wedding would fall through. She'd thought Clayton would be her first and last lover.

She shook her head as she walked toward MJ's in the center of town. She should be grateful that he wasn't. Even though she'd had no prior experience, she'd always felt he was a bit lacking in the sex department. And after Sam Brand, she was sure of it. Clayton had been too fast, clumsy, and definitely selfish. Even in her inexperienced state, she'd known how selfish he was. He'd left her nearly there more often than not, which had been completely frustrating. And he'd constantly blamed Lia for the lack of fireworks in bed. Calling her cold and frigid and boring. It had been cruel and had made her feel inadequate and belittled. But she had believed that things would improve after marriage. Looking back, Lia couldn't believe how naïve she had been. And definitely much too desperate to get that ring on her finger.

MJ's was usually close to empty this time on a Thursday, and she could immediately see that Daff wasn't there yet. She smiled at the waitress and made her way toward the back of the room, to her and Daff's usual midweek lunch table. This was a fairly new ritual, since Daff had quit her job only a few months ago, but it probably wouldn't go on for much longer. Daff, who was doing an online course in marketing, would be temporarily managing her boyfriend's sporting goods store while Spencer focused on launching his new store in the neighboring town of George. Her ultimate goal was to handle all the marketing and advertising for Spencer's business.

Lia had already put in an order for two coffees when her sister stepped into the restaurant. She made a beeline for their table, stopping to exchange a few words with the waitress before sitting across from Lia.

"That man is going to be the death of me," she complained without preamble, and Lia grinned. Daff liked to bitch and moan about Spencer, but Lia couldn't recall ever seeing her older sister happier.

"What's up?"

"He's still being really stubborn about me moving in with him," Daff said, her eyebrows furrowed and her face dark with displeasure. "I've already given Daisy notice." Daff had been talking about moving in with Spencer for months. The only problem was that Spencer seemed to have other ideas. He was more traditional than Daff and uneasy about the message living together would send to his fifteen-year-old half sister, Charlie.

"He's worried about Charlie," Lia said. It was really sweet how concerned Spencer was about appearances and making sure his sister had proper role models in her life.

"Charlie's a savvy girl—it's not like she doesn't know what Spencer and I get up to when he's at my place. Especially since he gets home close to two every morning. I'm getting fed up with sleeping apart. But he absolutely refuses to stay over. And do you know what he asked me the other night? He asked, 'What would your parents think if we moved in together?'"

Lia stifled a smile at her sister's absolute disgruntlement. It was a familiar rant, and Lia let it wash over her as Daff continued to huff and puff.

"It's just the way he is, Daff. You have to respect that about him," she said when her sister finally ran out of steam and Lia could get a word in. Daff's face softened.

"I know. And I love him for it. So damned much. I mean, the man is perfect. I just want us to move forward. I wish he'd hurry up and propose already." Lia snorted at her sister's words. Last year Daff would have run screaming in the opposite direction if anybody had mentioned marriage to her. But she was eager to take the next step with Spencer.

"Why don't you propose to him?" Lia asked curiously. It wasn't like Daff to sit around waiting for something she wanted.

"He absolutely forbade me to. Told me he was going to ask me, but only when he feels the time is right. The time was right four months ago. All of this now is just wasted time." Lia tried hard not to laugh. Her prickly older sister wasn't the most patient of people, and it was funny to see her like this.

"Anyway, I was wondering if you wanted to come shopping with Charlie and me on Saturday."

"Special occasion?"

"Charlie was invited to a friend's sixteenth birthday party. And Spencer is being dumb about it—he actually tried to tell her she couldn't go. Because there'll be *boys* at the party." Daff rolled her eyes. "I had a long private chat with him about trusting her and allowing her to spread her wings, blah blah blah, et cetera, et cetera. I'm so grown-up these days, it's sickening."

Lia laughed. Their waitress, an older woman named Suzy, brought the coffee and a huge glass of red wine for Daff. Lia eyed the glass with a raised brow, and Daff glared at her.

"Give me a break. I just went five rounds about cohabitation with my stubborn boyfriend, my lease is up in three weeks, and if Spencer won't let me move in with him, I'll have to move back home. So I deserve this glass of wine."

"Daisy will let you stay longer if you ask her."

"I know that, but Spencer doesn't, and I told him she's already found a new tenant for the place."

"Mason might tell Spencer the truth." Daisy's husband was Spencer's younger brother.

"I told Daisy I would mail her ugly caterpillars back to her, one broken piece at a time, if she or Mason let it slip." Lia laughed again. Daff was currently holding Daisy's ornamental—and sentimental—caterpillar collection hostage. Daisy had nowhere else to store them but in a cabinet at her old house, and Daff took full advantage of Daisy's fondness for her collection. But everybody—including Daisy—knew that Daff would never really destroy her baby sister's prized possessions.

"Anyway, so Saturday? Shopping?"

"Sure, count me in."

Suzy returned for their food orders, and both women gave the menu a cursory scan before ordering, steak and a baked potato for Daff and pasta for Lia.

"Hey, have you heard about Mason's buddy Sam Brand?"

Lia froze and slanted her sister a wary look. Daff was taking another sip of wine and didn't notice the look.

"What about him?"

"He's coming to Riversend for his convalescence."

Convalescence?

"Convalescence for?"

Daff choked on her wine and gaped at Lia. "You're shitting me, right?" Lia suppressed a sigh at the overreaction. Her sister could so often be both dramatic and crude. "Have you been living under a rock the past week? It's all over the news."

"I've been busy."

"With what? Reorganizing your underwear drawer? Needlepoint? Baking cakes?"

Wow. That was scathing even for Daff.

"I volunteer at the animal shelter, you know that. And at the youth center. And the retirement home. I've been helping Mrs. Salie with her Books Are Fun campaign." Mrs. Salie was the librarian. "And I help out at the day care center when I can."

"Yeah, yeah. You should start charging those people for your services," Daff said with a dismissive wave.

"That's not how volunteering works," Lia corrected primly, blowing on her hot coffee to cool it down. "Now tell me why Sam Brand is convalescing." She took a sip of her coffee. Still too hot. She blew on it again and took another mouthful.

"He was stabbed last week. Stabbed saving Laura Prentiss's life, can you imagine? I mean, I don't like the guy at all, but that's pretty cool. And so romantic, apparently. *Jesus,* Lia!" This last as Lia's coffee spewed from her lips and dribbled down her chin, fortunately not messing anywhere else. Daff chucked a napkin at her, and Lia dabbed at her face. Gosh, how embarrassing.

But the news that Sam Brand had been horrifically injured while saving a pop star was disturbing and unexpected.

"How badly was he hurt?"

"Daisy says he was in the ICU for three days—punctured lung, shattered bones in his right arm, and one of the stab wounds nearly nicked his femoral artery. The footage is all over YouTube. I watched it last night. Brand completely wrecked the guy, despite being stabbed in the process."

"Why did you say it's romantic? Isn't it his job?" Lia felt nauseous, and when Suzy chose that moment to bring their food, her stomach very nearly revolted at the sight of it. She doubted she'd be able to eat. The thought of a vital, healthy man like Sam Brand nearly dying so needlessly was repulsive.

"Sam Brand rarely does the bodyguarding thing anymore. He tends to work behind the scenes these days, but he made an exception for Laura Prentiss, and there have been rumors that they're an item. Neither of them has denied it, and now it's come out that when he heard she was being stalked, he *insisted* on being there to protect her. And he was." Daff, not the romantic type at all, sighed wistfully, and Lia stared at her. Falling in love had really done a number on her cynical sister.

"Anyway, Brand's asked to stay at Mason's cabin during his recovery, and Mason has obviously agreed to that. So he'll probably be here in the next month or so." Lia barely registered Daff's words, her mind on everything that she'd just learned.

Laura Prentiss. Well, she was certainly the kind of woman with whom Lia would have pictured Sam Brand: very beautiful, perfect body, perfect hair, perfect everything. She wore daring little outfits and was notorious for her controversial performances and her wild-child persona. Lia knew that Sam Brand hadn't exactly been spoiled for choice when he visited Riversend for the wedding. Lia had been one of the few young, single women around, but if he'd met her anywhere else, he would never have looked twice at her. She wasn't sexy, didn't dress anywhere near as provocatively as the Laura Prentisses of the world, and she didn't have the same sexual reputation as the other woman, either.

Balance had been restored to the universe. Sam Brand had found his perfect match and Lia, who had only recently started dating again, would soon find hers.

She was sure of it.

"*Another* date?" Millicent McGregor exclaimed five weeks later when she saw her middle daughter come downstairs dressed to the nines for the third time in less than a week. Lia self-consciously straightened her lightweight pink cardigan. It was a pretty, lacy thing that she had knitted herself. "You look lovely, my dear. Doesn't she look lovely, Andrew?"

Her father looked up from his book, and his salt-and-pepper brows furrowed.

"If you put as much effort into finding a job, you needn't be so concerned about finding a husband," he said bluntly, and Lia winced.

"Andrew!" her mother gasped, and he had the grace to look slightly shamefaced.

"I want what's best for my girls, you know that, Dahlia. And I'd rather you focus on finding a job and becoming self-sufficient than a man hunt. You don't need a man to take care of you. You're quite capable of being the captain of your own fate."

Wounded, Lia swallowed heavily and lowered her gaze to the floor. Did her father really see her as some kind of man hunter, looking for a mate to take care of her? When he looked at Lia, did he only see a deadbeat daughter without a job or prospects, searching for a man to mooch off?

"She still needs a social life," her mother defended. "You can't expect her to sit at home with us every night."

"She's thirty-two and she hasn't had a job in more than a year. Lia, I love you, you're beautiful and intelligent. But you have to take command of your life, my girl. Stop waiting around for things to happen for you and go out and *make* them happen."

"That's what I'm trying to do."

"You're husband hunting."

"It's just a date, Daddy," Lia said quietly, not even able to admit the truth of his words to herself.

All her life, Lia had been programmed to believe that marriage and kids were the keys to emotional fulfillment. Not by her parents but by teachers, her great-aunts, and other "well-meaning" adults. They had all lauded her prettiness but not much else. She'd grown up thinking that all she needed to complete her life was a husband and a family. It had been her sole goal after high school, finding the right man to grow old with. Teaching had been something she'd fallen into, a time filler while she waited for Mr. Right to come along and sweep her off her feet.

Her father was right—she *was* looking for a husband, but not because she needed a man to take care of her. She was lonely; she wanted a husband and children. She was a nurturer and needed to take care of people, not the other way around. It was one of the reasons she found such joy in doing her charity work. She felt needed, important when she was helping others . . . like more than just a pretty face.

"You're *husband* hunting," her father reiterated, interrupting her grim train of thought. "I don't want you to have to depend on anybody for anything. Not your mother and me, not your sisters, and definitely *not* a man. Take a leaf out of Daff's book—further your studies, aim higher."

He was using *Daff* as an example of model behavior? Lia's world really had flipped upside down in the last year and a half. *She* had always been the example for Daff. And now it seemed her position as the good daughter had been usurped by her foulmouthed older sister. How bizarre. She was tempted to tell her father about her studies, but she didn't think now was the right time.

"That's enough, Andrew." Lia was only vaguely aware of her mother's quiet voice and blinked rapidly to clear the blurriness from her eyes. Her father sighed heavily.

"Have a good time, sweetheart," he said, getting up to give her one of those wonderful bear hugs that had always comforted her so much as a child. She clung to him for a moment, and he dropped a kiss on her head before stepping back to chuck her chin gently. "You've been so unhappy lately and I just want you to be happy, Dahlia."

"I know, Daddy," she said with a small, sad smile. She went up onto her toes to kiss his craggy cheek. "Thank you."

Gregory Marsh was a quiet, studious-looking man. He was very tall and almost skeletally thin. He had thinning, sandy hair, an overbite, and an Adam's apple so pronounced he reminded her of Ichabod Crane. He was the bank manager at one of the small branches in Riversend and always wore ill-fitting gray suits and bow ties. She imagined he thought the ties were dashing, and that was true for *some* men. But because his huge Adam's apple poked out above the knot, Gregory's ties looked like they were strangling him.

After a series of disastrous dates with horribly abrasive and overly familiar men, she found Gregory's retiring personality relaxing and was willing to see where this could lead. Single men in her age group were few and far between, and Lia couldn't afford to be picky anymore. She had chosen to stay away from dating for more than a year after her non-wedding, and before that she'd been with Clayton. It was tough getting back into the swing of things.

This was her third date with Gregory, and he wasn't exactly a scintillating conversationalist—he had a monotonous voice and enthused about his stamp collection *a lot*. As usual, Lia found herself surreptitiously checking her watch after about an hour. One hour with Gregory tended to feel like three. But he was nice. Very nice. And polite. And nice. So pleasant.

Okay, in all honesty, he was boring. Really, really boring. And if he once again spoke of his rare 1876 one-penny Cape stamp—the pride of his collection—and the "exciting" online bidding war he'd won to obtain it, Lia was going to scream. Or pull her hair out. Or maybe (probably) she'd just grin and bear it and listen to the tedious story for the fourth time in three nights, because he was nice.

And he was single.

MJ's was crowded. He always brought her to MJ's. He saw no need to leave Riversend for dinner when they had a perfectly good dining establishment right there in town. Never mind that MJ's was a family restaurant with little variety to their menu. And that most nights the place was brimming with people they knew. She suspected the latter was the reason he enjoyed bringing her here. He always chose a table in the center of the huge room, where everybody could see them. She was Dahlia McGregor—not too long ago she'd been engaged to the heir to a multimillion-dollar family-run diamond company. She had been popular in high school, and had never exchanged more than a polite greeting with Gregory. Not until her friend Tilda had set them up on a date last week.

Lia didn't believe in false modesty; she knew that people often referred to her as the pretty McGregor sister. They had believed that she would be the one to settle down and marry first. *She* had believed that. She'd been on course to do that, before discovering that her fiancé was a low-life snake who had harassed Daisy. That news, added to his arrogance and selfishness and controlling behavior, had forced Lia into making the bravest and scariest decision of her life and canceling her wedding the day before the actual event.

People had been treating her like a broken doll since then and, until Sam Brand showed up and displayed not one iota of sympathy or concern for her "fragile" state, she had allowed it. Had felt like it was her due. Until she recognized that it was doing her more harm than good.

Brand had been the catalyst to release her from the depths of self-pity. His response to the news that her engagement had been broken had been so refreshing: *"Good to know you're a free agent, sweetheart. Married women are off-limits."*

That pragmatic and unsympathetic sentiment was all it had taken to lure her into bed with him. It would have been easy to blame the alcohol for her lowered inhibitions, but in all honesty, she had never made a more clearheaded or cynical decision in her life. And the rewards had been unforgettable and phenomenal. But at the same time, she had felt embarrassed by the tawdry encounter. And to repeat the mistake at the wedding? She shuddered at the recollection. Allowing him to take her in a filthy barn had been so sordid.

And *yet* the very memory of it had the power to bead her nipples and . . .

"Are you ready to go?" Gregory asked while Lia was still caught up in her confusingly raunchy and scandalous memories of Sam Brand.

"Yes," Lia said with a quick smile. He scrupulously added up the bill before telling her what her half would be and *generously* informing her that he would cover the tip. Lia tried not to cringe when he circled a possessive arm around her waist and steered her through the restaurant. She couldn't help feeling like a prized possession that he was showing off, an all-too-familiar feeling after Clayton's posturing.

Clayton had outright referred to her as his soon-to-be trophy wife, and Lia had initially thought it was a term of endearment. Until she'd recognized it for what it was—a claim of ownership. He'd seen her as nothing more than a thing, a shiny object to shelve in his trophy cabinet and neglect until he wanted to show her off when he played his games of one-upmanship with his friends.

Gregory led her to her car door and then caged her in by draping one arm over the roof of the small, silver hatchback Fiat and positioning his body in front of her, while her back was to the driver's door. He maneuvered her so quickly and expertly that she barely had time to react.

"Do you want to follow me home?" he asked softly. His free hand came up to cup her cheek, and she barely stopped herself from shuddering at the cold, clammy feel of his palm against her skin. His thumb ran over her lips, and she swallowed back a surge of actual nausea.

"It's getting late," she prevaricated. "I should get home."

"It's our third date, Lia," he said with a small smile, pressing closer. She could feel every sharp angle of his bony frame against her front, and when he actually had the nerve to grind his pelvis up against her . . . *yep*, that was his penis.

If her instinctive reaction to feeling his hard penis rubbing up against her was *eww*, then he was probably not the man for her. She tried to move her own hips away from his, but the car door limited her movements, and what had been an attempt to get away from him instead felt like a reciprocal thrust. He groaned.

"Oh yes, babe," he husked and mashed his lips up against hers. And then shoved his tongue down her throat. It took everything she had not to gag. Her eyes were wide open in horror and fixed on his passionate face so very, *very* close to hers. He had a fine smattering of blackheads on his forehead and a long, curly hair growing out of the mole just to the right of his left eye.

His hand moved down to her shoulder and then to her breast, squeezing too hard as he continued to thrust against her. When that cold, moist hand deftly slipped down her bodice and under her bra to cup her breast and thumb her unresponsive nipple, she finally snapped out of her horrified haze.

"Gregory, stop," she said firmly, flattening her hands against his bony chest and pushing. He was surprisingly strong and resisted at first. *"Stop."*

He finally released his hold on her, and his hand thankfully oozed its way out of her bodice. He was breathing heavily, his garlicky breath washing over her face in rapid pants. If he'd planned on sticking his tongue down her throat by the end of the evening, he could at least have refrained from the extra garlic on his pasta.

"God, that was good. Let's go to my place, babe." If anybody had placed wagers on his endearment of choice, *babe* would have been the *last* thing Lia chose. It sounded odd coming from him. Then again, the entire evening had taken a turn for the surreal, and Lia just wanted to escape.

"I can't. I have to go home."

"What, you have a curfew? Will your daddy ground you if you're home late?" he asked mockingly, and her eyes widened at the sarcasm. Well, Gregory had certainly devolved into an *a-hole* in no time at all.

"I—" Her phone tinkled discreetly, and she thankfully latched onto that excuse to look away from his flushed face. She kept her eyes carefully averted from the modest tent that was still pitched at the front of his trousers and opened her bag to retrieve her phone from its usual pocket. She peered at the screen and heaved a relieved sigh.

"It's my sister. I have to get this." She swiped at the screen. "Daff?"

"Lia?" Daff sounded completely harassed. "I have a huge favor to ask you. I bought some groceries to stock Mason's cabin with and I meant to drop them off and freshen up the place a bit. You know, put on bedding and open windows and stuff? But I forgot about Charlie's PTA meeting—why have a meeting during the school holiday anyway? If I was a teacher, I'd want the time off. Anyway, I promised Spencer I'd go with him. And it's running late. I won't be able to get it done tonight, and Sam Brand could arrive tomorrow or the day after. I don't want any of the food to spoil, and I wanted everything to be ready for him. Please could you—?"

"Of course," Lia said hurriedly. She caught Gregory's eyes and shook her head in fake apology. "I'll do it right now."

"Oh my God, thank you! You're a lifesaver." Lia tried not to wonder why Daisy had asked Daff to do it for her. Lia was usually the reliable one, the one everybody recruited when they wanted to get things done, and she couldn't prevent the small surge of resentment at Daff suddenly becoming everybody's go-to girl.

"The groceries are at Spencer's place. They're still bagged and in the kitchen. The key to the house is under the porch swing canopy. The cabin is unlocked—I stopped by earlier to make sure the electricity and plumbing are working."

"I'll take care of everything," Lia promised, just grateful for an excuse to get away from Gregory.

"Fabulous. Thanks, sis. You're awesome. I've got to go, we're about to speak with her math teacher." She hung up before Lia could respond. Lia looked at Gregory with feigned regret.

"I'm so sorry to cut this short, Gregory, but I have to go. Daff has asked me to help her out with an urgent matter."

"Anything I can do?" he asked, looking concerned, but Lia could see the impatience and anger in his gaze. Guy obviously thought he was going to get lucky tonight, and suddenly his date was bailing on him. Bummer. For *him*. Lia, on the other hand, couldn't wait to get out of here and away from him. She didn't think she wanted to see him again. They definitely were not compatible. But a tiny part of herself couldn't help but wonder if she would have been this picky before her experience with Brand. She hoped he hadn't spoiled her for all men. He had certainly raised her expectations much, *much* higher than before.

"No. It's something I have to do by myself," she said quickly.

"You can come around to my place afterward," he suggested.

"I'm pretty tired," she said with a fake yawn. "I think I'll head to bed afterward."

He looked miffed by that information.

"Thank you for a lovely evening," she said with a polite, strained smile. She turned to unlock her car door and thankfully he stepped away, allowing her to climb into the car.

Charlie's eight-month-old brown-and-white miniature pinscher/Chihuahua mix, Toffee, ran up to greet Lia enthusiastically when she let herself into the house. The dog ran for her tiny tennis ball, dropped it at Lia's feet, and stood watching her with an expectant tilt of the head.

"Sorry, girl, I can't play right now. Your family has left me a shed-load of work to do," Lia groaned, planting her hands on her hips as she took in the bags of groceries in Spencer's kitchen. Daff had bought up an entire store. Somewhere in Riversend a store manager had finally paid off his business loans and was probably planning his retirement trip to a small island in the Bahamas, thanks solely to Daff's extravagant spending today. Now Lia wondered if Daff actually had a PTA meeting or if she, Spencer, and Charlie were laughing their behinds off at getting Lia to do all this fetching and carrying in their stead.

She shook her head and, with Toffee—tennis ball in her mouth—dancing around her feet, started to lug the bags out to her car. It took four trips and ten minutes for her to get everything loaded up. After making certain that the forlorn-looking Toffee was safely inside the house, the drive was just a matter of taking a left turn and bringing the car to a stop a minute later. The places were only meters apart, but walking up and down the small incline with the bags would have taken a lot longer in the dark, on uneven terrain.

She let herself in through the kitchen door. The place had the musty smell of a home that had been unlived in for a few months. Mason and Daisy had moved to Grahamstown at the beginning of the year, just a couple of months after their November wedding. They were nicely settled into a pretty house outside the university town, where Daisy did locum work at a small veterinary practice and Mason had started his studies in March. Lia switched on the lights and opened a few windows to air the place out a bit. The mild late-April evening air had a slight autumnal nip to it, but nothing too extreme.

Lia got to work carrying the shopping into the kitchen, feeling like a scurrying ant with all the back-and-forth. She started unpacking everything, placing the groceries neatly in kitchen cabinets and the refrigerator. She was humming quietly to herself when the sound of a heavy tread behind her had her grabbing a knife from the block and whirling to face her would-be assailant.

"Great reflexes, princess," Sam Brand observed in amusement. He was in the living room, his hand curled over the top of an easy chair, obviously for balance, because he looked seriously wobbly. "But I'm pretty sure even I could disarm you in seconds, and I'm definitely not in peak condition at the moment. The key is to look like you mean to use the weapon. You look like just a cough would have you scampering off in the opposite direction."

"W-what are you doing here?"

"Well, I *was* taking a nap on the sofa. But you were making more noise than a herd of elephants," he said, sounding strained. His grip on the chair tightened so much she could see the white of his knuckles. He looked pale and sickly and much too thin. His right arm was in a sling and cradled against his chest.

"Oh good grief, sit down. Before you fall down," she said, finally overcoming the shock of seeing him here. And treating him like an invalid made her feel a little more in control of the unsettling situation.

"I'm fine," he maintained stubbornly. He was very far from fine. She was shocked by his appearance. This vital man, who had epitomized masculine fitness and perfection just six months ago, looked weak and shaky. It was disconcerting. She had attempted to watch that clip of the attack but couldn't get past the first thirty seconds. Just seeing that knife plunge downward and the look of shock on Sam's face had been . . . disturbing. She had switched it off and never tried to watch it again.

"You don't look fine," she pointed out, and he glared at her. It was the first time he'd ever looked less than charming.

"I've been stabbed, for fuck's sake," he gritted. "Of course I don't *look* fine. But regardless of how I look, I can damned well stand on my own two feet."

"Yes, but you don't have to do so right now," she said matter-of-factly. She felt completely flustered by his short-temperedness, but even while she told herself it was to be expected, she wasn't quite sure how to deal with it.

"Don't tell me what to do, princess," he said cuttingly, and she heaved an exasperated sigh before going back to her former task. The sooner she got this done, the sooner she could get out of here and back home. This evening had been an unmitigated disaster from start to finish, and she just wanted to crawl into bed and forget it had ever happened.

"Why are you here anyway?" he asked nastily, and she paused in the act of shoving some steak into the freezer to glance up at him. She was startled to discover that he had moved closer. How had he done that without her hearing? How could such a badly injured man move so stealthily? He was now leaning on the kitchen island, but the movement had clearly cost him dearly because he was even paler than before.

"Isn't it obvious?" Her voice was scathing, and a ghost of a smile touched his lips.

"I was led to believe your sister Daphne would be bringing me provisions on a weekly basis."

"*Daffodil* was busy tonight and won't be home till much later."

"Well, you don't have to unpack them. Just the delivery is fine. I'll take care of the rest." He pushed himself away from the island and swayed alarmingly for a few moments before gripping the countertop again.

Stubborn man. Lia shook her head in disgust before continuing with her task. She was about halfway through and would happily leave the rest for him to do if he didn't look on the verge of collapse. She just wanted to get out of here and pretend never to have seen him.

"We weren't expecting you today," she said a few moments later, after the silence grew too stressful. Considering how much she'd always longed for him to just shut up during their past encounters, it was uncanny how very uncomfortable she found his continued silence.

"I had to get out of London, the fucking press wouldn't leave me alone," he said, his voice bitter.

"Because you saved Laura Prentiss or because you're dating Laura Prentiss?" she found herself asking, then wished she hadn't. His private life was none of her concern, and she really didn't want to know about his relationship with the pop star. She kept her gaze averted but was relieved to hear a bar stool scrape back, followed by a few pained grunts as he settled into the high chair.

"Jealous, princess?" His voice oozed with smugness.

Ugh. She schooled her face into indifference before allowing herself to meet his eyes levelly.

"Of?" He winced theatrically at her cool rejoinder and clutched his hands to his chest.

"Ouch, the perfect pretty princess has some claws."

"Stop calling me a princess," she protested, and he merely smiled, if the grimace pulling his lips apart could be called that, and said not one word in response. She was relieved when she finally shelved the last grocery item and dusted her hands off in satisfaction.

"Well, that's the last of it. I see Daff has left a few emergency numbers on the refrigerator for you. I'll just shut the windows and leave you to it. Hope you feel better soon."

"Is *your* number on the fridge, luv?" he asked with a shadow of his roguish grin, and Lia cringed at the new endearment. She appreciated this one even less than *princess*.

"Of course not," she huffed, pushing a strand of hair back with the heel of her hand.

"Well, who am I supposed to call when I need a sponge bath?" He leered and she pursed her lips primly.

"I have to go," she said. "Good night."

"Before you leave, princess—" Lia paused, bracing herself for another lewd comment. "Where do you suppose I would find the bed linen?"

Crumbs! She remembered Daff mentioning that she hadn't yet made the bed. She chewed the inside of her cheek. She supposed she could get the linen for him and leave him to make the bed. She risked a quick glance at him—his pale face was gleaming with sweat, and there were lines of strain around his mouth and eyes.

He would probably keel over before he got the sheet on. She sighed and shook her head before whirling and marching up the stairs to the loft that housed the huge king-size bed. She noted his luggage on the floor at the foot of the bed and wondered how he had managed to get the bags up here.

She found the linen in the padded storage bench at the foot of the bed. She made quick work of the task and had the bed made in less than ten minutes. She was surprised that he hadn't followed her up the stairs and cautiously made her way back down, wondering why he was so quiet.

She found him seated in Mason's comfortable easy chair, looking completely wiped out, his lips thin and his eyes screwed shut. His breathing was shallow, and he seemed to be in a fair amount of pain.

"Are you okay?" she ventured tentatively.

"What the fuck do you think?" he snapped without opening his eyes. He was so different from the charmer of six months ago. It was unsettling. She now saw that practiced charm for the act that it was and knew that the real Sam Brand lay somewhere between that smooth talker and this short-tempered man.

"You're in pain, and in light of that, I'll let your language and your rudeness slide, but please be aware I won't tolerate it again."

"Well, shit, Miss Prissy Panties, have I offended your delicate sensibilities?"

"Can you get up without assistance?" she asked, ignoring his goading behavior.

"Of course I can!" he snarled, a bear with a sore paw. He heaved a huge sigh and then grimaced before opening his eyes to meet hers. His clear blue gaze was still penetrating despite his red-rimmed eyes. "I-I don't think I can."

She could see how much the admission hurt his pride, and she said nothing, merely held out her hand. He hesitated before taking it, his own large hand engulfing hers.

She tugged but he didn't budge, and she raised her eyebrows.

"You're going to have to help, Mr. Brand. I can't do this on my own." His hand tightened around hers, and his jaw dropped incredulously.

"Did you just fucking call me *Mister* Brand? Are we back to that? In light of the fact that I know what you look like naked—"

"You do *not*," she gasped. And he really didn't. The first time they were together, after her sister and Mason's mixed stag and hen party, they'd gone back to his hotel room, but like the encounter in the barn, they hadn't initially made it out of their clothes, and later, when they *had* stripped, the room had been completely dark.

"Semantics. I've been inside you—silly formalities between us would just be ridiculous. Call me Sam, for fuck's sake. Or Brand if that makes you feel better. Anything but mister. No point in pretending to be ingenuous."

Pretending? She was hardly pretending. She was pretty unsophisticated. Sam Brand was never supposed to reenter her life, and she had no clue how to handle the situation. Yes, she had been intimate with the man, but on the understanding that it would never happen again and that he would leave soon afterward. Now here he was, and she didn't know what to say to him or how to react around him.

Her hand was still in his; neither of them had a particularly firm grip on the other, but it was still alarmingly intimate. She tried to tug her hand free, but he tightened his fingers around hers.

CHAPTER THREE

"On three?" he asked, and she sighed before nodding. "Okay, one, two—*fuck*!"

He attempted to lever himself up on *three*, but because Lia had been expecting him to do so *after* three, she offered no resistance and tumbled gracelessly into his lap. She heard the agonized breath from his chest as she hit his injured arm on her way down and cringed at the unintentional pain she'd inflicted on him.

"Oh my *gosh*, I'm so sorry." His eyes shone with unshed tears of pain, and she felt close to crying herself at the sight of them. She patted ineffectually at his shoulders and face, her butt right in his crotch. He impatiently shoved her flapping hands away.

"Stop that!" he commanded curtly when she couldn't seem to control her stupidly waving hands. He corralled her wrists, grabbing both in his good hand and holding them in a tight grip. "Jesus, you're a fucking disaster zone."

Hurt by that unfair statement, Lia retreated into silence.

"Get off me, will you?" he muttered, and she tried to tug her hands free. He tightened his grip, probably just to show her how much control he had over the situation, before releasing her abruptly. She clumsily hauled herself out of his lap, unintentionally pushing at his hurt arm again, and he swore viciously at the contact.

"I'm sorry," she offered in a small voice once she was standing in front of him again. Her dignity in absolute shreds.

"Forget about it," he dismissed, despite the fact that he was trembling and beyond pale. He used his good hand on the arm of the chair and levered himself up with difficulty. She hovered, her hands instinctively coming out to steady him, but he shot her a warning glare. It took a great deal of effort, but he eventually stood hunched over in front of her.

"You can leave now," he said, his voice sounding shockingly weak. While she was tempted to flee and never return, Lia stood her ground.

"I'll wait until you're settled in bed."

"Looking to join me, are you?"

"Mr.—uh—Sam." She grimaced—that sounded too personal. "I prefer Brand." The words emerged from beneath her breath, and he bared his teeth in what she *supposed* could be taken as a smile.

"Go for it, as long as you drop the ridiculous *mister*."

"Anyway, *Brand*, we agreed in November that what was between us was just S-E-X." She spelled the word out self-consciously, feeling herself flushing as she did so. His gaze was riveted on her face, and it made her feel like a bug under a microscope. "And it was supposed to be just that one time—well, two times—and that was it. I never expected to see you again. Especially not so soon. I mean, I imagined you'd show up at Mason and Daisy's baby's christening. It's likely you'd be a godfather, but probably only to their second child, little Dianella. I think it's fair to assume Spencer would be godfather to their oldest, Delphinium. Godmother would be a toss-up between Daff and me. But because Daff is the oldest sister and she and Spencer are together, it would likely be the two of them. You and I would probably share guardianship of—" She stopped when his mouth dropped open and realized that she had gone off on a bizarre tangent. "What I meant to say was that I didn't expect to see you again. Not so soon. I thought by the time we met again, I'd be married with children of my own."

"Uh." The grunt emerged after a few moments when he seemed to realize that she was done speaking and some kind of response was required from him. "Daisy's pregnant?"

"Uhm. No." She flushed, embarrassed when he tilted his head and stared at her like she was a bizarre new species of insect. He shook his head incredulously before clearing his throat.

"You're engaged?" he asked, thankfully letting her weird little fiction about Daisy and Mason's possible future children slide.

"Well, not yet. But soon."

"Yeah?" His face was like granite and revealed not a single emotion. Not even pain. That was some feat, considering how protectively he was hunched over his arm. "Who's the lucky guy?"

"I haven't really *met* him yet," she said, feeling increasingly self-conscious. "At least I don't think so. I've been on a few dates with someone. And recently it got more serious." She bit back the surge of nausea at the thought of Gregory's cold, clammy hand on her nipple. Had that really happened just a few hours ago? It felt like years had passed since then. "The point is, I'm looking for someone serious. Someone to marry. I don't want you to think that we'll be picking up where we left off or anything. I mean, you probably wouldn't want to anyway, you've been dating Laura Prentiss, but just in case."

"Got it. You're husband hunting," he said matter-of-factly, still not revealing a single emotion. And did he have to use that term? Her father had as well. And it sounded incredibly predatory. "Look, princess, I'm knackered. Fascinating as this all is, I really can't deal with it right now. I need to get to bed, take some painkillers, and sleep for approximately fifty-seven hours."

"Oh. Of *course*! I'm so sorry. I'll leave very soon—I just want to be sure you manage the stairs okay. They're pretty steep."

He huffed impatiently and shrugged before limping his way to the staircase. She followed close behind, watching him anxiously. The limp reminded her of his extensive injuries. It went beyond the obvious cast on his arm. He'd been stabbed in several places. Gosh, the thought was sickening. He paused at the foot of the stairs and bent his head for a long moment before exhaling and taking the first step.

It took everything in Lia not to step forward to place a supportive arm around his waist. For one thing, she was pretty sure the gesture would *not* be appreciated, and for another, touching him didn't seem like a very wise course of action.

She waited for him to slowly progress up the first four stairs before setting foot on the first step.

"Don't fucking hover," he growled over his shoulder, more aware of her movements than she'd expected him to be.

"I'm not hovering," she protested. "Look, I'm *way* down here."

"What are you going to do? Catch me if I fall?" he asked, and she thought she could hear a touch of something close to amusement in his curt voice.

"I don't know. Something." He shook his head and refocused his energy and attention on getting upstairs. For every four stairs he took, she advanced another step. It was sixteen steps to the top, and she heaved a relieved breath when he finally reached the landing. She hastened to follow him, and when she got up to the loft, he was slipping the sling over his head. He tossed it—clear frustration in the gesture—on the bed and gingerly lowered his arm. It was encased in white plaster from his hand to just above his elbow. There were signatures scrawled all over the cast, and she found herself staring at those. Somehow she hadn't expected Brand to be the type of man to have his friends sign his cast.

She felt his eyes on her and reluctantly lifted her gaze to meet his. He looked exhausted and more than a little grim.

"They did these while I was out cold," he explained unexpectedly, lifting his arm with an almost embarrassed shrug.

"Who?"

"My colleagues, friends, and Lally." He cleared his throat self-consciously and shrugged again when he saw her confusion. "Laura Prentiss."

He had a pet name for her? And it was a lot more personal than just *princess*. She didn't have any right to feel envious about that. But now Lia couldn't help wondering if he actually remembered her name. Since he hadn't used it once since seeing her.

"I see," she said softly. Her eyes fell to the suitcases again. "Who brought these up here?"

"Driving service chauffeur," he explained. He cleared his throat again and awkwardly tugged at his T-shirt with his unencumbered hand.

"Let me help," she offered impulsively, and he hesitated for just a moment before dropping his arms and lifting his jaw. He looked stubborn and proud, and she knew how much it cost him to let her help.

She licked her lips nervously, ignoring the familiar flare of interest in his eyes at the gesture, and tugged at the hem of his shirt, holding her breath as she lifted the fabric over his sculpted torso. He was definitely much thinner than she remembered, but the muscle definition was still there. Once the pallor from his enforced confinement faded and he started eating properly again, he'd have no trouble getting back that lethal, lean, well-honed grace of before. Still, every fading bruise and bandage she revealed saddened her a little bit. He looked like he'd been through the wringer, and—if the involuntary deep, groaning sigh that emerged when she gently lifted his injured arm was any indication—he felt like it, too.

She was making her own involuntary sounds, soft, crooning, apologetic little noises as she eased the shirt over his cast. The sleeve had been removed, but despite the larger hole it was still a mission to get it off without jarring his arm. She released her breath gustily when she finally got it all the way off, but the next breath snagged in her throat as she took in the full impact of the damage on his chest, torso, and back.

Not all the knife wounds were still bandaged; the shallower gashes—on his left pec, just above his belly button, and over his left clavicle—had been stitched up and left to heal. The stitches had been removed already, but the scars still had the angry, swollen appearance of fresh wounds. Lia moaned and gently traced the tip of her index finger over the long, jagged cut on his pec, and his muscle jumped beneath her tentative touch.

"Don't." His gravelly voice breathed directly into her ear and startled her into jumping back.

"I'm sorry." That was *way* out of line. She didn't know what she was thinking. "I should go."

"Not going to help me with my jeans?" he asked, his face completely serious. "The buttons are tricky."

She hesitated, and her eyes involuntarily dropped to the fly of his jeans. To her horror, the generous bulge shifted beneath her gaze, quickly taking impressive shape down the length of his left thigh. She gulped and her eyes leapt back to his. Despite his obvious exhaustion, he was grinning broadly, a lascivious twinkle in his eyes.

"They'll be even harder to undo now," he said, his grin starting to look decidedly wicked.

"I'm sure you can manage," she squeaked before turning tail and getting out of there. His knowing chuckle followed her down the stairs and all the way out the front door, and even when she was in her car and halfway home, she could still hear it echoing around in her head.

Sam continued to laugh as he watched Dahlia McGregor's swift retreat. She was a weird little thing. He hadn't considered the fact that she would be around when he'd made the impulsive decision to come to Riversend. Truthfully, he hadn't given her much thought at all since their torrid encounter at Daisy and Mason's wedding. It would definitely be fair to say he'd almost forgotten about her entirely. But seeing her again tonight had reminded him how bizarrely hot he found that whole button-down librarian thing she had going on. This forced convalescence might not be as boring as he'd feared it would be.

He was going to be here for at least three months, and he had to pass the time somehow. Might as well pass it with the primly hot little Dahlia McGregor.

Lia was rattled. Her hands shook so badly she could barely get her key in the door. Thankfully the house was dark, which told her that her parents were both asleep. She definitely wasn't feeling up to speaking with either of them after the evening she'd just had.

First gropey Gregory and his peripatetic fingers, and then Brand's surprise reappearance back into her life. All in all, it was an evening she'd sooner forget. And yet—after she was settled in bed—she found herself constantly thinking of Sam Brand. Wondering how he was managing. He seemed to be in a lot of discomfort; would he be able to get any sleep? How would he cope in the morning? He would have difficulty dressing. She wondered if he was going to hire a nurse. Someone to help him out around the cabin until he was steadier on his feet.

She shook herself. It wasn't any of her business. She was sure Brand had it all figured out. Her phone buzzed, and she lifted it from the nightstand. It was from Daff.

Thanks for taking the groceries to the cabin.

No probs. Brand is there already.

No shit? Crap, I didn't make up the bed or anything. ☹
I took care of it.

Cool! Thanks, man. You're awesome.

Lia smiled fondly at that.

How was the PTA thing?

Ugh!!!!! Charlie's math teacher is an asshole. Spencer nearly hit the guy. Lunch at MJ's tomorrow? I'll tell you about it then.

It was unusual for them to meet on a Tuesday, but Lia didn't really have anything else happening after her usual errands in the morning.

Sounds good. See you then. Night.

Daff replied with a little snoozing emoticon, and Lia put her phone aside and lay on her back staring into the dark. She sighed heavily when her thoughts strayed to Gregory. She immediately shuddered and tried to push him back out of her mind. She had hoped that—despite the lack of chemistry between them—they could build a relationship, but after his earlier obnoxiousness, that likelihood was highly doubtful.

Her search for the right man would have to continue, and she might as well stop thinking about Brand and how attractive she still found him, despite his involvement with a gorgeous pop superstar. Because he was the polar opposite of the right man. He wasn't even in the same galaxy as the right man.

She just wished she could put him out of her mind as easily as she had Gregory. Thankfully, she wouldn't have to see either man again.

"Fuck! Fuck! *Fuuuuuck!*" Sam glared at his reflection in the steamy bathroom mirror and threw his razor across the room. Shaving was clearly not an option. He had sliced his face to ribbons, and he still had patches of dark stubble all over his jaw and cheeks. This was his first attempt at shaving himself since the attack—the nurses had taken care of it during his lengthy stay in the hospital. And then he'd spent five days after being discharged at home in his flat with a private nurse, reluctant to leave the country until he was sure Colby had a handle on everything.

He hadn't realized how wholly incapable he was of completing even the simplest of tasks until now. And it pissed him off. Luckily he should be rid of the fucking cast in another week or so, which was why he hadn't seen the need to hire a caregiver here. He hadn't anticipated how exhausting the journey would be, though. And he was knackered and completely out of sorts.

Even showering had been a bit of a disaster, since he hadn't remembered to cover his cast and had gotten it wet before comprehending he should probably wrap it in plastic.

He shook his head and stomped back into the bedroom, where he attempted to dress himself. He managed to struggle into underwear, socks, track pants, and a loose tank top and trainers, even though the effort left him panting and his bad arm aching.

He felt better after a decent night's sleep, and tackling the stairs today didn't feel like too much of a chore. The wound in his thigh pulled uncomfortably with each step, but it wasn't anything he couldn't manage. He wandered to the fridge, and a quick glance at the contents told him that everything would require cooking. He grimaced. Even with two functioning arms, he wasn't the greatest of cooks. Attempting a proper breakfast in his current state would only end in disaster.

On to plan B, then. Cornflakes. He hated cornflakes, it was a kid's meal, but it was that or toast, and he didn't fancy attempting to butter toast with his left hand. He grabbed a carton of milk and turned to put it on the island behind him and then reached for the orange juice. He somehow miscalculated the grab and fumbled. The carton went tumbling to the floor and exploded on impact.

"*Fucking* cock-sucking motherfucking son of a donkey's ball sac!" he yelled as he jumped out of the way. He got splashed anyway. Jesus!

"Uh. Knock, knock?" He swore again, the unfamiliar voice taking him by complete surprise. He didn't like being sneaked up on. In fact, he fucking hated it. Before the stabbing incident in London, nobody had gotten the jump on him. Ever.

He glared at the woman standing at the back door. She looked familiar. His confusion cleared when he recognized Daisy's oldest sister, Daphne. No, that was wrong. *Daffodil.* Stupid name.

She bore a striking similarity to Dahlia with her glossy, dark-brown hair, slender body, and pretty gray eyes, but she lacked her sister's appealing softness. This one had a cynical mouth and just somehow seemed more . . . angular. He couldn't figure out what it was. She looked sharp, while Dahlia looked round and cuddly. He reckoned cuddling Daffodil McGregor would be like trying to get cozy with a scorpion. She was well put together and dressed attractively—it was a look that usually appealed to him, sophisticated and sleek. But in comparison to Dahlia's fussy dress sense, it just left him cold.

Bizarre.

"Hey," he greeted with a nod, trying for insouciance, despite the bright-orange liquid pooling at his feet. "Daff, right?"

"Yes." Her voice wasn't particularly friendly, and he recalled that he hadn't exactly hit it off with her the first time around. She'd warned him to stay away from Dahlia. He didn't respond well to people who tried to tell him what to do. Her eyes dropped to his feet, and she sighed. "Having a shitty morning, I take it?"

He shrugged, as there was really no point in answering.

She turned away and stepped into the broom closet next to the guest bathroom before exiting seconds later with a mop and bucket.

"You don't have to—"

"If I don't, it won't get done." Her voice was curt, and he winced. There was no point in arguing—he couldn't clean it up himself. Not yet. Feeling like a helpless child, he stepped aside reluctantly and let her mop the floor.

"Get changed while I sort this out," she commanded him, her tone of voice grating as fuck. "I'll fix you some breakfast."

"Thanks," he muttered sullenly before kicking off his sodden trainers and padding out of the room and upstairs in his socks. He sank down onto the edge of the unmade bed and allowed his shoulders and head to slump for a few moments of self-pity before he shook himself and got up to hunt through his suitcase for a fresh pair of track pants.

It took him forever to get the wet pair off and the new pair on, and in that time he could smell fresh coffee on the brew. He sat for a moment and did his usual morning range of motion exercises for his broken arm. Wrist and shoulder rotations, fist flexing, and a host of other soft-core exercises designed to strengthen his arm.

"How do you like your eggs?" Daff's voice floated up from the kitchen, and he paced to the loft railing, still flexing his fist while rotating his wrist, to see what she was doing. The floor was clean and she was getting ingredients out of the fridge. God, was that bacon? He didn't care if her attitude stank, if she gave him bacon he'd probably drop to one knee and propose. He hadn't had a proper meal since yesterday's preflight breakfast in London. He was starving.

"Sunny side up," he called down, and she nodded without looking up. He took a few paces back and sat back down on the bed and lifted one foot to his knee to tug off a sock and then did the same with the other. He contemplated his bare feet for a few morose moments, curling his toes against the hardwood floor. He sat deep in thought for a while until the delicious aroma of frying bacon wafted up to his nose. He limped back downstairs—seriously, these stairs sucked balls—and noticed that her phone screen was lit up on the kitchen island. He sneaked a peek and saw Dahlia's name above a message—Still on for lunch?—and glanced at Daff, who had her back to him. He quickly tapped Dahlia's name—or Lia, as it said on the screen—and made a mental note of the number before making his way to the kitchen table and sinking heavily into a chair.

He watched Daff work. She wasn't exactly a domestic goddess, creating more dishes than he thought was entirely necessary for a simple breakfast of bacon, eggs, and toast.

"Thanks for doing this," he said. He hated feeling beholden to anybody.

"I promised Daisy I'd help out, but I'm not great at this, you'd be better off with—"

She stopped speaking so suddenly there was no doubt in his mind that she was referring to Dahlia.

"With?" he prompted.

"A nurse or something." He knew that wasn't what she'd been about to say, but he let it slide.

"I don't like having strangers hovering around me."

"*I'm* a stranger," she reminded.

"We're practically related," he exaggerated. "I don't mind having family around." She made a rude sound at the back of her throat, and he hid a grin when she unceremoniously thrust a plate and a mug of delicious-smelling coffee on the table in front of him. He groaned appreciatively and thanked her sincerely when she returned seconds later with cutlery and his toast.

Eating with his left hand was a messy affair, but he was getting used to it, and he was so hungry he didn't even care that she was there to witness his disgusting table manners. She had retreated to the other side of the kitchen, which wasn't very far, considering that this wasn't a huge cabin. She was propped against the kitchen sink, sipping coffee and watching him over the rim of her mug. Every time he looked up from his feast, it was to meet her narrowed gaze.

"What?" he finally snapped, his mouth full of toast and runny egg yolk.

"Just wondering why you came here, that's all," she said with a one-sided shrug. He gave his plastered arm a speaking look and chose not to respond to her comment. "It's just that you can go anywhere in the world to recuperate. Why Riversend?"

"Precisely." He nodded, sending her a condescending thumbs-up before mopping up more of the delicious yolk with his toast. When she turned her nose up like someone who'd just caught a whiff of something putrid, he grinned. "I could go anywhere, so this little bum-fuck town in the middle of nowhere is exactly the last place in the world anybody would look for me."

That offended her. *Good.* Served her right for digging around in something that was none of her business.

"I can't come here every day," she said coldly, draining her mug and slamming it down on the sink. "So you'll have to sort something else out."

"Don't you worry your pretty little head over it. I'll be fine," he said cheerfully, knowing exactly how much his patronizing words and voice would aggravate her. She pursed her lips and turned to rinse her mug beneath the faucet.

"Having a near-death experience hasn't exactly improved your personality."

"Nothing wrong with my personality to begin with," he dismissed. "And it was hardly a near-death experience. Just a bit of blood and drama. I had it all under control."

"I saw the footage; everybody is carrying on about what a hero you are. When, in fact, that guy had no business getting within a meter of Laura Prentiss, did he? You fucked up, didn't you?"

Sam's jaw clenched, and he glared at the woman staring at him with her challenging, defiant gaze. Of course she would see what very few others had seen. Sam and his team *had* fucked up, and it had nearly cost Sam and—worse—*Lally* their lives.

He shouldn't have been in the field at all. He had lost his edge, and these days he found managing the business a lot more rewarding than the mind-numbing boredom of trailing after some asshole playboy or ditzy pop star. Before they had gone their separate ways, Sam had dealt with the clients, the contracts, and management, while Mason had preferred handling the training program.

The arrangement had suited both men. After Mason had sold his half of the business, Sam had taken on his partner's workload until he could find someone to replace him. But he had been eager to relinquish the recruitment and training responsibilities once he had hired a suitable replacement for Mason. Sam didn't know why he had acquiesced to Lally's request, maybe because it had seemed like a cakewalk. Maybe a small part of him had been bored or restless. He wasn't entirely sure.

All he knew was that he hadn't assessed the threat properly, hadn't anticipated such extreme escalation from the letters to actual physical danger. It had been fucking inexcusable and a clear sign that Sam should probably stick to management. Still, having Daffodil McGregor point out his flaws was grating.

"Don't bother with the dishes," he said, hearing the ice in his voice. "I'm sure I'll manage to load the dishwasher. Thanks for breakfast." Daff's eyes flickered and the challenge faded, to be replaced by something resembling regret.

"Our numbers are on the fridge if you should need anything."

"I won't."

"Brand, look, I'm—"

"Thank you." His voice brooked no argument and she nodded before retreating through the back door.

Sam glared at the plate of half-eaten eggs and bacon in front of him, his appetite completely gone. The woman was a total viper. He didn't understand how she could be related to Daisy and Dahlia.

"Promise me you'll think about it," Aisha urged, and Lia stared at the woman, still a little stunned by the offer that she'd been presented with.

"Oh, I'll do *more* than think about it," Lia said with an incredulous shake of her head. "Aisha, this is . . . I can't tell you . . ." Abruptly overcome with emotion, Lia dropped her head into her hands and drew in a shuddering breath. She felt the other woman's arm circle her hunched shoulders and squeeze.

"Don't be silly, Lia, you have to know how much we—I—value you. And with you aiming to gain your BEd, it makes sense all round," she said, but her brusque voice had a telltale wobble in it. Aisha knew, better than Lia's own family, how lost she had felt since her engagement had ended. Lia had once, in a fit of depression and hopelessness, confided her feelings of inadequacy to Aisha. Soon after that, Aisha had started asking Lia to unofficially substitute for a couple of hours here and there. Getting a second chance at a career was priceless and gave her even greater incentive to complete her degree.

"Thank you," Lia whispered fiercely and wrapped her friend's pregnant bulk into a tight hug. The baby kicked in protest, and both women laughed. Lia stepped back and wiped her face self-consciously.

"I think you're late for your lunch," Aisha gently reminded her, and Lia nodded before reaching over to hug her again, this time a little gentler.

"I'll call you later," Lia said. Lia couldn't wait to tell Daff her news. She couldn't remember being more excited.

Her sister was waiting for her already, and because of her excitement, Lia didn't initially notice her sister's dark mood.

"Oh my gosh! Guess what, Daff!" she said as she sat down across from her sister.

"They finally cured assholitis?"

"No!" Lia squealed, before registering her words. "What?"

"Nothing, sorry. Forget about it. What has you so excited?"

"Aisha wants me to start working at the preschool again. After the vacation." Most of the schools had closed for a short first quarter break just that day, the preschool included. "Just half a day, twice a week for now, but it pays a small salary, and she eventually wants to offer me a full-time job as a caregiver, but of course she can't do that until I have a BEd."

"You already knew that," Daff pointed out, confused.

"Yes, but I always thought I'd have to leave Riversend to find work, but Aisha wants to spend less hours at work after the baby's born and Tumi is leaving at the end of the year, so there'll be a position for me."

"Yeah, but you can't really fill Tumi or Aisha's positions until you graduate."

"I know that, but they won't replace Tumi, so the other ladies and I will pick up the slack."

"It'll take at least four years," Daff reminded, clearly playing the devil's advocate.

"Actually," Lia said with a shy smile, "it'll only take about three. I've been doing an online degree."

Daff looked at her for a beat and then squealed. "Oh my God, you're such a secretive little cow! Why didn't you tell anyone? How long have you been doing this?"

"I've just started my second year," she admitted, and her smile widened when Daff squealed again. "I should have done this years ago, Daff. It's a calling. I just kept putting it off and expecting other things to fulfill and enrich my life. I should never have done that. I study at night and on weekends. I have money saved, Grammy and Grampa's trust, and with the extra I'll now be earning with this job, I can actually afford to rent Daisy's house . . . after you move out, of course. Or maybe we can be roomies."

Daff jumped up and rounded the table to give her a hug. Then she summoned Suzy over.

"We're celebrating, Suzy! Some bubbly, if you please. And not the cheap stuff, either! We're going to do this in style." Lia laughed at her sister's infectious happiness and felt silly for not telling Daff about the degree sooner.

"You should have told us—why didn't you?" her sister asked after sitting back down, and Lia shrugged uncomfortably.

"I don't know. After things ended with Clayton, I wanted to do something just for me. And I suppose I wanted to prove to myself that I could do it. Know what I mean? I didn't want to share it with anyone. Not yet."

"Silly. We would have been nothing but happy for you."

"I know. I'll tell Mom and Daddy soon, too."

"Well, my news seems like a damp squib compared to yours now," Daff complained good-naturedly. "But Spence has finally acknowledged that it would be best all round if I moved in with him and Charlie. So you and I won't be roomies. I never really thought you were interested in moving out, though. You're such a homebody."

"I'll still be a homebody, but in a different home." Lia could barely contain her excitement. "And I'm so happy for you, Daff. I can't believe it has taken Spencer this long to give in. You're like water dripping on rock, absolutely relentless."

"And I'm really happy you'll finally be chasing your dream, Lia. Who cares how long it took for you to get to this point? All that matters is that you're here now." Lia grinned—Daff could be so sage sometimes.

"So what happened at the PTA meeting last night?" Lia asked after they'd ordered their meals from Suzy.

"Oh my God, the drama," Daff said with her usual dramatic flair. "The asshole math teacher called Charlie an ill-mannered, ill-tempered, ill-bred . . . That was as far as he got before Spencer hulked out on him. I mean, it was pretty sexy. Spence doesn't get aggressive, but he was so pissed off that he seemed to expand to almost twice his size, and then he leaned down over the guy, like so . . ." Daff leaned over her wineglass and glared at it, reminding Lia a bit of Snoopy the beagle's vulture pose. "And said, all quiet like, 'I dare you to finish that sentence' . . . Oh my *God*, I could have jumped his bones right there and then. The teacher practically wet himself before he stuttered an apology and said something about Charlie needing to focus more in class and to stop being disruptive. Spencer just gave him a disgusted look and told him that if Charlie fails math he, Spencer, will hold the teacher *personally* accountable and that was that. We left. In grand style. I *did* jump his bones soon after. And he asked me to move in after that. He said that he hates not having me around all the time . . . still no proposal, but this is a step in the right direction."

"It definitely is." Lia nodded enthusiastically. Suzy brought the requested bubbly and their food, and there was silence between them as they took a moment to sauce and season their food. After which Daff lifted her glass of sparkling wine and urged the bashful Lia to do the same.

"To my little sister getting her degree!" she said with a grin.

"To my big sister, moving in with her man," Lia added, and they both giggled like schoolgirls before clinking their glasses together and taking a sip.

"So you saw Sam Brand last night?" Daff asked after the giggling had passed and they were focused on their food again, her voice much too casual. The subject change caught Lia by surprise, and she blinked before clearing her throat and nodding.

"Yes. He looks pretty rough." She avoided Daff's keen gaze and dug into her chicken schnitzel and mashed potatoes with what she hoped looked like relish. Quite honestly, the memory of how banged up and bruised Brand was made her lose her enthusiasm for the meal.

"I went around there this morning," Daff said between greedy bites from her huge burger. Lia waited while her sister took her sweet time before elaborating on her initial statement.

"And?" she finally prompted when it looked like Daff was going to scarf down the entire burger without pausing for breath.

"What?" Daff asked around a huge mouthful of meat and bread. "Oh." She swallowed and took a sip of water to wash it down. "He's such a jerk. I definitely don't like him—we'll make sure the cabin is stocked until he's able to get out and do some shopping himself, but I won't be going around to help him out with food prep or anything. I don't want to spend any more time around that douchebag than I have to. I don't care *what* Spencer says." The last was said so defiantly that Lia was willing to bet Spencer had already said quite a bit about her decision not to lend a neighborly hand to Brand in his time of need.

"He can't really do much with his dominant hand incapacitated," Lia said, recalling his frustration in attempting to get his shirt off the night before, and then she flushed when she recollected his chest once the shirt had actually come off. It took everything she had not to fan her flushed face.

"You okay? You look a little feverish," Daff asked, and Lia flushed even more.

"It's rather warm in here, isn't it?"

"Not noticeably."

"Anyway, I don't think I'll be seeing Gregory again," Lia said, desperate to change the subject.

"Gregory?" Daff looked blank, and Lia stared at her impatiently.

"*Gregory*, I mentioned him before. Several times, in fact. The bank manager?"

"Oh, *that* guy. For some reason I thought his name was Grant."

"Really? Do you ever listen when I talk?" It was exasperating how self-involved Daff could be at times.

"Well, you never sounded particularly enthusiastic when you spoke about him, I figured he wouldn't last long. So there was no point in really paying attention, was there? And look, I was right. You're not seeing him again. What was wrong with him? Did you fall asleep in the middle of dinner or something? Because that guy sounded boring."

"He had third-date expectations," Lia said primly.

"You went on three dates with that guy? He lasted longer than I expected. So he wanted to introduce his wiener to your hot pocket, did he?"

"*Must* you?" Lia asked. Daff could be so juvenile and vulgar sometimes.

"Did he want to holster his hot glue gun in your spasm chasm?" Daff continued solemnly and then snorted when Lia frowned at her.

"You're such a *child*," Lia chastised. "I'm never telling you anything again."

"Okay, okay. I'm sorry. I couldn't resist," Daff said, choking back her laughter. "Tell me what happened."

Lia pursed her lips and refused to comment, lifting a forkful of mashed potatoes to her mouth instead.

"Come on, Lia," she said coaxingly. "Don't be such a baby. I was just teasing. Tell me what Gilbert did."

"For cripes' sake! His name is Gregory."

"Lia, we've discussed this before . . . you *know* I can't take you seriously when you use words like *cripes*."

"Just because *you* like to swear doesn't mean I have to." Lia knew she sounded like an old woman, but seriously, her sister went a bit overboard with the language at times. It was so unladylike.

"Tell me about *Gregory*."

"Fine! He kissed me. And got a bit gropey." And just like that, Daff went as serious as a heart attack. All laughter fled from her eyes, and her expression froze. She could be a bit scary when she got into protective-big-sister mode.

"Do I have to find him and chop off his balls? Or did he listen when you told him to back off?"

"Of course he did. Eventually," Lia said carefully. Daff practically had smoke pouring from her nostrils, she was fuming so much.

"*Eventually?* What the fuck does that mean?"

"It wasn't anything serious, he touched my boob and kind of rubbed himself against me. But then you called and I had an excuse to go."

"You don't need an excuse, Lia. All you have to do is tell him no. And if he doesn't listen, knee him in the groin."

"I won't see him again."

"Not just this Gregory asshole. Any guy, Lia."

"I know, don't worry," Lia placated her, and Daff shook her head.

"It's hard not to. You're terrifyingly naïve at times, Lia. I worry about you." Her words made Lia bristle. She wished her family would stop seeing her as this helpless, sweet little girl who couldn't take care of herself.

"It's not your place to worry about me, Daff," she said, injecting enough frost in her voice to make her sister sit up and pay attention. "I'm not a child. And while I may have made a few stupid decisions in the past, I've *learned* from all of them. I never repeat my mistakes." Well, aside from that Sam Brand thing. But luckily nobody knew about that, and it definitely wouldn't happen again.

Daff didn't say anything for the longest time, merely stared at her, before shaking her head and shrugging.

"When are you thinking of moving into Daisy's place?" she asked. Another jarring subject change, and it took Lia a moment to adjust.

"I'm not sure. I haven't really spoken to Daisy about it yet. I hope she doesn't have a potential tenant in mind already."

"I doubt that."

"I'll call her tonight. When are you moving out?"

"Soon as I can. Wouldn't want Spence to change his mind." She was only half joking.

"He wouldn't."

"Yeah, I know, but I'm paranoid sometimes. Besides, I really can't wait for us to be under the same roof."

Lia smiled; it was strange to see her oldest sister so hopelessly in love. Daff had always been tough and self-sufficient. She had become jaded in recent years, but since she and Spencer had fallen in love, the hard edges Daff had been starting to develop had softened.

"You will be soon enough," Lia told her, and Daff grinned.

"I've turned into a total sap," Daff said with a rueful shake of her head.

"Total."

"Shut up."

~

I need your help! Lia stared blankly at the message on her screen later that evening. Her parents were chatting amiably in front of the television and Lia had been contemplating heading up to her room for an early bedtime when the cryptic message from the unknown number came through.

The second message appeared on the screen a moment later. It's Brand.

Of course it was.

How did you get my number? she texted back.

I have my ways. Seriously, princess, I need your help.

Lia bit her lip uncertainly as she stared at the screen. She was a sucker, and it seemed that even Brand knew that. She was picturing him sprawled at the bottom of the staircase, hurt even worse than before.

What's wrong? Are you hurt?

Kind of.

Now what on earth was that supposed to mean? Either he was hurt or not—there was no *kind of.*

You going to help me or not?

Wow. Bossy. Part of her wanted to switch off her phone and ignore his cryptic messages. But her conscience screamed at her not to leave the poor man to fend for himself. He was injured, and helping him was the right thing to do. Especially since it seemed like Daff wasn't going to.

What do you need? she found herself reluctantly asking. The reply came seconds later.

Can you come over?

It's really late.

It's 20:30

She very nearly responded that eight thirty was late for her but managed to stop the pathetic response just in time. She sighed. She didn't owe him anything, but she'd feel terrible if he was really in pain or in need and she just ignored his cry for help.

I'll be there in 10 minutes.

CHAPTER FOUR

Lia contemplated the mostly dark cabin for a long time before she finally stepped out of her car. She self-consciously patted her hair and smoothed down her skirt before throwing back her shoulders and walking up the path to the front door.

She knocked and waited a moment, but there was no response. Another knock yielded the same result. Concerned that he was hurt and incapable of answering, she tried the handle and was surprised when the door swung soundlessly inward. The only source of light was coming from the loft, and Lia tilted her head and stared at it for a moment, wondering if she should venture up there.

"Mis—Brand?" she called softly. Nothing. She raised her voice. *"Brand?"*

"Up here." She breathed a sigh of relief when his voice drifted down to her.

"I'm coming up," she warned, and she heard him swear in response to her words.

"I hope so, otherwise there'd be no fucking point in having you here, would there?"

So rude.

She made her way upstairs, not sure what to expect. When she got to the loft, all she found was an unmade bed with clothing scattered all over the floor. Jeez, what a slob. She curbed the uncharitable thought, reminding herself that he was injured and this was probably not a true reflection of what his living space usually looked like.

"Brand?"

"Here."

Crumbs! His voice was coming from the bathroom. Not good.

"Uh. What do you need?" she asked, and he swore again.

"*You.* Give me a hand, will you?" She heard water sloshing and grimaced.

"I don't think I should."

"Dahlia, for fuck's sake, this is embarrassing enough as it is. Don't make it worse."

Bracing herself for the worst, she pushed the slightly ajar door open and found Sam Brand sitting in the huge soaker tub with an extremely chagrined look on his face. He had his plastered arm draped over the side, and from her vantage point at the door all she could see was his head and chest.

"I seem to be having some difficulty getting out of this damned tub," he gritted out from between tightly clenched teeth. His red face rivaled hers.

"I should call Spencer."

"Fuck that! I don't need anyone else to know about this."

"You're injured, there's really nothing to be embarrassed about."

"You can help me; you've already seen me naked . . ."

"I haven't," she protested.

"Semantics. Just help me out of here, will you? My weak leg keeps slipping out from under me, the wound in my back hurts like hell, and I've already hit my arm on the rim about a dozen times." She winced in sympathy. He looked furious and disgruntled, but beneath it all she could see the humiliation and pain in his eyes. The vulnerability struck a tender chord and made her want to ease his discomfort and take care of him.

"Why didn't you shower?"

"Because I thought bathing would be easier with the cast. I didn't anticipate the difficulties of getting out of this deep fucking tub."

"I really think Spencer—"

"Lia!" It was the first time he'd ever called her that, and the surprise at hearing her name on his lips shut her up. She liked the sound of it in his deep, gravelly voice, and it sent a shocking frisson of awareness and heat sizzling down her spine. Well, that was completely inappropriate, given the situation. "The water is cold, princess. It took me a while to admit defeat."

"It's lucky you had your phone close by," she said, her eyes drifting to the phone, which he'd placed on the laundry basket beside the bath.

"Yeah."

"Uh, well, then. I think it would be easier if we drained the bath."

"How the hell would that be easier? I'd lose the buoyancy of the water."

"You said your leg keeps slipping, you need some traction. Trust me, this'll work." He didn't look convinced but reached forward and yanked the plug out. Lia took a step back and averted her eyes as the water level dropped at an alarming speed. They both remained awkwardly silent while the bath drained.

Lia's eyes darted around the bathroom, unable to rest on anything for too long, but she was excruciatingly aware of the fact that *Brand's* gaze never left her flushed face. Finally, after what seemed like hours, the last bit of water gurgled down the drain, but Lia was still unable to drop her eyes to the wet, naked man in the tub. He might have lost weight, but he was still a very virile man, with way too much sex appeal.

"You're going to have to look at me at some point, Princess Lia." He chuckled at his own nerdy pun, and Lia glanced heavenward, praying for strength. She took a deep, bracing breath and diverted her eyes down to his face, keeping her gaze very determinedly away from any other part of his body.

"You have to put a towel beneath your feet," she said and happily looked away from him to find a towel. She spotted one, a small hand towel draped through the metal loop beside the basin, much too quickly. She dampened it slightly beneath the basin faucet and handed it to him after one quick glance at his face.

She heard the squeaking of his wet body rubbing against the porcelain of the tub as he leaned forward to comply with her instruction.

"Done," he said, his voice strained. Right then, this was the tricky part. She removed her cardigan and hung it neatly over the towel rail. She was wearing a sweet, knee-length, pink floral dress with pretty little capped sleeves. It was one of her favorite dresses.

"Lift your arm," she instructed, keeping her voice as brusque as possible. He obeyed, lifting the heavy cast with a wince, and Lia ducked beneath the arm, draping it over her shoulders. She was bent at an awkward angle beside the tub. "Now bear down on the towel and use your other hand to push yourself up."

He did as she said, and with a huff of surprise from him, he stood with almost effortless ease. He was so startled by the smooth movement that he staggered a bit and she grunted as she took almost the full force of his weight while he ungracefully stepped out of the tub and unintentionally engulfed her in what could only be considered a bear hug. Lia's entire front was pressed up against his naked, wet chest and groin, and her cheek was pressed against his.

This time there was no escaping the dart of awareness, and now that he was safely delivered from his predicament, she knew he felt it, too. He tensed, and before he could move away, she felt the unmistakable stirring of his groin against her stomach.

"Did you miss me, princess?" His breath stirred the hair at her temple, and his voice rumbled in her ear, sending a delicious vibration through her body.

"Let me go," she demanded weakly. He didn't say anything more, just released her and stepped back. She couldn't help it, her eyes darted down to his groin, and she swallowed at the sight of his very impressive erection, which arched upward beautifully and kissed his abdomen just below his navel. She almost immediately redirected her gaze to his face, but judging from the amused smirk on his too-perfect mouth, he'd noticed her little lapse. She felt her cheeks heating and stepped farther away from him before turning blindly and reaching for a thick, fluffy towel draped on the towel rack on the rung below her cardigan. She tossed it back at him without a word, and he chuckled.

"I'm decent now," he said a moment a later.

She very much doubted that.

"I'll leave you to it, good night." She grabbed her cardigan and was halfway down the stairs when his voice halted her.

"Lia. Please don't leave. I want . . . I have . . ." His lack of articulation and the frustrated groan were enough to make her turn around and stare at him. He was standing on the landing, a towel wrapped around his lean waist, his beautiful chest still gleaming with the moisture from his bath. "I'd like to talk to you about something. Please."

She hesitated.

"Please." Three *please*s. She'd have to have a heart of stone to ignore the entreaty, and her shoulders sagged.

"Fine. But get dressed first."

"Thank you," he said, before turning away and limping toward the bed.

Lia made her way to the dark living room and switched on a lamp before curling up on the sofa and waiting. She listened to the rustling, interspersed with impatient swearing, coming from the loft, and a few moments later Brand's breathless and harassed voice called out to her.

"I'm dressed. Do you mind coming up here? I don't think I can manage the stairs again tonight."

Calling herself all kinds of fool, Lia complied. She took the stairs slowly, feeling like a condemned woman on her way to the executioner. He was sitting on the edge of the bed, dressed—if you could call it that—only in a pair of boxer briefs, with his legs spread and his forearms braced on his thighs as he contemplated the floor between his bare feet. He raised his blond head when he heard her tread on the landing.

"This is the best I can manage with just one arm," he said wryly. "Hope it doesn't offend your sensibilities, Miss Priss."

As if she hadn't *just* seen his penis.

She pursed her lips and said nothing at all in response to that.

"What did you want to talk about?"

"This, actually," he said, his crisp British accent particularly noticeable on those two words.

"I don't understand."

"I need help, Lia, and right now I find your company a damned sight more tolerable than anyone else's. I was hoping you'd be willing to assist me for just a couple of weeks until this cast comes off."

His request completely threw her, and she wasn't sure how to respond at all.

"You're gawking, princess. Not an attractive look."

"Why don't you hire a nurse?"

"Fuck that," he dismissed, and she heaved a sigh at the language—the man really had no filter. Then again, he probably didn't care about his crudity and how it offended her. "I'm not an invalid. I just need a bit of assistance, that's all. And I don't want strangers hovering around me all the time. You don't piss me off, I don't mind your company, and you don't talk my ear off."

"You barely know me. How do you know I *won't* do those things?"

"Look, Mason tells me you don't have a job at the moment. Well, I'm willing to pay you handsomely for just a little of your time." That made her pause. A supplemental income would come in handy if she was going to rent Daisy's house.

"How much of my time?" she asked and then regretted the question when his gaze sharpened. She would make a *terrible* poker player—she had no notion of playing her cards close to her chest.

"Well, I need someone to do some cooking for me. And I definitely need help shaving, as you can see I did a piss-poor job today." He lifted his strong cleft jaw to indicate the patches of dark stubble emerging. His beard seemed to be a shade or two darker than his hair. "And driving me around when I need to go to my doctor's appointments or just need to get the fuck out of here for a few hours. I don't do well in one confined space for too long, I'd go crazy."

"I won't be available on Tuesday and Friday mornings," she said, keeping her voice neutral.

"Why not?"

"I just got a part-time job at the preschool, they'll need me from eight till noon."

"I'm sure I'll be fine on those mornings."

"This is just a job? Nothing else? No funny business or anything?"

Sam bit back a grin at the question. He had her exactly where he wanted her, and smiling now would make her suspicious. He kept his face neutral, infusing just enough curiosity and confusion into his expression to set her mind at ease.

"Funny business?"

"You know."

"I'm afraid I don't." He added a faint frown into the mix, and she chewed on her luscious lower lip, looking uncertain. "You'll have to elaborate."

"I mean, you know? We have a history, and I just want to be sure that you don't expect the same thing from me again."

He couldn't play dumb anymore, she'd be onto him. He allowed his expression to clear.

"*Ah.* You mean no fucking," he said, and she winced. He covered his smile with his hand and pretend to clear his throat. "Of course not, princess. What kind of man would I be, offering to pay a nice girl like you for sex?"

She looked horrified by his words, as the connection clearly hadn't occurred to her before he said it.

"I didn't think you meant to pay me for it," she gasped.

"I mean, aside from the fact that I *don't* have to pay for it, never have, you're definitely not that type of woman."

"I didn't mean that. I just meant there'd be no flirting and stuff."

"I shall attempt to restrain myself. I know you're looking for a husband, and I have to tell you, I'm not husband material. Flirting with you might give you the wrong impression. I would hate that. I'm not the marrying kind, Lia." He kept his eyes level and his voice dead serious. This he needed to make absolutely clear to her, because he absolutely *did* intend to fuck her again. But not before his cast came off—he would use that time to get her primed and ready.

Basically it amounted to a week or two of foreplay, and by the time the cast came off and he was himself again, she would be so damned keen to get back into bed with him, she'd take him on any terms. Meantime, he was ready for a bit of fun and games with this prissy little schoolteacher.

"I really need your help, Lia," he said, injecting as much sincerity as he could into his voice. He meant it—he needed her help around the house, he needed her help with shaving and dressing, and he definitely needed her help to stave off boredom and keep him sane. Sam had a low threshold for boredom and was always busy doing something. This enforced rest was already hell, which meant he had to find ways to occupy his body and mind.

Of course, he would have been perfectly fine with having Spencer help him out of his ridiculous bathtub predicament. Sam had actually had the man's number up on his screen and had been a second away from calling when the thought of contacting Lia instead occurred to him. At that point it had been a no-brainer—the potential entertainment value alone had sold the idea. And while waiting for her, he'd come up with this plan.

Have her help him out around the house, butter her up, make her want him so badly that she'd be hot to trot for a blazing sexual adventure with him. By the time his cast came off, before they sealed the deal, so to speak, she'd definitely have no illusions about him being her Mr. Right. So she wouldn't be fabricating any happily ever after fantasies about them in her prissy little head when they wound up in bed again.

She still looked uncertain, so he sweetened the pot with an amount of money that would make most people sit up and pay attention.

"That seems excessive," she surprised him by saying. Okay, weird. If anything, the exorbitant amount had made her look a little more doubtful.

"It's a fair amount," he said, and she shook her head.

"It's daylight robbery." He blinked. What the fuck? "I can't take that much from you, Brand. You're in pain, you need help. To take all that money from someone so clearly in need would be unconscionable."

She shook her head and gave him a different number, half of his original offer. Was this chick for real? Seriously, she was unemployed and probably needed the money. He'd casually asked Mason to give him the rundown on the family last night. And had impatiently waited as his friend rambled on about his newfound sister, Charlie, then Daff and Spencer. Dr. and Mrs. McGregor. Lia had been last on the list, and Mason's information on her had been perfunctory at best.

"Lia, she's sweet. Very sincere, always wants to help people. She's been in a bit of a rut since her wedding fell through. Her asshole fiancé persuaded her to give up her job and she's been unemployed since then. A shame, really—according to Daisy, she really loved that job."

Mason had left it at that, and Sam didn't push the man for further information, knowing that to do so would alert Mason to the fact that he had more than just a passing interest in Lia.

"Right. Okay," he said in response to her last comment, still a bit at a loss after her refusal of his initial compensation. "Thanks."

"I'm just happy I'm the one you approached about this. Anyone else wouldn't have thought twice about fleecing you," she said with a sweet smile. "You have to be more careful."

"Yes." He felt a little wrong-footed and couldn't quite get his bearings. He cleared his throat, striving to regain control over the situation. "So I take it this means you'll do it?"

"I'll help you. I'll come around first thing in the morning to fix your breakfast and we can take it from there, okay?"

Just like that. She just took his word for it that there'd be no "funny business," asked for less money than he'd been willing to pay, and was willing to cook for him, *shave* him, and be his gofer/chauffeur for the next two weeks? It seemed too good to be true.

"Do you . . . uh . . . do you have any conditions or anything?"

"What do you mean, conditions? Like allergies or illnesses?" He stared at her, flummoxed by her bizarre turn of thought.

"No, of course not. I mean caveats to our agreement?"

"Oh." She laughed at her assumption, the delightful sound ending on the tiniest of snorts, and shook her head. "Sorry, that was a weird conclusion to leap to, wasn't it? No conditions. I just wanted to be sure there wouldn't be any, y'know . . ."

"Yeah. *Funny business*," he completed. And she nodded, flushing slightly.

"But it was silly of me to even think that. I mean, you're with Laura Prentiss now. And you know that I'm looking for something else, something you've already claimed to have no interest in whatsoever. So with that in mind, I think this arrangement will work out fine."

"You really think so?" he asked, fascinated, and his question made her pause and eye him in concern.

"You don't?"

"Well, we *do* have some mad chemistry between us." Pointing that out probably wasn't in his best interests, but he couldn't help himself. How could she just dismiss the overpowering sexual attraction between them?

"I'm sure we can overcome our baser urges. After all, I'm hardly your type and vice versa."

"So what's your *type*?"

"Not you."

What the fuck was that supposed to mean?

"So anybody else *but* me? That's a little insulting, princess."

"I didn't mean it like that, I just meant not someone like you. Someone so clearly not interested in commitment, or in settling down and having kids. You're the proverbial rolling stone, right? Well, I'm looking for a rock. Someone steady, reliable, interested in establishing some roots. And definitely not someone who gets stabbed for a living!"

"I don't get stabbed for a living," he protested. "I try very hard to do the exact opposite of that."

"And yet, if it comes down to it, you'd take the bullet or the stab wound for your client, right? Which, while commendable and brave as heck, is definitely not what I'm looking for."

"You'd rather have a coward?"

"I'd rather have a guy who'd put me, our kids, before any client. Who'd think twice before jumping in front of that bullet or placing himself in harm's way. I'd rather have him around than in an early grave."

"I'm trying to avoid an early grave, thank you very much," Sam said.

"Of course you are, but with what you do . . ." Her voice trailed off, and she shook her head regretfully.

"Your perfect cowardly man could walk in front of a bus and still wind up in an early grave. He could get some dread disease or electrocute himself making toast. There are no guarantees in this life."

"True. But his odds of living to a ripe old age are still better than yours," she said before wincing. "I'm sorry. That sounded really harsh."

"I'm really fucking careful," Sam said. He could hear the defensive heat in his own voice and tried to tone it down. He wasn't sure why he was letting this get to him. The Laura Prentiss job was never meant to be a permanent arrangement, and Sam had already admitted to himself that he didn't want to be in the field anymore. He could tell Lia that, but the more cynical side of him acknowledged that it was better if she thought he was the wrong man for her—it meant she'd have no expectations of more from him once they resumed intimacies. "I'm a professional. None of my officers, or I, go into a job prepared or willing to die. That fatalistic bullshit makes for a piss-poor CPO."

"CPO?"

"Close protection officer."

"I would just have gone with bodyguard."

"Yeah, well, you're wrong on a lot of fronts."

"I didn't mean to offend you," she said quietly. He shrugged.

"Since I'm quite clearly the exact opposite of everything you're looking for in a man, I'm surprised you fell into bed with me in the first place." Why was he pushing this? Sam wasn't sure. He was just stupidly and unexpectedly offended that she thought *everything* about him was wrong. He took snide satisfaction in the uncomfortable blush that lit up her face and kept his challenging gaze level.

"Well, I didn't say I don't find you attractive," she said carefully. "Most women would. You're very handsome and—and . . . charming when you choose to be. I was attracted to you and I thought I wouldn't see you again."

"At least not until baby Delphinium's christening," he mused and bit back a smile at her startled look.

He remembered that? People rarely paid attention to—much less remembered the details of—her weird little tangents, so for Brand to remember the exact name she'd used was a little unprecedented.

"Uh, that's right. So I thought why not—just once—do something a little out of the box and exciting before settling down into my normal, expected life?" Although nothing had really been going as expected in her life for the last couple of years. "I mean, you're a good-looking, experienced man, so obviously as a healthy, heterosexual woman, I'd find you attractive and intriguing."

"Good for a quick roll in the hay and nothing more? Why, princess, I feel cheap and used now." Did he? His voice was light and mocking, but there was an underlying seriousness in his face and eyes.

"That's all you wanted, a quick roll in the hay—you were quite clear on that. You're all for meaningless hookups, remember?"

His beautiful mouth quirked at the corners as he recognized his own words. He really was a very attractive man. He had dirty-blond hair, just a shade lighter than golden brown. Six months ago it had been clipped military short, but it was longer now and wavier than she'd expected and looked so thick and silky she itched to run her fingers through it. She liked how it fell over his broad forehead. He kept impatiently shoving his free hand through it to keep it out of his eyes. He had straight, intense eyebrows darker than his hair, slanted over piercing ice-blue eyes. He had creases—from laughter or the glare of the sun, she couldn't be sure which—radiating from the corner of his eyes that gave his rugged face a lived-in, masculine appeal. When she'd first seen him all those months ago, she'd concluded that he wasn't as handsome as the Carlisle brothers, but in her opinion he was much, *much* sexier. He was only about three or four inches taller than Lia's five foot seven inches, and before his injuries he had sported the spare, muscular build of a triathlete. Naturally he'd lost some of that muscle mass, but he could ill afford to lose the weight and she meant to help him regain some of it with her cooking.

"Yes, I do so enjoy a good, meaningless hookup," he said in response to her previous comment. "And I hope that after our raunchy encounters, you now appreciate the merits thereof as well."

In his very proper English accent, everything he said sounded ever so decent—until the words sank in. That was when she felt her cheeks heat up like a furnace. She hated blushing, she knew it made her look like a blotchy teen, but for some reason Sam Brand could make her light up like a beacon. It was ridiculous.

"Any time you want to revisit the sexy times with me, Lia . . ."

"That won't happen," she interrupted primly.

"Just thought I'd put it out there," he said with an unrepentant smile.

"I have to get home; my parents must be wondering where I am." She instantly regretted the words when his eyes widened in bemusement.

"Your parents? You live at home?"

"Not for long," she said self-consciously, but instead of staring at her like she was some kind of freak, a roguish grin lit up his wicked face.

"God, you just added another illicit element to that already sexy button-down librarian schoolmarm thing you've got going. Can you sneak me into your room for a make-out session while your parents are watching telly downstairs?"

Her jaw dropped, and he winced.

"Yeah, that's borderline deviant behavior, isn't it? Still, you're the walking answer to every man's forbidden prayer. All you have to do is tell me you went to Catholic school and were considering becoming a nun and I swear I won't be responsible for my actions."

"Ugh, I'm leaving. I'll see you in the morning."

"Good night, princess. Thanks for coming to my rescue."

Lia made her way to the stairs but paused on the landing to look back at him. He was still sitting on the edge of the bed, staring at her.

"Do you need anything before I leave? Something from the kitchen, perhaps?"

"A good-night kiss?" The lilt in his voice was so ridiculously hopeful that Lia couldn't bring herself to work up any kind of anger at the suggestion.

"I doubt you'll find one of those in the kitchen," she said, and he laughed.

"Tuck me in?"

"'Night, Brand," she said with a long-suffering sigh. Then, because boundaries were important, she felt obligated to remind, "And remember our agreement, no funny business. Asking for a kiss qualifies as funny business."

"Sorry, princess, it won't happen again. I'm just loopy after taking my pain meds. Send me a text when you get home safely so that I'll know not to send in the cavalry to come rescue you."

"Will do." He smiled at her response.

"Good night, Lia."

Sam woke up with a headache, a healthy appetite, and a huge hard-on. Dreams of Lia McGregor had definitely contributed to today's top-quality morning wood and were probably also at fault for the terrible headache pounding away beneath his skull. He hadn't slept very soundly—the constant dreams of Lia under him, over him, next to him, her mouth on him, her hands stroking and petting his body, had startled him awake throughout the night. And his frustration at finding himself alone in bed hadn't helped the situation.

He'd finally resorted to a hands-on session just before dawn. Most unsatisfying wank of his life. His left hand couldn't quite master the technique or grip—it was either too weak or too strong—and the whole experience had left him feeling irritated and unsated.

He stretched, groaned, and cracked open a sticky eyelid, confirming that it was indeed light outside. Something smelled *amazing*. He sniffed at the air . . . that was definitely bacon. Fully awake now, he pushed himself out of bed and limped his way over to the loft's waist-high glass wall. Lia was bustling around the kitchen, the bright morning sunlight catching the warm auburn notes in her dark-brown hair. From his vantage point high up in Mason's clever aerie, he could watch her unobserved for a few long moments. She really was pretty, with her expressive, thickly lashed gray eyes set beneath perfectly arched eyebrows. Her soft, full lips had a slight upward tilt that gave one the impression she was always on the verge of smiling, which contrasted sharply with the underlying sadness he sometimes glimpsed in her luminous eyes. High cheekbones and a delicate chin completed the pretty picture, and while she wasn't a raving beauty, her prettiness had a wholesome charm, which was *not* something that usually appealed to Sam. His attraction to her definitely stemmed from her prim and proper personality. That unconscious aura of untouchability and perfect poise she presented to the world challenged him, and Sam was fundamentally incapable of backing down from a challenge.

Even now he felt everything in him tightening in anticipation of their next encounter. He found himself grinning like an idiot at the prospect of talking to her again, which was bound to be entertaining. It always was.

"Morning," he called, and she nearly dropped a skillet in fright. She carefully placed it on the stove top and stared up at him in admonition.

"You scared me," she chastised.

"You knew I was up here," he pointed out.

"I thought you were asleep."

"I'm not."

"Maybe you should get dressed," she suggested, her face bright red as she kept her eyes determinedly above his waist. Sam snorted, only now registering his nudity and the fact that his erection had found renewed vigor in her presence.

"You know I need help dressing," he said, injecting a fair amount of misery into his voice. Her eyes flickered with sympathy for a moment before they narrowed and the concern in her pretty face transformed into a full-on glare.

"You were wearing boxer briefs when I left last night," she reminded. "You managed to get out of them without a problem. You can get into them with equal ease, I'm sure."

Busted.

"You're a heartless woman, Dahlia McGregor," he said on a dejected sigh before turning around. He grinned at the sound of her gasp, hoping she enjoyed the cheeky eyeful of ass he'd so considerately gifted her with.

"Breakfast will be ready in five minutes," she called.

Lia ran a shaky hand over her face and muffled a groan behind her fingers. This was probably the most ill-advised thing she'd ever done in her life. Why did she think she could handle this? Sam Brand was too good-looking, too sexy, and too darned arrogant and self-assured by far, and Lia had been an idiot for thinking she could handle him.

She took a moment to compose herself before sucking in a bracing breath.

"Woman up, Lia. You can handle two weeks. The man is as weak as a puppy, for goodness' sake. Get over this." Ineffectual and unconvincing pep talk over, she shook herself and went back to work.

She had everything prepared when she heard Brand's footsteps coming down the stairs. She threw back her shoulders and turned to face him with a bright smile, which immediately faltered when she noted first his naked chest, then his scowl, and finally the scrap of fabric he had clutched in his left hand.

"Trouble?" He didn't bother answering her, merely shoved his left hand in her direction. It was clutching a cotton shirt. She took the shirt gingerly and shook it out to assess it. The left sleeve was inside out, as if he'd had his arm in it and then pulled it back out without much care. The right sleeve was cut down the seam to allow the cast to slide in with ease. But clearly, Brand hadn't found it very easy, if his lethal glower was anything to go by.

Lia didn't say anything. She dragged the left sleeve the right side out and shook the shirt vigorously to get rid of the creases.

"Hold out your left arm," she instructed, keeping her voice crisp and businesslike. He obeyed sullenly and she slid the sleeve up before focusing on the other arm. She made short work of that, too, and soon found herself standing in front of him, way too close for comfort, while she buttoned the shirt. She was so aware of his closeness, his heat, and the wonderful, masculine smell of his cologne that she couldn't control the shaking of her fingers and she botched the job. He said nothing when she had to start over, just stood quietly, his breath ruffling the hair at her temple. The tips of her fingers inadvertently brushed against the silky skin of his chest and he shuddered, his breath escaping on a slightly muffled groan.

"Sorry," she murmured, her voice quivering. She tried to take more care not to touch him, but she was swiftly turning into a wreck, her hands shaking almost uncontrollably now. She paused and let her hands fall to her sides, where she clenched them into fists to regain some semblance of control, before she attempted the task again.

She was on the last button and nearly jumped out of her skin when he reached out and brushed his fingertips against her cheek.

"You have flour on your face," he explained, his voice ridiculously gravelly.

Lia left the top two buttons unfastened and stepped away from his heat, patting at her hectically flushed cheeks in what she hoped looked like an attempt to dust any residual flour from her face. Rather than what it truly was—a really flustered move to cool down and gather her composure.

After a moment of frantic confusion, she finally took a long look at him before frowning.

"Well, this is completely impractical," she noted. The split shirt-sleeve hung uselessly from his shoulder. "Whose bright idea was this?"

"My mother altered some of my clothing to help me acclimate to my infirmity," he said. Lia immediately felt bad for her harsh observation—and an overwhelming curiosity about his mother.

Sam watched the play of emotions on Lia's face. She wanted to ask him about his mother. He was sure of it. He hoped she resisted the impulse. He didn't particularly want to discuss his private life with her—it wasn't any of her business. She was meant to be a distraction, even if she didn't quite know that yet, and nosing her way into his private affairs would make her more of a nuisance than a distraction.

"I have to remove this sleeve," she finally said, her natural reserve kicking in, and Sam barely refrained from exhaling a relieved sigh. Instead he cast a rueful glance down at the ruined sleeve. He had packed mostly loose tank tops, which were easy enough to get into, but his mother had taken it upon herself to destroy several of his expensive dress shirts during one of her—as usual, ill-advised—acts of maternal concern. And because she'd been hovering and helping like a concerned mama bear during the packing process, Sam couldn't bring himself to leave the mangled shirts behind.

He'd had no intention of ever wearing them, precisely because buttoning them up with his left hand was a tedious process and the useless split sleeve looked ridiculous. In typical *Mimsy* fashion, she hadn't thought things through, but he had politely thanked her for her help rather than hurt her feelings by pointing out the flaws in her plan. Now he found himself silently thanking her for ruining some of his best shirts, because they suited his purpose.

Sam was turned on by how very turned on *Lia* had been. And try though she might, she couldn't hide her reaction from him. The uneven breathing, the trembling fingers, the hectic flush in her cheeks—though Miss McGregor could dissemble as much as she wanted, Sam knew exactly how performing such an intimate task for him had affected her. But Sam was dangerously susceptible to falling prey to his own little game. If his response to the shirt thing was any indication, he would go stir-crazy with lust long before his cast came off.

"Something smells fantastic." He forced a cheerful note into his hoarse voice, and it seemed to snap her back to the present.

"*Yes.* Yes, of course! Your breakfast. Please have a seat, I'll just—just . . ." She paused and inhaled deeply, patting at her flushed cheeks again. "Uh, just get rid of this sleeve and feed you. I've left a lasagna in the fridge for lunch, and I'll pop around with your dinner this evening."

The flurry of words made him frown.

"You're not staying?" he asked shortly, and her mouth snapped shut as she stared at him in surprise.

"No. Of course not. I have a lot of errands to run this morning."

"Then what the fuck am I paying you for?" He was seriously aggravated that she'd just swan off and leave him on his own all day.

"Cooking, cleaning, doing some driving, and maybe helping you with some of the more difficult tasks. I do have a life, you know? I didn't expect to have to stay here all day and wipe the sweat from your fevered brow," she said tartly, and Sam bit back a smile at the show of defiance.

"What kind of errands?"

"Various errands," she hedged. Why was she hedging? What did she have to hide?

"I'll join you," he decided.

"You'd be bored."

"I'll be bored here, too; I'd rather be bored with you than alone."

"It's not a good idea. You should rest."

"I've rested enough. I'll go crazy in this place by myself all day."

"You should have thought of that before coming here."

"That's a very uncharitable sentiment, princess."

"*Fine*, you can tag along"—as if he were a child—"but not one word of complaint when you find yourself bored out of your mind."

"That's the spirit," he praised, and she glared at him. How adorable was that? The cutest little glare ever. It made him smile, which made her forehead wrinkle even more.

She shook her head, grumbling beneath her breath as she turned away to rummage through one of the drawers. She returned moments later, clutching a pair of kitchen shears.

"Sit down," she commanded, and he meekly dropped into one of the kitchen chairs. He was starting to like this bossy streak of hers. She made short work of the sleeve, and Sam tried not to wince when she tossed the remnants of his Dior into the garbage.

She bustled around a bit more before returning with a mug of coffee clutched in one hand and a plate in the other.

"It's probably gone cold by now," she said, and Sam straightened in anticipation, hoping whatever it was tasted as good as it smelled. He didn't even care if it had cooled down. He was starving. She handed him the mug, which he accepted with a grateful smile, and carefully placed the plate in front of him, before turning away and picking up a small bowl and another plate from the counter next to the stove top. She positioned those on the table as well.

Sam barely registered her movements as he blinked down at the first plate in consternation. It was . . . *food*. Of that he was certain. It smelled good, looked good, but . . .

"Why the fuck is my breakfast frowning at me?" He could hear the outraged confusion in his own voice. It very accurately reflected what he was feeling. His perfectly fried sunny-side-up eggs were the eyes, crispy rashers of bacon formed frowny eyebrows above them, four grilled tomato wedges were angled into a downturned mouth, and the solitary button mushroom in the center of the plate could only be the nose. There were a few more buttery mushrooms tucked into a bowl beside the plate of toast. The stack of pancakes she popped down next to the toast seemed like overkill, but Sam wasn't going to complain about the sheer volume of food. Not when it all looked and smelled so good.

But that face . . . He frowned up at Lia, who was blushing again. She slid her eyes away from his and sucked her luscious bottom lip into her mouth. It very nearly succeeded in drawing his attention from his angry-looking breakfast, but one glance down at his plate was enough to distract him from the urge to suck that lip into his own mouth.

"Sorry, I . . . it was an impulse. You kind of annoyed me just now." He nearly laughed at that reluctant confession. If she found *that* annoying, his meals were going to look permanently pissed off with him. She didn't strike him as a very impulsive person, so that information was neatly tucked away for further scrutiny later. Right now, despite the frowny face, he was looking forward to devouring his delicious-smelling breakfast.

"Yeah, I get that a lot," he said agreeably and tucked into his meal with gusto, destroying the censorious bastard on his plate in no time at all. He even managed to down a couple of pancakes after polishing off the eggs and bacon. No sense having them go to waste. And he needed to regain some weight.

Lia was at the sink, doing dishes, and Sam watched her while he ate. She was wearing a perfectly pretty knee-length dress. This one was pastel pink with thinner straps at the shoulders and a white flounce at the hem. Ice cream on a hot summer's day—that's what she reminded him of. She wore a frilly white pinafore apron to protect the dress, and the combination made her look like a 1960s housewife.

She turned and caught him staring, and the bright-red flush on her cheeks clashed with the delicate pink of her dress.

"Are you done?" she asked, nodding down at his plate, where nothing but a few streaks of yolk remained of the angry face.

"Yes, thank you. That was quite delicious, princess. You're a good cook."

"Any idiot can make a couple of fried eggs, pancakes, and some bacon."

"True, but few can make them taste this good." The compliment flustered her, that much was obvious. She patted at her already neat hair—she always seemed to be patting at things when she was out of sorts—and picked up the empty dishes from the table.

"I'll clean these and we can get going. You may want to grab a jacket, it's a bit chilly today."

Sam cast a dubious look outside. The sun was out, the sky was blue, and there wasn't a breeze stirring so much as a leaf on the massive cherry tree outside the kitchen window.

"If you say so," he acquiesced gracefully. He wasn't about to argue when he'd already gotten his way.

CHAPTER FIVE

"What is this place?" Sam asked ten minutes later. Lia had brought her tiny, ancient car to a stop outside a beautiful Cape Dutch–style building off the main road of the tiny town of Riversend. A discreet plaque on the wall just below the house number told him that this wasn't a private residence, but he wasn't close enough to read it.

There really wasn't much going on in this town. Lia had pointed out the "hot spots"—pub, eatery, Methodist church, random shops, Catholic church, Spencer Carlisle's huge sporting goods store, Anglican church, library, mosque, grocery store, her father's veterinary practice—in very little time. It certainly unsettled a veteran sinner like Sam to be around so *many* places of worship.

Once they'd turned off Main Road into the "suburbs," it had been nothing but cute house after cute house. Before they reached their mystery destination, she'd pointed out Daisy's little dollhouse, telling him she, Lia, would be moving there soon.

"Twice a week, I come here to play the piano for an hour or so."

"The piano?" he repeated dumbly, and she nodded, flipping the sun visor down and using the mirror to apply bubblegum-flavored lip gloss to her soft, pink mouth. The gloss gave her lips a juicy sheen, tempting Sam to sample that bubblegum taste with his own lips and tongue. She wore very little makeup, just a bit of eyeliner and that lightly rose-tinted gloss, accentuating her two best features.

God, he desperately wanted to kiss her!

He averted his eyes and shifted uncomfortably, willing his unwelcome erection away. This was highly inconvenient; *she* was supposed to be growing more sexually aware of *him*, not vice versa. He forced himself to push away the memory of her beautiful, soft mouth planting sweet kisses all over his naked chest and ran an embarrassingly shaky hand through his hair. It needed cutting—maybe he could convince Lia to do it for him. He nearly groaned at the thought, the idea of her hands in his hair and on his scalp sending a shudder of anticipatory pleasure down his spine.

Rein it in, for fuck's sake! he commanded himself sternly. This was getting ridiculous.

"I didn't know you played the piano," he heard himself say and was grateful that his lizard brain had kicked in and his fight instinct had flickered to life. He really couldn't continue to sit here mutely fantasizing about stripping that prim little dress from her neatly proportioned body and fucking her senseless. It was adolescent and uncouth.

"I'm a passable player, nothing special. I'm the only one available to do it at this time of the day," she said with a shrug, grabbing her handbag and letting herself out of the car. Sam fumbled with his seat belt and the door handle, and by the time he staggered out of the car, she was halfway up the path toward the building. She set the car alarm when she heard his door close, not bothering to turn and check if he was following her.

A little disgruntled by this lack of concern, Sam felt his brow lower into an irritable scowl but continued to follow her like a lost puppy. He wasn't used to having so little control over a situation, and for some reason he'd expected Lia to be fawning all over his injured ass. In fact, he'd placed bets with himself that he'd be irritated with her fretting less than halfway through the day. She struck him as a fusser . . . but there'd been nary a fuss in sight all morning. And Sam irrationally found himself irritated by the absence of what he now considered his due.

He shook his head and grumbled beneath his breath as he trudged up to where she stood waiting by the door. Oh, okay, scratch that, she wasn't waiting, the door was opening and she was totally going inside . . . without him.

For fuck's sake!

He hastened his pace and caught up before the door shut in his face. A pretty young woman, with complex-looking cornrows and wearing what looked like a nurse's uniform, smiled at him questioningly.

"I'm with her." He nodded toward Lia, who was chatting with another uniformed woman a few paces ahead of them. What was this place? The woman—her name tag identified her as Prudence Magubane—quirked her head as she assessed him.

"With Lia?" she asked.

"The one and only," he affirmed, and her smile widened.

"Welcome to Sunset Manor. We're glad you can join us for the afternoon musicale. Our residents will be so pleased to see a new face."

Residents?

"Happy to be here, I'm sure," he said gallantly, while wondering what the hell he'd gotten himself into. He nodded at Prudence before hastening to catch up with Lia.

"Please be nice," she said beneath her breath once he was beside her, and he frowned, a little insulted by her comment. He'd never aspired to be *nice* in his life, but he wouldn't go out of his way to be an arsehole, for God's sake. What did she take him for? Some callow misanthrope without any social graces? He could lay on the charm when he wanted to. She knew that better than most.

"I don't do nice, princess. I do charming, charismatic, sexy, fascinating—"

"Conceited," she interrupted.

"I would have gone with honest," he said, laying it on thick.

"All right, fine. Be charming and charismatic. Just don't be dismissive, okay?" she said, stopping outside a pair of large, closed double doors. A sign above the doors read **CAFETERIA** in bold letters. She threw back her shoulders without a further word and pushed the doors open. Sam followed and came to a complete standstill just inside the room.

The cafeteria was filled with senior citizens. Men and women whose ages appeared to range from sixty-five to ninety, maybe older. They were all dressed to the nines, and they all greeted Lia exuberantly. Lia was smiling, that huge, beautiful, open smile that he had last seen at her sister's wedding. It had captivated him then and did the same now. He couldn't take his eyes off her beaming face as she greeted everybody by name, asking after grandchildren, pets, and ailments.

This wasn't at all what he'd been expecting, and while half of him wanted to flee before the silver brigade caught sight of him, the other half just wanted to stare at her and bask in all that warmth and radiance.

Still, whatever *this* was, it clearly wasn't his scene, and he tore his gaze from Lia and took one backtracking step before he was spotted. A little old lady with a walker beamed at him and, with more speed than he would have believed possible, came up to chat.

"Hello there, are you our Lia's young man? She's never brought a boy to our afternoon soirees before. I'm Alison Bryson. I hope you'll save a dance for me." She stuck out her hand, and before he quite knew what he was doing, he took her palm in his. He smiled down at the lovely old girl and bent at the waist, lifting the back of her hand to his mouth to drop a kiss onto her paper-thin skin.

"Enchanted, I'm sure," he purred, and she giggled girlishly. "My name's Sam, and I'm *always* happy to dance with a beautiful woman."

"Silly boy," she tittered. "Aren't you the charmer?"

A few of the others drifted over and introduced themselves, avidly interested in Sam, wanting to know if he was Lia's "gentleman friend." They were a friendly and cheerful group and couldn't stop lauding Sam's "sweetheart." She was such a "dear thing" with a "kind heart" and a "gentle spirit" and a "wonderful pianist with very talented fingers." Sam didn't know about the rest of it, but they were spot on about her talented fingers. He suppressed a shudder at the inappropriate memory of her hand tightening around his . . .

"—member?" Sam blinked, reddened, and shook himself before focusing on the dapper gentleman decked out in a neatly pressed three-piece suit and a white fedora.

"I'm sorry, I didn't catch that," he apologized.

"I asked if you were willing to become a member of our Sunday night poker club," the man, Bertie, repeated patiently. Obviously used to repeating himself in this half-deaf crowd.

"Uh? I'm not too . . ."

"You do play, right?"

"Of course, but I probably won't be in Riversend for very long."

"You won't? What about our Lia? You're not the love-them-and-leave-them type, are you? That doesn't sit right with me at all, young man! She's a good, decent girl." The man looked seriously affronted at the thought of Sam abandoning Lia.

"We're not—"

"Brand and I are just friends," Lia's voice intervened, and Sam had never been more grateful for an extraction from a volatile—potentially hostile—situation before. "I'm helping him while he recovers from his injuries. He got stabbed saving his *girlfriend* from an attacker."

Oohs and ahhs followed that revelation, and the crowd pressed in around him, wanting to know more. He sent a panicked look at Lia, whose lips quirked in amusement before she clapped her hands like a schoolteacher bringing a disruptive class to order. She moved to the piano and plucked one of several binders up from the top of the instrument.

"Why don't we start?" She looked down at the binder. "I'm taking requests from Set B today." Her words definitely distracted them, and she smiled and mouthed *you're welcome* at Sam before sitting down in front of the old upright piano in the corner. The requests came thick and fast, and she grinned before settling on "Moon River." Lia was right; her playing was passable at best. She hit the occasional wrong note, and it reminded Sam of the dance classes his mother had insisted he attend when he was a boy, but it was good enough to dance to. Soon all the debonair silver foxes present were approaching their giggling, coquettish ladies and requesting the "honor" of this dance. It was so sweet it practically gave Sam a toothache, but at the same time, he couldn't help finding the entire scene poignant and charming.

The women outnumbered the men, and the few ladies who were left without a partner watched the dancing couples wistfully. Sam spotted Alison Bryson huddled among the wallflowers and made his way toward her.

"I believe this dance is mine," he said with a bow. The corny gesture was worth it just to see her face light up. He gathered her frail body into his arms, maintaining a polite distance between them, and slowly, mindful of the fact that she had to dance without her walker, waltzed her around the floor. It was awkward with her limp and his cast, but they fared quite admirably despite that.

Lia played song after song. The sheets in Set B ranged from "Fly Me to the Moon" to "Great Balls of Fire" and even "Hey Ya!" by Outkast. The seniors loved it. She watched Brand surreptitiously as he made his way from one wallflower to the next, and by the end of the hour every woman present had had at least one partnered dance. At one point, with one of the livelier songs, he'd divided his attention between three different partners at the same time.

Lia didn't know what she'd expected, but it certainly wasn't Brand throwing himself into the experience so wholeheartedly. She'd expected reticence, surliness, possible lurking in the corner . . . instead he'd been the life of the party, and by the time they left he'd promised Bertie he'd be the fourth at this week's poker match, begged Edith to bake one of her famous chocolate mousse cakes for him, oohed over Alison's pictures of her grandbabies, and allowed at least five of the seniors—that Lia had seen—to sign his cast.

To say that he'd been a hit would be understating it.

He had a definite bounce in his step when they walked back to the car and grinned at her once they were both buckled up and she had the engine running again.

"You thought I was going to hate that, didn't you?" he asked, his voice challenging. She watched him contemplatively, tilting her head slightly as a thought occurred to her.

"I did, and you knew that. Is that why you laid it on so thick? Did you pretend to enjoy yourself just to prove me wrong? Because they all genuinely liked you, Brand. I would hate to have them disappointed if you start breaking promises."

"What promises?"

"Bertie's poker night, for one."

"About that . . ." Lia braced herself, waiting for the inevitable excuse, knowing *she* would be the one who would have to break the news to Bertie. "I'm going to need a ride on Sunday night."

"What?" she asked blankly.

"To the poker thing. I can't drive myself, you're going to have to bring me."

"You're actually going?"

"Lia, I can be a prick . . . but you don't know me well enough to assume I make promises I won't keep." His voice was like ice, and Lia chewed the inside of her cheek while she looked at him for another long moment, trying to gauge how much of what she'd presumed about this man was accurate.

"You're right, I'm sorry. Thank you for making sure they all had a good time."

"Not my usual scene, but I enjoyed it. Where to next?"

For a small town, Riversend had way too many homeless creatures in its animal shelter—dogs, cats, a couple of parrots, a pony, two donkeys, countless chickens, an African rock python, and a freaking porcupine. Lia spent time grooming the long-haired cats and dogs, talking to them soothingly while she gently combed the knots from their coats. The animals, clearly starved for affection, loved it, and Sam could see it broke a piece of her heart every time she had to return one to its cage. While she was busy with that, one of the animal minders, Siphiso, introduced Sam to a few of the rehab dogs. They were all potential adoptees with abusive backgrounds who had to be rehabilitated before they could be cleared for adoption. Siphiso explained that less than half of the rehab dogs wound up in loving homes even after being cleared. People were too reticent to take a large dog with a violent past into their homes.

"This is Trevor," Siphiso said as they came up to yet another large pen. A huge chocolate-and-white boxer crouched in the farthest corner of the cage. His body language was hostile—tail down, ears and hackles up, and teeth bared. He looked both terrifying and terrified, and Sam felt something inside him break at the sight of the thin, cowering, angry animal. His white muzzle was covered in scars; there were thick ridges of scar tissue all over his torso and back.

"What happened to you, my boy?" Sam asked beneath his breath, hearing the hitch in his voice.

"He was a fighting dog. Somebody found him on the side of the road—he was stabbed many times. Possibly by his owner because he's a bad fighter. Or by a competitor because he's too good. He's very angry. Doesn't trust anybody. Dr. Gunnerson-Smythe wanted to give him a chance and said we should try rehab, but he's been with us for nearly four months now and still trusts no one."

"Christ," Sam swore shakily, sinking to his haunches in front of the pen. "Hey, boy. Trevor? That's a shitty name. We'll pick a new one, okay? New name for a new life."

"Trevor *is* his new name." Lia's voice sounded quietly behind him. She nodded at Siphiso with a smile, and the man waved and walked off, leaving them alone. Lia crouched down beside Sam, uncaring of the fact that her white hem was touching the dirty floor.

"No wonder he's given up on life," Sam said, but he couldn't summon up enough cheer to make the words humorous. Instead they sounded dull and despairing. He continued to look at the dog, who didn't even have enough interest in his surroundings to maintain his hostility. He just huffed a sigh and sank to the floor, huddling on his thin blanket and cushion and watching them with wary eyes. Stabbed, for fuck's sake. What kind of motherfucker stabbed an animal? Sam felt an affinity with the dog. It sucked balls to be stabbed.

"We have to go," Lia whispered after a few long, silent moments. Sam wrested his gaze from the wretched creature in the corner of the pen and gratefully pinned them on her lovely face.

"*How* do you do this every week?"

"Every day," she corrected, and he swore shakily.

"How?"

"How can I not?" she asked simply, and he shook his head before one last, quick look at Trevor. He pushed himself up, ignoring the twinges in his leg and back, and strode out without a backward glance.

Brand didn't say a word in the car as Lia drove them to MJ's for lunch. She should have warned him about the shelter. She hadn't expected it to affect him as deeply as it clearly had. Something about Trevor seemed to have resonated with him. The dog didn't have much time left. He wasn't responding to any of the conventional rehabilitation techniques, and Dr. Gunnerson-Smythe, the shelter's vet, had begun making the warning noises he usually made just before an animal was about to be put to sleep.

"I'm sorry," she said after parking the car, and he blinked, like someone coming out of a deep sleep.

"I beg your pardon?" His words nearly made her smile—they were so innately British.

"About the shelter. I should have warned you or something." He shook his head.

"People can be dicks," he muttered. "You help the victims of that dickery. Try to make their lives a little happier. It's commendable. Nothing to be sorry about."

"You weren't prepared for it."

"Nothing you said could have prepared me for that. It's just one of those things you have to see for yourself."

"Did you have dogs as a boy?"

"Not even a goldfish."

"Seriously? That's . . ." It was surprising, was what it was. He'd been so deeply affected by Trevor's plight, Lia had been certain that he must have had at least one dog in the past. "It's unexpected."

"My mum and I moved around a lot when I was a kid, not the best life for a pet," he said, and her eyes narrowed. Not the best life for a child, either, if you asked her. "And then when I was older, I joined the army. Did that for a while. Then started the agency with Mason. There was never time for any pets."

"I see."

"Where are we?" he asked, changing the subject without any finesse whatsoever.

"MJ's. For lunch."

"Great. I'm a little hungry. All that dancing earlier has worked up quite an appetite."

~

Sam's eyes took in every aspect of the town's local eatery. There were a few people dotted around the place, mostly women and kids. The tension, always present when he entered a new place for the first time, left his back and shoulders as he ascertained that there were no immediate threats present. He rolled his neck in an attempt to loosen up even more. All eyes were on them, and he knew the exact moment when that registered with Lia and she started to doubt her decision to bring him here.

He went straight to a round table dead center in the place and politely drew back the chair and ushered her into it. He made a deliberate show of it, knowing that the last thing she wanted was to draw any kind of attention.

"So where to after this?" Sam asked after they were both seated. Lia couldn't seem to meet his eyes, which annoyed him a little. He remembered her being equally evasive when he first met her—of course, back then he'd considered it a challenge. But while he enjoyed a challenge, he didn't enjoy the tedium of going through the same motions over again. He wanted to get all the boring shit out of the way and move straight back into bed with her. He didn't doubt for a moment that he'd be able to convince her to pick up where they'd left off in November, but first he had to play this ridiculous game with her. Where she got to act innocent and outraged for a hot second in order to appease the outdated moralistic code she operated by. He didn't know if he had the patience for that.

He watched cynically as she fiddled with a saltshaker, still coyly denying him her pretty eyes.

"I'm stopping by the library for story hour," she muttered, *finally* lifting those luminous gray eyes to his.

"Story hour?" he repeated blankly, trying very hard *not* to be affected by that beautiful gaze.

"It's part of the Books Are Fun campaign that the head librarian and I have devised. It's a grassroots program aimed at elementary school children. I read to them every week from whatever our spotlight book is, and after that we encourage the children to read or even act out the scene I just read."

"It's almost inevitable that I get to see you in a library," Sam said with a grin. "It was written in the stars, you know."

Predictably, she blushed, and Sam refrained from rolling his eyes. He didn't want her to be predictable. Predictability was tiresome, and he needed Lia to be interesting, exciting. He needed her to surprise him and keep him on his toes.

He wasn't sure how long his interest in her would last, but with her shyness and her sweetness and her do-goodness, he was pretty sure it would wane in short order. He wanted to at least sample her charms a few more times before the inevitable boredom set in.

He was reevaluating his time line. Waiting two weeks before sleeping with her was perhaps a bit unrealistic.

"I have to get there in an hour, before the first graders get out of school, so that I can set up. I don't mean to rush you, but this is going to have to be a fast lunch."

"And maybe you want to get me out of here before more of the townsfolk wander in and spot us together?" Another blush. He stifled a sigh.

So sweet. And *so* expected.

Lia wasn't sure what had changed, but the interested and disarming Sam Brand of that morning disappeared sometime between lunch and the library. Instead of charming everyone he came into contact with, he barely acknowledged them. He stifled yawns and seemed distracted and just plain rude. The children were clearly intimidated by him and kept well away. Mrs. Salie, the librarian, smiled and introduced herself warmly. All she got in response was a curt "how do you do?" without a smile or a handshake in sight.

Lia ushered him into the farthest corner of the reading room and hoped that the children would forget he was there. But the more he sat there and glowered, the more annoyed she became.

By the time the kids' parents came to pick them up, she was fuming so much she wasn't quite sure what to do with herself. She rarely lost her temper and never raised her voice, but right now both of those seemed not just possible but highly probable.

She was silent on the drive back, ignoring his attempts at conversation, and when they got back to the cabin, she swiveled in the driver's seat and glowered at him. The expression felt heavy and unfamiliar on her face, and she wasn't sure how it looked. Lia frowned, she glared, she froze with a stare, but she rarely full-on glowered. She was tempted to glance in the rearview mirror to check if it looked as awful as it felt but didn't want to spoil the effect, especially not with him blinking at her in surprise.

"What did I do to earn this look?" he asked, and she'd swear he sounded amused, even though his bland expression didn't change at all. That annoyed her even more.

"You were so rude. I asked you to be nice. I asked you not to be dismissive, and yet you were both."

"To be fair, you made those requests before the senior citizens' dance."

"Would it have been *such* a stretch for you to behave like a civilized human being all the way through the afternoon? You scared the children."

"Hardly."

"This may seem like some kind of joke to you, Brand, and maybe it all seemed small and trite, but the people we met today, the things we did, are important to me. This is my life, not some show I put on exclusively to entertain you."

"It wasn't my scene," he said, his voice sounding sulky, and she felt her brow lower even more.

"Perhaps not, but you're not a child! For heaven's sake, the first graders I read to this afternoon would have more success in hiding their bad mood than you did."

She sighed heavily.

"I'll see you in the morning. Have a good evening," she said, wanting him out of her car. He frowned.

"Whoa, what about my dinner?"

"Since we had lunch at MJ's, you can have the lasagna I prepared for your lunch as dinner."

"What about other things? What if I need help with . . . stuff?"

"I'm sure you'll cope," she said, trying to keep her voice steady. "Stay out of the tub, but keep the cast dry if you decide to hop into the shower."

"I won't be able to get out of this shirt. Can you help me with these buttons at least?"

She worried her lower lip with her teeth, contemplating the buttons for a moment. She didn't want to, she really didn't want to, but when she raised her eyes to his, he looked so hopeful and kind of sad and pitiful at the same time. She knew he was playing her, she *knew* it, but there were a lot of buttons on that shirt.

"Look, I'm sorry I was a dick this afternoon. I was tired and in a bit of pain, and those kids were so energetic, just looking at them exhausted me."

It was a terrible apology and so insincere she was a little insulted he thought she'd believe a word of it.

"I'll help you with that shirt, but only because of our agreement. *I* don't go back on my word."

"Meaning I do?" He managed to look quite offended by her implication, but Lia wasn't going to apologize.

"If the shoe fits." She shrugged, unbuckling her seat belt and exiting the car before he could respond.

She was in the cabin and gulping down a glass of water in the kitchen by the time he finally made his way inside.

"For the record," he said, coming out guns, eyes, and temper blazing, "I didn't go back on my word. I made that promise at the old-age place . . ."

"Retirement home," she corrected primly, ignoring his glower at the amendment. "And excuse me for expecting civility from you. I now know not to make that mistake again."

~

Well, this was interesting; Sam hadn't expected her to have a temper. He liked it. It definitely wasn't boring. He liked the way her eyes sparked when she was annoyed, and he liked that dark, pissed-off little glower that merely reinforced the stern librarian look he found so fascinating. He liked not knowing what her next move or words would be.

She slammed the glass down on the counter and stalked—that was the only word he could think of to describe that angry movement—toward him. Before he could say a word, her hands were on him and he had a brief moment of "hell yes!" before he realized that she was attacking his shirt buttons. And not in a passionate "I want to rip your shirt off and jump your bones" kind of way, but in a focused, "no button will be popped today" boring kind of way.

Still, he couldn't resist the urge to make some kind of comment.

"Why, princess, you seem a little desperate to get me naked. I must say, the feeling's entirely mutual."

"Shut up," she gritted from between clenched teeth and then looked instantly appalled with herself for her bad manners. Her hands dropped from his shirt, leaving it half-unbuttoned. "Look, stop saying things like that, okay? It's . . . what about your girlfriend? How would she feel if she knew you were making these comments?"

"My girlfriend?" *Shit.* He couldn't believe she actually believed all that crap in the press about him and Lally. He sighed and recognized that he would get a lot further with her if she knew that he didn't have some woman waiting in the wings for him back home. But part of him knew, too, that the only reason she'd felt comfortable enough to take this job in the first place was because she thought he was involved with someone. He was also enough of an ass to immediately grasp the positives of having some fictional woman back home. It would give him an easy out once he was ready to move on from Lia. No messy aftermath, just a "hey, you knew there was someone else." Yet, at the same time, he understood that he wouldn't get anywhere close to bedding Lia McGregor if she thought it meant hurting a third party.

He had to consider this carefully.

"Lally and I are . . . We're not together."

"Did you break up?" she asked with a sympathetic wince, and Sam—feeling like a dick—swallowed as he considered his response.

"She has someone else in my place now . . ." Technically that was true. She had Chambers as her new CPO.

"I'm sorry," Lia said, her eyes alive with sympathy, making him feel like even more of a douchebag.

"But maybe someday we could reestablish our relationship."

"Do you love her?"

"I cared for her," he said honestly. Another technical truth—it was his job to care for her.

"It gets easier," she placated, and her words reminded him that she'd once been engaged and he now wondered about that broken engagement.

"Does it? Did it for you?" Her eyes flickered, and for a fleeting moment an expression of such abject sadness crossed her face that Sam felt his gut clench in reaction to it. He didn't like knowing that pretty, sweet Lia had once felt such pain, and he quite uncharacteristically wanted to wrap his arms around her and hold her close until she felt better.

"It did, yes," she said softly, as her hands went back to his shirt to resume unbuttoning. This time her movements were slower and less angry.

"Why did your engagement end?"

"Various reasons."

"What was the main reason?"

"He said awful things to Daisy. Touched her in inappropriate ways, made her feel unattractive and victimized at the same time."

Sam tensed, pissed off at the thought of some fucker doing something like that to his friend's lovely wife. And then even *more* pissed off at the thought of how truly awful Lia must have felt when she learned the truth about the man she was going to marry.

"I hope Mason fucked him up," he stated vehemently, and Lia smiled, the expression too grim for her pretty face.

"Mason gut punched him and, if rumors are to be believed, promised Clayton that he'd be defecating his own teeth for a week if he kept messing with Daisy."

It was satisfying to know that the bastard had received some form of comeuppance, but a large part of Sam wanted to find the prick and beat him to a pulp—not for what he'd done to Daisy, but for what he'd done to Lia. For the sadness still evident in her eyes when she thought about the guy.

"But even before I heard about what he'd been doing to Daisy, I had doubts. I felt . . . He was so controlling. And he never really seemed interested in me. I was just an object, a trophy he got to show off to his friends. He blatantly showered other women with compliments when we were out together and then told me how I should dress more like them or act like them. He even—" She caught herself before completing the thought and blushed furiously. This particular blush fascinated the hell out of him—he wanted to know what had caused it and was frustrated when she stopped so abruptly.

"He even what?" he prompted, and she swallowed audibly before shaking her head.

"It was nothing. Lift your arm." The detached instruction startled him and he looked down, surprised to see that she had unbuttoned the shirt completely. He obediently lifted his arm and refocused his gaze on her face. She carefully tugged the shirt over his cast until it was hanging from just his left shoulder. Sam carelessly shrugged the rest of the way out of the thing, trying to figure out how to keep her talking. But he could tell that she wasn't going to divulge any further information, and he knew pushing her on the subject would probably have the opposite intended effect.

"I have to go. The lasagna just needs to be heated. Three minutes in the microwave should do it. I've also prepared a salad to go with it. I'll see you in the morning."

"You don't want to join me for dinner?"

"No, thank you, I have plans."

"Anything exciting?"

"Nothing that would interest you."

"More of your do-gooding? What is it this time? Cupcakes for Christians? Doughnuts for the deaf? Hugs for hookers?"

"Nothing so commendable," she said in a wobbly voice, clearly fighting back a laugh. "I have a date."

Sam's knee-jerk reaction to that was a resounding "hell no!" He wanted her focus on him and him alone. He vaguely recalled her mentioning a guy the other night. Something about it getting serious recently. He did *not* like the thought of some other guy kissing her and touching her. Sam was too territorial to share.

"Who's the lucky guy?" The words felt like sand in his mouth, and he spat them out in much the same way he would actual sand.

"Just a guy."

"Your Mr. Right?"

"Maybe. I'm not sure yet. We've only been on a few dates." She cleared her throat and nervously twirled her car keys on her index finger. She seemed evasive, and he wondered what she was hiding. Sam tilted his head and watched her speculatively. He'd find out eventually—he just needed to figure out the best way to extract that information from her.

"Thanks for today," he said, and she nodded. "Sorry about being an arsehole at the library."

"You were in pain; I suppose it's understandable."

Could it really be *that* easy to secure her forgiveness on something that she'd been fuming about less than half an hour ago?

"Anyway . . ." Another nervous throat clearing. "Have a good evening."

She left before he could say anything further.

Of course she didn't have a date, especially not with Gregory again. Lia had just needed an excuse to get out of there as quickly as possible. She'd been so angry with him for his behavior at the library, but his confidences about his relationship with Laura Prentiss had taken the wind clear out of her sails. Add his naked chest into the equation, and she'd found herself revealing unnecessary things—almost admitting to the humiliating fact that Clayton had been so controlling that he'd even chosen her wedding dress—and then telling blatant lies just to get out of there.

It hadn't been her most shining moment.

When she got home, she found her mother in the kitchen.

"Hello, dear, would you like the spoon?" her mother asked, offering her a chocolate batter–covered wooden spoon, and Lia groaned.

"You *know* I do," she said, grabbing the spoon with both hands. This was one of the perks of being the only one still living at home—she didn't have to share the bowl, the spoon, or the mixing blades with her sisters. All this chocolatey goodness was hers alone. It was almost enough to make her reconsider her decision to move out.

"Yum," she crooned after a few happy licks of the unexpected treat. "What's the occasion?"

"I'm not baking this one for us. It's for Mason's friend Sam. Daisy asked me to check how he's doing, and I thought I'd bake him a cake, poor boy."

Now was probably the time to admit that she'd been helping him out. She grimaced—she really didn't want to. Her mother had this uncanny ability to sniff out secrets and half-truths. Still, if her mother was going around there tomorrow, Brand would probably mention it, and then the older woman would wonder why Lia hadn't said something.

"I've been helping him out a bit around the house and stuff," she said supercasually. The spoon had been licked bare and she pounced on the bowl, grabbing a smaller spoon with which to scoop up the gooey, delicious leftover batter.

"Have you? That's nice of you. I didn't think you knew him that well."

"I don't, but he *was* my partner at the wedding, so I kind of know him. And he needs help. It's the right thing to do. I'm just helping him out with some meals and stuff."

"What stuff?"

"Sorry?" Her mother's question flustered her, and Lia's eyes widened over the top of her spoon.

"That's the second time you've mentioned helping him with 'stuff,' I just wondered what kind of stuff you meant."

"You know cleaning, cooking, and . . . stuff." Her mother's brow lowered in puzzlement, and Lia focused on scooping up another spoonful of chocolate, deliberately evading her mother's curious gaze.

"What aren't you saying?" Millicent McGregor asked bluntly, and Lia grimaced. Maybe partial honesty would help.

"It's embarrassing," she said uncomfortably. Her words received no response, just a look. An expectant, mom look, complete with raised brows, pursed lips, folded arms, and a tapping foot. "I help him d-dress sometimes."

She felt her cheeks heating and knew she probably resembled a ripe tomato right now. Her mother's expression cleared and she laughed, the sound almost relieved.

"Good grief, Dahlia. You had me thinking you were helping him with his dangerous bodyguarding stuff. Maybe handling his gun, or contacting his *contacts*." She whispered the last word, and Lia felt her own brows shoot up.

"So . . . what kind of contacts do you expect him to have, Mother?" she asked curiously.

"You know . . ." Her mother's voice was still a furtive whisper. "Shady kinds."

"I'm sure his business is entirely legal and aboveboard, Mom."

"Oh, I don't mean to imply otherwise." The other woman looked flustered. "But the nature of his business may necessitate him sometimes being in contact with shady individuals." She laughed airily and waved a dismissive hand. "But of course, it's nothing like that, you're just helping him dress and undress. Well, if you're already helping him out, then I suppose you can take the cake to him tomorrow."

"Sure," Lia said agreeably, happy to keep her mother and Sam from ever speaking. She finished the bowl and looked around for the mixing blades but found them in the sink, soaking in some soapy water. "Why didn't you save these for me?"

"Don't be greedy, Dahlia. You know your father has a sweet tooth, too. I had to share some of it with him."

Dahlia sighed, disappointed.

"I'm going to grab a shower." She dashed out of the room before her mother could ask her any more questions about her arrangement with Brand.

CHAPTER SIX

Sam was thinking about Lia, and he wanted her to be thinking of him, too. He didn't want her out with some dick who would try to weasel his way into her bed by the end of the evening. The thought of this anonymous fucker touching her really burned, and Sam couldn't stop thinking about it, wondering where she was, what they were doing, how they were doing it.

Anyone would think he was jealous, but he wasn't . . . he was just *possessive.* Right now, Lia McGregor belonged to him. Whether she knew it or not. He picked up his phone. If he called her, even texted her, it would take her out of whatever moment she was sharing with her Mr. Perfect. It would force her to think of *Sam.*

He was about to call her when a short, authoritative knock sounded on the back door. Sam nearly dropped his phone in surprise at the unexpected sound, and his head whipped around to look at the door while his entire body went on alert. The handle was turning and he winced, feeling like an idiot for not remembering to check if it was secure. He crouched, ignoring the twinges coming from his various healing wounds, and stealthily moved toward the door. Ready to do battle if it came to that.

The door swung inward and Spencer Carlisle stepped over the threshold. He paused when he saw Sam's half-crouching stance and lifted his arms slightly, bringing Sam's attention to the six-pack of beer clutched in the man's right hand.

"I come in peace, I promise," the guy said with something close to a grin, and Sam relaxed, feeling like an idiot. "You military types ever switch off?"

"Only when we're dead, mate," Sam said easily, stepping forward with the intention of offering his hand until he remembered that his arm was in a cast. The other man seemed to understand his intention, though, and nodded in acknowledgment.

"Brought you some beer. Noticed that Daff didn't include any in her shopping."

"Couldn't come at a better time," Sam groaned appreciatively.

"I have conditions." The man's words reminded Sam of Lia's misunderstanding of his question the other night, and he grinned at the recollection.

"Something funny?" Spencer asked.

"Yeah, but it's unrelated to this. What conditions?" Spencer gave him an assessing look before shrugging.

"Daff and Charlie are watching a chick flick. I needed to get away from all the sighing and crying," Spencer informed him with an intimidating frown. He had dark hair and thick, straight, dark brows that made him look pretty damned formidable. He was a huge guy, probably four or five inches taller than Sam, and massively built. Sam understood that he'd once been a rugby player, a forward lock, so he was lean and solid at the same time. Physically he'd make a pretty intimidating CPO, but from what Sam had observed since meeting the man for the first time in November, he lacked a soldier's edge. He was huge and intimidating on the outside with not an aggressive bone in him. He also never had more than two words to say, so Sam was surprised that the man had approached him and was being so damned chatty.

"Want to watch something manlier?" Sam asked, and Spencer nodded.

"There's a *Fast and Furious* movie on at seven thirty," he stated, and Sam glanced at the kitchen clock and nodded.

"Make yourself at home, I'll see if your fiancée bought any snacks."

"Girlfriend," Spencer corrected uncomfortably, red darkening the back of his neck and the tips of his ears.

"Beg your pardon?"

"She's not my fiancée . . . *yet*."

"Ah." Sam opened and closed a few of the kitchen cabinets, searching for something salty. He found a packet of crisps and a can of pretzels on the same shelf and grabbed them both. "Mate, would you mind getting a bowl or something? Kind of incapacitated over here."

Spencer grunted and went on the hunt, finding a couple of bowls in short order. He emptied the crisps and pretzels into the bowls, carried everything into the living room, and dumped them onto the coffee table in front of the huge television. Mason had a great setup—digital surround sound, seventy-seven-inch organic LED television, PS4, and music all hooked up to the same system. It was man cave central, and Sam had been so preoccupied with Lia that he hadn't even thought to check it all out before now.

"This is a sweet setup," he said, and Spencer grunted again—it sounded like agreement. He was a taciturn fucker, but that was okay. Sam appreciated the quiet companionship he offered.

They settled in, Sam spread out on the sofa and Spencer sprawled in the easy chair, and were soon absorbed in the loud, improbable movie. The crazy car stunts, gunfights, and hand-to-hand combat scenes were completely unrealistic, and Sam picked them all apart in his head, finding the *exact* moment in each action sequence where the character should have died a horrible death. Gravity, physics, and the limitations of the human body were terrible equalizers.

Still, he enjoyed the loud, chaotic movie for what it was, a couple of hours of pure escapism. Spencer didn't speak at all, just kept his focus on the screen, systematically making his way through his share of the snacks and beers. He was great, undemanding company.

When the movie ended, Spencer stretched and yawned. "Need anything before I go?" he asked.

"No, thanks. I think I've got it all covered."

"Daff says she won't be . . ."

"Won't be helping out? Yeah, I know. She doesn't like me."

Spencer grimaced and shrugged. "Hmm." That's all he had to say on the matter, and Sam could respect that—the opinionated, borderline unlikable woman was the guy's almost fiancée, after all.

"It's fine. Lia's offered to help out with meals and cleaning." Another formidable frown from the big guy.

"She has?"

"Yes."

The frown deepened as Spencer absorbed that information, but again he offered no opinion.

"I'll drop around again tomorrow night. I think Daff and Charlie are planning some kind of makeup tutorial with some of Charlie's friends." The look of panic and absolute horror in his eyes was comical, and Sam grinned.

"See you then."

"Hmm."

Another long night of interrupted sleep with crazy, sexy dreams starring Lia McGregor had Sam waking up irritated and horny the next morning. Again he could smell coffee brewing, and he sat up in bed, willing his erection away. He was in a foul mood, and not even the smell of waffles and bacon could dispel his aggravation.

He prowled downstairs and found her at the stove, her back to him. Her hair was up in a neat ponytail and she was wearing a knee-length mint-green pencil skirt with a plain white cotton blouse. On her feet she wore a pair of modest beige pumps. She looked neat and fresh, and all Sam wanted to do was go up behind her and wrap his arms around her. He wanted to turn her around and devour her mouth and mess up all that pristine neatness. Ruin all that prim goodness with just the touch of his hands and mouth.

He would take her down to the floor, push that skirt up over her thighs, pull down her panties, and claim her right there. He had the almost violent, primal urge to do just that, right here and now. He actually took a step toward her, cock hard, hands reaching . . . when she turned around and spotted him. Her smile stopped him dead in his tracks. A beautiful, innocent, and genuinely delighted smile.

"Oh, good morning," she greeted, not knowing how very close he'd come to ravishing her on the fucking floor like a wild beast. "I trust you slept well?"

"No," he growled and turned away from her. Any other morning he'd flirt and try to charm her, but not today, not after the frustrating night he'd just had. He was in an unpredictable mood. He didn't trust himself not to say or do something stupid and scare her off.

"Oh. Well, I'm sorry to hear that. Were you in pain?"

"Yes." Serious pain. All night long. The type of pain that could only be assuaged inside her body.

"Oh no. What can I do to help?"

He laughed bitterly and glared at her over his shoulder.

"*Don't* fucking ask me that," he growled, feeling like a wounded animal, and her eyes widened.

"I don't understand."

"Yeah, no shit," he muttered angrily, and she pinned him with an annoyed frown.

"What's your problem today?" she asked sharply, and he snorted a sarcastic laugh and stood with his arms spread, inviting her to look her fill. He was wearing only boxer briefs this morning, and she'd very stoically kept her eyes on his face since he'd joined her in the kitchen.

"I'd say that my *problem* is pretty fucking self-evident," he growled, and her eyes did a quick sortie down his body and then very swiftly scampered back up to the safety of his face. Her cheeks had gone bloodred, and her breathing was coming in alarmed little pants.

"Oh. Well. I'm sorry." Her words stymied him, and he stared at her for an instant before his arms dropped back down to his sides.

"What are you sorry for?"

"I'm sorry about what happened between you and Laura Prentiss and that she isn't here to help you with . . . with . . . uh, *that*."

"She's not, but you are."

"What?" she gasped, her shock genuine, if the absolutely appalled expression on her face was anything to go by. "Women aren't interchangeable, Brand. What an awful thing to say."

"I never said they were, Lia," he gritted, completely frustrated with the way this was going. It was too damned soon to be talking about this, to be suggesting this, but he'd been betrayed by his lack of patience and his own adolescent response to the woman in front of him.

"Look," he began, praying for patience, while at the same time knowing that he was going to completely fuck up his already ill-conceived plan with his next words. "Remember how your one stipulation to our agreement was no 'funny business'?"

"Of course," she said warily.

"Well, I'm afraid there's going to be some funny business. Possibly a *lot* of funny business. Right now, Lally is quite the furthest thing from my mind, princess. You're the one responsible for this hard-on. You and your closet full of schoolmarm outfits. You and your neat little body and your prim lips and your dated sensibilities. I want you back in my bed. For however long I find myself here. I want you to stop your search for Mr. Right and focus on me . . . *only* me. But I want you to remember that I'm Mr. Wrong and not refocus your romantic attentions on me."

"Is that all?" She tried for sarcasm, but her voice was breathless and lacked heat. She looked dazed, not sure how to respond to his words.

He didn't even know how to respond to his words—he was as shocked by them as she clearly was.

"Fuck me, not by a long shot, princess. I want to lean you over the kitchen counter, push your skirt up over your firm little bum, and pull down your panties, then I want to bury myself in you and lose myself in your tight heat until we both come."

He went quiet and there was nothing but silence in the kitchen as they watched each other. She swallowed audibly and licked her lips.

"That's . . ." Her voice emerged on a husky note and she cleared her throat. "Uh, that's a lot, Brand. I don't know what to say to that."

"You can say 'fudge it,' throw caution and inhibitions to the wind, and fuck me?"

"I can't," she said, her voice carrying just the slightest hint of regret.

"Why not? Where's the harm in it?"

"I'm not made that way. I don't have casual flings."

"I can think of at least two separate occasions when you did."

"That was different. It was meant to be just then. Just that one time."

"It was twice."

"I think of it as one extended encounter."

"Can't we extend it even further? Can't we just continue where we left off? Just a consensual, adult sexual encounter that started in November and will end when I leave."

"No. I don't think so. That was then. This is now. Things have changed."

"What things?"

"For one thing you've been in a serious relationship since then . . ." She paused, and her eyes widened. "Oh my goodness, please don't tell me you were involved with her when we first met."

"I'm a one-woman-at-a-time kind of guy, Lia, so no, I wasn't involved with anyone else when we first fucked."

She winced. "Just so you know, that kind of language does nothing to endear you to me."

"Just so *you* know, I don't actually give a fuck. I'm not proposing marriage here, Lia. Just sex. And that means taking me just the way I am, crude, crass, and common. I won't pretend to be something I'm not just to appease your delicate constitution."

Her lips thinned, and her jaw went up.

"And *I've* changed," she said. "Back then I was . . . unsure. Still rebounding from my failed engagement . . ."

"It was more than a year later, wasn't it?" he asked incredulously.

"I don't bounce back very quickly. Anyway, I was vulnerable, and you were lucky enough to capitalize on that vulnerability."

He laughed at that, the sound cynical. Was this woman for real?

"Is *that* what you told yourself? That I took advantage of your vulnerability."

"No. I needed something to make me feel better about myself, and you were there. I suppose I took advantage of *you*. You were . . . you were my rebound guy."

He choked back another laugh at that. He liked that. He liked that she was proud enough to want to turn the tables on him.

"Sure, I like that. I like being your rebound guy. I can keep being that."

"I don't need a rebound guy anymore. I did the rebound thing. I need something else now. Someone else. Someone who'll stick. Who'll want to start a life and a family with me."

"Boring shit that can wait a few more months," he dismissed. "I was your rebound guy, now let me be your final fling guy. Let me be the last wild thing you do before you settle down."

"I . . . no." She looked away and swallowed again. "No, thank you. Your breakfast is ready. Please have a seat."

Always so fucking polite. He dragged a chair back and sank down at the table. Did she really think the conversation was over? Just like that? Apparently so—she smoothed her hands down the front of her pristine pinafore apron and smiled serenely at him, her eyes carefully blank. He returned the smile with a glare and watched in grim satisfaction as her expression faltered. She turned away and picked up a couple of plates. She crossed the short distance between them and placed his breakfast neatly in front of him before turning away to retrieve a mug for his coffee.

Sam stared down at his plate resignedly. She'd shaped roses out of a couple of strawberries and centered them on top of a stack of waffles. More freshly sliced fruit was prettily placed in a separate bowl. She returned with his coffee and a side plate of crispy bacon.

"Stop turning my meals into weird little pictures, it's fucking pointless," he groused before spearing his fork into the stupid flower and bringing it to his mouth. He chomped it down without ceremony, and she sucked her lower lip into her mouth and contemplated him for a long moment.

"It's a habit. But from now on I'll try to remember that you have no soul and take no enjoyment from pointless, pretty things."

"It's food—as long as it's edible, I don't care about the presentation," he said defensively, feeling like a dick now.

"*I* care about the presentation," she said softly, her voice carrying a hint of stubborn defiance that surprised him. "I take pride in my accomplishments, Brand. And while they might seem completely pointless and dumb to you, I do it because it makes *me* happy. And I couldn't care less what you think about it."

"I'm sorry," Sam said begrudgingly. He was being a prick, he knew it, but sexual frustration, combined with constant pain and discomfort, were not conducive to charm and good behavior. It was a poor excuse, but it was the only one he had. He wanted to say more, but those were the only two words that came out and, in the end, the only words that really mattered.

She nodded an acknowledgment of his apology, looking somewhat mollified, and Sam went back to his breakfast.

"I brought a chicken pie for lunch. It needs to go in the oven—the heating instructions are on the container. Oh, and my mother baked you a cake. Chocolate fudge—she says she hopes you enjoy it." She nodded toward the island, where a beautifully iced, decadent-looking chocolate cake stood on display on a glass cake stand.

"Please send her my thanks," he said. "Why'd you bring the pie? I thought we'd be spending the day together again."

Lia did her best not to gape at the unsettling man. There he sat, in nothing but his underwear, after presenting her with the most ridiculous proposition and then insulting her food, still expecting to accompany her on her day's errands? It was confusing and contradictory and strange.

Worse, she had been so tempted to take him up on his invitation for a final fling. Nothing was stopping her—she didn't have a man in her life, and she was a consenting adult with the usual wants and needs. Why not take him up on the offer? He was attractive, and he was *very* good in bed. And despite his current contrariness and his extreme rudeness, he was often an entertaining, if enigmatic, companion.

If they were up front about this being nothing more than a fling, then neither would have any expectation of more from the other. He wasn't ever going to be the right man for her, she knew that. So why not simply enjoy him and what they could have together?

"Well?" he prompted, impatient with her silence, and Lia blinked, coming back to the present with a jolt.

"You didn't seem to enjoy yesterday; I didn't think you'd want to go with me again."

"I want to see Spike again."

"Who?"

"The boxer, Titan."

"His name is Trevor," she reminded him frostily, and he wrinkled his nose.

"That's a terrible name for a dog. Who names a dog *Trevor*? You might as well have called him Clive. Or Norman. Or Claude. Anyway, I wanted to see how he's doing today. You *did* say you go to the animal shelter every day, right?"

"Yes."

"And the old folks?"

"I see the seniors twice a week, Mondays and Wednesdays."

"Pity. The dancing was great exercise. So what's happening today? Animals and . . . ?"

"Just the animal shelter, and then I'll be dropping some blankets and clothes off at the homeless shelter."

"I can help with that. I have one good arm," he said. He seemed desperate, and she wondered about that. Maybe he was the type of person who preferred activity over their own thoughts. It was strange, and she wanted to ask him about it but stopped before she formulated the question.

It wasn't her business.

"I'm leaving in twenty minutes. If you're not done by then, I'm going without you," she said, and he grinned before scooping a huge portion of waffles into his mouth.

"These waffles are brilliant, princess," he said between bites. "Make them yourself?"

"Of course." She helped herself to some coffee and sipped while she waited for him to finish. He was done in less than five minutes and excused himself to shower and get dressed. Thank goodness.

She was getting way too used to seeing him in his underwear.

He required help with his shirt again. Another one of those ridiculous dress shirts, and she found herself once again cutting the ruined sleeve away. She worked quickly, with barely a quake in her fingers, even though she was even more aware of the heat from his chest after their earlier conversation. Worse, she found herself wanting to stroke that silky skin, kiss it . . . possibly *lick* it.

Crumbs! She was completely losing it. She desperately needed to pull herself together. After fastening the last button, she patted her hot cheeks in an attempt to cool them down.

"You okay?" he asked her softly, and she nearly jumped out of her skin at the unexpected sound of his voice. He'd stood so docilely while she was buttoning him up; now she looked up at him and caught the wicked glint in his eyes and the hint of a smile on his lips and knew that he'd been well aware of her reaction to him.

His thick, uneven stubble hadn't been shaved in at least two days, and it was beginning to enter the short beard phase. It was a shade or so darker than his dirty-blond hair and made him look even more rugged and masculine than usual. She would never have believed that possible. Not when he was already so unbelievably and unfairly sexy.

"I'm fine, thank you," she said stiffly. She was stronger than this—she would not let this man, no matter how lethally attractive he was, unsettle her so.

"Liar," he said with a roguish little grin, and she cleared her throat and stepped away from him. "Any time you want to rip my clothes off, Lia, I'll be right here waiting."

"Don't be ridiculous," she said with what she hoped sounded like scorn and grabbed her car keys. "Let's go."

The animal shelter was their first stop of the day, and Brand made a beeline for Trevor's pen, chatting amiably with Siphiso along the way.

Lia went through her usual Thursday routine, walking some of the smaller dogs, playing with the puppies, and cuddling the seniors. The older dogs were least likely to be adopted, and it broke Lia's heart every time she visited them because she wasn't sure which ones would still be around when she returned the following week.

The time she spent at the shelter was nearly up when she realized that she hadn't seen Brand since their arrival. She spotted Siphiso and asked him about it.

"Oh, Mr. Brand? He's still with Trevor."

"Still? He's been there all this time?"

"He asked if he could sit with him."

"What do you mean, sit with him? Like, in the pen?" Her voice raised in alarm, and Siphiso smiled.

"No, he's just sitting outside the pen, talking and talking. Trevor moved a little closer."

"He *did*?"

"Just a little." Siphiso grinned happily.

"Oh gosh." Lia's hands went to her mouth. It was the only reaction Trevor had shown to anyone in months. Immediately she worried. What if Trevor chose to trust Brand? What if Brand simply upped and left one day and Trevor felt abandoned again? She wasn't sure if she should encourage this. But maybe it would pave the way for Trevor to open up to other people.

She hastened to Trevor's pen and found Brand sitting flat on his butt, facing the pen, back against the wall with his legs drawn up and his arms resting on his spread knees. He was still talking. His voice sounded hoarse, and he seemed to be discussing a *movie* with the dog. An animal movie. One that she recognized.

"'Baa-ram-ewe, to your own self be true' and I shit you not, mate, those fuckin' sheep moved for him. Nice and neat like, straight into their pen. It was pretty cool." He stopped talking abruptly and tensed when Trevor tensed, the dog sensing Lia's presence before Brand did. His eyes lifted to hers, and he grinned sheepishly.

"Are you telling him about *Babe*?" she asked disbelievingly, and he wrinkled his nose self-consciously, melting her heart.

"We've already worked our way through a couple of real dog movies."

"Such as?"

"The one where the three dogs get lost and have to find their way home."

"I believe it was two dogs and a cat."

"I didn't want to upset him by using the *C* word," he said lightly.

"I see."

"And the one about the huskies that get left behind and have to fend for themselves. But in my version, all of the dogs were rescued."

This was so unexpectedly sweet. Lia wasn't sure what to make of it. He kept his voice low and soothing while he spoke with her, even though Trevor had withdrawn and crept back to his corner, his eyes wary as they watched her every move. Lia took her cues from Brand and kept her own voice quiet while she spoke.

"Are we leaving?" he asked, and she nodded. His eyes went back to Trevor, and he heaved a sigh before struggling to his feet. She reached over to help him, but he shook off her hold. Surprising, considering he always seemed to actively seek her hand whenever he wanted to get out of chairs.

"I'll see you tomorrow morning, mate," he promised Trevor.

Naturally *everybody* at the homeless shelter knew Lia and wanted to chat with her. Sam was starting to comprehend that she was considered something of a saint by the good citizens of Riversend. It pissed him off a little, because they all seemed to *want* something from her. Even when she was in the middle of one thing, they were already buttering her up to do the next thing.

He'd noticed it with the old folks—yes, she was there to play the piano twice a week, but then there were all the requests that she fetch things, bring things, fix things, make things. At the animal shelter, they'd asked her to organize a fund-raiser, some kind of annual fete that apparently *only* Lia could do right. At the library, after she'd finished reading to the kids, the librarian had asked if Lia would mind baking—not buying or just bringing, but *baking*—confectioneries for the next adult-literacy class. Lia, of course, had said yes. Because Lia seemed incapable of refusing anybody anything. Anybody except Sam, of course. She was quite comfortable telling him no.

Now he watched, increasingly irritated, as the man they called Oom—which apparently meant "uncle"—Herbert asked Lia if she would mind terribly fetching another few boxes of donated goods from the Catholic church. Lia's face lit up with a warm smile.

"Of course I don't mind," she said sweetly, and Sam's teeth gritted in annoyance. It was none of his business—after he left they would continue taking advantage of her because she allowed it. If she enjoyed being the town's general lackey, then far be it for him to intercede.

A lanky guy, about Sam's age, wearing a sweater-vest, a tight-looking bow tie, and a pin-striped short-sleeved shirt, approached Lia as she was sorting through some of the clean blankets that had been donated to the shelter. Sam, who was standing to one side, not helping, not interfering, and not really talking to anyone, immediately stood upright, his gaze sharpening as he took in every aspect of this newcomer. He didn't like the proprietary way the man was looking at Lia, and he liked it even less when the skinny bastard touched her. Not just touched her—encircled his bony hand around her arm before she even knew he was there. The shock on her face spurred Sam into action, and he was beside her in three seconds flat.

The other man was taller than Sam, but he was skeletally thin and Sam knew how to intimidate with nothing but a glare and an open, loose-limbed stance. Legs braced apart, shoulders back, hands loosely hanging at his sides, he looked combat ready. He *was* combat ready, despite his injuries. If this guy didn't move his hand from Lia's arm very soon, Sam was going to fuck him the hell up.

"Problem here?" he asked grimly, and Lia blinked from the other guy to Sam, looking completely confused. She pulled her arm out of the other man's hold, and Sam relaxed marginally.

"Who are you?" the taller man asked resentfully, his huge Adam's apple bobbing as he swallowed.

"Brand. You?"

"Gregory Marsh. Dahlia and I are seeing each other."

Sam looked at Lia and raised his eyebrows at her. She looked uncomfortable and slanted her eyes away from his.

Really? This guy? This was the guy with whom she was getting serious? Okay, so this was a small town and maybe there weren't many eligible men around, but Lia was . . . she was *Lia*, and this guy was not worthy of her. Not because he was weird-looking and smelled funny, but because he didn't look at her like she meant the world to him. He didn't look like he'd appreciate strawberry flowers on his waffles or breakfast faces, and maybe Sam didn't appreciate those things, either, but it was already established that Sam was the wrong man for her. If this was an example of the kind of man she considered *right*, then she was going to have to reevaluate her wish list. Because this guy was all kinds of wrong for Lia.

"Gregory, what are you doing here?" she asked uncomfortably.

"I saw you come in, and since you haven't been answering my texts, I thought I'd come over and ask you in person if you'd like to have dinner tonight."

"I-I . . . can't." Brand watched the uncomfortable little exchange with extreme interest. Lia didn't *seem* all that into her Mr. Right. What was that all about?

"Why not?" Good old Greg practically snarled the question, his gaze sliding to Sam, who made no secret of his avid curiosity. Once again the other man's hand went around Lia's arm, and Sam heard the low growl in the back of his throat. The other two heard it as well, and both of them looked at him in shock. Truth be told, Sam was a bit shocked as well. But the sight of that arsehole's bony hands on Lia's soft skin pissed him off and made him want to get violent. Luckily for Greg, he released Lia's arm, but he shifted so that he was standing between Lia and Sam. He lowered his voice, but Sam still heard every word. As he was certain Gregory intended him to.

"The other night was so good. I can't stop thinking about it. Your soft skin, your sweet mouth . . . the way you rubbed against my . . ."

"Stop it," Lia hissed. "That wasn't what you imagined it to be."

"Why are you doing this? Are you playing hard to get? Or are you just a cocktease?"

Lia gasped, and Sam's temper snapped.

"Not very gentlemanly of you, mate," he chastised, grabbing the back of Gregory's scrawny neck and yanking him away from Lia. "Fuck off out of here before I snap you in two. Don't let the cast on my arm fool you—I'm pretty capable of breaking parts of you if I want to."

The guy gave him a terrified look but still managed to get a word in before he scuttled off back to whatever fucking hole he'd crept out of.

"I know we have something, Lia. Call me."

The encounter had drawn stares, and Sam met every curious pair of eyes challengingly before everybody looked away and pretended to go back to what they were doing before.

"Seriously, Lia? *That* guy? He's the guy you were getting serious about?" Lia winced and refused to meet his eyes.

"You're going to have to look at me sometime, sunshine," he said, surprising himself with the endearment. It suited her much more than the more aloof "princess" did. The endearment startled her into looking at him, and he smiled at her. "Tell me about Gregory."

"Not now," she said, her furtive gaze going around the room, where everybody was looking at everything *but* Lia and Sam.

"Then I believe it's time for lunch."

It was only as they were walking into MJ's that it finally registered with Lia that it was Thursday and that Daff was waiting for her at their usual table. The expression on her sister's face darkened when she saw Brand, and when Lia looked at the man walking beside her, she saw that his face bore a similar expression to Daff's.

Well, they would have to suck it up and play nice, because Lia was angry and irritable after Gregory's confrontation and she really, really needed a glass of wine or something to soothe her nerves.

She didn't acknowledge either of them when she sat down, merely summoned Suzy over and ordered a glass of red wine, leaving both of her lunch companions to stare at her in surprise.

"*What?* I can't have some wine with my lunch?" she snapped, and Daff's eyebrows went straight to her hairline.

"Okay, asshole, what did you do to upset her?"

"*Me?* Ask her creepy boyfriend, Ichabod Crane. He's the one who came slithering over and embarrassed her in front of half the town."

"Icha—wait, do you mean Grantley Marsh?" Daff asked Sam with wide eyes.

"Gregory," Lia corrected automatically. Daff ignored her interjection, keeping her eyes on Brand's face.

"Lanky fucker, wears bow ties, has the beginnings of a comb-over and a gigantic Adam's apple?" Brand elaborated for Daff's benefit.

"Ugh, where did you run into him?"

"Homeless shelter," Brand said concisely. Lia refrained from saying anything. Her drink arrived and she smiled gratefully at Suzy before downing half the huge glass in one gulp.

"Oh, of course, the bank's across the street from the homeless shelter," Daff breathed with a slight shake of her head before elaborating. "He's the bank manager."

"That explains that, then."

"And he *confronted* Lia?" Daff looked completely thrown by that information. Like someone had just told her that they'd taught a monkey to talk.

"Full on," Brand said grimly, his face going dark at the recollection. "Grabbed her arm and asked her why she hasn't been returning his texts. Why haven't you been returning his texts, Lia? I thought he was your guy?"

"That bastard?" Daff asked, her voice dripping with scorn. "No way. He's a handsy asshole who thinks grinding himself up against an unwilling woman counts as foreplay."

"What?" Brand's eyes narrowed and his head whipped to Lia as if seeking confirmation, but she didn't feel like confirming or denying anything. She just wanted to drink her wine and pretend the other two weren't there. She averted her gaze and stared off into the middle distance. Refusing to acknowledge either of them until the wine had mellowed her mood a bit. But apparently her refusal to speak was enough of a confirmation for Brand, if his next words were anything to go by. "That *motherfucker*! I should have torn him apart."

He looked set to do so, too, Lia observed, taking another calming sip of wine. His good palm braced against the tabletop, as if he meant to push himself up and go Gregory hunting. She'd never seen him look so angry before, and she found it both gratifying that all that rage was on her behalf and intimidating when she knew he was fully capable of maiming or killing with his bare hands.

"Calm down, Brand, it's none of your business," she said, injecting a measure of unruffled coolness into her only slightly shaky voice.

"What did he do?" Brand asked, his voice still holding that dangerous edge.

"Nothing. We just kissed, that's all."

"'We'? As in you and he? As in you were a willing participant in this embrace?" he asked tersely, and she shrugged.

"I knew he was going to kiss me. I was prepared for it."

"Prepared? What the fuck does that even mean?"

"Lip gloss? Breath mints? Tongue exercises?" Daff asked, also seeking further clarification, and Lia glared at her sister, who was *so* not helping.

"Did you wear the juicy bubblegum-flavored lip gloss for him?" Brand growled dangerously, and both Lia and Daff gaped at him.

"What? *No!* That's not what I meant. I meant I knew he was going to kiss me. It was our third date, and I expected some kind of physical escalation from him."

"How far did this 'physical escalation' go, sunshine?" More dangerous growling, combined with lip curling and nostril flaring. He was fascinating, like a territorial male animal.

"A kiss. Our first. With tongue." She wrinkled her nose at the recollection. "He'd had garlic, though, so it wasn't exactly what I'd been hoping for."

"And that's all? A disgusting, garlic-flavored kiss."

"This is really none of your concern, Brand," she tried again, not comfortable discussing this with him, but this time Daff chimed in.

"Oh, he grabbed her tit and rubbed himself against her," she elaborated, clearly *wanting* Brand to kill Gregory and go to prison for murder, thereby effectively killing two birds with one stone. Her sister could be pretty devious at times.

Brand swore and was halfway out of his seat this time before Lia sighed and clamped a hand around his left wrist.

"Sit *down*, Brand. You don't get to play this role in my life."

"What role?" he asked between clenched teeth.

"Hero." The word made him pause, and his eyes narrowed before he released a furious breath and sat down heavily.

"We're letting the matter go now," she said, quite proud of her level voice as she aimed a warning look at both Daff and Brand.

"If he approaches you again . . . ," Brand said, his voice fading as he left the rest unspoken.

"If he approaches me again, I'll deal with it. *Me.* Not you," she said calmly and confidently. Her answer seemed to frustrate him and he looked set to argue, but Daff cleared her throat, bringing his attention to her.

"So why are you hanging out with my sister today, Brand?" Daff asked pointedly.

"She's showing me around town," he said after a beat, allowing the subject change as he picked up the laminated menu.

"How *exciting*. There's so much to see," she said acerbically, and Lia rolled her eyes.

"I've enjoyed the last couple of days," Brand surprised them by saying. "We've gone dancing, seen a bit of theater, some of the local animals."

Daff choked on a sip of water and laughed, the sound genuinely amused. "I'm going to take a stab in the dark here and say you've been to the retirement home and the animal shelter. Not sure what the theater thing is."

"The Books Are Fun campaign," Brand supplied with a grin. "The kids act out scenes from a book." More laughter from Daff.

"So did you and Spence have fun last night?" Spencer had visited him last night? Brand hadn't mentioned that. Lia didn't know why that news surprised her or why she felt a little betrayed that she had to hear about it secondhand.

"Yeah."

"I hear you're having another male-bonding session tonight?"

"Well, if what he tells me is true, he'll need it." Daff's lips tilted at the corners at his response.

"I'm doing makeup tutorials with Charlie and a few of her besties tonight. She's been so bored this holiday, she's driving us a little crazy," she informed Lia. "Want to join us? We'll be doing facials and having virgin cocktails. Well, virgin for the girls, but I'm totally slipping some rum in my daiquiris."

"That sounds like fun," Lia said with a grin.

"We can have a few extra drinks because it's a *holiday* tomorrow. Freedom Day, baby!"

"I completely forgot about that," Lia gasped, and Daff chuckled. After the excitement and ups and downs of the last week, the national holiday had completely slipped her mind.

"Does this mean we can't go and see Tyrion?" Brand asked, worried.

"His name is Trevor, and because of the holiday the shelter will have an adoption fair tomorrow. I'll be helping them with that. I just lost track of the dates."

"I think Tyrion is a cool name. Or maybe Drogon. Drogon is an awesome name."

"You're not naming him after a *Game of Thrones* character."

"Why not? *Game of Thrones* is great. We have a few of the actors on our client list."

"Oh my . . . which ones?" Daff asked breathily. "Jon Snow? Can you introduce me? Spencer knows I'd probably throw him over for that bite-size hunk."

"Can't tell you that," Brand said with a grin. "It's confidential."

"The dog has a name," Lia said pointedly, ignoring the deliberate diversion. "It's Trevor."

"You need to give the guy a fair shake in life—he's disadvantaged with a name like *Trevor*. It doesn't sound cool. It doesn't suit his personality."

"We don't know what his real personality is yet beneath all that fear and anger."

"I'm pretty sure it's not that of a Trevor."

"Cripes, you're irritating!"

Brand paused and stared at her in fascination.

"Did you just say *cripes*?" he asked, and Daff chuckled. For a moment the two shared a looked of mutual amusement at Lia's expense. She didn't like this sudden camaraderie between them, especially not if it meant them teaming up against her.

"Right?" Daff asked on a laugh. "I told her I can't take her seriously when she uses words like that."

"You both think you're *so* special with your f-bombs and your s-bombs and your c-words and . . ."

"Which c-words?" Daff asked curiously. "There are a few."

"All of them. Shut up, I'm making a point."

Daff gasped in exaggerated horror. "So rude, Lia."

"Anyway, you both think you're so special. But you're not, you're just . . . just *crude*. It doesn't make you edgy and cool or anything. It just means you can't properly express yourselves in a meaningful or eloquent way."

"And *cripes* is a meaningful and eloquent word?" Brand asked, his voice low and trembling slightly. Daff laughed again and quickly stifled it behind a hand when Lia shot her a glare.

"I'm no longer participating in this juvenile conversation," she said with a haughty sniff and ushered Suzy over to place her order.

"Chicken Kiev and salad for me please, Suzy," she said and folded her hands primly, one on top of the other, as she watched Brand hastily pick the oh-so-manly rump steak and baked potato. Daff ordered a burger and fries. Last year, for about a minute, her sister had gone on some crazy diet and ordered only salads. Thankfully, she'd come to her senses and was eating normally again. Spencer and his insistence on feeding her properly had contributed to Daff's return to normalcy.

Lia wasn't quite sure what had gone on with Daff last year, but all the turmoil and drastic life changes had resulted in a much happier woman. Her sister smiled and laughed more often and just looked like a heavy burden had been lifted from her shoulders. It pleased Lia to know her sisters were happy and settled, she just wished . . .

She sighed softly. Wishes had proven to be futile. Her ridiculous and childish expectation of a happily ever after with the man of her dreams had long ago been extinguished and replaced by the desire to just have *anyone* to care for. Someone who would care for her in return. She didn't need the grand romance that both Daisy and Daff had found. Not anymore. She would settle for something warm and cozy. Like a pair of old winter socks. Comfortable and a bit slouchy. Not quite a perfect fit, but just enough to make her feel content.

But even that modest dream seemed destined never to come true. She would be the daughter who wound up taking care of her parents. Living with them, growing old with them . . . After all the truly terrible dates she'd been on over the last few months, she was starting to believe that there were no husband or children in the cards for her.

The unsavory business with Gregory had just been the rotten cherry on the pile of excrement that was her dating history. She was getting heartily fed up with playing relationship roulette with her love life.

She sighed again and stared at Brand over the rim of her wineglass as he chatted with Daff. He looked relaxed, but still so masculine and predatory and absolutely sexy. Just looking at him and thinking of his words that morning made everything inside her clench in anticipation.

If she was destined to be alone forever, then why not take what he was offering? Why not make some exciting and wild and crazy memories to cherish when she was old and curled up in her lonely spinster bed? What if Brand was her last chance at something different? Something less than ordinary?

He looked up and caught her eye, and he smiled at her. A warm, enticing smile. The stubble over the indent in his cheek darkened as the groove deepened with the movement of his mouth.

"You're looking gloomy, sunshine."

"Then perhaps you should rethink your latest nickname?" she suggested, and his smile became a full-fledged grin.

"Nah. Even when you're gloomy, there are still hints of sunshine peeking through behind the clouds."

"Oh my God. You're so corny. Lia, do not fall for any of this smarmy shit, okay?" Daff protested dramatically, and Brand turned that grin on her.

"I'm using my best material here, McGregor," he teased, and she rolled her eyes.

"Did Laura Prentiss actually fall for your lines?" she asked pointedly, and the other woman's name shook Lia. How could she have forgotten about Laura Prentiss? He hadn't given her definitive answers on his relationship, and Lia was *not* going to be anybody's *other* woman. Ew, no. That would be gross.

The food arrived and Lia tried to put the entire train of thought firmly out of her mind. But as she ate and they talked, she couldn't help but think about it. If he and Laura Prentiss were really through, then why not go for it? He'd been her rebound guy—maybe she could return the favor and be his rebound girl.

CHAPTER SEVEN

"Not much of a talker, are you?" Sam observed later that evening after he and Spencer were three beers in and about halfway through another action flick. This time Keanu Reeves was destroying the assholes who'd killed his dog. Spencer, in the process of taking a thirsty sip of beer, cocked an eyebrow and lowered the bottle to level a look at him.

"Hmm." For a second Sam reckoned that was the only response he'd get. The man hadn't said more than two words to him since his arrival forty minutes ago. But Spencer's lips quirked and he contemplated Sam for a moment before saying, his voice droll, "What gave it away?"

Sam chuckled appreciatively.

"I don't know, maybe the fact that it took me about half an hour to appreciate that you'd managed to glean which drink I'd prefer, what movie I wanted to watch, *and* what I wanted for dinner, all without asking a single question. And yet I fucking *know* I had choices." Spencer's lips tilted into a full-on grin. It wasn't an exaggeration to say the guy hadn't asked a single question.

Drinks were easy—he'd held up a beer and a bottle of scotch with a tilt of his head, and Sam had reached for the beer. Same with food, both microwavable choices—pizza or lasagna. But the movie, that was when shit had gotten freaky. He'd scrolled through Mason's selection, stopped at *John Wick*, looked at Sam, and grunted. Just a grunt. But the sound had been a question, Sam was sure of it—why else would he have responded with "Yeah, sure. I haven't seen that one yet"?

Uncanny fucker.

"How can Mason be such a garrulous bastard when he was raised by someone like you? I can't figure it out." Sam shook his head in wonder.

"*You* ever get a word in edgewise when Mason's on a roll?" the other man suddenly asked, his deep voice hoarse from lack of use, and Sam snorted at the pithy response.

"Touché," he said, chuckling.

"It was easier just to be quiet with Mason around. He spoke enough for both of us. Besides, you hear more, see more when you're not always mouthing off about insignificant shit."

"Hear and see what?" Sam asked, and Spencer reached for the remote and paused the movie. Then he leaned forward, forearms resting on his thighs, and watched Sam for a long, uncomfortable moment.

"You and Lia. You disappeared from the stag party and the wedding together," Spencer shocked him by saying.

"Didn't know you were so interested in my movements, big guy," he joked weakly, and Spencer lifted a heavy brow in response to that.

"Couldn't give a fuck about your movements, bro. But Lia's going to be my sister. She's already family, and I take care of my own."

Sam cleared his throat.

"She can take care of herself," he said quietly.

"Hmm." The sound was nothing more than a deep rumble, and Sam had no idea what it was supposed to mean.

Spencer leaned back, still not taking his eyes off Sam's face, and took a long drink from his beer. Sam, who had been trained in both interrogation techniques and resistance, had never felt more uncomfortable in his life before. This guy was good. He was wasted peddling sporting goods in this tiny town. A shame he lacked that military edge—with it he would definitely have made an excellent addition to Sam's team.

"You're not ambidextrous," Spencer observed, waving his bottle at Sam's injured arm, and Sam was thrown by the abrupt change in topic. Seriously, Spencer Carlisle was good at this.

"I'm not," Sam agreed, waiting to see where the man was going with this.

"But you're not as helpless as you want to seem. You're comfortable enough with the use of your left arm, even if it's not your dominant arm, to manage small tasks. So why do you need Lia's help?" Sam cleared his throat, and this time *he* took a long, thirsty drink from his beer. It was such a transparent delaying technique he was embarrassed by it. He preferred Spencer when he was silently observing and not delivering an opinion. That guy was manageable; this one was . . . Well, he was a fucking big brother. An overprotective, intimidating big brother.

"That's between Lia and me," Sam finally responded, and Spencer narrowed his eyes, not happy with the answer—that much was clear.

"I don't like to waste words," Spencer said heavily, and Sam snorted at that obvious statement. "So consider everything said."

"What do you mean?"

"The warnings and the threats. Consider them said."

Ah.

Well, that was much more effective than any of the words Spencer might have used, because with Sam's much too extensive knowledge of torture techniques—anything his own mind came up with to fill in the gap was probably a lot worse than whatever Spencer could devise. Although Sam had seen the lengths even the mildest of men would go to in order to protect their family.

Right then.

"Noted."

"Hmm." The sound was filled with satisfaction, and Spencer reached for the remote and unpaused the movie. He went back to his previous relaxed demeanor as if the exchange hadn't happened, and

Sam watched him for a moment before sighing and refocusing on John Wick's implausible ass-kickery.

The rest of the evening passed amicably; they didn't speak much, and after his previous unsettling conversation with Spencer Carlisle, Sam was okay with that. Instead they exchanged manly grunts and growls, and that was that. It was all quite satisfying, actually.

They watched another movie after *John Wick*, and Spencer got up to leave before the credits started rolling.

"Do you think the coast is clear?" Sam asked when he saw Spencer check his watch.

"No idea. How long does this kind of shit last generally?"

"How the fuck would I know, mate? I don't exactly go for regular mani-pedis and bikini waxes." Spencer paled comically at that, and Sam fought back a grin. The badass he'd encountered earlier was nowhere to be found.

"You don't think they're waxing their . . . down theres, do you? They're *kids*."

Sam laughed at that—the guy looked positively squeamish at the thought. He took pity on Spencer and shook his head. "From what I gathered, it would be facials and makeup and pretend cocktails. Unfathomable girlie shit."

"Great. I should be getting back."

"Thanks for the company," Sam said sincerely, and Spencer waved his thanks aside.

"I'll pop around tomorrow to see if there's anything you need . . ."

"Actually, Spencer, there *is* something," Sam said on a wince as he ran his hands over his unruly stubble. The other man stopped, stared at him, and then grinned as understanding dawned.

"Guess we'll be doing our own manly makeover," he said unexpectedly, and Sam was startled for a moment before he started chuckling.

"Guess so."

The teenage gigglefest came to an end when Spencer returned home. Well, it didn't so much end as change locations. The girls, all five of Charlie's *closest* friends, and Toffee filed upstairs and into Charlie's room. The door slammed, the music went on, and the volume went up. Spencer groaned, heaved a huge sigh, and pinched the bridge of his nose.

Lia and Daff laughed at his reaction. Daff enfolded him in a hug.

"Oh, poor baby, it's not that bad. Soon you'll be so used to the noise you won't even notice they're there." A high-pitched squeal made an instant liar out of her, and she grimaced. It was Charlie's first sleepover, and Spencer didn't look too comfortable having a bunch of high-pitched teens in his home.

"Why did we agree to this again?"

"Because we love her and it's healthy for her to have close female friends. They can enjoy themselves here in a safe environment."

"Hmm." He didn't sound convinced.

"What did you and your man crush get up to?"

"Movies, makeovers . . . or would you call that a male over?" Lia's eyes widened as she tried to make sense of his statement.

"Wait, what?" Daff gawked, and Spencer grinned proudly. Looking smug that he had some information that could surprise her.

"We drank, watched a movie, and I did his manscaping." Lia choked on her spit, and Daff snorted.

"Oh, my love," Daff murmured, her voice low and sympathetic. She had only recently started calling him that, and Lia could tell that Spencer absolutely adored it—he practically preened every time she used it. "That definitely doesn't mean what you want it to mean."

"What?" Spencer stared at her blankly.

"Manscaping," Daff elaborated patiently, and Lia was starting to shake as she tried to control her laughter. Poor Spencer looked completely baffled and the tips of his ears were starting to go pink, as if he realized that he might have used the wrong pop-culture reference. Again.

Lia lifted her hand to her mouth; the laughter couldn't be contained any longer and actually exploded through her fingers. Spencer sighed in resignation.

"It means his pubes, doesn't it?" At his question, Lia doubled over the kitchen counter and held on for dear life.

"Mostly," Daff said, still looking completely earnest and compassionate, her hand stroking up and down Spencer's broad back. "But it *can* also mean chest hair. Back hair. Ear hair. Butt hair. I suppose it's just general male grooming and appearance."

"Fuck," Spencer said, the word soft and heartfelt and just so, so funny. He glared at Lia, who was still bent over and laughing uncontrollably. "Shut up, Lia. Eighty-nine percent of the time you make the same kind of mistakes."

"Y-yes," Lia gasped, her voice hoarse and breathless as she tried to control her laughter. "B-but not this time."

"This is why I prefer to keep my mouth shut," Spencer muttered, and Daff finally lost it. She hugged him and laughed, and because the sound was so joyful, Spencer lost his look of disgruntled resignation.

"Oh, you beautiful man." Daff laughed. "This is why I love you. You're hilarious. And a fantastic sport."

Spencer grinned and enfolded his arms around her.

"Are those the only reasons you love me?" he asked into her hair, and Daff settled snugly into his arms and rested her cheek against his broad chest.

"Tip of the iceberg," Daff crooned.

"Well, then, elaborate, darling."

Lia knew that they were on the verge of forgetting her very existence, and she sighed wistfully before bidding them both good night. They were aware enough to separate and give her a proper farewell, but

Lia could tell from the dazed expressions on both of their faces that they'd be resuming the "conversation" the second she drove off.

She went as far as the end of the drive, took the left turn, and then stopped at the entrance to Mason's driveway. The cabin wasn't completely dark—the loft lights were still on, and Lia wondered what he was doing. She considered her life, her desire for more, and her recognition that there would be no more. This was it.

Maybe it was defeatist; maybe it was simply her way of talking herself into this fling with Brand. She needed an excuse, a way to make herself feel better for doing something so completely uncharacteristic. Telling herself that this was a rebound thing for him and a last chance for some sexual excitement for her was that excuse.

It would benefit both of them. And when it was over, they'd walk away from it without looking back. None the worse for wear.

Decision—crazy, insane, off-kilter, and totally uncharacteristic decision—made, Lia turned her car into the driveway and drove the short distance to the front door. Once there, she sat for another long while, on her phone, making a list. She needed guidelines, a set of rules to keep her in check. To remind her not to get emotionally involved and to keep her cognizant of the fact that this was nothing more than a short-term, mutually satisfying arrangement.

Sam was ready for bed. He had made one last check of the perimeter—uh, *cabin*, old habits—and was ready to head upstairs when a soft knock sounded on the front door. For an instant he froze, not sure if it was an actual knock—the wind was picking up and it could be something loose on the porch—then it sounded again. Three uncertain little raps on the wood. He knew who it was. Of course he knew who it was, but he couldn't quite bring himself to believe that he'd actually convinced her to come. She hadn't looked at all into his suggestion that morning.

Sam stared at the door for a moment longer, feeling oddly uncertain. He mentally cataloged his toiletry bag, trying to remember if he'd packed condoms. Why would he pack condoms? He'd come here to recuperate, not to find a fuck buddy. But he never went anywhere without condoms, so . . .

The knock sounded again. Even fainter than before, and he swore. What the hell was he doing? She was probably talking herself out of this with every passing second. He surged to the door and yanked it open. The suddenness of the gesture shocked her, and she blinked at him apprehensively. He could tell from her stance that she had been in the process of leaving and heaved a sigh of relief that he'd come to his senses before she could do that.

"Hey," he said, his voice a little overeager, and he toned it down. "Uh, Lia. You're here."

"Yes."

Jesus, woman. Give me something to work with, he lamented silently.

"Great, I'm glad. Come in." He stepped aside and she slowly stepped over the threshold, looking very much like someone heading for the guillotine. Yeah, well, that wasn't sexy at all. He needed to get her a bit more relaxed. "Would you like a drink?"

"I need to know," she said, her shaky voice filled with resolve. "Laura Prentiss."

Sam sighed. For fuck's sake, not this again!

"I told you before, the relationship we had is over." It was the most honest way he could think of to phrase it.

"You were my rebound guy, Brand. And I suspect . . . I feel you need a rebound girl. And I want . . . I'm happy to . . . I think I can be that for you."

So many stops and starts as she tried to find the perfect way to phrase that, but Sam didn't like the way her statement sat with him. It felt completely wrong.

"Are you sacrificing yourself or something? Returning a favor?"

"No," she hastened to assure him, her eyes wide and earnest. "Of course not. I mean, maybe that's part of it, but I want to do this for me, too."

"Why?" Damn it, why had he asked? What did it matter what her reasons were as long as he got her into bed? He didn't understand his weird reaction to this. He should have her in his arms already; his mouth should be on hers, his hands on her naked skin. Why was she even still *dressed*?

"I'm not going to find him," she said on a whisper, looking miserable, and his brows lowered in confusion.

"Find who?"

"The guy. My guy. I won't find a Mason or a Spencer. I was happy to settle for a Gregory—"

"Over my dead *body*," he interrupted furiously, and she smiled absently.

"Before I saw how very similar to my ex-fiancé he is," she added. "I was okay with a man I didn't really love or feel attracted to. I thought that those feelings would grow eventually, but I don't think I'm even going to find Mr. Okay, much less Mr. Right. Not anytime soon, at least. Maybe not ever. I'm just tired of all the bad dates and the dashed hopes. After Gregory . . ." She paused before shaking her head. "I just need a break."

"So you're giving up?" he asked disbelievingly, and she shrugged.

"For now. For this, with you."

"I'm not the guy you're looking for, Lia," he stressed urgently. "I'm not even a great Mr. All Right for Now. If we're going to do this, you can't get attached. If you do, you'll get hurt, and I don't want to hurt you."

She smiled warmly, the expression dispelling some of her previous misery. He didn't like seeing her miserable. It was disturbing and should never happen again.

"I know that, Brand," she said, the gentle reassurance in her voice matching the tranquil smile. "But I was thinking about what you said, about you being the last wild thing I do before I settle down . . . and I decided that I want that. I want to be your rebound girl and you'll be my wild thing. Consider my caution thrown to the wind. I figure it would be nice to have something like this to look back on when I'm old. To know I was willing to do something uncharacteristic and fun, just because why the heck not?"

"You're not exactly old and decrepit, Lia. I doubt this will be your *last* wild thing," he amended, and her smile widened, but the edges were tinged with sadness.

"I'm not known for my spontaneity, Brand. I think one per lifetime is my limit."

"And yet this is the third—"

"No," she interrupted quickly. "It's one extended extemporaneous walk on the wild side."

"I'll help you," he suddenly decided, not sure what the fuck he was promising but just hating to see such abject defeat in her normally sparkling eyes.

"What?"

"While we're *flinging*, so to speak, I'll help you find that guy."

"That's crazy. And also quite amoral. I won't be dating men while we're involved."

"You can date them, just don't sleep with them. When you find a guy you *want* to sleep with, we end our thing."

"That's too bizarre; I don't like it."

"It'll be part of your new wild-woman persona. You can date one guy while sleeping with another."

"It feels dishonest. Why are we discussing this? I came here for a fling and you're—you're . . ." A delicate frown settled between her brows as she tried to think of a way to describe what she was feeling. "You're copblocking me."

"What?" He blinked, not sure he'd heard her properly.

"You heard me," she whispered angrily, and his lips quirked.

"No, sunshine, I'm not really sure I did."

"I said you're *cop*blocking me." Her cheeks were bright pink, and in that moment Sam watched his good intentions curl up and float away right before his eyes. The sexy, shy librarian was back, and he wanted her *badly*.

"And what does that mean, sunshine?" he asked, keeping his voice gentle, and she flushed as she struggled to frame a response.

"You know what it means, I just replaced the *other* word," she confessed, and he grinned.

"Oh, you mean *cock*?" He bit back a laugh at her pained groan.

"Just stop doing it," she admonished, and he nodded solemnly.

"No more cockblocking. Got it." His eyes ran over her face, and he felt his lips stretch into a full smile. God, she was absolutely gorgeous. His breath hitched and he palmed her cheek with his good hand. "You're sure about this, right? Because I don't do regrets."

Her breath shuddered from her chest and he recognized that she'd been holding it. Her lips parted and his eyes dropped to them—they looked full, *juicy*, and he wondered if she'd applied some of that gloss before knocking on his door. Applied it for him. He groaned as he understood that he could finally sample that bubblegum flavor. All it took to go from thought to action was a single breath before his lips were on hers. She sighed and moved closer and opened up for him. It was the only way he could think of to describe it—she just tilted back her head, softened her mouth, and let him in.

It was fucking fantastic. He couldn't quite remember if the last time had been like this. He couldn't remember if they'd kissed. This felt like a first kiss, and he couldn't remember the last time a first kiss had held this kind of significance for him. It terrified him but at the same time made him want more . . . so much more.

He wanted to wrap her close, but the cast on his arm hampered him and he made a frustrated sound in the back of his throat as he lifted his mouth from hers. Her lips followed his, soft, lush, and completely ravished. They still wanted more and they pouted when he moved his mouth out of reach. Her eyes fluttered open and those luminous gray irises were almost completely obscured by the black of her pupils. She looked dewy, aroused, ready . . . and Sam wasn't sure this could be slow or even gentle. He just needed to get through the logistics.

"Help me," he grated, and her eyes regained focus as they registered the frustration on his face. He was tugging at the hem of his tank top and she said something, he couldn't be sure what, but it sounded like *cripes* or *crumbs*. It made him smile, and he wondered at the lightness he felt in this moment. He was hard, he was burning up, he wanted to rip her clothes off and fuck her right where she stood—and at the same time he felt elated. Like a kid at a carnival, he felt excited, happy, nervous, and ready all at the same time.

She helped him drag the tank up and over his cast and then looked at it for a moment before placing it neatly to one side.

"At some point," she said primly, despite the alarming wobble in her voice, "you and I are going to discuss the fact that you were just wearing a tank top. Why have we been struggling with those button-up shirts whe . . ." She stopped abruptly, and he could see exactly when the truth hit her. She gasped softly. "You *deliberately* made me struggle with those shirts, didn't you?"

He laughed and then, because he couldn't stand the separation any longer, kissed her again. Outrage forgotten, she wrapped her arms around his waist, burrowed against his chest, and, again, gave him everything with that one kiss. He plucked at her clothing with his free hand, groaning at how ineffectual his attempts were, and she made soothing sounds, her hands stroking up and down his bare back, her fingernails alternately digging in and lightly scraping.

"Brand," she said, her voice muffled against his lips. "Let me."

"What?" he asked dazedly, lifting his head to look down at her, worshipping her with his eyes.

"Let me. Please let me do this, just while you're in that cast. I can . . ."

"You want to drive, sunshine?" he asked lightly, understanding where she was going with this, and she flushed before nodding. He grinned, loving the thought of it. He threw himself back on the sofa and spread his arms invitingly. "Then have at it."

Sam wasn't sure what to expect when he so brazenly invited her to take over, but it certainly wasn't what he got. She licked her lips, those juicy, bubblegum-flavored lips, and her hands fell to her blouse. She was still in that mint-green pencil skirt and white top that had so turned him on that morning, and he watched with bated breath as she flicked open one pearly button at a time. Her movements weren't seductive so much as efficient, and that was even more of a turn-on than any blatant attempt at seduction would have been. He watched as she tugged her blouse off, folded it, and placed it aside. His greedy eyes drank in every aspect of the neat, pretty figure now revealed to his gaze. The sweet little nipped-in waist, the cute indent of her belly button, and then her modest cleavage in a pretty, lacy white front-fastening bra.

She didn't need much support. The bra seemed entirely superfluous, but it was still such a turn-on to imagine peeling it off her and revealing the loveliness beneath. She didn't touch the bra, though, instead she kicked her foot back and his throat went dry as she tugged off one sensible pump and then the other. His cock twitched urgently when she skimmed her hands under her ass-hugging mint skirt and hitched it to just below her thighs in order to access her panties.

Sam growled when she performed a tug and then a shimmy and her lacy white panties dropped to her ankles. She stepped out of them and again folded them and placed them atop her blouse. Still none of this was overtly sexy, just efficient as hell. She barely looked at him while she did her sensible little striptease, while Sam couldn't take his eyes off her. When he was himself again, he was going to strip her slowly and kiss every single silky strip of newly revealed skin until she was begging him for release.

"Undo your hair for me," Sam begged hoarsely, startling her into looking at him. She went bright pink, and he comprehended that one of the reasons she was so determinedly avoiding eye contact was because this was hard for her. It explained the efficiency and the lack of artifice. She didn't know how to seduce but in her innocence succeeded in seducing him more effectively than any other woman had before her. Her hands went up to her ponytail, and he winced when she tugged the rubber band off without any care or concern for the silky stuff bound within. Her soft, sleek hair fell to her shoulders like a dark-brown curtain, and Sam ached to trail his fingers through it, yearned to bury his face and nose in it.

"Beautiful," he encouraged softly, and she smiled, running her splayed fingers through the mass before allowing it to settle again.

"Show me your breasts," he begged, his voice a whisper. "Please."

"No," she said, her voice stubborn. He scowled, irritated by her disobedience, but instantly forgave her when she fell to her knees on the floor in front of the sofa where he sat and wriggled between his splayed knees. Her forearms rested on his thighs, and she looked up at him earnestly. "I'm quite . . ."

She sucked on her lip and swallowed back whatever she'd been about to say, and Sam groaned in despair.

"Don't withhold your words from me now, Lia. I want to know what you're thinking."

"I'm quite *wet*," she confessed, her voice low. She seemed embarrassed by the confession, and the sound that emerged from Sam's throat was equal parts amusement and despair. "I don't remember being this wet before."

"God, I want to touch you," he moaned. "Taste you."

"You will," she promised. "But before you do, I think it's prudent we do this."

This turned out to be palming his thick erection through the thin material of his boxer briefs. She gave another one of those shuddery little sighs that Sam found so damned erotic and finally reached under the elastic waist and wrapped her small, soft hand around his rampant hardness. Sam hissed and arched into her touch, damned near coming in her hand.

She pushed the material of his shorts out of the way and gently released his hardness and watched in satisfaction as it throbbed against his stomach. Her face was so close to it, he could feel her breath on his sensitive flesh, and part of him was desperate for her to take him in her mouth, but another part wanted something else, wanted to experience the tightness of her body again. Right now, he wanted that *much* more than her mouth. She stood up and straddled his knees, tugging her tight skirt up to her thighs. Her crotch was level with his eyes, but he couldn't see her—her skirt was still modestly covering the part of her he now craved the most.

"Give me your hand," she urged, and he held up his left hand. She took it in her much smaller right hand and without any warning whatsoever pushed it beneath her skirt. They both hissed sharply when his hand made contact with her moist heat, and she moaned when he found her clit. Her lower lip caught between her teeth when he clumsily stroked her, his left hand heavy and uncooperative and definitely not equal to this most important of tasks.

He tried his best and she didn't mind his clumsiness at all—she looked like a fucking goddess, her pelvis gently thrusting against his questing touch as her hands went to her breasts and unclipped the fastening of her bra. Her palms immediately cupped the small mounds, completely obscuring them from view, and her head tilted back as she worked herself back and forth over his fingers.

"Do you have a condom?" she suddenly asked on a broken breath, and Sam snapped out of his erotic fog as he hazily registered that his fucking condoms were upstairs in the bathroom.

"They're upstairs," he groaned. She was still rubbing herself against his hand, and Sam couldn't seem to focus on anything else. She pointed to the sofa beside him.

"Brand . . . my bag. I have a couple of condoms."

"You do?" *Really?* That was unexpected, to say the least. She blushed and shrugged, striving for unconcern when she looked embarrassed as hell.

"I stole them from Daff and Spencer's medicine chest tonight," she confessed, and Sam choked back a laugh at that revelation. Sam had to withdraw his hand from all that wonderful heat in order to grab the bag, and Lia moaned at the loss. When he fumbled around in her bag, she took it from him impatiently and withdrew the condoms herself.

That move finally revealed her pretty little pink-tipped breasts to his greedy gaze, and while she struggled to tear open a foil packet, he leaned forward and tugged one of her hard nipples into his mouth for a sample. But a mere taste wouldn't do, and soon he was feasting. He was vaguely aware of Lia wrapping her arms around his head and encouraging him to suckle harder—something he was very happy to do. His clumsy left hand crept back beneath her skirt, this time not content to just stroke; he plundered her with his fingers, easing the way for the invasion to come.

"Oh yes, oh yes. Oh *thank you* . . ." This last was moaned as she clenched tightly around his fingers when her orgasm took her. He couldn't recall ever being thanked during sex before, and Sam grinned. It was so typically and charmingly Lia. She slumped heavily against him, her legs giving in until she was straddling his lap, her heat within touching distance of his throbbing shaft.

"Think you can get that condom on me now, sunshine?" he asked, his voice strained.

"Give me just one moment, please," she begged breathlessly, her voice muffled by his throat.

"I fear we might not have a moment," Sam said, fighting the urge to smile. That spurred her into action; she pushed herself up and stared at him with barely focusing eyes. She looked drugged, dazed, and a little bit devastated. But despite that, she managed to get him sheathed in the condom, her hands fumbling even more than his left hand had. Sam wasn't certain how he managed to keep himself from coming in her hands, but he was damned proud of his restraint.

Proud until she lifted herself up and over him, proud until he found himself completely engulfed in her tight heat, proud for all of the thirty seconds it took before he came, violently and messily and quite fucking spectacularly. She was in the middle of her upward stroke and he gripped her skirt with his good hand and dragged her back down onto his spasming cock. Kept her down while he emptied himself inside her.

"Oh my sweet, sweet *Christ*," he groaned, his hand leaving her skirt and burying itself in her hair. He pulled her close until her face was nestled in the spot where his shoulder met his neck. She happily nuzzled him there and sighed contentedly.

"That was nice," she murmured happily, and he found himself glaring at the wall. *Nice?* Seriously?

He nudged her up and she lifted her butt lazily while he tugged off the condom and clumsily knotted it, setting it aside for later. She sat back down on his lap, her wet nakedness smooshing against his wet nakedness. She didn't seem to mind.

"What did you do with the other one?" she asked drowsily, and he shifted to look down into her very contented face.

"What do you mean?"

"The condom. That night in the barn?" His brow furrowed.

"You're seriously asking me about that right now?"

"Yes. It bugged me for a while after that. I kept picturing one of the poor farmworkers picking it up. Or my father." She shuddered delicately at that thought.

"I didn't leave it in the barn. That's disgusting." He was offended that she'd even think that about him.

"Well, then, what did you do with it?"

He wrinkled his nose. "Put it in my pocket and discarded it when I got to a bathroom."

"Oh. Good." She wriggled a bit to get more comfortable, and of course it had a predictable effect on his body. She pushed herself up and peered at him through her messy hair. She moved against him, this time with more purpose, and he sucked his breath in through his teeth at the delightful friction.

"More?" she asked hopefully, and he grinned.

"Sunshine, we're just getting started."

Hours and hours and *so* many orgasms later, Lia sat up in bed with a contented sigh and stared down at the man who had satisfied her so completely tonight. He was wiped out, fast asleep, spread-eagled on his back with his arms thrown out on either side of him. He had dragged her close just before falling asleep, tucking her against his side, but she had wriggled away almost immediately, because it felt dangerously close to cuddling and cuddling was a huge no-no.

Because Sam didn't have the use of his right arm and because he wasn't as physically adept as usual, Lia had been on top every time. Sam had been very vocal in both his appreciation of her and his demands. Still, she knew he wanted to do more and that his current weakness frustrated him. But despite that, it had still been streets ahead of anything she'd experienced with Clayton. Lia sighed again and shifted her legs over the edge of the bed and pushed herself up.

"Where are you going?" The gravelly voice sent shivers up her spine, and she fought the urge to climb back onto the bed with him.

"Home. It's late. Or early," she rectified with a giggle. "Take your pick."

"You should stay," he growled, and she laughed outright at that.

"I don't think so. But thanks for the offer." She leaned over and planted a kiss on his lips. Just because she could. And because he looked rumpled and sleepy and gorgeous. His left hand lifted to the back of her head and kept her there while he deepened the kiss. She made a small sound of surrender, and her hands went to his chest and then smoothed up over his shoulders and his throat until she was cupping his jaw.

She took another taste, her tongue lazily sweeping over his lush lower lip before, with a reluctant sigh, she lifted her head. His eyes caught and held hers.

"You okay?"

"More than okay," she said with a smile. "This was a good idea. I feel fantastic. Thank you."

He chuckled.

"Always so polite, sunshine. I've never been thanked for sex before."

"I was thanking you for the orgasms," she corrected primly, feeling brazen, and was pleased when his laugh deepened.

"Never been thanked for an orgasm, either."

"Well, I'm happy to rectify that oversight," she said with a blush. "I should go."

She gathered her clothes and, despite already being stark naked, took them to the en suite and dressed there. His laughter followed her into the bathroom.

When she emerged from the bathroom, it was to find him clad in a pair of briefs and sitting on the edge of the bed.

"You sure I can't convince you to stay?"

"We're flinging, remember? Staying over doesn't fall within the fling guidelines."

"You have guidelines? How do you have guidelines? Where would you even find them?"

"On the internet." He gaped at her.

"Seriously?"

"Yes."

"You found *actual* guidelines?" He couldn't seem to wrap his head around that idea.

"A few. I chose different ones from different lists and tailored a set of rules to suit our situation. Is that weird?"

"A little." He nodded and then smiled. "But I suppose it's also practical. Maybe you should share this list with me? I should know the rules so that I don't overstep."

"Of course *you* won't overstep. I think men kind of live by these rules when they're involved with someone unimportant."

"You're not unimportant," he snapped, actually sounding offended. "I've never called you unimportant."

"I only meant—"

"I'm just not ready for a relationship. I'll never be ready for a relationship. I don't believe in marriage and long-term monogamy. It's unnatural. But that doesn't mean that I think less of you. I think you're pretty fucking great."

"That's nice of you," she said, smiling weakly before clearing her throat.

She didn't look convinced, and that frustrated Sam. He didn't want her to think that she was just some random place-filler chick. The thought made him pause, because essentially she was exactly that. A fun, sweet bit of short-term entertainment . . . He'd been adamant that she not romanticize this arrangement between them, and she was doing exactly the right thing in establishing a clear set of guidelines up front about what they could expect from each other and this *fling*, for lack of a better word.

But why did it make him feel so damned uneasy and unsatisfied? He wasn't sure. He watched as she gathered her things, feeling a hollowness settle in his gut as she turned to him and rewarded him with another of those beautiful, sweet smiles.

"I'll see you in the morning," she promised, and he nodded. He didn't want to speak, not when the only words that would come out were more pleas for her to stay.

She hesitated and looked like she was about to say something else. Sam waited, hoping she'd change her mind about leaving, but in the end she said nothing. Just nodded at him and left.

He listened to her car start up, the cold engine coughing a bit before it turned over, and he instantly worried about her safety in that ancient Fiat. He checked the time and was shocked when he saw that it was after three. It was much too late for her to be out alone.

He immediately started pacing and, after ten minutes had passed, picked up his phone and called her. She answered on the second ring.

"Brand? Are you okay?" He shuddered in relief when he heard her concerned voice.

"That's *my* line, sunshine. I didn't know it was this late—you shouldn't have left this time of night."

"The roads were quiet; I was home in five minutes."

"Next time you stay the night."

"No. I'll leave earlier." He didn't much care for that answer and seethed silently in response to it.

"Brand? You still there?"

"Yes," he gritted.

"Did you call to find out if I got home safely?"

"Yes."

"That's really sweet, thank you for your concern."

"You're always so polite," he said, for lack of anything better to say, and she laughed.

"I don't know how to be any other way."

"I like it," he said, and then before he could stop himself, "I like you."

She didn't respond to that, and he sighed. That was probably for the best. He was in an odd mood. He didn't understand himself right now.

"Lia?"

"Yes?"

"Thank you. For the orgasms." He heard her harshly inhaled breath and smiled.

"Y-you're, um . . . you're *quite* welcome." His smile widened into a grin.

"Lia?"

"Yes?"

"I can practically *hear* you blushing." His observation startled an exasperated laugh out of her.

"Good night, Brand."

"'Night, sunshine."

CHAPTER EIGHT

Dahlia Rose McGregor's List of Rules for an Effective Short-Term Fling (STF)

- ☐ RULE 1—Absolutely! Do NOT! Fall in love!
- ☐ RULE 2—No cuddling.
- ☐ RULE 3—Don't leave anything behind. Keep your clothes in your own closet!
- ☐ RULE 4—No sleepovers.
- ☐ RULE 5—No meaningful postcoital conversation.
- ☐ RULE 6—Do not introduce to family (too late!).
- ☐ RULE 7—No gifts given or received.
- ☐ RULE 8—When it's over, it's over.
- ☐ RULE 9—No regrets or shame.

"Good morning," Lia greeted Sam with a bright smile when he came downstairs the following morning. He looked exhausted, and she figured they had probably overdone it the night before. The man was recovering from some pretty horrific injuries, and while he had performed admirably last night, four times had perhaps been a bit extreme.

"Hey." He nodded, grabbing a long wooden spoon and inserting the end of it between his cast and his wrist. His eyes practically rolled back in his head when he reached the itch that had been bothering him. “God, I can’t wait for this fucking thing to come off!”

“When is your doctor’s appointment?” she asked. He dragged the spoon out and dropped it on the table before sitting down and looking at her.

“Next week. Wednesday or Thursday.”

“I need to know exactly where and when so that I can rearrange my schedule,” she said, dropping a coffee in front of him. He groaned appreciatively and hooked his palm around the mug to drag it closer. He inhaled deeply, just savoring the aroma for a long moment before lifting it to take a sip. He opened his eyes and met hers over the rim of the mug.

“Your coffee is the best,” he complimented, and she smiled. His gaze raked over her, going from her sensible beige kitten-heeled Mary Janes, up over her legs, farther up over the knee-length skirt of her pink gingham dress. It was a simple, strappy dress with a sweetheart neckline and small buttons all the way down the front, from neck to hem. She’d combined it with one of her favorite lacy white cardigans.

“You look pretty,” he observed, and she dropped her gaze. His words made her feel shy and a bit self-conscious.

“Thank you.” She picked up a damp cloth and started wiping down kitchen surfaces, busywork to keep her hands occupied. “I see you’ve managed to dress yourself today.”

He glanced down at himself and grinned unrepentantly.

“I figured I was busted.”

“*So* busted,” she said with a mock glare. “So what was the point of the shirt sham?”

“Shirt sham? I like that,” he said with a chuckle. “I wanted to make you hot for me. And I thought if you got to see my pecs and abs every day, you’d start throwing yourself at me.”

“Pecs and abs?” she scoffed, trying to hide her smile. “In case it’s escaped your notice, you’re as thin as the proverbial rail at the moment.”

"Wow, does my fragile male ego mean nothing to you, woman?" he asked woefully, and she rolled her eyes. "I'll have you know, my manly form is making a comeback thanks to your smashing meals."

"Good to know," she said, unable to fight the smile any longer. "Then you'd better eat up."

She placed his full English breakfast on the table in front of him, and he looked down with an expectant grin. The smile faded abruptly and Lia looked at his plate, wondering if there was a hair in his food or some other bit of nastiness that she hadn't noticed.

~

Sam stared down at his perfectly delicious-looking, perfectly ordinary plate of food. No faces or flowers this morning. Just two eggs, bacon, mushrooms, sausages, and toast. For a second he wondered if she was upset with him over something, but then he remembered his dickishness of the previous morning. She was just giving him what he'd demanded—edible food without any pointless, pretty fripperies.

And yet . . . he felt ripped off. He didn't understand why he felt that way, and he damned well didn't like it.

"Is everything okay?" she asked, and he blinked and forced a smile.

"Yes, this looks marvelous," he enthused, stabbing his fork into a mushroom with more force than was necessary. Some stupid, irrational part of him wondered what she would have created for him if he hadn't ranted at her yesterday and felt bereft that he would never know the answer.

The food was amazing as always, and he savored every bite, watching her while she bustled around and cleaned the room. She looked fresh and lovely this morning. Not at all like a woman who'd only gotten about four hours' sleep and had spent most of the previous night thrusting away on top of him.

The memory of her riding his cock so damned beautifully made his throat dry, and the appendage in question hardened painfully. She had her back to him and her hands in soapy water. Sam got up and stalked toward her until he was directly behind her, his crotch just above her tight, round butt. His left hand went to her hip and pulled her firmly back against him.

"What time are we leaving?" he asked, bringing his mouth to her ear.

"We c-can leave anytime we like. It's just the animal shelter today."

"I want to fuck you," he said.

"Yes."

"Right here. Right now."

"Ye-es." The word trembled out of her mouth on a soft sigh and he nipped her earlobe before dragging the skirt of her dress up over her thighs and then over her peachy little bum. He groaned when he caught sight of the plain white panties. His hand roughly yanked the soft cotton garment down her thighs, leaving her lush, already damp nudity completely revealed to his gaze.

"Move to the island," he commanded hoarsely, and she obeyed without question. The movement lacked grace, but they both stumbled from the sink to the island, Sam steering her with his hand. When they reached their destination, he placed the flat of his hand gently between her shoulder blades and guided her down, until she was leaning over the island, her cheek resting on the back of one hand while the other curled over the front edge of the countertop.

She didn't say a word, merely waited, and he sucked in a breath at the picture she made. Prim, perfect Lia McGregor bent over the kitchen counter, dress hiked up, legs spread, and panties pooled around one ankle, ready and waiting for his cock.

Sam groaned, unable to go another second without being inside her. He was wearing track pants with an elasticized waist, and he shoved them down to his hips without any problem. He'd had the forethought to put a condom in his pocket that morning, and he didn't know how the hell he did it, but he managed to get the thing on without her help.

He gripped his shaft and positioned himself at her sweet, hot little entrance before dropping his hand to her hip and pushing. She was ready for him, dripping for him, despite the lack of foreplay, and he moaned as all that tight hotness closed around him. She whimpered once he was fully sheathed, and the helpless little sound drove Sam quite mad with desire. He dragged himself out without much finesse before surging back in with a hard, almost violent thrust. Another little whimper from her, and he cursed.

"This is going to be rough, sunshine," he managed to warn her tightly, and she clenched around him.

"Good." Her voice was muffled against her hand. "Thank you."

The thank-you sent him completely over the edge, and he grunted before losing himself completely. Years of experience, of technique, of laudable bedroom skills went flying out the window to be replaced by sheer, primal animal instinct. All he felt was the need to mate, to claim, to mark someone as irrevocably his. He felt her come, more than once, and he felt a rush of possessive pleasure that he could satisfy her like that. It was the resultant swell of pure happiness that sent him into his own blinding orgasm.

When it was over, when he came to himself again, it was to stare down at Lia, then at his surroundings in dazed shock. He didn't feel right. He stepped away from her and turned his back to tug off the condom and adjust his pants. His movements were automatic but felt sluggish, like none of his limbs belonged to him. He was hazily aware of Lia moving behind him, heard her still labored breathing along with the rustling of fabric as she straightened her clothes and probably fixed her hair. But he couldn't seem to move. He stood frozen in the middle of the kitchen, not quite sure what to do or where to go next.

"Brand?" Her quizzical voice seemed to come from far away, and he blinked and then blinked again. His confusion abruptly wore off as everything snapped into focus again. He'd been in the process of discarding the condom. He went to the upstairs bathroom to complete the task and then sat on the side of the tub for a moment to gather his faculties.

He shouldn't have left her alone immediately after sex like that, he suddenly thought.

It was an arsehole move. He moved to the basin and dashed water on his face, roughly toweling it dry before hurrying back downstairs. She was at the sink again, and he frowned at her narrow back. How could she just go back to doing the dishes after *that*?

They should at least talk about what happened.

"Lia?" He kept his voice gentle. "You okay?"

She lifted her hands out of the water and dried them on a dish towel before turning to face him. Her eyes were serious, but she had a smile on her face; the effect was jarring and he was shocked to recognize that this was not a genuine smile. When had he become so familiar with her that he could tell her smiles apart?

"That was something else, Brand," she said, her voice teasing, while her eyes remained completely solemn.

"I'm sorry. It was a bit . . . much."

"It was intense, but I'd be lying if I said I didn't enjoy it."

"Maybe we should talk about it?" She shook her head, another one of those horrible fake smiles on her beautiful lips.

"No. We shouldn't."

"Another one of your rules?" he asked, unable to disguise the frustration in his voice.

"Uh-huh. Number five, to be exact."

"How many are there?"

"Nine."

"I want to read them."

"I'll send you the abridged notes," she promised. "I'm nearly done, let's leave in five minutes."

Because Lia had no other errands that day, they spent a couple of hours at the animal shelter. Brand went straight to Trevor, while Lia helped out with the adoption fair.

Her father was at the shelter today as well. He was a busy man who ran his own practice and the free clinic he and Daisy had started in Inkululeko, the township, but he spent a lot of his free time at the shelter, and Dr. Gunnerson-Smythe often called him in to consult on the more complex cases. The shelter simply didn't have the time or resources to cope with complicated veterinary cases, and if not for her father, a lot of animals with potentially treatable problems would have been put down.

Lia and her father had waved at each other in acknowledgment but hadn't really spoken all morning, each busy with their own tasks. Lia was interviewing potential pet families and her father was administering treatment to some of his patients, a task he would have had to squeeze in on Saturday, after his free clinic, if not for the holiday.

Lia lost track of her father and concentrated on her own task. It was a busy, tiring morning for her, and only after the rush had passed did she realize that she hadn't seen Brand since their arrival. She stretched, ignoring the Brand-related aches and twinges in so many unfamiliar places, and handed off the last of the adoption questionnaires to Sarah, the receptionist.

"I think we did well today," she said with a smile. "At least ten adoptions, if I'm not mistaken."

"Minky found a home," Sarah said, her eyes bright with excitement. Minky was one of their golden oldies, a plump ten-year-old miniature dachshund with soulful black eyes and a graying muzzle.

"That's wonderful, who wants her?"

"An elderly couple. They lost their Labrador to old age a year ago, came in six months ago to fill out an adoption form, and then decided they weren't ready. They came in again today, took one look at Minky, and fell completely in love. It was mutual, too—Minky looked like she wanted to crawl into the old lady's lap and stay there forever."

Lia was still smiling over the news when she went looking for Brand. The smile faded in an instant when she found him amiably chatting with her father. They were both standing outside Trevor's pen, looking like longtime buddies as they talked and laughed. Her father saw her first and smiled fondly.

"Ah, here she is," he said, and Lia swallowed down a surge of panic.

Here she is? What did he mean by that? Were they talking about her? *Why* were they talking about her? And how could Brand be looking at her with so much heat in his eyes with her father standing right there beside him? It was unnerving.

She smiled nervously and her father wrapped an arm around her shoulders and hugged her to his side, dropping a kiss on her head.

"Your mother tells me you've been helping Sam out," her father said, sounding pleased enough about that.

"Yes, until his cast comes off."

"She's always been my sweetest girl," he told Sam proudly, and the younger man's eyes dropped to her painfully embarrassed face.

Brand, damn him, smiled, and Lia caught the wicked glint in his eyes, even if her father didn't.

"Is that so?" he asked, his voice perfectly neutral.

"Daisy was a bit of an introvert, always focused on her studies. Daff was . . . is . . ." Her father smiled fondly and shook his head. "Well, I'm sure you've met Daff."

Brand's smile widened, and he laughed.

"Say no more," he joked.

"But Lia, never a harsh word to say about anyone, always happy to help out. She'll take good care of you."

"Oh, she has definitely been taking very good care of me," Brand said agreeably, nothing at all lascivious in his voice or in his words, but Lia still stared daggers at him.

"Your mother tells me Daff, Spencer, and Charlie are coming around for a braai later, Lia. Bring Sam."

"I will." Lia nodded obediently, even though the last thing she wanted was for her STF to hang out with her family. Her father shook Sam's hand firmly before taking his leave.

"How was your visit with Trevor today?" Lia asked.

"Great, he sat a little closer than he did yesterday. Showed interest in the treats I brought but wasn't ready to take them from me."

"That's good," Lia said, even while she was still troubled over what it could mean if Trevor bonded with him and he left.

"So a braai is a barbecue, right?" he asked, and she nodded.

"Brace yourself," she warned lightly. "You won't know what to do with all the meat."

"Sounds fantastic." He grinned. He cast a furtive look left and then right down the quiet corridor that housed the rehab pens before leaning toward her and whispering, "Time to get back to the cabin for a quickie before we hang out with your parents?"

Lia sucked in a breath as her legs wobbled and her stomach flipped at the words.

"I think that's doable," she said, her voice emerging on an embarrassingly husky note.

"I think *you're* doable." He leered comically and she laughed breathlessly before taking his left hand in both of hers and tugging him toward her. He went willingly, and when she stepped into his arms for a quick, stolen kiss, *he* was the one who hiked in his breath and groaned helplessly.

Lia dashed home for a shower and a quick change of clothing after her and Brand's afternoon quickie turned into an hours-long sexual odyssey. At the rate they were going, Lia was fairly certain their sexual chemistry would fizzle out in a matter of days. Surely something this hot and potent couldn't last.

As she stood beneath the shower, she explored her body in wonder. It was the same unremarkable set of arms and legs and breasts as before, and yet she felt like she had never really known what it was capable of. It was ridiculous how sensitive and responsive this body was to Brand's touch—she was almost dreading the prospect of the cast coming off, because he was already pretty lethal without the use of both hands.

Her phone buzzed while she was dressing, and she picked it up with a dreamy smile, expecting it to be from Brand. But the text wasn't from him—it was from Daff.

> Hey, Spencer tells me Daddy invited Brand (eye-roll emoji). Easier for us to drive him to the farm. Meet you there.

Lia beat back the swell of dissatisfaction at the message, telling herself she had no right to be disappointed that he wouldn't be with her. It was a short drive and it definitely made more sense for him to go with Daff, Spencer, and Charlie.

She was still in her room when she heard Spencer's truck drive up, and she ran her hands down the front of her skirt before heading downstairs to join everybody. She pinpointed Brand's exact location in seconds, giving him an impersonal smile before moving her eyes along. She avoided even casting her gaze in his general direction after that, instead going up to her mother, Charlie, and Daff and joining them in setting up the picnic table.

"Aunty Millie, are we expecting more guests?" Charlie asked their mother suddenly, and Lia and Daff both looked at the pretty teen in surprise. She widened her eyes at them before pointing at the table. "There are extra place settings. You guys aren't very observant."

Lia's eyes dropped to the long table, where two extra plates were set out.

"Are we expecting company, Mom?" Daff asked curiously.

"Not exactly," their mother said with a smile, and Daff's eyes narrowed at the cryptic response.

She was about to probe further when a couple of familiar dogs came scrambling through the open patio doors, rolling over each other in their eagerness to greet everybody present. For a moment Lia stared at them in blank confusion until Charlie's delighted squeal snapped her out of her perplexed daze.

"Peaches! Cooper!" the girl screamed, dropping to her knees and opening her arms until the two dogs threw themselves at her and laved her with their overeager tongues. Charlie's own dog, Toffee, huddled beneath the table, watching the commotion nervously.

"Oh my *gosh*," Lia said in wonder as the implication of the dogs' unexpected presence finally sank in. Her eyes flew to the door and her squeal was almost identical to Charlie's when Daisy and Mason stepped onto the porch. The next ten minutes flew by in a confusion of hugs, kisses, and muddled talking as everyone demanded to know why they hadn't been told about this visit. It was crazy and wonderful all at the same time.

At some point in the middle of the chaotic family reunion, Lia glanced up at Brand. He remained standing to one side, a beer in his hand as he watched the happy gathering with a grin on his face. Content to let the family get reacquainted before going to greet his longtime friend. He met Lia's eyes, and that inevitable heat sparked between them. His smile turned sensuous, and he acknowledged the spark by lifting his bottle to her in a slight salute before breaking the short, intense staring contest.

Lia shook herself and focused on Daisy and Mason, whom none of them had seen in four months.

"We wanted to surprise you guys," Daisy was saying, her voice breathless with excitement. "But we also didn't want to say anything because I wasn't sure I'd get the time off."

"How long are you staying?" Daff asked.

"The entire week. The second semester starts the week after next, so we'll drive back next Monday."

"And since Daff moved in with Spencer, we'll be staying at Daisy's house," Mason said and grinned at Brand. "In case you're wondering if I'm evicting your injured ass."

"How long have you been here?" Lia asked.

"We've literally *just* arrived. Mom and Daddy knew we were coming, of course," Daisy said.

"You poor kids must be exhausted," their mother said sympathetically. It was a long drive from Grahamstown to Riversend.

"A little. The clinic was open for a few hours this morning, so I was at work and then we did some last-minute packing and shopping before we left. It's been a long day," Daisy said, and Mason wrapped his arm around her shoulders and pulled her close to drop a kiss on top of her curly head.

Sam watched the happy little family tableau with a smile. There was a lot of love and affection in this group. Mason and Spencer looked like they'd been a part of this family for years, they were so welcome and at ease with everybody. Sam felt the slightest dart of envy. It was a rogue, anomalous emotion that he couldn't explain. He wasn't a happy-family kind of guy. This wasn't something he coveted or aspired to, but still . . . it had to be nice to be so accepted and loved. It had only ever been Sam and his mother, with the occasional stepfather thrown in the mix. He and his mom had been a great team—that was all he'd ever needed. He'd never desired anything more, and he didn't see the point in wanting more now. Not when he knew he wasn't suited for it at all.

Mason finally managed to extricate himself from the rest of the group and wandered over to Sam. He cast a critical look over Sam's body before shaking his head and grinning.

"You look like shit," he observed before stepping up to give Sam a quick hug, mindful of his injured arm.

"At least in my case it's temporary. You *always* look like shit," Sam countered. The banter with the guy, who was essentially his best friend, felt familiar, and they both grinned again.

"Fuck off," Mason said without heat, reaching into the cooler behind Sam and helping himself to a beer. "How you doing, bro?"

"Been better," Sam admitted. "But it's not as bad as it was."

"You settled in at the cabin?"

"Yeah, thanks for that. Are you sure you're okay with me staying there? I can stay at Daisy's place until after you leave again."

"Nah. It's cool. Daisy and I will only be using that place as a base. We'll probably spend most of our time at Spencer's or the in-laws'." Mason's eyes roamed over the assembled group, continuously circling back to Daisy. "Fuck, it's good to be back home. I didn't even know how much I missed everyone until we walked through that door."

"You have a great family, mate," Sam said and was shocked to hear that previous envy creep into his voice.

"They are pretty fucking fantastic. And I see they've welcomed you into the fold."

"Temporarily."

"This family doesn't do temporary."

"But I do," Sam reminded, and Mason grimaced at him.

"Yeah, good luck with that," he said, taking a sip from his beer. His eyes were back on Daisy and then fell to his brother, who was teasing their young sister, Charlie, about something. Mason's face lit up. "'Scuse me for a second. Spence might need backup."

Sam nodded and watched as Mason waded into whatever was going on between Spencer and their teenage half sister. The girl, with her almond-shaped emerald eyes, flawless brown skin, and thick black curls was exotically pretty but still bore a striking resemblance to her brothers. Mason tucked an arm around her waist and hoisted her up over his shoulder like a sack of potatoes. She laughed and squealed at the indignity of it all, trying to maintain her adolescent cool while giggling like a child.

"It's hard to believe she's been in their lives for less than a year, isn't it?" Lia said, and Sam glanced down at her, unsurprised that she'd finally, *inevitably*, made her way to his side.

"Hello there, Miss Priss," he greeted softly, his eyes taking in her cap-sleeved, knee-length, sky-blue dress with the high neck and slightly flared skirt. "You're looking very pretty and proper this evening, and you *know* what that does to my blood pressure."

She kept her eyes straight ahead, but he could see her breathing change while a hectic flush bled into her skin.

"Maybe we should retreat to the barn?" he suggested wickedly. "I have very fond memories of that barn. We could do a reenactment. What do you say?"

"Be good. This isn't appropriate behavior for this setting," she said firmly, and he groaned.

"I *love* it when you speak etiquette to me, sunshine. It's like you *want* me to take you to a dark spot around the corner, pin you to the wall, and have my nasty way with you." She didn't say anything, just turned her head and looked at him, and Sam bit back a groan at the expression in her eyes. So much mute longing, heat, and lust. Her pupils were dilated and her breathing was much too fast. She licked her lips, ran her eyes over his face, down his throat, then his chest until they dipped to his crotch. And stayed there. He felt her gaze like a touch and, embarrassingly, despite the crowd all around them, felt himself harden like a teenage boy.

Shit! His silly little game had backfired severely, because he suddenly found himself on the receiving end of an unspoken sensual assault.

"Later," she promised, her voice low and throaty and meant only for his ears.

Sam groaned and willed his erection away as she walked away from him without a backward glance.

~

Lia was happy to spend time with Daisy and Mason again. She had missed her baby sister fiercely, but part of her couldn't wait for the braai to end so that she could collect on the promise she'd been seeing in Brand's eyes all evening. How could she still want him so desperately after last night and this afternoon? It was like a dull ache that faded but never truly went away. And every time she looked at him and met those smoldering eyes, the ache intensified sharply.

Her dad was the self-proclaimed braaimaster for the evening, and even though Spencer and Mason constantly tried to take over the grill, he kept them at bay with sharp, humorous reprimands.

"My house, my braai. You youngsters think you know everything. Stand aside and watch a true master at work." He ignored the good-natured heckles from the younger men, talking his way through his barbecuing process as if he were tutoring children.

Meanwhile, the women were sitting around the patio table, catching up and fussing over Charlie, who pretended to struggle out of affectionate hugs even while everyone could see she loved the attention. It was a lovely evening and every effort was made to include Brand, even though he held himself slightly apart.

Lia knew that he couldn't feel left out—her family was much too welcoming for that. She wondered if the entire scene was a little too cozy and domesticated for a man like Sam Brand. He had an in-built reserve that she had noticed at the wedding. He seemed quite happy to be an impartial, if pleasant, observer. He joked, participated in conversations, and was very at home with the men, but there was always an aloofness to him.

When dinner was finally served, everyone—barring Charlie, of course—had a nice alcoholic buzz going. Conversation around the table was loud and cheerful, and when her mother brought out a chocolate cheesecake for dessert, the atmosphere mellowed, everybody just content to be there and hang out.

"I have something to say," Spencer suddenly proclaimed, his voice a little too loud and a little too nervous. Everybody immediately paid attention. Spencer wasn't the type to willingly address a crowd. Not even family, so this was unusual to say the least. Daff had a perplexed frown on her face as she watched him get up and speak to the table. "This wasn't planned, but it feels right because . . . because we're all here."

He turned to look down at Daff, whose eyes widened.

"Spencer, what are you doing?" she asked warily.

He grinned.

"Maybe, as gestures go, it's not so grand . . . but you know me, darling, I'm not great at grand," he said, and Daff gasped at his words. Her hands flew to her mouth when he dropped to one knee in front of her, and this time everybody else gasped. "Daffodil McGregor, I've been carrying this around with me for months. Everywhere I go, I've had it close to my heart. I couldn't decide what type of gesture would most reflect my love for you, but then I realized that there just isn't one big enough. You're the beat of my heart and the sun in my sky. You're my everything, and I love you." His voice was starting to wobble, and his cheeks and ears were going pink, but he forged ahead, lifting a ring that Lia was too far away to see. "Would you do me the honor of being my wife?"

Daff just looked at him, eyes wide, face frozen, hands still covering her mouth. She didn't seem to be breathing. She didn't answer, and Spencer started to look nervous.

"Uh, Daff? Marry me? Will you?" She leaned forward to palm his face in her hands.

"You sound like Yoda," she said with a little giggle before planting a huge kiss on his lips. "And yes, Spencer Carlisle, my big, wonderful man . . . marry you, I will."

Everybody cheered and got up to engulf the couple in kisses and hugs. Lia's eyes welled up; she felt overwhelming happiness for her oldest sister. They were a wonderful couple and belonged together . . . but . . . she also felt a stab of loneliness when she realized that this kind of relationship with someone was farther and farther out of reach for her.

She moved forward to kiss her sister and hug Spencer and then fawned over the beautiful rose-gold ring, with its pear-shaped peach sapphire. It was delicate and feminine and understated and simply perfect for Daff. The evening, which had been winding down, found new life, and talk turned to weddings and honeymoons. Lia kept smiling, kept enthusing, was happy to say yes to Daff's request that she be her maid of honor. And all the while tried to keep the vicious talons of envy at bay. It was unbecoming and it was ugly.

Her face was starting to ache with the effort it took to keep smiling, and her head was starting to pound. She kept her gaze away from Brand's, not sure she even wanted to lose herself in his arms tonight. All she wanted to do was curl up and cry and hate herself for being so petty and pathetic and stupid.

Sam didn't know how none of Lia's family could see how very much she was hurting. He knew how much she wanted what Daff and Daisy had. And he couldn't understand how Lia, with her strawberry flowers, her gentle disposition, and her sweet, ladylike dresses, had not been snatched up by some grateful guy yet. Why was she having so much difficulty finding this Mr. Right of hers?

Sam knew the only reason she'd agreed to this thing with him was because she felt the right man was no longer on the horizon for her. She had compromised some unspoken rule of hers and had instead chosen to have some fun with someone she recognized was completely wrong for her. Sam knew he was being a selfish bastard in reaping the rewards of her broken dreams, but he was only human—and a weak one when it came to resisting her appeal. And he would continue to enjoy her until she either ended it or he left, whichever came first.

He watched her laugh, joke, and make suggestions, while the sadness in her eyes never dissipated. It was surprisingly distressing for him to see her like this. He didn't want her sad. He wanted her stern or disapproving, happy or angry, turned on and consumed by desire . . . anything but this absolute heartbreak in her beautiful eyes. He wanted to take her to bed and distract her from the world and its disappointments.

But he couldn't. Not right now. Right now he had to watch her put on a brave face and get sucked into planning her sister's wedding.

The evening finally ended because Daisy and Mason were both absolutely exhausted. Everybody, with the exception of Dr. McGregor, who had his free clinic in the township, planned on meeting for breakfast at the farm in the morning, and Lia's mother insisted that Brand join them. Daff and Spencer promised to bring him. Everybody departed in a flurry of goodbyes until it was just Lia left with her parents. Luckily cleaning up had been a group effort, so there wasn't much to do but bid her happy parents good night.

When she was finally in the privacy of her own room, Lia sank onto her bed and wrapped her arms around her shuddering body.

"Get a grip, you idiot," she scolded herself. "Your sister's getting married—it's a wonderful thing."

What was wrong with her? Was she really this self-absorbed? She swiped at a couple of errant tears and loathed herself for being this way. There were other things in life. Marriage wasn't the key to happiness, she knew that. She'd very nearly made the stupidest mistake of her life because of her eagerness to get married and start a family. If she'd followed through with that wedding, she'd be completely miserable now.

She would allow herself this one moment of self-pity, and then she would move on. She was better than this, stronger and less pitiful than this.

Her phone beeped, and she reached for it. A message from Brand.

I could send you pics of my dick so that you'd know exactly what I'm in the mood for, but even I'm not that crass. Shocking, I know.

She snorted and swiped at a tear with the back of her hand, then thumbed a response.

€===3?? She smiled through the sheen of tears.

LIA!! WTF? That is in no way an accurate rendering of my cock. It should be at least €=====3!!

She giggled, surprising herself with the lighthearted sound. He was incorrigible and unapologetically crude at times. But she was getting used to it and even finding it funny and refreshing. He was base and obscene and somewhat shocking, but she liked his honesty.

My apologies. Will have to reacquaint myself with the appendage in question, so as to refresh my memory. She blushed while she typed the words, hesitated for a moment, and then sent the text.

His response was almost instant.

Get over here right now! You should be here, riding my cock, not moping alone in your childhood bedroom.

How did he know she was moping? She didn't want to ask, didn't want to talk about anything meaningful. She and Trevor the boxer were in the same boat right now—both in serious danger of becoming way too attached to someone who would be leaving soon.

She reminded herself of Rule One and Rule Eight, possibly the most important rules on her list. No falling in love, and accepting that the end of their fling wasn't a matter of if, but of when. Keeping things casual and physical only would be the best way to ensure that there would be no danger of falling in love.

I'm on my way, she promised. A quick shower and change of clothes later and she was sneaking out of the house like a teenager. Her parents weren't nosy about her private life, but they would still be concerned if they saw her leaving at this time of night. And Lia would rather not be confronted with difficult questions she had no way of answering right now.

Sam was waiting for her by the front door like some overeager schoolboy. When he heard the car drive up, he flung the door open and watched her exit the vehicle. She had changed her clothing and was now wearing a flowery slip dress—risqué for her, as it was an inch above her knees—a pair of strappy sandals, and a green cardigan. He could tell that she wasn't wearing a bra, and his mouth went dry as he wondered if she was naked on the bottom, too.

She didn't say a word, simply launched herself at him, plastering her lips to his desperately, muffling his greeting as her tongue plunged into his mouth. His arm went around her and pinned her close, his hand landing in the small of her back and fisting the fabric of her dress. He was keen to discover if she was wearing panties, but she slipped out of his hold before he knew what her intentions were and pushed him back into the cabin. She shut the door and then turned to look at him again, her expression wild and unfocused. Her eyes drank in his face, and he opened his mouth to speak again, not sure how to react to this marginal aggression. He liked it and wanted to see where she was going with it, but he wasn't quite sure if she was okay.

She was tugging at his tank, dragging it up over his chest and kissing his skin as it was revealed. They awkwardly managed to remove it completely before she was on her knees and yanking at his drawstring gym pants. She fumbled impatiently with the ties and finally got them undone. She shoved his pants down past his thighs and reached beneath the waistband of his boxers to free his rampant cock. She was moving entirely too fast, and he was about to pull her back up to take control and slow things down, when she took him into her mouth.

He groaned and fell back against the wall, thumping his head in the process. He didn't even register the pain as she continued to lick and suck her way up and down his shaft.

"Fuuuuck. Don't stop," he implored, and she looked up at him with those gorgeous eyes. There was too much vulnerability in them—this didn't feel right. It killed Sam, but he reached down and encircled her arm with his hand and pulled her up. She released him reluctantly, and despite the absolute pain he felt at the interrupted blow job, he gave her a gentle smile.

"Please," she whispered. "Please let me."

"Ssh," he responded before claiming her lips again. But this time the kiss was softer, deeper, filled with the tenderness and reverence she deserved. When it ended she shook her head.

"No. Not like that. I want hard. I want rough. No gentleness. Not tonight." Her words made him frown. Her texts had put him in a playful, sexy mood . . . he hadn't been expecting another frantic coupling. They'd had plenty of those over the last twenty-four hours. He wanted fun and flirty tonight. But clearly Lia needed something else.

She kissed him again, and her hand dropped to his straining length. Sam hissed at her touch, but she quickly released him and turned to stand with her back against the wall.

"Here. Like you said earlier. Up against the wall." Sam made a feral sound at the back of his throat and moved to cage her body with his, placing his good arm against the wall while he kept his cast out of the way for fear of hurting her with it.

"There's a condom in my pocket. Put it on me, then wrap your arms around my neck and your legs around my waist," he urged hoarsely, and she obeyed without hesitation. Her back was supported against the wall while she hung on to him with her arms and legs.

He grunted in satisfaction and reached between them—gratified to discover she wasn't wearing panties after all—to take his shaft in hand and position himself at her entrance. He braced his arm against the wall above her head for support and entered her with one long, delicious stroke.

They both cried out when he was fully sheathed, and he stood like that for a moment until she wriggled against him.

"Do it," she urged. "Hard and fast, please."

"Fuck me, it drives me wild when you say *please*," he growled against her mouth and gave her exactly what she asked for.

It was hot and hard and fast and dirty. And it was over sooner than Sam would have liked. They ended on a rare mutual, mind-blowing orgasm that left them sagging against each other for a second before they ran out of strength and slowly melted to the floor.

Afterward they sat side by side, breathing heavily, with their backs against the wall.

"You okay, sunshine?" he asked after he'd finally managed to regulate his breathing.

"Thank you," she said softly. "I really needed that."

Which didn't exactly answer his question.

"Do you want to talk?" he asked softly. "About earlier? About the engagement."

She turned her head and looked at him for a long, unfathomable moment, a small frown furrowing her brow while her teeth worried her lower lip.

"I have to get home," she said.

"Lia . . ."

"I'll see you at breakfast." She leaned over and gave him a quick, wholly unsatisfying peck on the lips before pushing herself up from the floor.

"Lia. Wait . . ." She didn't; she picked up her little cardigan and bag where she had dropped them at the front door and was gone before he even managed to get up off the floor.

He wasn't sure he liked these fucking rules of hers. It was amazing how much he'd learned about her over the last few days and how he knew that this behavior, this reluctance to share her thoughts, was completely aberrant for her.

He had enjoyed the Lia who had already envisioned her unborn nieces and made up names for them. Who had happily shared her misconceptions about his job and had sweetly sympathized with him about his supposed breakup. He wanted that Lia back. Sure, the sex they had now was scorching hot, but it left him feeling oddly hollow when she wouldn't exchange a single meaningful word with him afterward. He was confusing himself with these unprecedented longings. Sam didn't like discussing feelings with women at any time, and especially not after sex. He didn't want to know their thoughts and emotions, and he for damned sure didn't want to talk about his.

So why the fuck was he so concerned about how Lia McGregor was feeling right now? It was bizarre, and he didn't like it.

CHAPTER NINE

Family breakfast at the McGregor homestead was as noisy and vibrant as dinner had been. Everybody was loud and boisterous and talking over one another in an attempt to be heard. Sam enjoyed it because it meant that he got overlooked in the confusion. Which left him to watch Lia. She was quieter than the rest, speaking only when she had an opinion to offer.

Once again she barely acknowledged his existence, and it made him want to say or do something outrageous to catch her attention. He didn't, though; instead he minded his manners like a champ and resisted the impulse to get a rise out of her. Still, it grated that she pretended he wasn't even there, but he knew it was probably another one of her ridiculous rules.

Because he was so intent on watching her, he noticed the flare of panic and discomfort in her eyes before Daisy's words registered. It made him sit up and pay attention to the conversation.

"Who told you that?" Lia was asking Daisy, and the younger woman shrugged amiably.

"Daff. She said you wanted to move into my house. You'll want to get rid of Daff's crap first, though—apparently she doesn't know that moving out means you have to take all your stuff to your new place."

"Come on, Daisy, Spencer asked me to move in on Monday, I packed a bag that same night and he hasn't been rid of me since. I didn't want to give him a chance to change his mind again," Daff protested, and Daisy's eyebrows flew up. "I'll get around to the rest of it soon."

"You gave notice last month," Daisy said. "I thought you moved out weeks ago."

"Spencer wouldn't let me move in," Daff said, and all eyes shifted to Spencer, who shrugged uncomfortably.

"I thought we'd be setting a bad example for Charlie," he muttered, and Charlie laughed.

"Please, like I don't know what sex is."

"Let's pretend you don't know what it is and leave it at that," Mason said with a glower.

"Hmm. Until you're at least thirty-eight," Spencer agreed, and Charlie rolled her eyes at them.

"You're moving out, Lia?" Millicent McGregor asked, bringing the conversation back to the topic that had interested Brand in the first place.

"I thought it was a good idea," Lia said uncomfortably.

"Of course, I understand your desire to live your life without feeling like your parents are constantly monitoring your every move. Especially now that you have a gentleman friend that you're calling on, but we're going to miss you," her mother said, and Sam suddenly understood where Lia got her sometimes quaint turns of phrase. Millicent had a delightfully old-fashioned way of wording things. The older woman's actual meaning didn't register until he saw Lia's fiery blush.

"Gentleman friend?" Daisy asked with wide eyes, her voice escalating on each syllable. "Lia! Have you been keeping secrets from me? Is it Gregory? Have things been going well with him?"

"You know about that douche?" Daff asked incredulously.

"Unlike *some* people at this table—*Daff*—Daisy actually listens when I speak," Lia said self-consciously, still battling a fiery blush.

"Why is he a douche?" Daisy asked. "What did I miss?"

"Nothing," Lia said softly.

"Let's just say we call him Gropey Gregory around these parts now," Daff said with a frown. Lia looked so perfectly miserable that Sam had to curb the impulse to tell Daff to shut the fuck up about that prick Gregory. This was clearly not a topic Lia felt comfortable discussing right now.

"What did he do?" Mason asked dangerously, and Spencer sat up and paid attention, too, both men clearly protective of all the McGregor women.

"He won't be bothering her again," Sam felt compelled to say. It wasn't their place to feel protective over Lia, especially not since the problem had pretty much been resolved already.

The table went silent as all eyes flew to him. Wow, uncomfortable. Sam shifted slightly and cleared his throat. Not sure what to say beneath the weight of expectation in all those gazes. The only one not looking at him—*still*—was Lia. And that was driving him crazy.

"Explain," Mason demanded curtly, and Sam huffed an impatient breath.

"I had a firm word with him." Mason grinned at the explanation—Sam's "firm word" was good enough for him.

"But I don't understand," Mrs. McGregor said blankly. "If you and this Gregory aren't getting serious, then where did you go last night?"

Lia could feel her face flame, and she wasn't sure how to respond to that. She didn't want to lie to her family, especially not while they were all staring at her in avid interest and concern.

"I . . . uh . . . I . . ."

"I'm afraid I'm to blame for that, ma'am," Brand said suddenly, and Lia's eyes flew to his apologetic face in horror. "I was having some difficulty last night and couldn't find my pain medication. I messaged Lia and asked if she knew where I'd put them. Turns out, she had them in her handbag. She was kind enough to bring them to me. I know it was late and I wouldn't have asked her to come if I weren't in pretty extreme discomfort."

Her mother looked mollified by his explanation, but everybody else, even Charlie, was glancing between Lia and Sam with varying degrees of skepticism and outright disbelief on their faces.

"Why would you have his medication in the first place?" Daisy asked in confusion, and Lia patted nervously at her hair before replying.

"Uh. I've been helping him out with some of his household chores and stuff. Just until his arm is out of the cast."

"I see," Daisy said, even though she still looked completely confused. "I just thought Daff was going to lend a hand, because she's closer."

"Daff got busy helping Spencer with the business, and since I'm often at loose ends, I thought I'd lend a hand."

"What do you mean, 'often at loose ends'?" Sam surprised her by asking disbelievingly. "You're the busiest person I know. You're helping every single charity organization in town. I'm shocked you ever have a free moment to yourself."

"Right?" Daff agreed. "I told her they take advantage of her good nature. They just keep piling on the tasks and Lia seems completely incapable of saying no."

"I noticed that about her," Brand said with a nod, and Lia frowned. Daff and Brand always seemed to find common ground over her shortcomings, which was getting a bit tedious.

"I told her she should charge them for her services," Daff said, and Brand snorted.

"I'm quite capable of saying no," Lia said levelly. "I just reserve it for people who annoy me, and right now that's a pretty short list. *When* did you say you needed me to pick Charlie up from soccer practice again,

Daff? I'm afraid something urgent has just come up on that day and I won't be able to make it."

"You don't even remember what day it is," Daff spluttered.

"I'm busy on *all* the days," she said breezily. When Sam laughed, she pinned him with a glare. "Oh, and maybe you can fix your own breakfast tomorrow, Brand. I'm afraid I'll be much too busy updating my Facebook settings at that time." She shifted her gaze back to Daff before continuing, "I don't only spend my time helping out charity organizations. Remember that next time you ask me to do you a 'quick favor.'"

She put her newfound glower to good use and deliberately dismissed them by turning to Daisy, who was grinning widely.

"So would you be okay with me renting your house?"

"Of course I'm fine with it," Daisy said warmly. "Happy it's staying in the family. So much better than renting to strangers."

"Thanks, Deedee," she said.

Sam watched as Lia pointedly continued to ignore both Daff and him. Her setdown of them had been both gentle and effective, and Sam would have high-fived her for the eloquent little barb if he hadn't been one of the recipients of said slight. Still, he couldn't help silently cheering her spirited response.

He'd let her stew for now. Later, he'd take great pleasure in reminding her of the perks involved in preparing his breakfast.

"When's the cast coming off, Brand?" Mason asked, and Sam shrugged.

"I'm going to Knysna next week to have this one removed and the arm X-rayed. They'll probably recast it, but they'll be able to tell me how much longer I'll be stuck wearing this thing."

"Yeah, you must be missing the water, hey?" Mason said sympathetically, before elaborating for the rest of the room. "I swear to God, Brand's part fish. Swimming, scuba diving, surfing, parasailing, paddle-boarding, kayaking—anything on or in water, Brand has done it. Guy goes stir-crazy if he can't swim a million laps a day."

"How did you manage in Afghanistan?" Daisy asked curiously, and Sam felt his skin grow tight at the memory.

"Badly. I hated every second of it. I'm not cut out for all that sand. I would have preferred to be deployed to Bali, really. Or Bimini. Maybe the Seychelles."

His response got a laugh from everybody except Lia, who still looked a bit miffed at him. He sent her a cheeky little wink, and her eyes widened in horror. She immediately glanced around guiltily to see if anyone else had noticed. Nobody had, of course, Sam was a little more careful than that.

Talk turned to more general topics after that, and breakfast ended soon after.

"Brand, you want to join Spencer and me later?" Mason asked. "We're heading out to the local watering hole for a catch-up and some drinks."

Sam cast a quick glance at Lia, gauging her reaction. She kept her face carefully averted and was talking to Charlie about something, but he knew she was listening to every word.

"I think I'll leave you two to do a bit of brotherly bonding," he said. "I have plans to take my injured, pain-riddled ass to bed for a couple of hours." *Preferably not alone.*

"If you decide to join us, text me. We'll be at Ralphie's after seven tonight."

"Thanks," Sam said with an appreciative grin.

Still mad at me, sunshine? The text from Brand came while Lia, her sisters, her mother, and Charlie were discussing ideas for Daff and Spencer's wedding. The couple hadn't settled on a date yet, they just knew they wanted a spring wedding. Possibly in October. Daff wanted something low-key, without fuss or frills, which was pretty much in keeping with her personality. Considering that just six months ago she'd been adamant about never getting married, it was a pretty big step for her to even consider a wedding ceremony, so everybody was playing it cool, even though Lia knew her mother was dying for more fanfare.

Lia, happy for a distraction from all this wedding talk, stared down at her phone for a moment before quickly typing a reply.

Maybe. Not sure. She ignored the animated conversation and feminine laughter swirling around her as she waited for the response.

Gutted. Does this mean I don't get to play with your (. Y .) and (|) tonight? Lia choked back a laugh at the text and tried very hard not to blush.

Maybe. Not sure, she replied.

God, you're brutal. Throw me a bone, sunshine. Just one little bone for my not so little boner. She clamped her lips between her teeth to prevent the smile but she knew she was fighting a losing battle. He was completely incorrigible.

I'll see you at seven.

Can't wait.

"Lia, you're the color of a ripe tomato. What's going on?" Daisy asked curiously, and Lia practically jumped out of her skin. Unbelievably, she had completely forgotten the other women were there. She quickly lowered her phone, screen down, to her lap and smiled at Daisy while waving her free hand in front of her flushed face.

"It's just a little hot in here, that's all," she said, and they all gaped at her.

"If you're menopausal, maybe," Daff said and glanced at her mother. "No offense, Mom."

Their mother snorted.

"If you think I'm still menopausal, you're deluded, my girl. I'm fifty-eight. I went through menopause four years ago."

"I wasn't sure if it was still a sensitive subject or not," Daff said, and the older woman laughed.

"It was never a sensitive subject. Now, focus on the subject at hand, please. I'm definitely interested in knowing why your sister looks like someone who got caught with her hand in the cookie jar."

"I'm just hot, that's all," Lia protested, while her cheeks brightened even more.

"Why are you hiding your phone?" Charlie asked gleefully. Lia sent her a mock wounded look, which the girl completely ignored.

"Why *are* you hiding your phone?" Daff repeated.

"I'm not. I'm thirsty," she prevaricated desperately, pushing herself up from the table and getting a bottle of juice from the refrigerator. "Anybody else want a drink?"

"Oh my God, I don't think I've ever seen you full-on *lie* before," Daff gasped, her eyes alive with unholy pleasure. "You're terrible at it. Never do it again."

"Do you have a man friend you're not telling us about?" Daisy asked astutely.

"I'd rather not discuss this right now," Lia said, pouring her orange juice into a glass and taking a thirsty gulp. The pulp made her cough, and she'd never been so grateful for that uncomfortable tickle in the back of her throat. Sometimes having her family so involved in her life could be trying, but she knew they only wanted her happiness after her failed engagement. She also knew none of them would approve of her involvement with Brand, because they knew as well as she did that it would never be anything more than it currently was. And they would worry she was setting herself up for more pain.

They would all be filled with well-meaning advice and concern, but they wouldn't be telling her anything she didn't already know. Lia would rather they never knew about what was going on between her and Brand.

"Lia—" Daff began, but Lia cut her off with a look. For once, Daff paid attention to the clear warning in Lia's eyes, and her mouth snapped shut.

"I'm not prepared to discuss this. Can we please focus on the wedding?" Daisy and Daff exchanged troubled looks, while Charlie just stared at Lia like she'd never seen her before. Her mother was staring, too, but her eyes were thoughtful, which made Lia feel incredibly uncomfortable.

Daisy, bless her tactful soul, quickly adjusted the subject back to engagement parties and weddings, and Lia was left alone. But she knew this wouldn't be the end of the matter. Her sisters were too persistent and stubborn for that.

When she went around to the cabin just before seven that evening, it was to find the door unlocked and Brand nowhere in sight. She stood uncertainly in the living room for a moment before a god-awful racket alerted her to the fact that he was upstairs in the loft. She followed the unidentifiable noise until she found him lying flat on his back on a workout mat, with his hands folded over his flat, taut stomach and his eyes closed. He was wearing a pair of gym shorts and nothing else. His entire body gleamed with sweat, and Lia bit back a moan at the sight of all that honed, masculine strength. His injuries may have weakened him, but he was still a beautiful specimen of masculinity.

She finally identified the source of the racket as *singing*. Brand's singing, to be precise. He was wearing earbuds, which were attached to a tiny iPod that he had strapped around his left bicep, and he was singing along to . . . it *kind* of sounded like Bon Jovi's "Livin' on a Prayer." Sam Brand had many talents, but singing was definitely not one of them. The man had a singing voice that would make dogs howl and small animals flee in terror. It was actually kind of cute how singularly terrible his voice was, especially since he was singing along with such gusto.

Some sixth sense must have alerted him to her presence, because his eyes shot open abruptly and he stopped his caterwauling immediately upon spotting her. His face lit up with a huge welcoming grin and he leapt—well, okay, semileapt, and winced while he was doing it—to his feet.

"Sunshine," he greeted warmly, engulfing her in his arms and planting a smacking kiss on her lips. She laughingly pushed him off.

"You're sweaty and you *smell*," she complained.

"You don't like my manly musk?" He sounded injured, but the twinkle in his eyes belied his tone of voice.

"Go take a shower."

"Only if you join me," he husked, grabbing a handful of her butt and lifting her to his straining crotch. She laughed helplessly.

"Brand, there'll be no hanky-panky in the shower while you're wearing that cast. You'll get it wet for sure."

"I don't care, as long as I get you wet in the process."

"You're absolutely irredeemable," she said with a wry shake of her head. "Go get cleaned up. Have you eaten yet?"

"Not since breakfast."

"You shouldn't skip meals," she fussed. "And why are you so sweaty anyway? What have you been doing?"

"Working out. I need to rebuild my strength in order to keep up with you."

"Do you think it's wise to go back to your exercise regimen so soon?"

"It's that or go fucking crazy. I needed to blow off some steam. I didn't do anything too strenuous, just some stretches and core exercises.

And it nearly kicked my arse, so I'm happy I got to it. Just shows how out of shape I've gotten."

"I just don't think it's wise."

"I have to get to it eventually. I'm not used to sitting around on my butt doing nothing all day."

"Maybe you should clear it with your doctor first," Lia suggested.

"It's cute that you're worried about me, sunshine. I didn't think you cared." They both went awkwardly silent after that cavalier statement, and Lia cleared her throat while trying to think of the best response.

"Of course I care, I would hate to see you reinjure yourself and add to my workload," she teased, and he winced theatrically.

"Ouch," he cried, clutching a hand to his chest. "You cut me, sunshine. You cut me deeper than any knife-wielding dickbag ever could."

Lia giggled, the sound ending on an embarrassing snort.

"You're such a drama queen. Go shower while I sort out your dinner."

"You're sure you don't want to join me?"

"Quite." He grinned at the concise answer before turning from her and deliberately pushing his gym shorts down past his hips and then over his tight butt. Lia couldn't take her eyes off that firm behind as he stepped out of the shorts and cast a glance over his shoulder.

"Pity, look at what you're missing out on." He turned so that his body was in profile to hers, showing off the thick, impressive erection that curved up toward his belly button. He reached down and gave it a couple of long, languorous strokes before meeting her eyes and giving her a wicked smile.

"I'll save it for you," he promised, and Lia, her eyes glued to the movement of his hand, gulped and nodded.

"You do that," she squeaked, sounding a bit like Minnie Mouse. He chuckled knowingly before turning away and strolling unhurriedly into the bathroom. Only after he'd shut the door behind him and Lia exhaled on a shaky gasp did she realize that she'd been holding her breath.

Wow, just *wow*. How was he so good at turning her on with so little effort? It was almost embarrassing. She shook herself, ignoring her beaded nipples and shaking legs, and made her way downstairs to make his dinner.

Brand insisted she join him in eating the delicious spaghetti bolognese she'd whipped up. Despite having prepared his meals before, this was the first time Lia actually found herself eating one of those meals with him, and it felt way too cozy and domesticated for comfort. Especially when he started chatting about Daff and Spencer's engagement and Mason and Daisy's unexpected visit. The small talk went against her list of rules, and she was reticent in her responses. She could tell that her unresponsiveness was beginning to frustrate Sam, but she didn't really know how to fix the situation.

Not much of a drinker, she took a tiny sip of red wine to fortify herself and another undignified slurp of pasta. *Lady and the Tramp* had it so wrong—this was the least romantic meal on the face of the planet. Then again, she wasn't exactly striving for romance here, so it was best to get those kinds of thoughts out of her head right now.

"Tell me about the guidelines," Brand unexpectedly requested, and she blinked, a little surprised.

"What do you mean?" she hedged, and his icy eyes snapped impatiently.

"You know what I mean, Lia." He so rarely used her name that it took her aback to hear it emerge from his mouth. "These so-called rules for a successful fling that you seem to be adhering to so religiously."

"You should thank me for sticking to the rules. Things can get messy very quickly without rules, Brand."

"You don't fucking have to tell me that, sunshine. I've been following rules most of my life. I'd just like to know what they are so that I know when I'm not overstepping. Attempting to have a decent conversation is *clearly* making you uncomfortable, which means that I'm probably breaching one of your sacred rules, so how about letting me know what the fuck they are?"

"They're pretty basic," she said. "The usual stuff. Like—um—no giving or receiving gifts. I mean, that's an obvious one, isn't it?"

"Is it?" He didn't sound convinced, but she ignored him and continued hesitantly.

"And not leaving stuff behind. Like clothing and things. It would feel too intimate. And no sleeping over. That's a big no-no. I did have no introductions to the family down as well, but that horse has pretty much bolted from the barn."

"Why wouldn't you want me to meet your family?" He seemed offended. "I'm a likable guy."

"Of course you are. But introducing your fling to your parents is a stupid thing to do—they'd have expectations. But I wasn't the one who introduced you. You met them in your capacity as Mason and Daisy's friend, so that's a bullet dodged, I suppose. And naturally, you wouldn't introduce me to your family and friends."

"Naturally." Again, he sounded offended. Or maybe defensive. She wasn't sure which. His reaction just seemed . . . *off.* And she couldn't pinpoint why. She'd expected his agreement, even approval, on these stipulations. But she couldn't get an accurate read on his mood at all.

"Also, it's good to remind yourself, when you go into something like this, that there's an expiration date. It's going to end. So better to maintain an emotional and intellectual distance. I like you, but I don't want to find myself liking you *more* than I already do."

"And that's why you won't allow yourself to have a conversation with me? In case, God forbid, you find yourself liking me more?"

Or loving you. She kept the words unspoken and stared at him mutely, allowing him to draw his own conclusions.

"It would complicate things if we became friends."

"Well, I thought we were friends and I fucking *like* you, Lia. Sue me. I wouldn't be attracted to you if I didn't like you!"

"You barely knew me the first time we did it, Brand," she reminded him, and his face darkened.

"That doesn't count," he said, and she tilted her head as she tried to figure him out.

"Why not?"

"It just doesn't. I like you now. I consider you a friend. Sorry for fucking up your rules!"

~

Sam didn't know why he was so pissed off. He just was. She wouldn't talk to him because she didn't want to be his friend? What in the actual fuck? He was outrageously offended by that, and he had no clue why. So what if he'd never been friends with any of his past lovers? They'd all just served an obvious purpose. He fucked them a few times and then he moved on. No friendship required. Just an understanding that it was an extremely finite, mutually pleasurable arrangement. Still, sometimes things tended to get messy, and on the surface Lia's rules made sense. In fact, he would have been thrilled if some of his former partners had adopted the same mind-set.

But inexplicably, all Sam wanted to do was find a hard copy of her fucking rules and tear them the hell up, right in front of her. Then burn the pieces and piss on them to put out the fire.

"Any other rules I need to be cognizant of?" he asked tightly, and she sucked her lower lip into her mouth before nodding.

"No sleeping over, as you know. And no postcoital cuddling."

Postcoital? How fucking clinical that sounded. Well, that certainly explained why she dashed out of his arms every time they finished.

Sam wasn't a cuddler, he didn't give a fuck about cuddling . . . but what if he wanted to hold her close for easy access in case he got horny again? She obviously hadn't considered that, which was incredibly selfish of her. And what if he fell asleep for a brief moment while he was holding her? What if *she* did? Sex was a natural soporific; these considerations were well within the realm of possibility.

"You can't like me," she insisted. "Not really. You don't even know me."

"Sure I do, you're my Miss Priss." Sam didn't know where the possessive pronoun came from, but it made him wince because she wasn't *his* anything. He'd never considered any woman his.

Ever.

And he wasn't about to start now.

He was starting to gain a new appreciation for these rules of hers. If it meant keeping things in perspective, he was all for it. Using a possessive pronoun in relation to a woman was dangerous. He needed to rein that shit in. *Fast.*

But seriously, the embargo on talking would have to go.

"I'm all for these rules of yours, they make sense, but you can't expect us not to talk. That's ridiculous."

"Why?"

"Because I don't see the point of banning casual conversation. I'm an awesome guy, I'll give you that," he said, knowing his lack of modesty would get a smile out of her. She fought against it, but her lips quirked at the arrogant proclamation. "And many women in your position have displayed appalling lack of judgment and poor taste by falling in love with me. But you're more intelligent than most of them, and the mere act of talking is not going to make you fall in love with me. Quite the opposite, probably. And trust me, I've spoken to many, many women and I haven't fallen in love with a single one of them. And I'm not about to start now."

"Don't worry, Brand, there's no danger of me falling in love with you, either, that's not what concerns me . . . it's the intimacy. It would feel too much like a relationship. And it can become confusing. I'd like things to remain clear-cut and uncomplicated between us."

"Want to keep me firmly in the fuck buddy category, do you? I can respect that. But even though I'm only a booty call, so to speak, you still have to spend some time with me outside of bed. And I'll be damned if I'll sit in silence when we're in the car, or sharing a meal, or with your family."

She was quiet as she mulled over his words, a cute little furrow coming and going between her brows.

"What about keeping things friendly but casual?" Sam suggested. "No personal conversations?"

"What constitutes a personal conversation?" he asked. She stared down at her half-eaten meal and prodded the remaining pasta with her fork. Absently playing with her food while she considered his question.

"Questions about previous relationships, maybe?"

"Is that a question or a statement?"

"Statement?" The questioning lilt at the end of the word made him grin.

"Okay, what else?"

"I don't know. If it feels inappropriate, I'll let you know that it's out of bounds."

"Seems fair." He watched her push her food around her plate for a while longer. "You going to finish that?"

"I think I'm done," she said, meeting his eyes without hesitation.

"Yeah?" he breathed, his eyes dropping to her mouth, and he dragged his chair closer to hers. "Well, *I'm* just getting started."

It was the last thing either of them said for a very long while.

Sam awoke when he felt Lia carefully extricating herself from his arms and climbing out of bed. He frowned and opened his eyes to watch her fumble around in the dimly lit room for her clothes. Once again she made her way to the bathroom to dress, and he pushed himself up to glare at the frosted glass pocket door that led to the en suite.

Despite three intense—and extremely satisfying—sessions since dinner, he didn't want her to leave. He had an insatiable appetite for Lia, and he would rather she stayed close while he worked it out of his system. He knew her hunger for him was equal to his own, and he didn't understand why she limited their portions in this way. Didn't she recognize that in doing so, she would only lengthen the duration of their fling?

She exited the bathroom, fully dressed, and stopped abruptly when she saw that he was awake.

"I didn't mean to disturb you."

"Stay."

"No. I can't. It's close to midnight. I don't want my family to know about this. And if I'm here till all hours of the night, they'll figure it out."

"It's none of their business. You can fuck whomever the hell you want."

"They'll be concerned."

"Would they think I'm some rapey monster and you're my innocent victim?"

"No, of course not. That's not why they'd be concerned."

"Why then?"

She hesitated, and Sam knew he was venturing into forbidden territory.

"Because of Clayton," she finally admitted, shocking him by actually replying. "Because of how I was after the engagement ended. They'll worry that when this ends, I'll react in the same way."

"How were you after the engagement ended?" he asked, and she smiled. The expression was both sweet and sad.

"That's out of bounds," she said, the words quiet, and Sam bit back his instinctive profane response.

"Of course it is," he responded, unable to keep the bitterness out of his voice. He could tell his reaction confused her—truthfully, it confused him, too. But he hated not knowing something so integral about her. Even though he knew he shouldn't *want* to know. He should like not knowing.

"I'll see you in the morning," she said, and he nodded grimly. Then he watched as she turned to leave, even while everything in him wanted to snatch her back and keep her with him.

"Lia?" he called, just as she reached the landing. She stopped and looked back at him. "Text me when you get home."

She nodded and then she was gone.

"Psst!" Lia jumped in fright at the urgent hissing sound coming from her right. She'd just exited the cabin and the surrounding woods were dark aside from the porch light and the few lights coming from Spencer's house.

A little freaked out, Lia contemplated dashing back inside or making a run for her car, which was parked just a few yards away. Clearly the cabin was the sensible choice, and she turned to flee back inside when the hiss came again. This time accompanied by words.

"Psst! Lia!"

"Crumbs," she muttered beneath her breath when she recognized Daff's voice. She should probably have known that her oldest sister would eventually figure out what was going on. Especially since Lia had stupidly made no real effort to hide her car from view. She turned in resignation, and her eyes widened when Daff emerged from between two of the cherry trees that separated Spencer's property from Mason's.

"What the fuck are you doing here?" Daff asked, her voice still pitched low, and Lia's eyebrows flew to her hairline.

"Me? It's the middle of the night. Have you been standing outside in the cold all this time waiting for me to come out? And *what* are you wearing?"

"Don't deflect," Daff said, folding her arms over her chest. Her plaid-covered chest. She seemed to be wearing a man's pajama top. And fluffy rabbit slippers. She looked so unlike herself that Lia couldn't stop staring at her in bemusement. "I knew something was up when Brand spun that bullshit story about his pain meds. How can you be sleeping with him? He's bad news, Lia. He's a player!" She spat out the last word as if it were the vilest insult she could come up with, and Lia laughed, which—if Daff's shocked expression was anything to go by—completely threw her sister.

"I know that," she said, holding her hands up in a placating manner. "Everybody knows that, which is why he's perfect."

"I don't get it," Daff admitted, and Lia snorted.

"I don't want to have a relationship with him, I just want to have some stress-free fun." Daff gaped at her like she had grown an extra head, and Lia sighed. "I've always been so good. I just wanted to try something different. This thing with Brand is temporary, and there's no danger of me mistaking it for anything else. He can't hurt me because I already know what to expect from him. It'll end, he'll leave, we'll both move on."

"What if you fall in love?"

"With *Sam Brand*?" Lia forced a hearty laugh that sounded genuine enough to fool her sister. Truth was, she hadn't really expected to like Brand this much. He was fun, witty, arrogant, supremely self-confident, and genuinely likable. She needed to tread carefully, and despite what she'd told Brand earlier about there being no danger of her falling in love with him, she had to guard her heart more closely than she'd expected to.

"It's all happened so fast, Lia. I hope you know what you're doing."

"Not *that* fast," Lia admitted with a blush. "We kind of, sort of . . ."

"What? Spit it out."

"At the wedding, we . . ."

"*No!* Oh my God! Are you serious? Are you telling me you and Brand had sex at our sister's wedding?"

"And at the hen party." Lia wasn't sure why she was admitting this, but since Daff knew this much, she might as well know the rest. She was gaping at Lia like she didn't know her at all, and some part of Lia enjoyed shocking her jaded older sister. It made her feel daring and interesting and unpredictable.

"What the fuck is going on out here?" Brand yanked open his front door and glared at them. His hair was sexily mussed, his chest was bare, and he was wearing a pair of boxer briefs. Lia immediately salivated at the sight of all that beautifully tanned nakedness and forced herself to focus on Daff, who was giving Brand her version of a death stare.

"You dick! I told you to stay away from my sister, didn't I?" she seethed, and Brand's chest heaved in exasperation.

"You did." He nodded.

"You *did*?" Lia gasped at the same time.

"I did. When we first met him and he wouldn't stop staring at you," Daff confirmed, then focused on Brand again. "But you just couldn't keep it in your pants, could you?"

"To be fair," Brand said, his voice measured, "neither could she."

Lia snort laughed, then clapped a hand over her mouth. She should probably be offended or shocked by the comment, but little Brand said shocked her anymore. He just entertained her. Daff, however, looked totally stunned and for once seemed lost for words.

"Why are you spying on us?" Brand demanded to know.

"Please, I have better things to do with my time. I couldn't sleep and came out for some fresh air when I saw Lia's car, and then *Lia* herself coming out of the cabin. At frickin' midnight. How can you send her home this time of night—have you no regard for her safety?"

Brand's eyes were troubled as they ran over Lia's body.

"*I* wanted her to stay. But I'm pretty sure she thinks she'll catch cooties or something if she stays the night."

"Can't say I blame her," Daff muttered beneath her breath.

"Oh, *come* on!" Brand protested in exasperation. "Stop acting like I'm some cheesy silent-movie villain. Your sister and I are adults, engaged in a mutually beneficial relationship—"

"Fling," Lia corrected, uncomfortable with the *R* word in this context. Brand sent her an annoyed glare.

"The point is, we know what we're doing, and it's none of your business."

"Fine, whatever," Daff said, throwing up her hands in irritation. "Fling away. But let's be clear, Brand, you hurt her and I'll castrate you."

"Oh, for heaven's sake," Lia muttered. "Stop this, both of you. Daff, the castration thing's a bit much."

"I don't think so," Daff said belligerently.

"Brand's right, this is none of your business. I appreciate your concern and I love you for it, but I'm fine. I know what I'm doing."

"Famous last words," Daff muttered.

"Look, just . . . keep this to yourself, okay? I don't need the whole family trying to give me their well-intentioned advice, and Brand doesn't need to be threatened by every member of the family. It's unnecessary. He's not doing anything I haven't explicitly agreed to."

"Very explicitly," he emphasized smugly, and Lia flashed him an irritated look.

"Brand," she warned, and he shrugged before folding his arms over his chest. "Daff, you owe me. I didn't tell Daisy about you and Spencer when you were doing your no-strings thing. And you know how difficult it is for me to lie."

"I do, which is why I'm having a hard time believing you've successfully kept this from us for so long."

"It's different—nobody knew about it, nobody asked questions. I didn't have to say a word."

"Until Brand had to cover for you with the bullshit pain meds story."

"Look, just keep it to yourself, okay? Please."

"Fine. But you can't expect me to keep it from Spencer."

"Spencer, uh . . . ," Brand started to say, then stopped abruptly, and both women looked at him curiously.

"What about Spencer?" Daff asked, and Brand shrugged.

"Nothing. He's a good guy."

"Fine, you can tell Spencer, but no one else," Lia agreed.

"I hope to God this works out the way you're both expecting it to. I don't want you to get hurt, Lia."

"Hey, what about me?" Brand mock pouted, but Daff wasn't amused.

"Trust me, I'll take great pleasure in hurting you if you make her shed one tear."

"I won't," he promised, suddenly dead serious. "I would hate to make her cry."

Daff watched him for a long moment before finally nodding.

"Fine, I'm going to have to take you at your word. For now. I'm starting to freeze my butt off, so I think I'll head back home. Lia, let me know when you're home safe. Good night."

They both bade her good night and watched her retreat back to the bigger house about a hundred yards away.

"Spencer already knows," Brand told Lia, surprising her with the information. "But I didn't want to throw the guy under the bus. Wouldn't want her to take her bad mood out on him."

"How does he know?" Lia asked, and Brand lifted his shoulders.

"Apparently he's known since the stag. He's an observant bastard."

"Daff's not going to like that he didn't tell her."

"He won't tell her if he knows what's good for him."

Lia laughed at that response. "Oh, he'll tell her, and she'll be angry for two seconds, which he'll deserve for keeping a secret like that from her in the first place. But they'll be fine."

Brand reached out to cup her face, and she lifted her eyes to his. "You okay? I know this wasn't ideal."

"I'm fine," Lia admitted with a serene smile, because she really was. This encounter with Daff had shown Lia that she was stronger than she knew. She tended to back away from confrontation, but she was proud of the way she'd stood her ground with Daff.

Brand surprised her with a gentle kiss before resting his forehead on hers.

"Stay?"

"No." She kissed him and stepped away from him. "Good night, Brand."

He said nothing, merely watched her moodily as she got into her car and drove away. He was still standing on the porch watching as she took the turn toward town.

CHAPTER TEN

To Daff's extreme irritation and Lia's discomfort, the rest of the family started inviting Brand to absolutely every family gathering. Sunday lunch, a potluck dinner on Monday. Tuesday was another holiday—International Workers' Day—which meant yet another family cookout. Their mother and Daisy fawned over him and fussed over his injuries, and Lia suspected Charlie had a bad case of hero worship. The teen had so many questions about Laura Prentiss and a few of his other well-known high-profile clients. Mason, of course, had a long-standing friendship with him, and Spencer was in the honeymoon phase of a budding bromance with the guy.

Even their father enjoyed discussing football with him, the older man being a fan of the English Premier League. Brand, of course, knew a few of the players personally—information their father found ridiculously impressive. When Mason pointed out that he knew some of the same people, their father had dismissed him by saying his information wasn't as current.

Lia knew it annoyed Daff no end that everybody *liked* him so much—she never had anything to say to Brand, and when she did speak to him it was short and to the point. Lia also avoided speaking to him in front of her family, but only because she was terrified she'd seem too familiar with him, which would raise questions about the nature of their relationship.

She could tell that Brand disliked her polite indifference, but he never attempted to breach the distance she maintained, thankfully respecting her boundaries. When he got her alone, though, he couldn't keep his hands off her. And whenever they finished and she prepared to leave, he'd invite her to stay. It was getting harder for Lia to deny that one-word request, which made it all the more important for her to maintain her resolve.

Wednesday afternoon, after their visit to the animal shelter and the retirement home, Lia drove him to Knysna for his doctor's appointment. He was becoming increasingly popular with the seniors. He'd been a graceful loser at Sunday night poker and every lady's favorite dance partner at the Monday and Wednesday seniors' dance.

He was . . . nice. Against her better judgment, and despite her careful observance of the rules, Lia was starting to like him more with each passing day.

"This is an exceptionally beautiful part of the world," Brand was saying as he watched the passing scenery. "So verdant, but with all these stunning ocean views. I think, once we get the South African division up and running, I'll get a holiday home here."

"It's a sound investment—this is a great place to live or vacation," Lia agreed, keeping her voice neutral and her eyes on the road. But her heart was racing at the thought of Brand being a regular in the area and possibly in her life.

"You can come stay with me whenever I'm in town," he suggested with a sidelong smile, and she shook her head, refusing to meet his eyes.

"No. I won't do that." She sensed his scrutiny, and her fingers clenched around the steering wheel. "You know there's an expiration date on this thing between us. Once you leave, it's over. I'm not going to be your woman in this particular port."

"What the fuck does that even mean?" he asked, the frustration and anger in his voice surprising her.

"It was a play on words," she explained. "You know? That whole woman-in-every-port thing?"

"And you think I have a woman in every port?"

"Don't you?"

"No, Lia. I'm not quite the man whore you seem to think I am. I don't have an international harem of willing ladies on standby for sex every time I happen to wander into their part of the world. Any man who does is an arsehole." His vehemence surprised her, and she sent him a quick, confused look before refocusing on the road. He intercepted her look and heaved a huge, gusty sigh. The sound was filled with annoyance.

"Why does that surprise you?" he asked, and she shook her head.

"I can't figure you out, that's all."

"Here's a little tidbit for your consideration: the last person I fucked before coming back to Riversend was *you*."

She resisted the urge to full-on stare at him as she navigated past a couple of long-haul trucks and then shook her head in disbelief.

"That's a blatant lie," she denied, giving him a venomous look. "I don't care if you're a player, Brand. This whole thing between us works because of the type of man you are. You don't have to fabricate BS stories to make me think more of you."

"Why would you think I'm lying?" he practically yelled, sounding completely affronted.

"Because of Laura Prentiss," she yelled back, shocking herself by raising her voice.

"Fuck," she heard him swear, the word low and vehement. "Lally doesn't count. At all."

"What? Why not?"

"Jesus." She saw him lift his left hand to the back of his neck and massage his nape. "Because she and I . . ."

"Oh my God," Lia breathed, interrupting him. Feeling like blinders had been ripped from her eyes. "Oh my *God*! You're in love with her, aren't you? You don't consider what you do with her in such base terms because it's more special."

"What the fuck?" Complete disbelief in his voice. "Lia, are you shitting me with this? Where do you come up with this bullshit?"

"It's true, isn't it? How could you do all those things with me when you're in love with someone else?"

"I'm not in love with Lally, for fuck's sake! Stop saying that. Lally and I aren't even together . . ."

"We're here," she interrupted him frostily as she pulled the car into a vacant spot outside the orthopedist's office. "You'd better get in there or you'll be late for your appointment."

"We're not done talking about this," he insisted, and she released the steering wheel to pin him with what she hoped was a completely indifferent look.

"I think we are. I'm going to get some lunch. Text me when you're done." She pulled the key from the ignition and tossed it into his lap. "Lock the car, please. See you later."

She left before he could say another word and walked brusquely toward the city center to find a restaurant. She didn't have an appetite but needed to process what had just happened. If Brand really had feelings for Laura Prentiss, then Lia was doing the unthinkable—she was placing herself squarely in the middle of a possibly redeemable relationship.

Combined with the nickname and the obvious reluctance to discuss her and his supposed breakup with the woman, Lia should have seen this coming a mile away. Lia had offered to be his rebound girl, but if he loved the woman, there was so much more at stake. If he stood any chance of getting back with her before, Lia could quite possibly have ruined it by getting involved with him.

Sam stared dispassionately at his skinny, pale right arm. It looked completely alien to him and smelled pretty funky as well. It had healed enough over the last six weeks for the doctor to feel comfortable about not recasting the limb. The genteel older man had bombarded Sam with a list of aftercare instructions and had recommended a few good physiotherapists in the area for rehab.

Sam sent Lia a text to let her know he was done. He thought about their earlier conversation . . . or was that an argument? He didn't know how to categorize that particular exchange of words, because it had been so fucking peculiar. Lia had a penchant for seeing things a certain way and then stating them as fact without anything to back up her words. The stuff about Daisy and Mason's future kids had been cute, but this shit about Lally and Sam was so far out there, he wasn't sure how to respond to her words. Or even if he wanted to respond. It was probably Sam's fault for fostering the belief that he and Lally were involved in the first place, but nothing he had ever said or done had hinted at him being in love with Lally.

He waited in the doctor's reception area, ignoring the flirtatious glances the receptionist was casting his way, keeping his eyes glued to the huge plate-glass window. When he saw Lia walking toward the doctor's office, he felt an odd, twisting sensation in his chest. The feeling was unfamiliar and freaked him out a little, but he knew it had something to do with Lia and the way she was dressed—pretty and fresh in a plain turquoise knee-length A-line summer dress. And the way she walked—shoulders back, chin up, hips swaying gently with each step. And definitely the way she looked—sweet and wholesome with her sun-kissed freckled nose, her glossy brown hair, worn in a loose ponytail, and her earnest gray eyes, so luminous and expressive a man could lose himself in them.

She was lovely.

Lovely wasn't a word Sam typically used. But it perfectly described Dahlia McGregor.

So fucking lovely.

He was absently rubbing his chest, trying to ease the crazy, unfamiliar flutter, watching as every step brought her closer to him. She looked pensive and remained unaware of his scrutiny until he exited the doctor's office to meet her at the door. She stopped and lifted her eyes to his. Sam's breath stalled. He felt nervous . . . he wasn't sure why.

Her eyes moved over his face and then down to his arm, and a genuinely happy smile lit up her face.

"The cast is gone," she pointed out unnecessarily, and he grinned sheepishly, lifting his puny arm like a kid showing off a scrape.

"It looks like shit," he said, his voice rough, and she laughed.

"Not for long, I'm sure. You'll have it whipped into shape in no time at all."

"Lia—"

"Sam—" They spoke simultaneously, but it didn't escape Sam's notice that she'd used his name. He liked it. He more than liked it. He wanted her to continue calling him that. He wanted to hear her shout it out when he made her come.

"Me first?" he asked, trying to ignore his reaction to the sound of his name on her lips. She nodded. "Lally and I were never involved. It was something the press fabricated, and neither of us cared enough to correct them. In fact, we figured it might even deter her stalker." He laughed self-deprecatingly and lifted his arm. "It clearly didn't."

"Why did you say you were? I mean, I understand why you didn't correct the press, but why did you lie to *me*?" she asked in confusion, and Sam felt a stab of remorse. He felt like a bastard, and he inhaled deeply.

"Okay, this is going to make me sound like a prick, and maybe I am a prick. No, I definitely am . . . but I thought it might help me get you into bed. If you knew we weren't involved, you would rescind your offer to be my rebound girl. Since I didn't really need a rebound girl."

"Okay, the rebound thing *may* have been one of a few deciding factors," she admitted uncomfortably. Her honesty winning out again. "I thought it was an adequate excuse to allow myself to enjoy you, in a guilt-free, uncommitted way. But when I thought you were in love with her, I felt terrible about getting in the way of a potential reconciliation."

"She's a client. Nothing more."

"You have a nickname for her."

"Everybody who knows her personally calls her Lally. How the fuck did you make the leap that I was in love with her?"

"You mean aside from the fact that you deliberately misled me about the nature of your relationship with her?" she asked pointedly, and he felt an uncharacteristic swell of remorse. She continued before he could reply. "Mainly because you always use the *F* word when you refer to our intimate encounters. I thought maybe you considered your interludes with her in a different, more romantic light."

"Your thought processes are so bizarre and so fucking fascinating," he mused, shaking his head. He dropped an arm around her shoulders and dragged her over to drop a kiss on her head.

"I'm not sure how I feel about this," she said, and his brow lowered.

"What do you mean?"

"I don't like that you lied to me," she explained. "I feel . . . I don't like it."

"Lia, it was a lie of omission. If that. *You* were the one who decided that Lally and I were together. I never said we were. Nothing I said was overtly dishonest."

"Your very carefully worded responses to any of my questions relating to your relationship with Laura Prentiss were completely dishonest and you know that."

"God, first you're pissed off with me for supposedly being in love with Lally and then you're pissed off with me because I'm not? You're being irrational, Lia."

"I'm angry with you for lying," she corrected. "That's not a small thing."

"I didn't lie!"

"You *did*."

"What does it fucking matter?" he finally asked, his voice raised and bordering on a shout. "We were having fun. Enjoying each other. None of it was serious, why are you acting like this is some huge betrayal? I'm not your boyfriend, *princess*! My relationship, or lack thereof, with Laura Prentiss has no bearing on us. Frankly, it's none of your goddamned business—yours is a temporary presence in my life and I don't owe you any explanations."

His words made her blink, pause, and retreat. He watched it happen—a complete emotional withdrawal—and he couldn't blame her. He swallowed, almost tasting the words he'd just spewed at her. They were acrid and foul. Completely unpalatable. He opened his mouth to say something else. Something less . . . something more . . .

Just *something*.

But she'd turned away from him and was heading back to the parking lot, her back ramrod straight while her cute ponytail swayed perkily with each step she took. He stood watching her uncertainly for a moment before following her.

They spent the first half of the twenty-minute drive back in strained silence. Finally deciding that he needed to say something—apologize at least—Sam opened his mouth to talk.

"Lia." She leaned forward and turned on the radio. An overly cheerful DJ was discussing the weather with his cohost, and they were both way too fucking enthusiastic about it. Sam took the hint and shut his mouth, and the second half of the drive was filled with annoying DJ chatter.

When she brought the car to a standstill in front of the cabin, Sam pointedly turned down the radio and shifted to face her. She kept her gaze straight ahead.

"Look, I'm sorry, okay? I shouldn't have kept the truth from you. I didn't even have a legitimate reason for doing so, it just seemed like—"

"Brand"—she turned to meet his eyes, and he tried not to flinch at the distance he saw in hers—"you're right. You don't owe me any apologies and certainly no explanations. I overstepped. It was out of bounds. I think, since your arm is out of its cast, you don't need me anymore. So why don't we call this experiment of ours a partial success and move on from there?"

Fuck.

"I still hate doing my own cooking," he pointed out. "And I paid you for two weeks' help."

"In light of our situation and the intimacy, I don't feel right accepting your money. I'll be returning it."

"No. For fuck's sake, Lia. You only agreed to help me because of that money. You clearly needed it for something."

"I didn't earn it, and to accept it after what happened between us just feels wrong."

"Look, we don't have to end things. I mean now that everything's out in the open, it'll be better. No more secrets, right?"

"I have to get back to my studies," she shocked him by saying, and he was confused for a moment.

"Studies?"

"I've been doing an online bachelor of education degree. My eventual goal is to be a properly qualified foundation phase educator. Preschool teacher, really. I've been on a midterm break, but I have a couple of assignments to complete before the new semester starts next week."

"That's fantastic, Lia." Her lips quirked slightly in acknowledgment of his sincere compliment.

"Thank you. But I'll be busy, so it's probably best to end our fling."

"I don't want to end it." He knew he sounded petulant, but fuck it, he wasn't anywhere close to getting her out of his system. "You're just punishing me because I don't meet your crazy high morality standard. News flash, princess, nobody can ever meet those impossibly high standards."

He was starting to recognize that he only ever called her "princess" when he was annoyed with her. Maybe because she put on that prim, unapproachable, high-and-mighty façade whenever she was upset about something. It rubbed him the wrong way.

"Brand, let's not make this unpleasant. I'd like it if we could remain civil and respectful of each other."

"God, you're cold! As frigid as a fucking iceberg." She paled and flinched at his words, which instantly made him regret saying them. He had meant that she was harsh and unyielding in her decision making, but he wasn't sure that was how she took it. And that bothered him. Especially when he considered within which other context those words could be used. Somebody had called her frigid—*sexually* frigid—and Sam was willing to bet it was that prick she was once engaged to. Again, he felt a burning urge to find the bastard and fuck him the hell up.

"Please," she was saying, her voice quiet. "I have to get home."

"Sunshine," he began tentatively, keeping his voice low and sincere, "I'm sorry. I didn't mean for things to go this way. I'm going to miss the hell out of you."

She smiled, but it was one of those horrible ones that didn't reach her eyes.

"Thank you for saying that."

The prim little thank-you absolutely shredded him, and he fought the urge to gather her into his arms and simply hold her.

"Fuck." He heard his voice falter on the word. "I'm seriously going to miss you, sunshine."

"Goodbye, Brand."

He had no choice—he took another lingering look at her downcast profile before acquiescing to her wishes and leaving the car. Sam stood watching, the heel of his hand pressing against his chest, as she drove away without a backward glance.

Just because Lia had ended their fling did *not* mean that Brand would magically disappear from her life.

Ha, if only. She managed to avoid him at the animal shelter by changing her visiting times, but she knew, from Siphiso, that he came to see Trevor every day.

And she saw him again just three nights later, having dinner at MJ's with Daisy and Mason. Lia immediately felt awkward because she was meeting Michael Kendrick, a local accountant, for dinner. It was a blind date—one of the residents from the retirement home had been pushing Lia to meet her grandson for months. And yesterday—after making the less than rational decision to get back on the dating horse, so to speak—she'd asked Mrs. Kendrick for his details. She didn't know anything about him other than the fact that he was an accountant and—according to his grandmother—a very handsome boy.

Lia halted when she spotted Brand, her first instinct to turn around and wait for Michael outside. She would suggest they go to Ralphie's for a drink instead. But Daisy caught her eye and waved enthusiastically. Biting back a groan, Lia pasted a smile on her face and waved back. Mason and Brand looked up, too, and she could see the subtle shift in the latter's body language when he saw her.

When Daisy beckoned her toward them, Lia sighed and reluctantly walked over to their table.

"Hey, wanna join us?" Daisy asked, and Lia, diligently avoiding Brand's eyes, shook her head, hoping she looked reluctant enough.

"Thanks for the invitation, but I have a date." She sneaked a glance at Brand and was surprised to see his brow lower at her words.

"You can both join us," Brand suggested, and this time she met his eyes directly, trying to prevent her sister and brother-in-law from seeing the daggers she was throwing at him.

"I don't think so."

"A *date*? Who is he? Anyone I know?" Daisy asked eagerly.

"I don't think so. His name's Michael Kendrick."

"Mikey? I know him, we were in the same grade." Which meant that he was about twenty-eight, four years younger than Lia. Not a deal breaker or anything, just disconcerting. Most guys in their thirties were married already anyway, so it was actually surprising that this was the first younger man she'd encountered since she had started dating again.

"Doing a bit of cradle snatching, are you, Lia?" Brand's voice was as smooth as silk, and Lia tried very hard not to react to his comment.

"Younger men have so much more *stamina*, though, don't they?"

Gah! Had she really just said that? She didn't make insinuations about sex in public, or in private, for that matter, no matter how mild. Daisy looked startled by her comment, Mason was grinning, and Brand looked angry. She didn't think she had ever seen him angry before. Charming, in pain, turned on, tired, and grumpy, but never truly angry.

He opened his mouth, looking like he was about to say something scathing, when a deep voice, coming from behind Daff, interrupted him.

"Dahlia?" Lia spun around and then smiled as she looked up at the tall, very handsome man standing behind her. He had dark hair, a well-maintained beard, and deep-set brown eyes. "I'm Michael. Nice to meet you."

"How did you know it was me?" Lia asked in confusion, still a bit awed by his height and good looks. Blind dates were supposed to be disappointing, but Michael Kendrick exceeded expectations by a mile. She heard Brand make an irritable sound and ignored him.

"You said you'd be wearing a pink cardigan," he said with a kind smile. "Although I'd say it's more fuchsia, don't you agree? It's a very pretty cardigan—did you make it yourself?"

Lia looked down at her bright cardigan and blushed.

"Yes, I did. I knit . . . as a hobby. I like to make pretty things. I put a lot of them away, as gifts, or, you know, for the future and . . ." She was babbling. She cleared her throat, her voice tapering off, and took a deep breath, her eyes meeting Brand's. He was watching her intently, so she shifted her gaze back to Michael's patient stare.

"Hi, Daisy, long time no see," Michael said, smiling at her sister and bending down to drop a kiss on her cheek. Oddly enough, Mason, who was usually absurdly possessive over Daisy, remained completely relaxed through the interaction.

"Hello, Mikey. Nice to see you again. This is my husband, Mason, and his friend Sam." The two men stood up to shake hands with Michael.

"We should find our own table, Michael," Lia said, and he grinned, looking quite roguish.

"We should . . . although maybe we could join this table? Unless you all are expecting more people?"

Daisy looked hesitant, her eyes widening as she looked at Lia, who was frantically shaking her head behind Michael's back.

"Not at all," Brand said pleasantly. "More than enough space for you two at our table."

Sam kept his eyes on Lia's miserable face as she and her *date* joined their table. He shouldn't have intervened—he should have let them go off to their own table. But he was trying to protect her. Initially, after learning about her date, he'd felt an irrational spurt of possessiveness at the thought of Lia out with some undeserving bloke. Worse, what if she liked the guy? What if there was a second date and a third? What if it became a thing? Sam didn't like that idea, because it would completely eliminate the possibility of any renewal of future intimate interactions between Lia and him.

Then this Kendrick guy showed up and he was tall, dark, and handsome. A slightly younger stud. He could tell from Lia's reaction that the guy had made a strong first impression, and all Sam had wanted to do was sabotage the whole fucking evening.

But then Kendrick had opened his mouth and called Lia's pink cardigan *fuchsia*. What the fuck was a fuchsia? At first Sam wasn't sure if the guy was referring to the wool or the design until it had clicked that he meant the color. And then the guy had turned to the table, his eyes had gone over Mason, checking him out quite thoroughly, before his gaze had fallen on Sam and lingered. Sam knew that look—he had perfected that look. The surreptitious and appreciative once-over.

Sam wasn't sure why the guy was on a date with Lia, but he was pissed off for a different reason now. He didn't know what Kendrick's deal was, maybe he was into guys and girls, whatever. But this asshole was blatantly checking Mason and Sam out, which was more than a little disrespectful to Lia. Not cool. She should be the man's sole focus this evening.

Sam wasn't going to allow this dick to play fast and loose with Lia's feelings. *Not on my fucking watch!* he told himself. Sam knew it wasn't his place to be watching over Lia. She wouldn't want or appreciate it. Especially since his motives weren't at all altruistic.

But that was why Sam had invited them to join the group, and Lia could stare daggers at him all night if she wanted to, but at least she wasn't going to develop feelings for a guy who didn't look set to return them. He tried to ignore the hypocrisy in the sentiment—the longer he and Lia had kept *flinging*, the more likely she was to develop feelings for Sam. No matter her protestations to the contrary. So maybe there was more than one prick sitting at the table tonight. Sam was honest enough to acknowledge that and selfish enough to dismiss the feelings of guilt that accompanied that self-awareness.

Daisy and Mason looked a bit awkward at the sudden inclusion of a clearly reluctant Lia and her date to their table. Mason was giving him curious sidelong looks, but Sam avoided his friend's eyes.

"So Michael," he began amiably. "What do you do?"

"I'm a senior accountant at Rutger, Powell & Lee."

"Is that a local firm?" he asked, and Michael nodded, his eyes on Sam.

"It is. You have an accent. English?"

"Yes. How did you meet Lia?"

"Through my grandmother. You look familiar. You're that guy, aren't you? The one who saved Laura Prentiss. You're a bodyguard."

"Close protection officer," Sam corrected. "And yes, I'm that guy. Is your grandmother Mrs. Kendrick at the old-age home?"

"Retirement home," Lia corrected, her voice short, and he smiled at her.

"Sorry, the retirement home. She dances a mean waltz."

"You know her?" the guy asked, his eyes widening in shock.

"Yes, I see her twice a week at the dance recitals." He watched Kendrick process the words and then immediately retreat. No more borderline flirtatious looks and interested questions. Granny Kendrick probably didn't know that Michael liked men. Sad that the guy hid his true self from his family.

Kendrick *finally* seemed to remember his date and started asking Lia all the usual questions. He was polite but distant and his eyes kept roaming around the room and lingering on a few of the other men in the restaurant. Lia smiled, her expression artificially bright, as she put on a first-date show for the guy. Not seeming to notice that the guy, while friendly and polite, seemed not even the slightest bit interested in her. But Sam could tell she was nervous and that his presence made her uncomfortable and abruptly felt like a shit for putting her in that position.

He should have backed off, let them have their dinner, and had a private conversation with her about Kendrick later. As a friend.

Mason and Daisy were making small talk with Lia and Kendrick while Sam, a headache developing, sat silently and observed.

~

Lia didn't know how, but somehow the awkward evening managed to pass pleasantly enough. Something in Brand had changed during his intense exchange with Michael, because he had been quiet for most of the evening after that, only answering questions when he was addressed directly. He kept rubbing his forehead and his eyes were narrowed against the light, and she wondered if he were in pain. She verged on asking him more than once but always thought the better of it and continued to keep her focus on her date.

Michael was nice. She had found his exchange with Brand a bit odd and had felt completely excluded from their conversation, but she soon became the man's main focus.

She liked him, but she wasn't attracted to him. And truthfully, he didn't seem all that interested in her. He spent a lot of time talking to Mason, who looked uncomfortable but kept the conversation pleasant. Oh well, at least Michael wasn't boring like Gregory.

Lia and Michael were stiltedly discussing their mutual interest in ikebana when Daisy loudly proclaimed that she was going to the ladies' room and then gave Lia a pointed look.

"Uh. Me too?" Daisy nodded and Lia placed her napkin on the table before excusing herself. She followed Daisy into the unisex restroom and watched as her sister checked all the stalls before turning to glare at her.

"What's up, Daisy?"

"Seriously, Lia? *Seriously?*"

"I don't understand."

"Look, Mikey's a nice guy, I've always liked him, but even back in school he never seemed all that into girls. I always thought he was just shy. But he's cute, there were opportunities but he never seemed to take them. And tonight, I finally understand why. He's spent more time chatting with Mason and full-on flirting with Sam, than he has with you."

"What? Are you saying he's not into women?"

"I don't know. I just feel that you deserve more than a guy who doesn't seem to even notice you as a sexual being."

"It's a first date and it's awkward with all of you there. Things aren't progressing the way a normal first date would."

"He hasn't even looked at your boobs! Not once!"

"He's a gentleman. And this top isn't exactly meant to tempt a man's eyes in that direction." She was wearing a high-collared blouse with a soft, flowing skirt tonight. Not unattractive, but not exactly designed to set a man on fire with lust.

"Please, no man is that much of a gentleman. If your boobs aren't tempting, why have Brand's eyes not strayed from them most of the evening?"

"They haven't?" Naturally she had been aware of his gaze all evening, but she had been too busy not looking at Brand to know where his eyes were focused.

"Oh, there may have been a slight break between dinner and dessert, but they've constantly wandered to your boobs throughout the night."

"Michael's not gay."

"Maybe not, maybe he likes girls, too, but the man's tongue nearly fell out when he saw Brand. Now call me crazy, but I think your date should be reacting that way to *you*, not to one of your dinner companions. Look, I don't want you to get your hopes up about this guy only to be disappointed, okay?"

Lia nodded miserably as she considered her conversation with Michael tonight. He'd been very nice and very friendly, but also distant and polite. Not exactly showing an interest in her at all.

Even if Daisy was wrong and he wasn't interested in Brand, he definitely wasn't into Lia, and, honestly, she wasn't into him, either. Her shoulders fell, and Daisy hugged her.

"I'm sorry, Lia," she said, genuinely contrite. "I was hoping you'd clue in before I had to spell it out for you."

"That's okay. I've been having no luck dating at all."

"Well, if all else fails, at least you know Brand thinks your boobies are riveting," Daisy teased, and Lia fought back a blush.

"Shut up," she mumbled, too scared to say much more than that for fear of alerting her sister to the fact that Brand was most likely staring at her breasts because he knew how they looked naked.

"Brand's a nice enough guy, but such a player. Mason once told me that he's a prick—'scuse the French—with women."

"Oh?"

"Yes, a real love-'em-and-leave-'em type. Once he moves on, which is usually after just a few weeks, he deletes all pictures, contact details, and correspondence from them off his phone and computer. He erases them from his life, as if they never existed. Never mentions them again."

"Is that so?" Lia asked faintly, wondering if Sam had erased her number yet.

"Yes." Daisy turned to check her makeup and met Lia's eyes in the mirror. "But the weird thing is the women are aware of his terms, and for the most part they're happy enough to move on afterward. There have been a few who went a bit stalkery, though, wouldn't accept that he meant it when he told them it was over."

"What did he do?" Lia asked breathlessly.

"Mason says restraining orders and stern lectures from the police usually did the trick."

How humiliating for those women.

"We should probably head back," Lia said, feeling a bit queasy after the reveal about Michael and the information about Brand.

Dinner ended soon after the women returned to the table. Lia kept her interaction with Michael light and friendly. They argued amicably over the bill until she charmingly relented and allowed him to cover their portion of the meal.

"I'll chat with you tomorrow, Daisy," Lia promised, giving her sister a hug and a kiss. She followed that up with a hug for Mason.

"Good night, Brand," she said curtly, still not meeting his eyes.

"I'll be seeing you, Lia. Take care, Kendrick."

Michael barely looked at Brand, just nodded, before he politely escorted Lia out of the restaurant and to her car.

"I had a nice evening," he said, his voice neutral.

"Me too," she said, wrapping her cardigan around her to ward off the chill in the air.

"Maybe we can do it again sometime?" he suggested when they reached her car.

"Maybe." He nodded at her response. Both silently acknowledging that there would be no future interaction between them.

"Good night, Michael."

"'Night, Lia." He held the door for her and closed it after she had climbed into her car. Lia silently wished him well as she drove off and left him standing in the nearly empty parking lot.

I'm sorry I fucked up your evening, sunshine. The message came about half an hour after Lia got home from her date. She stared at the screen and all she felt was a weird relief that he hadn't yet deleted her number from his phone.

You didn't.

I did. I shouldn't have interfered. She read the message a couple of times, and a few minutes elapsed before she responded.

I'm sorry my date flirted with you. Her phone rang thirty seconds later, and his name popped onto the screen. She accepted the call immediately.

"Brand?"

"The guy was a dick. He shouldn't have gone out with you and flirted with other people," he said, his gravelly voice thick with annoyance.

"You knew, didn't you? That's why you invited us to sit at the table."

"I didn't like that he was playing you. It pissed me off."

"I think it's really sad that he feels like he has to pretend to be something he's not."

"Yeah, well, he can fucking pretend with someone else." Why did he sound so indignant about something that had no direct effect on him?

"Well, no harm done," Lia said, her voice deliberately light. "Part and parcel of being lost in the dating wilderness again."

"So this wasn't a one-off thing? You're definitely dating again?"

"I know I must seem like an indecisive idiot."

"No. Just hopeful." His voice was heartbreakingly gentle. "I'm glad you haven't given up on that hope, Lia."

"I feel so stupid," she admitted softly. "I keep putting myself out there and then this."

"How are you meeting these guys?" he asked curiously, and she drew in a huge breath as she tried to settle her erratic emotions and concentrate on answering his question.

"Well, Michael was obviously through Mrs. Kendrick, and Gregory is my friend Tilda's brother's colleague."

"So you have a network of connections? Like an analog dating site?"

"More like an old-fashioned matchmaking ring," she corrected with a laugh. "And it's safer than online dating, because murdering me would mean they'd have to murder the friend who set us up, too, in order to cover up the crime."

"Jesus, that's fucking grim. Don't talk like that." He sounded genuinely freaked out, and she laughed again, more heartily this time.

"I'll be perfectly safe, Brand. You don't have to worry."

"Do you have your next date set up already?"

"Of course not. How awful would that be? Like I was anticipating failure with Michael before even going on a first date with him. I'm not that pessimistic."

"It's good to plan ahead."

"No, this is stressful enough without thinking about more than one date simultaneously. I prefer taking it one guy at a time. It feels less cold-blooded."

"You're dangerously naïve, sunshine."

"And you're hopelessly cynical, Brand."

"Will you let me know when you go on your next date?" he asked, not responding to her statement. She snorted in answer to his question.

"Of course not. And have you show up at all of my dates like some overprotective father figure? I don't think so! I already have a dad, and he trusts me to make the right decisions." That was true, even though she had often failed in her decision making. Her father—both her parents, really—remained supportive.

"I just want you to be safe. Look, I know we're not *flinging* anymore, but I did promise you I'd help you find your man, remember?"

"I remember. I also remember telling you that the thought of an arrangement like that made me uncomfortable."

"Yeah, but only because we were fucking."

"Brand, you're not going to be my Mr. Matchmaker, okay?" she said in her most no-nonsense voice. "I told you before . . . you don't get to play this role in my life. I don't need you to be my hero."

"Lia?"

"Yes?"

"Will you come over?" His voice was gruff, and Lia sighed and shook her head.

"No." She hung up without saying good night.

CHAPTER ELEVEN

Brand was at the animal shelter the following morning when she stopped by. Which led her to conclude that he'd changed his usual visiting time to coincide with hers. He was with Trevor, as usual. According to Siphiso, the dog had started taking treats from Brand. Not every time, but he would venture forward with every third offer or so. It was slow going, but it was definite progress, which meant that Trevor was now a viable contender for rehabilitation and no longer an immediate candidate for euthanasia.

Lia ran into Brand when she was visiting the rehab dogs. He was sitting inside Trevor's pen, animatedly chatting with the dog. Lia's heart leapt in fear at the sight of him sitting inside the cage.

"Are you sure that's safe?" she asked without any preliminaries. Brand's face lit up when he saw her.

"Hey, sunshine. I was just talking about you."

She chose to ignore that, keeping her eyes glued on Trevor. The dog's head and ears were down, and he was staring at her warily.

"Should you be in there? He has a history of aggression."

"Somebody has to take the first step and trust him. He was just scared before. He's a pretty mellow guy. Aren't you, Tyson?"

"Do the handlers know that you're in here?"

"Siphiso knows, he stayed for a while and observed. He left a couple of minutes ago. It's sweet that you're worried about me, sunshine."

"I'd worry about anybody foolish enough to expose themselves to a potentially dangerous animal."

"Danger is my middle name," he joked. And she shook her head.

"I'm all too aware of that," she said quietly. "But if he acts out toward you, it's a strike against him, and the more strikes he has, the more likely he is to be put down."

Brand paled and glanced at the dog.

"Don't say stuff like that in front of him. You'll scare him. I'm pretty fucking terrified myself—I didn't know what the stakes were."

"How could you not? What do you think happens to the animals who can't find homes? Space and resources are limited, Brand."

"That's barbaric," he growled. His obvious agitation was starting to upset the dog, and he got up carefully and stepped out of the pen. He took Lia's elbow and led her farther down the corridor.

"If it makes you feel better, your interactions with Trevor have been a lifeline for the dog. I've just heard that they're reevaluating his rehabilitation potential," Lia said, gentling her tone.

"He's a great dog," Brand said, looking relieved. "I'm glad he'll have the opportunity to prove that."

Lia tilted her head and ran her eyes over his disheveled form. He was wearing a pair of baggy running shorts that ended just above his knees, along with a T-shirt that looked damp in spots. His hair was also darkened—from water or sweat, she wasn't sure which.

"How did you get here?" she asked curiously.

"Well, since I find myself without transportation lately, I started running again," he said with a grin, the grooves in his cheeks deepening wickedly.

"You jogged here," she repeated flatly.

"Nah, jogging is for pussies, I run. But it kind of wiped me out. It felt farther than it probably was. Which probably means I'm the pussy now."

"Possibly because you're still recovering?"

"I can't keep using that whole recovery thing as an excuse not to get back into shape." He shrugged.

"You planning to run home?"

"When I get my wind back," he said, resting his hands on his hips.

Lia sighed. "I'm leaving in ten minutes, after I've visited my golden oldies. If you want a ride, be ready at that time."

"Cool, I'll hang out with Figaro a bit longer, then."

"Figaro? Seriously?"

"What? I know all kinds of cultural and classy shit. My mom dragged me to countless operas when she found herself between boyfriends, husbands, or toy boys."

"Your mother has toy boys?"

"Yeah, her current plaything is twenty-seven. Dumb as a bag of rocks, poor guy. And she'll probably be on to her next young gun by the time I see her again."

"How does that make you feel?" Lia asked, despite herself. Then reminded herself that they weren't flinging anymore, so *maybe* it was okay to ask him personal questions now?

"As long as she's happy, I have no beef with it. She gave up on the whole marriage thing after her fifth husband and tried dating for a while, but that didn't work out, either. So she has her man, or boy, as it were, of the moment. Which seems to be working out well for her. It's not harming anyone. If I thought they were taking advantage of her, I'd step in, but most of these guys are really, *really* lacking in the intellect department. And wouldn't know how to mastermind a scheme to deprive her of her money if their lives depended on it. Mom's not really interested in their brains, if you know what I mean. They offer a laugh and some companionship."

"And she's happy?"

"Happy enough." Lia frowned as she considered the information. The notion of having a series of sex-only relationships, like the one she'd had with Brand, was not at all appealing to her, and she couldn't fathom living her life going from one meaningless sexual encounter to the next.

It gave her some insight into Sam Brand, though. He'd grown up with a mother who went from one relationship to the next. No wonder he thought permanent relationships were a waste of time. He'd never seen one that worked.

"Why are you staring at me like that?" he asked suddenly, and Lia blinked.

"Like what?"

"I don't know, like *that*. Like you're trying to figure something out."

"I'm not. I was just wondering what it was like growing up like that. Did you have a stable father figure in your life?"

"Aside from my actual father, you mean?" he asked mockingly, and Lia's eyes widened.

"Oh, I didn't know—"

"What, that I have a dad? Of course I do. Joseph Joshua Brand, JJ to his mates. Great guy. Gets along with everybody. Awesome dad . . . to his three kids from his second marriage. Me, I get to see him once a year . . . if that. I spent the occasional school holiday with him when I was a kid. Trying to fit in with his other family. God, my half brothers are stuck so far up their own arses, I'll be shocked if they even know what the sun looks like."

"Is he still with his second wife?"

"Oh yes, they're full on into the happy family thing. Married for twenty-seven years and going strong. Rita, my stepmother, is quite nice. Hard to believe she bred such douchebags."

"You preferred your mother's lifestyle to your father's stable home life?"

"Lifestyle?" He raised his brows at the word, and Lia flushed, recognizing how unintentionally judgmental her use of the word sounded.

"I mean . . ."

"My mother is a warm, loving woman. I never lacked for anything, especially not love. Which, I'm sure you will agree, is the key ingredient to any happy family."

"Yes, of course. I'm sorry. I didn't mean to offend."

"Not everybody has the same overwhelming drive to marry and have kids that you do, Lia. Some of us are actually quite happy to never go anywhere near the outdated institution of marriage."

"You don't think your parents' divorce or your mother's serial partners have contributed toward this belief?" She winced at her own question—she could perhaps have phrased it a bit more tactfully. But Brand surprised her by laughing heartily.

"God no, I would never look to my mother as any kind of model example when it comes to relationships. She's an unapologetic train wreck at romance. I have known many happily married couples; my dad and Rita, my grandparents—on both sides, all sadly passed on now—friends, even my douchey half brothers, who have somehow managed to find awesome women willing to marry them, all happily married for years. I'm quite familiar with what marital bliss looks like. I just don't want that for myself. I'm not willing to give up my work or my freedom for any woman."

"And you don't want children?"

"I'm too fucking selfish. My entire life would have to revolve around them, wouldn't it? Around their wants and needs. I can't imagine that. I like doing my own thing too much."

Lia was aware that she was staring at him again, but she couldn't help it. Daff had once held the same life philosophy, but her sister's adamant anti-marriage stance had definitely hidden some pretty deep-rooted insecurities. Sam Brand didn't look like a man with insecurities. He looked like a man who knew exactly what he wanted from life, and a wife and family were most definitely *not* in the cards.

"Um. Okay, so ten minutes?" she reminded. The interesting exchange had revealed so much more about Brand than she had learned over the course of the last week. She needed time to process.

"Yeah. See you then." He nodded, his eyes already back on Trevor.

"Stay?" Sam knew he was pushing it asking her to stay, but she was tempted, he could see it in her eyes. She opened her mouth to speak, then thought the better of it. Her eyes met his mutely for a long moment before she shook her head.

"You know I won't." He didn't push her, merely nodded.

"Are you okay?" he asked. "After last night?"

"Completely over it," she said with a smile that didn't quite reach her eyes.

"Do you have another date lined up?"

"Not going to tell you that, Brand," she said, and it frustrated the hell out of him that she could be meeting some potential creep show tonight and he had no clue where she would be or with whom.

"Come on, sunshine. I just want you to be safe."

"I'll be fine."

"So you *do* have a date?" She laughed, genuine amusement in the sound. It ended on that adorable little snort.

"Stop asking, Brand."

"Will you call me? If you need help?" Another snort laugh.

"You don't have a car," she pointed out. "I'll call Mason. Or Spencer."

He swore beneath his breath, feeling completely useless and incapable of defending her if she needed him.

"Call me anyway, okay? I'll see you around, sunshine."

"Take care, Brand." After hearing her use his first name the other day, he was desperate for her to say it again. But disappointingly, she'd stuck with *Brand* since then. He wanted to ask her to call him Sam but wasn't sure how that would go over with her. She was such a prickly thing, with her weird rules and hang-ups about everything.

He moved into the cabin, still bothered by her infuriating stubbornness, rotating the shoulder and wrist on his weak arm. He had an appointment with a physiotherapist early next week and would have to arrange for a car or a driving service to take him to Knysna. He was delaying the task because he hoped to convince Lia to drive him. But now he wondered if he should keep a car on standby every day in case she needed him.

He missed her. Not only her presence in his bed, but her companionship as well. And that despite her adamant insistence that they not have a decent conversation. He had fucked up badly with her, handled a delicate situation tactlessly. It had been misguided and pointless to lie about his relationship with Lally in the first place, and he sorely regretted it now. Especially since it had cost him his fling, or whatever the fuck it was, with Lia.

He had a long, hot shower, trying to work the kinks out of his aching body. He shouldn't have pushed as hard as he did today. But he was impatient to get back to normal, back to his life and his work. This place and its overly friendly people were starting to mess with his brain. All his interactions with Lia, as an example, had been way more intense than anything he would normally have with a woman. For a brief insane moment, this afternoon, he'd actually considered adopting Trevor himself. Which would have been a mistake, since he didn't have the time to dedicate to a dog.

Sam also found himself enjoying the McGregor/Carlisle clan way too much. He liked the instant welcome and acceptance he'd received from them. And on Monday and Wednesday he'd *actually* looked forward to hanging out with Bertie, Alison, and the rest of the seniors.

Sam didn't recognize himself, and it was highly disturbing. This vacation had been way too long, and it was time to touch base with Colby.

"I would never consider marrying someone who isn't prepared to have my mother move in with us," Peter Baker explained earnestly, greedily shoveling a forkful of apple pie into his mouth before continuing to talk. He had a thick black beard, and pieces of pastry kept falling and getting trapped in the hair. In fact, he was quite . . . *hirsute*. His shirt was unbuttoned at the top, and a thick carpet of hair trailed up from the collar to meet the beard hairs in his neck. That, combined with the mop of overlong hair on his head, gave him a distinctly ursine appearance.

And while some women might find that appealing, Lia imagined what it would be like to kiss him with all that hair on his face. She kept picturing it getting into her mouth and stuck between her teeth. Ugh, what if she swallowed a stray hair? She shuddered and could barely concentrate on what he was saying. Which was probably a blessing, since he hadn't stopped talking about his mother all evening.

"Do you like cooking?" he suddenly asked, and Lia blinked, tuning back into the conversation. It had been a while since he'd asked her something.

"What?"

"Cooking. Do you cook?"

"Yes. I enjoy it."

"You should get my mother to give you her chocolate cake recipe. It's the best. Maybe you can bake a cake for me sometime. But only after you get the recipe from my mother."

Right. Where was Thandiwe, the waitress, with that check? Lia was about ready to leave.

"I make a pretty decent chocolate cake myself," she said.

"I'm sure it's nice," he said, blatant dismissal in his voice. "But my mother has this special way of mixing the batter that makes it unbeatable. She won a baking competition with that cake."

Lia made a show of looking at her watch.

"Oh wow, it's getting pretty late. I should get home. I have work in the morning."

"Really? I thought you were unemployed. Truthfully, I would prefer a woman who stayed home after we have kids. My mother will help raise them, of course."

"I work at the preschool on Tuesdays and Fridays," Lia said frostily, offended that this guy wanted her to stay at home with his future kids and his mother. It took her a moment to recognize that it was pretty much in line with the life she had once desperately wanted. Now—and not because she found Peter Baker and his unknown mother completely unlikable—she couldn't imagine staying home permanently. She admired women who did and would happily take years off to spend with her children, but she would always want to go back to teaching.

"You do? Nina didn't mention that." Her friend Nina Clark had reluctantly set her up with Peter. Pretty much at Lia's insistence. She had warned Lia that he probably wasn't the guy she was looking for. But Nina had once, ages ago, mentioned her boyfriend's single friend Peter, and Lia had called her this morning and asked her to set up a blind date with the man. Next time she'd listen to her friends when they told her a guy wasn't for her. Nina would only give her a resounding "I told you so" when she heard about this disastrous evening.

"It's not common knowledge yet. I plan to become a fully qualified preschool teacher, and the job will eventually become permanent." Part of her really hoped he'd realize that the schools were closed and clue in to the fact that he was being brushed off.

"Will you give it up when you start popping out babies?" he asked crassly, and Lia fortified herself with a gulp of wine and shook her head.

"No. Anyway, it's really late. I have to get home. Thank you so much for a lovely evening, but I don't think we have much in common. So we probably won't be seeing each other again." She summoned Thandiwe over, and the young woman, who had been waiting for her signal, astutely guessing that Lia would want to make a break for it, hastened over with the bill.

"Thanks, Thandiwe," she said gratefully. The woman was very familiar with the McGregor sisters—she'd been interning at their father's practice for the last few years and would be leaving for college soon to study veterinary medicine. She only rarely worked shifts at MJ's anymore, concentrating on her studies instead, but Lia was grateful that she was here tonight. She'd been hovering for most of the night, clearly not caring much for Peter Baker.

They split the bill.

"I'll walk you to your car," Peter said, and Lia shook her head. Seriously? How could this guy be so thick-skinned? She'd just told him they wouldn't be seeing each other again.

"No, that's fine. You go ahead. Thandiwe works with my father, and I need to get something from her for him."

"I can wait," he said.

"Oh yes, I have Inkululeko's dog vaccination charts for you," Thandiwe said, catching on quickly. "I have to ask you to wait five minutes, though. I just need to take table ten's order."

"Yes, of course, no problem," Lia said with a smile. "I need to use the restroom."

He still didn't budge.

"Thandiwe, do you have a, uh . . . *sanitary* towel for me, please? I didn't bring any," Lia asked in a not quite lowered voice. In fact, her voice had just enough volume to swivel a few heads at the tables closest to theirs. But these were desperate times. She fought back a blush and ignored Peter, who shifted uncomfortably at her question.

"Oh, no sanitary towels," Thandiwe said regretfully. "Only tampons, I'm afraid."

"Oh, great, that's . . ."

"Anyway, good night," Peter said, surging to his feet. "I'll call you in the morning."

He left without looking back, and Lia face-palmed while Thandiwe burst into laughter.

"Oh, good grief! I thought he was *never* going to leave," Lia lamented, which only made Thandiwe laugh louder. "I didn't want him to walk me to my car, I figured he'd try to kiss me."

"He had food in his beard," Thandiwe said, wrinkling her nose in disgust.

"I *know.*"

"Wait five minutes before leaving. Did you park right outside?"

"Yes, within sight of the door."

"I'll walk you to the door and watch you leave," Thandiwe suggested, and Lia grinned.

"Thanks, Thandiwe, you've been an absolute star."

⁓

She was in bed when her phone rang. A look at the screen confirmed that it was Brand.

"Brand. It's late. I'm trying to get some sleep."

"It's barely ten. I'm surprised you're at home already. Spencer mentioned that you had a date tonight."

"Why are you and Spencer discussing—" Lia bit off the rest of the sentence and sighed. "You know what? Never mind. If you thought I'd still be out on my date, why are you calling me?"

Silence.

"Brand? Why are you calling?"

"I was just checking if you were okay."

"I'm fine."

"I've seen all kinds of shit, Lia. I know what kind of dangerous losers are out there."

"He was hardly dangerous," Lia scoffed.

"But he *was* a loser?" he guessed astutely, and Lia grimaced.

"He lives with his mother."

"You live with your parents," he pointed out, and she laughed. Acknowledging the hit. Her comment had been hypocritical.

"I have plans to move out. He wants his mother to move in with us after we get married."

"Wait, why are you discussing marriage with some arsehole you just met?" Brand asked, his voice dangerously low.

"Maybe it was love at first sight?" she suggested lightly. More silence. This time it thundered.

"How old is he?" Brand asked, ending the loaded silence.

"Thirty-nine. He's an electrical engineer. He expects his wife to stay home and take care of the kids. His mom will help out, of course. He likes her cooking, so his wife will have to learn her recipes. He's allergic to all animal fur. Even bird dander. So absolutely no pets. He likes a woman who takes care of her figure and who keeps her hair and nails—"

"*Stop*, for God's sake! Don't tell me you'll be seeing this fucker again!"

"Not likely," she said, laughing. "He wants this perfect wife but can't even be bothered to keep his beard neat or wear a clean shirt on a date. And I plan to teach—it's not something I'm willing to give up again. Not for anyone."

"Sunshine, you're turning me on with all this delicious assertiveness. I may be developing a librarian dominatrix fantasy right as we speak."

"Shut *up*," Lia said, rolling her eyes but smiling despite herself. "Now if you don't mind, I'd like to get some sleep."

"You could come over and sleep next to me."

"For heaven's sake, Brand!"

"So that's a no?"

"You know it is. Good night."

"'Night, sunshine. See you in the morning."

Paul West chewed with his mouth open . . . but that wasn't the deal breaker. Chewing with an open mouth she could handle; watching bits of food being masticated was tolerable. She really wasn't that picky. After the first civil half hour, she had relaxed and sent Billie Greenspan, the friend who had organized this particular date with one of her boyfriend's cricketing buddies, a thumbs-up emoji. But that had been before the first course had been ordered, when Paul West had smiled sweetly and been charming. Before he had started chewing with his mouth open and *before* he had started in on his very favorite subject of conversation.

". . . but I told that bitch, I *told* her, if she takes the dog, I'd take her to court so fast her head would spin. No, seriously, she thinks she can cheat on me with that Neanderthal and then get the dog? She can fucking think again!" Yes, what Lia couldn't quite handle was the conversation.

"You must really love the dog." Lia managed to get a word in edgewise. He liked animals—that was something, wasn't it? Plus, he was a good dresser: nice tie and jacket. Passably good-looking. But—

"I fucking hate that little psychotic mutt. He bites any chance he gets. No, he's headed for the pound."

"But then why do you want him?" Lia was appalled and he shrugged, shoveling another forkful of food into his open mouth. He then started talking with his mouth full . . . *ugh*.

"Because she wants him, and *she* wants him because I want him. In truth, neither of us really wants the little bastard." The poor dog. Lia felt sorry for it, having two such selfish individuals for owners. "I have him at the moment. She had to get away for the weekend, she said. Told me if I was so desperate for the dog, I could keep him for a couple of days. But he's done nothing but whine and bark since I got him."

"Where is he now?"

"In the car."

"*What?* You can't leave a dog in the car for hours at a time."

"Yeah, maybe not in summer, but come on, it's not like he's going to die out there in this cool weather."

"Yes, but . . ."

"Don't tell me how to take care of my own dog, sister. Now, are we going to screw tonight or what?"

"Hey, Brand," Lia answered her phone with a despondent sigh an hour later.

"Bad?"

"Unbelievably bad. I didn't think they could get worse than the guy with the Oedipal thing going on, but this one . . . what a horrid individual. Hates his ex-wife but couldn't stop talking about her at all."

"Yeah?"

"And . . ." A whine interrupted what she'd been about to say, and she stared down into a pair of concerned eyes looking up at her from her lap.

"What's that sound?"

"That's Yappy the yorkie."

"What?"

"He asked me to look after his dog."

Well, his exact words had been *"If you're so fucking worried about the mongrel, you take him. I can't wait to tell that bitch I gave the little asshole away."*

"Wait, *what*? Your date asked you to look after his dog?"

"Well, he kind of stormed out, then came back in, said 'good riddance,' and dumped the dog in my arms before storming back out. Leaving me to take care of both the bill and Yappy."

"Jesus, Lia!"

"Tonight was a bit of a low point," she confessed on a whisper, her voice hitching as a tear trickled down her cheek.

"Oh, sunshine, I'm so sorry," he groaned. "Please don't cry, okay? This motherfucker isn't worth it."

"It's not that, it's just . . . I don't understand why I can't meet someone nice. It shouldn't be this hard. It was so easy before Clayton—I had so many romantic opportunities with lovely men. After three years away from the dating scene, it feels like the viable prospects in the pool of single men have mostly disappeared. Probably all happily married by now. And the only ones left are these horrible . . ." She stopped, shaking her head, and impatiently swiping at the tears with the heel of her free hand. She was annoyed with herself for allowing this to affect her so strongly. "I'm sorry. I'm being silly."

He groaned again.

"Please come over," he said, his voice raw.

"It's not a good idea. Good night, Brand."

"Lia . . ." She hung up on him before he could complete his sentence. Her phone buzzed seconds later, and she smiled when she looked at the screen and saw the kissy face emoji. She didn't reply, but for some reason, the silly little emoji made her feel slightly better.

~

Yappy was an instant hit with Lia's mother and became a welcome and immediately loved addition to the family's always-growing menagerie. Millicent McGregor hadn't had a special fur baby of her own in many years, but she and Yappy adopted each other at first sight. When Lia called Billie and told her what happened, her friend was both apologetic and livid at the same time.

Brand had sent her an early-morning text, asking if she was okay, and Lia had responded with just a thumbs-up emoji. After three embarrassing and disastrous dates in three nights, she was starting to miss her former arrangement with Brand. At least there was no uncertainty there. She knew what to expect from him and vice versa.

She sighed and got ready for dinner at Daisy and Mason's. The couple would be leaving in two days' time, and they were cramming as much family time in as they could.

~

Lia was looking forward to putting the last three nights out of her mind and spending an entertaining evening with her sisters and the Carlisles.

For some reason, it didn't occur to her that Brand would be there as well. But he was the one who opened the door for her, welcoming her with a huge smile.

"Hey, sunshine, you're looking beautiful as always." Lia looked down at her plain yellow dress and gray cardigan combination. She looked ordinary, but Brand definitely had a gleam in his eye while his gaze perused her from top to bottom.

"Uh, thanks. You look nice, too." That much was true. He was wearing a pair of jeans that were slightly loose on his thinner frame and a T-shirt with sneakers.

"When I heard you were going to be here, I made an effort to look good," he joked, and she smiled in response.

"What did you bring?" he asked nosily, taking the foil-covered bowl from her as he let her in. Daisy's tiny house—soon to be Lia's tiny rental—seemed overcrowded with everybody crammed in there. Their parents were in Knysna, enjoying a preplanned romantic date night, and weren't there to add to the chaotic throng.

"It's just a salad," she replied, and he lifted a corner of the foil to peer into the bowl.

"Fucking fantastic! Tomato and cucumber roses." Why did he sound so absolutely delighted by that fact?

"Some people actually appreciate my pointless pretty food," she said with a smile, inviting him to join in on the self-deprecating joke.

"I was a prick, Lia," he said, his voice alive with contrition. "I missed your little flowers the moment you stopped making them for me."

"Really?" He was having her on again. What a ridiculous and unnecessary lie to tell.

"I know you don't believe me, but yeah, really." How odd—he seemed sincere and Lia found herself actually believing him. He made a show of looking her over and then grinned.

"Where's your new little buddy?"

"What?" she asked, confused.

"The dog?"

"Oh! My mom fell in love with him, he's hers now. He's at home, she didn't want to leave him so soon after getting him, but she and our dad have been planning this evening for weeks. So he's in one of the spare rooms with some toys and treats."

"It may not have been under ideal circumstances for you, but he's lucky he found his way to your family."

"Thank you," she said self-consciously before shifting her eyes from his and smiling at Daisy, who came over to give her a casual hug and a glass of white wine.

"Yay, you're here! Please, please, *please* get Daff out of my kitchen, I'm gone four months and she thinks she's a *chef*? She's burning something as we speak." Sure enough, the acrid smell of burned meat wafted toward them, and Lia laughed. Daff wasn't a great cook, but she couldn't accept being less than amazing at anything and was now on a mission to prove to herself and everybody else that she could create passably good meals.

Tonight's offering didn't smell passable or good, it just smelled inedible, and Lia, being the peacekeeper in the family, immediately made her way over to her older sister to ease her away from the stove.

Spencer was chatting with Mason and grinned as he watched Lia join Daff in the kitchen. The man knew better than to intervene.

Charlie had latched onto Brand and was peppering him with questions about some pop star or another. Thankfully not Laura Prentiss this time. If Lia never heard that woman's name again, it would be too soon. Brand was patiently answering the teen's questions, even though Lia was pretty sure the girl had asked him the exact same things on Sunday.

"What's cooking?" Lia asked, sipping her wine as she glanced down to see what Daff was slaving over. She tried not to cringe at the sight of the meat sticking to the bottom of the pot.

"Burned offerings," Daff said on a sigh.

"You giving up?"

"Yeah, not even you can save this, Lia. And Deedee's in a panic that I'm going to burn the house down."

"She's not," Lia said kindly, and then amended, "Well, not *really*."

Daff laughed and shook her head.

"Meh, I'd rather be drinking anyway," Daff said, taking a slurp of her red wine to prove her point. She shifted the pot off the heat and turned off the gas. She hooked her arm through Lia's and nodded toward Brand, who was still chatting with Charlie. "So I hear you've been out and about town with several different men. Does that mean the fling's over?"

"Yes." There was nothing more to add, really.

"That was pretty fast." The sheer astonishment on Daff's face made Lia uncomfortable.

"Says the woman who once had a three-night *thing* with Spencer."

"Well, that was different, wasn't it? There were feelings developing between us. The no-strings-sex thing didn't suit the parameters of our changing relationship."

"It doesn't matter, Brand and I are done. It was fun, but it's over now. I thought I'd start dating again and spend more time on my studies. I have to hand in a couple of assignments when the semester begins again."

"And you're okay?" Lia considered the question. Was she okay? Yes, she was. In fact, her fling with Brand had been less stressful and humiliating than her foray back into the dating pool. Okay, so getting sexually involved with a man on a casual basis was very far away from normal for her, but she found Sam Brand incredibly attractive. And more than that, she *liked* him. And maybe she should stop trying to overanalyze every aspect of that attraction and just enjoy it.

"I'm fine," she said in response to Daff's concerned question, while her eyes sought Brand out again. She considered his dishonesty about his relationship with Laura Prentiss and her visceral reaction to him lying about it. She had been angry, but that anger had been out of proportion to the nature of their relationship. She was the one who had put a moratorium on conversations of a personal nature, and, whatever his relationship with the pop star, it was personal. And when he'd tried to tell her it was none of her business, she'd taken offense. Taken offense when he'd chosen to implement one of her own rules.

Her mind switched to thoughts of his concern for her over the last few days, his phone calls and texts, his genuine supportiveness last night, and the interest he still had in her. And she concluded that maybe it wouldn't be so bad to grab this non-relationship with Brand with both hands and just run with it.

"Hey! Lia! You still with us?"

"What?" Lia shook her head and looked at Daff, who was snapping her fingers in front of Lia's face. "Oh, sorry. I was thinking."

"About?"

"I have plenty of free time for studying. And I can always go back to dating later."

"What do you . . ." Daff began, then tracked Lia's line of sight to Brand, who was laughing at something Charlie had said. "Crap. Seriously? Lia, don't let him break your heart, okay?"

"Don't worry, sissy. This thing between Brand and me has a very limited time line. I'm well aware of that. My heart's under lock and key. But . . . I enjoy him. I don't see why I can't continue to enjoy him until he leaves."

"Oh *man*," she heard Daff breathe.

Lia smiled widely. Gosh, she felt light as a feather.

She was watching him again. Brand wasn't sure what to make of that. Lia had been staring at him all evening. She'd been generous with her smiles, too. Those beautiful, genuine smiles that he so enjoyed. When they finally sat down around the small, crowded dinner table, he found himself sitting between Lia and Charlie. He felt like he was sitting way, *way* too close to Lia. Her arm brushed against his every time she moved, and when she spoke with him, which was often, she leaned in close enough for him to breathe in her tantalizing scent and trapped his eyes with her beguiling gray stare. It was driving him insane. He was uncomfortably erect and trying very hard to keep his reaction hidden from the rest of the group.

When she touched his arm with her fingertips and he nearly jumped out of his skin, his reaction drew every eye at the table and Sam mumbled an apology, feeling his cheeks heat in the process.

"I just wanted you to pass the salt," Lia murmured into his ear, her voice husky with amusement. Her mouth was so close, he could feel her warm breath wash over his temple, and he swallowed down a groan.

She was fucking killing him.

She excused herself and sauntered off to the bathroom, and Sam bit back another groan as he watched the seductive sway of her hips. He felt a kick on his shins and identified the assailant as Daff. He glared at her and she glared back, raising her eyebrows meaningfully at the same time. He knew she was trying to warn him not to stare so blatantly at Lia.

His phone buzzed; he lifted it to glance down at the screen and nearly swallowed his tongue when he saw the message.

I miss your €====3!!

He blinked. Then gaped at the message for a long moment.

"Bad news, bru?" Mason asked in concern, and Sam immediately switched off the screen and dropped the phone facedown on the table.

"Uh, no. Just unexpected." His phone buzzed again, and he fumbled for it. He couldn't resist a quick glance and felt his face redden.

Do you miss my (|)?

What in God's name was she trying to do to him?

"Brand? What the fuck is going on with you?"

"Mason, language," Daisy reprimanded in a long-suffering voice, obviously knowing it wouldn't make a difference.

"Sorry, angel," Mason apologized, lifting Daisy's hand to his lips for a quick kiss.

"I, uh . . . ," Sam began to say, but his words stalled when Lia strolled back into the dining room, not betraying by a flicker of an eyelid what she'd been up to. Mason and Spencer, with that fucking old-fashioned courtesy of theirs, both stood up when Lia sat down. Sam lifted his butt an inch from his seat as a nod toward good manners before sitting down again. No way was he standing up in his current state.

"It's something that I'll be seeing to later," he continued pointedly, answering Mason's question and still not looking at Lia. She went back to her dinner like nothing was amiss.

"Anything I can help with?" Mason asked, and Sam choked on a sip of wine.

"No, thanks. I can definitely take care of it myself. Uh, Lia—" He dared a look at her and she met his eyes guilelessly, her eyebrows raised in question. "Mind passing the salt back, please? I missed the hell out of it."

"What a weird thing to miss," Charlie observed, and Lia coughed delicately, her face pinkening slightly as she caught his meaning.

"Not really," he said, smiling at Charlie. "I adore salt. Can't get enough of it. Could eat it for days."

This time it was Lia who choked on nothing but her spit, and Sam hid a grin as Charlie wrinkled her nose.

"That's really bad for your health," she said, concerned. "You can get high blood pressure, high cholesterol. Think of your heart and your kidneys."

"You're a smart kid. Don't worry, I understand that everything is better in moderation. No matter how tempted one is to overindulge."

The rest of dinner continued uneventfully. Lia thankfully kept her hands to herself, barely acknowledging him, while Sam manfully fought to get his erection under control. Thankfully, he was decent again by the time the meal ended and surreptitiously watched as Lia sat chatting and joking with her sisters and Charlie—inevitably discussing Daff and Spencer's pending nuptials—while the men cleaned up the kitchen.

She left a full half hour before the rest of the party disbanded, citing tiredness. Sam watched her leave, waited ten minutes, and finally took the opportunity to send her a message.

I want you. He knew the text lacked finesse, but he wasn't a sweet talker by nature. He had at least refrained from using the word *fuck* in the text. Which, for him, was as romantic as it got.

I know. He didn't have to wait long for that two-word response, and he glared at his phone screen, annoyed that she was being so fucking stingy with her words.

While he was glaring at the screen, another word popped up.

Soon.

The promise had him champing at the bit, and he waited impatiently while Spencer and Daff—his ride home—chatted their way through another drink. Charlie kept herself busy by taking selfies and random other pics for her Instagram account. Thankfully, she was respectful enough not to include Sam in her pictures. He didn't want anyone to know where he was spending his convalescence.

Sam tried not to show his impatience and kept up his end of the conversation, but he was relieved when Spencer playfully prodded Daff in her side and suggested they get a move on.

CHAPTER TWELVE

Lia had parked her car around back so that it wouldn't be visible to Spence and Daff when they dropped Brand off. She had let herself in, using the spare key that Mason and Daisy kept hidden under a loose brick on the porch step, and sat waiting in the dark, cold living room.

She heard the car drive up, and her heart sped up in excitement at the thought of seeing Brand again, of being with him, of touching him and being touched. She was trembling in anticipation.

Her phone buzzed, and she glanced down at the screen and smiled.

Get your gorgeous butt over here, sunshine. I fucking ache for you.

The front door opened, and she stood up. He didn't see her—his eyes were on his phone, waiting for her response.

"I ache for you, too." His head jerked up, and the living room light flashed on. She blinked rapidly as she tried to adjust to the sudden brightness. Before she knew it, she was in his arms and he was groaning and kissing her.

Deeply, passionately, and voraciously eating her mouth.

Neither of them said a word. She wore nothing beneath her coat, and when he pushed it down, he said a worshipful prayer of thanks before kissing and suckling her naked flesh. He was so familiar with what worked for her that he immediately homed in on her erogenous zones, and her knees buckled at the intense responses he was so good at drawing from her.

Before they knew it, they were lying on the thick rug in front of the cold hearth, entangled in each other's arms. His injured arm was still weak, but he was a more confident and masterful lover with the use of both arms and it gave her a taste of what was to come once he regained full use of the limb. For now, his right hand made up for its previous lack of participation by stroking and touching and playing with her nipples, her sensitive skin, her highly sensitized femininity. It was amazing, and he gifted her with two orgasms before he even got partially naked.

"Sunshine, I love the sounds you make when you come," he whispered against her lips. "Soft and breathless and desperate."

"Make me come again," she begged, her hands drifting down to his straining crotch. "Make me come with this."

He groaned, the sound low and frantic. He fumbled with his fly, his right hand still clumsy, and she reached out to help him with the task. His hot, hard length spilled into her hands, and she latched onto it, stroking it eagerly. He arched out of her touch.

"Sunshine, you're killing me. No touching for now, okay?"

She lifted her hands to his head instead and tugged him down for another kiss. And while their lips and tongues entangled, he entered her with one swift, deep stroke. Lia cried out against his mouth and raised her knees to cradle him closer.

"Oh, Brand," she moaned, and he stopped thrusting, holding himself still inside her. She sobbed and pushed herself up against him, wanting more.

"Sam," he muttered. "I want to hear it. Call me Sam." She was too desperate to give the command much thought, her entire being focused on his delicious heat inside her. She needed him to move, to give her what she was so frantic for, and she would do or say anything in this moment for the culmination she craved.

"Sam," she whispered, and he buried his face in her neck and thrust into her. "Sam." Another thrust.

"Oh my God, *Sam*."

He sobbed and thrust even deeper than before.

"Sam, please . . ." She bit into his shoulder, planted her feet on the floor, and lifted her hips to meet his thrusts. When she finally came, she screamed his name. A long, drawn-out cry. One syllable stretched out into nine.

Not Brand.

But *Sam*.

Sam couldn't catch his breath. He held Lia close, cradling her in his arms like she was the most precious thing in his life, and he felt like he was slowly asphyxiating, because he just couldn't fucking breathe.

He finally moved, leaving her wet warmth and automatically reaching down to discard the condom when he comprehended that there wasn't one. Which a) explained why the entire encounter had been so fucking amazing and intense and b) was completely unprecedented for him.

"Fuck," he swore vehemently. "Fuck, fuck, *fuuuuck*!"

"What's wrong?" she asked groggily, sitting up and pushing her messy hair out of her face.

"I forgot the condom." She gasped softly at his revelation.

"I thought things felt a bit . . . damper than usual," she said tactfully. "Um. I don't have anything to worry about, do I?"

"What?" He was still a bit dazed, and it took him a moment to register her question. "Jesus. *No.* Of course not. I'm sorry. I was tested for everything when I was in the hospital. All clear. And you've been my only partner since last November."

"Oh. Well, I've never had a partner other than Clayton," she confessed. "And he always used a condom. I did have tests after our breakup, because I wasn't sure how much I could trust him."

"So that only leaves, uh . . . the *other* thing." God, this was awkward, especially when she stared at him with those innocent gray eyes.

"Other thing?"

"You know? Pregnancy?" She inhaled sharply, and her hands automatically flew to her tummy in a protective gesture. Oddly, the instinctive movement elicited an unmistakable wrench of possessiveness in Sam.

"Pregnancy?" she mused, her eyes bright. "A baby? Imagine that, a little blond boy or girl. Probably stubborn and charming in equal measure."

Sam swallowed, trying to ease the dryness in his throat and mouth as he envisioned said child. A little brown-haired girl with gray eyes and a beautiful smile. She would be a sweet little thing, always laughing and . . .

He shook his head violently. What the fuck was wrong with him? Why the hell was he picturing babies?

"Of course, I won't expect you to be involved or anything. Don't worry. I can raise him or her myself."

Over my dead body! He felt himself glowering in response to her claim, pissed off that she would automatically exclude him from his kid's life. He was about to vehemently tell her that she would do no such thing when she lifted a hand to her mouth and giggled.

"Oh my gosh, the look on your face!" He stared at her, confused. Maybe she was hysterical at the prospect of an unplanned pregnancy. He couldn't believe he'd been so careless. He never forgot the condom—well, aside from that time in the barn with her, but that had been a fraught encounter and he'd remembered the condom after only a few strokes. This time . . . okay, this time had been fraught as well. But still, this was fucking inexcusable. He found himself considering all possibilities. He would take care of her. Despite her claims that he didn't have to. If she was pregnant, she and the baby were his responsibility, he would—

"Brand, I'm on the pill." His thoughts came to a screeching halt at her revelation, and it took a moment for him to process her words.

"What?"

"The pill." He didn't know why, but the information startled him.

"You are?"

"Yes, I went on it a week before my wedding date in a futile attempt to stave off a wedding-day period. I found it convenient to stay on the pill after that. It kept my cycle regular."

"Why didn't you mention it before now?"

"Well, I figured—considering the nature of our relationship—that it would be best for us to continue using condoms. I'm sorry, I shouldn't have teased you. I just couldn't resist. You looked terrified. I feel kind of bad now."

Terrified? Far from it. Stunned by his own carelessness, maybe. Overwhelmed by the notion that a whole new person could result from that carelessness and a steely resolve to be part of said new person's life if it came to that.

What *had* terrified him was the inexplicable pang of disappointment he felt when the possibility of that baby had disappeared with just a few words.

He watched Lia gather her coat and push herself up from the floor. She was getting ready to leave.

"Stay," he whispered, getting up as well. She paused in the act of shrugging into the coat and stared at him for a long moment.

"No."

"Lia, we have to rethink these guidelines of yours."

"Agreed. We can discuss them tomorrow and find a list that works for both of us, but this one rule remains sacrosanct. No sleeping over, Brand."

"I'd prefer it if you called me Sam."

"Why?"

"Because it's my name."

"So's Brand. Mason calls you Brand."

"You're not Mason."

"How am I different from Mason?"

"I'm not sleeping with Mason, for starters."

"You're not sleeping with me, either."

"Fine. *Jesus!* I'm not fucking Mason. Look, call me Sam, okay? I just . . . I like it more."

"If it means that much to you, you should tell Daisy and Mason to use Sam. You shouldn't be called Brand if you dislike it. I'll tell—"

"Christ, Lia. I don't give a fuck what name they use. I like it when *you* call me Sam." He watched her process the words, chewing the inside of her cheek as she considered what he'd said.

"Okay," she decided. "Sam."

"Thanks."

"I'll be around tomorrow morning to fix your breakfast," she informed him.

"You don't have to do that."

"I know," she said easily. "But I want to."

She walked toward the door and Sam watched her go, frustrated that she wouldn't stay.

"Lia, don't get me wrong . . . I love that we're back on the coitus carousel, but why did you change your mind about us? Was it because of the shitty dates?" he asked before she reached for the doorknob. She turned to face him, leaning back against the door as she considered his words.

"Not really, it was mostly because I want this. And I was talking myself out of having it because it didn't suit the image I had of the Dahlia McGregor I should be."

"And which Dahlia McGregor is that?"

"The same Dahlia who saved herself for the man she was supposed to marry." She shook her head and laughed self-deprecatingly, the sound ending on that little snort he was growing to like more and more. "And look how that turned out. Not the engagement, but the actual intimate act. Clayton was . . . unsatisfactory, to say the least. A fast fumbler. And then he blamed my lack of enthusiasm on me. If I'd gone through with the wedding, uh . . . *sex* would have remained a disappointment to me. I would never have known how much better it could be."

She hesitated and blushed before saying *sex*. Still so shy about verbalizing certain words when she seemed so comfortable sending naughty texts to him. Not to mention how expressive she was during sex. He found that idiosyncrasy positively adorable.

"It made me think, and I recognized that I don't want to go back to being that willfully ignorant Dahlia McGregor again. I like what we do together. I understand that it's temporary, and I intend to enjoy it while it lasts. Without guilt or shame."

"What about my lie about Lally? You were pretty pissed off about it."

"I was being a total hypocrite. I told you that personal conversations were off-limits and then I got irritated with you for not divulging the truth about your personal business. I don't like being lied to, but it was none of my business in the first place. As long as you're not cheating on someone and making me an accomplice in that act. I wouldn't stand for that."

"So we're flinging again?"

"Until you get sick of me, or I get sick of you, or you leave. Whichever comes first."

"One day, when you meet the man of your dreams, you won't regret having a wild, crazy fuckfest with me, will you?"

She winced at the description, and Sam grinned unrepentantly.

"Nope. He should be thankful that I've gained useful experience that will contribute toward his pleasure in the bedroom."

The thought of Lia in bed with someone else had the immediate power to wipe every trace of humor away, and Sam attempted to conceal his overwhelmingly negative reaction from her.

"But like I said," she continued, "I doubt there's a man of my dreams out there. I'm pursuing other goals right now."

"Don't let a few fucked-up dates put you off, sunshine. If you don't wind up married with kids down the line, I'd be surprised. Any guy would be lucky to have you, Lia."

"Thank you for saying that, Sam. But I've decided it's not that important anymore. Like I said, other goals." She considered her words and knew that they were the absolute truth. Her obsession with finding the right man and living the perfect life was waning with every step she took down this unknown path with Sam. Her self-worth was no longer tied up in being Mrs. Somebody. It was all about Dahlia McGregor and the life she was creating for herself. She pushed herself away from the door. "I'll see you in the morning. Good night."

She was gone before he could get his own *good night* out.

⁓

The following morning, she was already in the kitchen when he came downstairs wearing his running clothes.

"Morning, sunshine," he greeted, his voice still thick with sleep. He came up behind her and hooked an arm around her waist, pulling her back to his front and dropping a kiss into the cove of her neck. Lia reached up and cupped his jaw, tilting her head to allow him greater access to her neck.

"Morning. Your breakfast will be ready in half an hour."

"I wanted to take a quick run, think you can push it to forty-five minutes?"

"Yes. Don't overdo it."

"I won't, need to save some of my energy for you." He gave her an additional hug, stepped away, and spared a little squeeze for one of her breasts before heading out the back door.

Lia sighed and went upstairs to make up his bed and tidy up the place a bit before she started his breakfast. But she looked at the mess for a moment and snorted.

Yeah, right, she *so* wasn't his maid. This inclination she had to tidy up after others had to stop. She might as well put that new resolve into practice now. Food was one thing—she wouldn't want the guy to get malnourished, and she enjoyed cooking. But fixing other people's messes? That was about to stop right now.

He returned close to an hour later, looking hot and sweaty and so unutterably sexy that Lia could do nothing but stare for a long moment.

"Sorry it took so long, I ran into Mason in town and we got to talking. Did I ruin breakfast?"

"Uh-uh, I haven't started it yet. You grab a shower and I'll fix something."

"Thanks, sunshine." He grinned. "You're joining me for breakfast, right?"

"I've eaten."

"I prefer having breakfast with you."

"I'll have a cup of coffee while you eat. We need to talk anyway."

"That never bodes well," he said with a frown, and she grinned.

"You're the one who wanted to rethink the guidelines," she reminded, and his face cleared.

"Definitely. I'll be down in a jiff." Lia bit back a grin at the quintessentially English expression.

He was down in less than ten minutes, wearing a pair of jeans and a gray Henley. He smelled amazing—she loved his woodsy aftershave—his hair was damp and his jaw freshly shaved. The hollows in his face were starting to fill out, and he was looking healthier and handsomer every day.

"What's for breakfast?" he asked, squeezing her butt on his way to the table. He sat down, folded his hands on the tabletop, and watched her expectantly.

"Pancakes," she said. She put the stack of pancakes in front of him and was gratified by the delighted smile that lit up his face.

"How did you do this?" he asked, his voice filled with boyish wonder. "They look like snowflakes. They're amazing."

He couldn't stop staring at the lacy pancakes she had so painstakingly made for him, and Lia was happy that she'd gone to the effort.

"What other patterns can you make?"

"The options are pretty limited when it comes to design. I can make snowflakes, hearts, these round doily-type ones, flowers. I keep experimenting to see what other designs I can come up with. But they can be pretty disastrous at times."

"They're perfectly golden, how do you manage that? I burn the edges even on normal pancakes."

"Practice. They taste good, too," she said pointedly, pushing a bowl of freshly cut fruit toward him. "So dig in."

"It seems a shame to eat them."

"They were made to be eaten," she encouraged, taking a sip of coffee and watching him over the rim as he poured syrup on his pancakes and then added the fresh fruit. She held her breath when he scooped the first forkful into his mouth and released it when his eyes closed involuntarily. That was a good sign.

"This is so fucking good," he said, his mouth full.

“Glad to hear it,” she said and watched him devour the rest in very little time. After a contented sigh, he finally put his fork down and reached for his coffee.

“So . . . guidelines,” he said.

“What were your thoughts?”

“You know I want you to sleep over.”

“Nope. That one’s not negotiable.”

“Well, if I can’t have that, then I want to be able to talk about shit.”

“What kind of stuff?”

“All kinds. Whatever strikes our fancy. Nothing is off-limits.”

“It seems foolish.”

“I don’t think so.”

“Fine. Although I’d like it stated, for the record, that I think this is unwise.”

“Noted. No more dates while we’re together.”

“Ugh, no. I’m off that for a while.”

“And . . . I’d also like to snuggle after sex.”

“*No!* Why?” she asked, completely horrified at the notion.

“Because you’re cuddly and because it’s relaxing.”

“I didn’t take you for a cuddler.”

“There’s a lot you don’t know about me,” he pointed out smugly.

There’s a lot I don’t know about me, either, Sam conceded to himself. Such as the fact that he enjoyed a snuggle after sex—where the fuck had that load of bullshit come from? He wasn’t a snuggler. He was a retreat-to-his-own-side-of-the-bed-immediately-after-orgasm kind of guy. Good sex was hot and sticky and disturbingly moist. Not ideal circumstances during which to snuggle up with somebody.

Maybe he just wanted to fuck with her guidelines, and since there was already one he couldn't touch and the others made sense, this was the only other one he could change.

He watched her shoulders lift as she sighed.

"Fine. But once again, I don't think it's a great idea."

"Stop worrying so much, sunshine, we'll be fine." She smiled at his appeasing words, but she didn't look at all convinced. "Now, what will we do today? A long, lazy Sunday stretching ahead of us endlessly. So many options. We could fuck in the kitchen. Maybe in the living room? Definitely the shower, you owe me a shower shag. Then we could . . ."

"Sorry to throw a wrench in your big plans there, mister," she interrupted lightly. "But it's Daisy and Mason's last day in Riversend, so *I'll* be spending the day with my family. Knowing how they feel about you, I've no doubt I'll see you there."

"Can we at least do the shower thing?" he asked wistfully, and she grinned before cupping his jaw with her hands, leaning over to kiss him.

"Tonight, I promise."

"Lia, I'm glad we're doing this again. I've missed you."

"You've seen me every day." She laughed, and he grimaced.

"You know what I mean," he said gruffly, looking almost embarrassed, and Lia nodded.

"I know. I've missed you, too."

Daisy and Mason left the following morning. The family all gathered at the farm, before work and school, for an early breakfast before the couple hit the road. Lia, Daff, and their mother finalized some plans to meet Daisy in Cape Town in a month's time for a weekend of bridesmaid and wedding dress shopping. Then, sooner than anyone would have liked, the couple and their dogs were on the road back to Grahamstown again.

"Spence and I have to get to work," Daff said, her voice curt but husky with unshed tears. "Brand, we'll drive you back to the cabin."

"Don't you have to drop Charlie off at school?" Sam asked, his eyes moving to the young girl, who was already in her school uniform.

"It'll be tight, but we can do both," Daff said.

"I'll drop him off, no need for you guys to rush around like that," Lia said, and Daff's eyebrows rose.

"Oh, how *accommodating* of you, Lia," Daff said, her voice alive with sarcasm. And Lia's eyes narrowed.

"I aim to please," Lia said with a bland smile.

"I'm sure you do," Daff said smoothly, and Spencer rolled his eyes before taking her elbow.

"Thanks, Lia, 'preciate it," he muttered. "Let's go, darling."

Lia and Sam left soon after Daff and Spencer.

"I'm off to the retirement home later. You joining me?" Lia asked while they were en route to the cabin.

"What time?"

"In about an hour or so," she said, and he made an approving sound in the back of his throat.

"Want to work off that huge breakfast?" he asked playfully, and she laughed. She had to admit flinging with Sam was surprisingly fun and stress-free. She loved his body and what he could do with it and enjoyed his company. He was a great guy. He was also an expert cuddler—immediately after sex last night he had gathered her into his arms and tucked her close.

Lia had fallen asleep during their first postsex snuggle session. And he hadn't awoken her. Luckily she had slept only an hour and then, despite his protests that it was too late for her to leave, had gone home. She had to be careful not to do that again.

Her parents had eyed her speculatively this morning, but neither of them questioned her whereabouts. As long as she let them know she was safe. Thankfully, she would be moving into Daisy's house on the weekend and would no longer have to feel like a teenager creeping upstairs on bare feet.

"Well, you *did* miss your run this morning," Lia said in response to Sam's question. "You'll need the exercise."

"I can always count on you to have my best interests at heart," he quipped.

"Of course, I'm selfless like that," she retorted with a serene smile, and he chuckled, tugging at her hair.

"Get us to the cabin quickly, sunshine. I don't want to waste a second more in this car than we have to."

"You're a great dancer. I didn't take you for the sort of guy who could fox-trot," Lia said after they left the retirement home later that morning, and Sam grinned.

"Considering all the dance classes my mom made me take when I was a kid, it would be a disgrace if I didn't at least know the fox-trot."

"Dance classes? How long did you have to take them?" Lia asked, intrigued by that morsel of information. She had to admit, lifting the ban on personal conversations was proving to be fascinating. Especially when he revealed such diverting snippets about himself.

"From nine years old to sixteen. I was pretty proficient by the time I quit. Junior ballroom champion three years in a row. If I'm going to do something, I like to do it right. It helped that the girls were pretty and often wore leotards and tights."

"Did you?" she asked wickedly.

"Did I what?"

"Wear leotards and tights?"

"Of course I did." He nodded, then in typically arrogant fashion added, "I fucking rocked those tights. The girls couldn't get enough of my muscled thighs and manly bulge."

"Why did you stop?" she asked, ignoring his last comment.

"Well, I didn't want to be a professional dancer, so I didn't see the point in continuing. My mother enrolled me in the class because she thought it was a good skill for a *young gentleman* to have. My mother loves dancing. She's great at it—she competed at a semiprofessional level for a few years. When she was between partners, she liked me to escort her to some of the high-end parties she often attended. And that meant not embarrassing her on the dance floor." He grinned before continuing, "She'd inevitably meet her next man at one of those parties."

Lia still couldn't get over his easy acceptance of his mother's constantly changing male companions. But she found it quite charming how much he seemed to adore his mother.

"You and your mother seem close," she observed.

"Well, due to the transient nature of her relationships, in the end it always boiled down to just the two of us. I won't say she was the ideal mother, she's a little too neurotic for that, but she was fun, lovable, and supportive."

"But how did you cope without a stable home life?"

"My mother *was* my stability. As long as she and I were together, we were home." Lia pondered that answer for a moment. It was an incredibly sweet sentiment and completely melted her heart.

"So how are things going with Trevor?" she asked, deliberately changing the subject.

"He's awesome. He's been taking treats from me more regularly, and they're moving his usual walk time today so that I can take him for a stroll. Apparently his on-leash skills are pretty terrible, and because of his temperament and his lack of discipline they've had trouble controlling him. Dr. Gunnerson-Smythe wants to see if I'll have more luck with him."

"You've already done wonders with him, Sam," Lia said.

"I think he's going to make someone an amazing pet someday. He just needs some time to learn to trust."

Lia smiled, fighting to keep the concern from her eyes. Trevor was learning to trust Sam, and she was very worried that once Sam left, the dog would regress. She knew that everybody at the shelter thought that Sam would wind up adopting Trevor, which was why they allowed him so much leeway with the dog. Lia wasn't sure if she should intervene.

"Do you think maybe he's becoming too attached to you?" she asked tentatively, and he went quiet.

"He needs help," he said, his voice cooling significantly. "I'm helping."

"But—"

"He's better off now than he was when I first got here. That's amazing progress in just a month. Way I see it, that's a good thing."

"I'm just a bit concerned that he'll backslide when you leave."

"He'll be fine," Sam insisted.

He was out of the car seconds after she parked at the animal shelter.

"See you later, sunshine," he promised before rushing off to see Trevor. He barely limped at all anymore, recovering some of the sexy, pantherlike grace that she remembered from their first meeting.

She followed him into the building at a slower pace, her thoughts still in turmoil. For now, she would leave him to work with Trevor. She hoped that he would get the dog to a point where Trevor would start to trust others as well.

The move into Daisy's quaint little house right on the edge of town was much smoother than Lia had anticipated. It helped that the house was fully furnished and that Lia had little furniture of her own to move. The depressing fact was that she had managed to pack up thirty-two years of her life in just a few boxes. Seeing her scant personal possessions made Lia more determined than ever to remain on this path of positivity and growth.

She enjoyed the sense of purpose her studies gave her and loved her few hours at the preschool during the week. She eagerly soaked in everything Aisha and the other teachers told her and taught her. Because she was trying to balance her time between studying and Sam, she had reduced her time at the library and the homeless shelter. She didn't want to give up the senior dances and the animal shelter, so she had been forced to choose which projects would get less of her time. She comforted herself with the knowledge that she would pick up the slack again after Sam left.

Her eyes strayed to where he was sharing a pizza with Spencer in the living room of Daisy's—*Lia's*—house. She found herself staring at him all the time. Because of his daily run, he had all but lost the sickbed pallor, his skin taking on the healthy golden tone of before. He was also starting to fill out his clothes better, and over the last week she had felt the difference in his body and in his strength during their lovemaking . . . Her thoughts crashed to an abrupt halt at that word.

Lovemaking?

Don't you start using words like love *in relation to Sam Brand, you idiot,* she berated herself harshly.

She tore her eyes away from his handsome, laughing face and went back to unpacking the boxes Spencer and Sam had carried into the house for her earlier. Essentially, aside from her electronics, bedding, and few knickknacks here and there, the boxes contained mostly clothes, books, and framed photos.

"You should have kept your wedding presents," Daff said as she stood with her hands on her hips, surveying the sad collection of small to medium-size boxes.

"That would have been so tacky," Lia scoffed.

Daff scrounged through one of the boxes, squealed, and extracted a gigantic green dildo.

"Oh my *God*, remember this?" she asked, giggling. And Lia went scarlet.

"Put that away! Charlie's in the backyard!" The girl was playing fetch with Toffee.

"I've seen her biology textbook—girl knows what a penis looks like."

"I remember that thing," Spencer said, his voice amused. "Someone gave it to you at your hen night. I remember telling Mason that it looks like the Hulk's cock."

Lia made a grab for it, but Daff held it above her head and the silicone member jiggled in her grip.

"*Why* do you still have this, Dahlia McGregor, you bad, bad girl?"

"Why *do* you still have that?" Sam repeated, before adding, "It's not like you need it."

"Oh my gosh, you all are irritating me so much right now," Lia complained, and Daff chortled in glee.

"Did you keep the other stuff?" Daff pressed.

"What other stuff?" Sam asked, his voice alive with curiosity.

"Fuzzy handcuffs, right, Lia?" Daff prompted. "Crotchless panties, edible condoms, and a crapload of other stuff."

"I didn't," Lia admitted uncomfortably.

"Pity," Sam said, and she glared at him.

"If you got rid of the rest, why keep this?" Daff pressed, shaking the dildo for emphasis.

"Have you ever tried getting rid of something like that?" Lia finally asked, exasperated. "I couldn't chuck it out at home—what if Daddy saw it in the trash can? And what if someone spotted me throwing it away in town? You know how the homeless guys always scavenge in the garbage! And they all know me from the shelter. And what trash do I throw it in anyway? Is it recyclable? In the end, it was easier to just keep it."

"You should really stop overthinking everything, sunshine," Sam said, his voice gentle.

"Easy for you to say, *you* don't care about your reputation."

"I do," he corrected quietly. "I have a professional reputation to maintain. An expected image to project for the sake of my business. I care about that."

"Of course," Lia said, contrite. "I'm sorry. My comment was uncalled for."

"Daff, would you mind putting that thing away?" Spencer pleaded, his eyes on the dildo in Daff's grip. "It's making me uncomfortable."

"Uncomfortable?" she repeated, her eyes sparking with interest. "In what way?"

Spencer cast an awkward glance at Sam and Lia before shifting his eyes to meet Daff's again. Whatever she saw in his gaze actually made her blush and she cleared her throat before, with a wicked grin at Spencer, giving the sex toy one last squeeze and dropping it back in the box.

Fortunately, the subject was dropped along with the dildo, and after finishing the pizza, Daff and Spencer were ready to leave. They called Charlie and offered Sam a lift home.

"I think I'll stay a little longer. I'm sure Lia wouldn't mind giving me a ride home in exchange for my help." Daff glanced at Charlie, and Lia knew the girl was the only reason her sister refrained from calling BS on his words. Daff was a straight shooter and liked to call a spade a spade. She settled for rolling her eyes to let him know exactly what she thought of his words.

"I thought they'd never leave," Sam said, his voice husky with desire, as they waved the car off a short while later. "I think we should christen every room in this house tonight."

"It's only three rooms, really, since the kitchen and living room are open plan," Lia babbled and then yelped when he dropped his hand on her butt and squeezed.

"Living room sofa and kitchen counter. They're separate rooms to me."

He positioned himself in front of her, dropping his free hand to her other butt cheek and squeezing and lifting her behind until her crotch was in line with his.

"We have a lot to get done tonight, Lia," he said sternly. "Let's not dawdle."

In the end they managed living room, kitchen, shower, and bed. They now lay sprawled, naked and exhausted on top of the bedcovers, both on their backs and staring up at the ceiling. Lia was on his left, her head tucked into the nook between his shoulder and arm, one hand resting on his flat, ridged abdomen and the other pillowing her cheek on his shoulder. His arm was hooked around her shoulders, and his fingers were idly tracing up and down her side, from the swell of her breast to the dip of her waist and back, and his other arm was draped across his stomach and with his hand over hers.

Aside from explicit instructions from both of them about what felt good where, they hadn't really spoken since the shower and were both content to just lie in companionable silence for the moment.

"I had an imaginary puppy once," he admitted, his voice even more gravelly than usual.

"What was his name?" Lia asked softly.

"Rex. I was six, so no points for imagination. I can't remember much about him—my mother said he was my best friend for nearly a year, and when she divorced husband number four, I cried for days because we'd moved out and I was heartbroken because we'd left Rex behind."

Lia frowned and stroked his chest, wondering why he was telling her this. Her heart broke for the confused little boy who had lost his only friend but she wasn't sure how to respond to his words.

"My mother offered to buy me a *real* puppy after that, but I refused. I was scared that the next time we moved that dog would be left behind, too."

"I see," Lia murmured.

"I'm very busy with work," he said, and the non sequitur made her blink in surprise. "Even when I'm not in the field, I spend long hours in the office. I can't have a dog. I know you think I should adopt Trevor." It was the first time he'd ever used the dog's real name. "But I can't. He'd spend too much time alone. My hope is that he'll learn to trust others through me and find that special someone who'll be willing to take him into their heart."

Now she wondered if he was referring only to the dog, or if his words were a gentle reminder to Lia not to get too attached.

"I'm sure he will," she said, keeping her voice low and soothing. "You've worked wonders with him, Sam."

"Lia—"

"I should get you home," she interrupted, not wanting to hear him expand his confessional to include his relationship with her.

"I could stay."

"No, you can't, Sam."

"For fuck's sake, Lia. We'll just be sleeping in the same bed, it's not a big deal."

"It is to me. Maybe *you're* used to spending the night with just any woman, but to me, sleeping with someone is more intimate than just having sex with them. It's . . . it's . . ." Her voice trailed off, and she wasn't quite sure how to express her feelings on the matter. "It means more to sleep with someone. We're having fun, and I don't want it to be more than fun. I don't want it to mean more."

He sighed, the sound rife with frustration, and levered himself out of bed. His movements were graceful and an indication of just how much better he was. He would be leaving soon, that much was evident. He was healing by leaps and bounds, and she was sure he wouldn't be staying for the entirety of his three-month convalescence. He'd be gone in a matter of mere weeks, and it was important for her to keep sight of that.

This last week with him had been wonderful. They'd spent as much time together as possible; she never got tired of his body, and he never seemed to grow bored with her, either. Every time they were intimate felt like the first time. She would have expected that desperate edge to wane by now, but instead it seemed to be growing more intense.

Frighteningly, she had to remind herself on a daily basis not to fall in love with him, that this wasn't real. That it was nothing but casual fun.

He's not for you.

Don't get used to this.

He'll be leaving soon.

Don't like him too much.

Don't love him even a little.

A daily mantra, five quick, magical incantations with which to safeguard her heart. But the scariest part of it all was that she didn't think they were working.

CHAPTER THIRTEEN

"What?" Sam exploded, and he heard Colby sigh on the other end of the line.

"She's been receiving them intermittently for the last month or so," the woman continued, and Sam rubbed his fingers over his forehead, trying to ward off the headache that was forming.

"Why did no one tell me?" he growled.

"Because you were out of commission. Quite frankly, I didn't want to tell you now, but Chambers was concerned about the threat she received last night. Somehow the note was slipped into her underwear drawer. Chambers has put extra security on her house and two more CPOs on her."

Lally had been receiving death threats again, same MO as Marshall Weathers, the fucker who had stabbed Sam, but that bastard was still in jail and awaiting trial.

"It could be Weathers," Sam suggested, "getting someone to do his dirty work for him."

"That's a distinct possibility," Colby said, "and the police are investigating that angle, but the general consensus for now is that it's possible but not likely."

"Fuck it," Sam muttered beneath his breath. "Okay, tell Chambers to keep the extra security around her house and the additional CPOs on her. Do *not* let her run roughshod over him. Cancel all public appearances, aside from concerts, until the police have concluded their investigation into Weathers's activities in prison."

"She's not going to like that."

"I don't give a single fuck what she likes or doesn't like. We're taking this seriously, especially since she's already been attacked once. I'll get packed up and head back—"

"No." Colby's tone was frosty, and Sam's mouth dropped open.

"I beg your pardon?" he asked incredulously.

"You heard me, you're not coming back early. You pay us to solve problems. We have it under control. But Chambers has a point about your needing to know about it."

"How fucking commendable of you to *allow* me to know about the shit going on with my own company."

"Yeah, I thought so, too," Colby said agreeably, and Sam glared at the wall at her response. "Look, if we think the place is going to fall apart without you, we'll let you know. For now, we have it in hand."

She gave him updates on a few other contracts before ringing off, after another stern admonishment that he was not to come home.

Sam stared at the lit screen of the phone for a long moment before putting it aside. He felt *strange*. He knew that if he'd heard this news just a few weeks ago, nothing Colby said would have prevented him from packing his bags and heading home. Injuries be damned. But today, the threat to pack up and go back had mostly been posturing.

Because he wasn't ready to go home.

He had poker with Bertie and the guys on Sunday. He had promised Mrs. Beecham at the retirement home that he would teach her and a few others the Viennese waltz next week. Trevor—he had started to accept the dumb name for the dog because the animal was so mild mannered it actually suited him—was learning to sit and stay. Sam and Spencer were planning a *Fast and Furious* marathon on the weekend after the women left.

And Lia . . .

His thoughts stuttered to a halt.

Lia. There was Lia.

They were nearly a month into their fling, and it was still nowhere near over. He had stopped asking her to stay every night . . . but he hadn't stopped *wanting* her to stay. Watching her leave every night was becoming increasingly difficult. He wanted to keep her with him—he was starting to resent every moment she spent apart from him. She would be going away with her mother, Daff, and Charlie on the weekend, and Sam was dreading the prospect of not having her around for two days.

So yes, Sam wasn't quite prepared to leave Lia yet. Not at all.

He threw his head back against the sofa cushion and stared at the vaulted ceiling of the cabin.

"What the fuck are you doing, Sam?" he asked himself beneath his breath. "This is not the life for you, mate."

"Talking to yourself, Sam?" Lia's soft voice asked from the kitchen, and he sat up, startled. She smiled at his reaction.

"Ha! Did I manage to sneak up on you, Mr. Special Ops Close Personal Protection Man?" she teased, clearly delighted, and despite himself, Sam felt his lips quirk upward in a smile. She was so fucking cute.

"Close protection officer, sunshine," he corrected.

"You know what I meant," she said, airily dismissive. He jumped to his feet and walked toward her, loving the way her eyes stayed on his as he drew closer. He hooked an arm around her waist and tugged her into his embrace, dropping his mouth onto hers for a hungry kiss.

"Fuck, you taste good," he growled when he lifted his head. "Strawberries? Where's the bubblegum?"

She laughed and pushed at his chest until he released her.

"I'm out of bubblegum lip gloss. I thought I'd give the strawberry flavor a try."

"You taste good no matter what," he said truthfully, and then allowed his eyes to drift over her neatly dressed body. "And no matter *where*."

He grinned when his words elicited a blush.

Predictable—he adored that about her.

The thought made him start, and his eyes widened. He had once thought her predictability would become boring, but he now recognized that he hadn't *once* found himself bored with Lia. Not with Lia, nor with her family or the people she knew. And not with the town, which he was starting to explore more now that he was getting better. It was a beautiful place, and the ocean called to him. He wanted to try out the surf as soon as he was stronger.

He liked it here. He hadn't ever expected to like it here.

"Sam?" Lia snapped her fingers in front of his eyes, and he shook his head and smiled at her. "Where did you go?"

"Just down the road a way," he joked.

"I don't feel like cooking this morning. MJ's for breakfast?" she suggested, and he frowned.

"Are you okay?"

"A bit of a headache and a bit wheezy. I think I'm getting a cold, that's all," she dismissed. Sam looked at her again—she had shadows under her eyes, and despite her immaculate appearance, he could see how tired she was. It was as close to frazzled as he'd ever seen her.

"Why don't I fix you something?" he offered.

"You can cook?" she asked, surprised.

"Not as well or as prettily as you, but it's edible. Sound good?" She nodded and trudged to the living room. There was none of the usual crisp pep in her step, and she sank to the sofa and kicked off her shoes. Usually Lia would remove them and neatly place them side by side. For her to not even care where they landed was very uncharacteristic.

He watched as she curled up onto her side on the sofa, tucking her hand under her cheek to watch him.

"What are you going to make?" she asked, and, trying to put aside his concern, he forced a smile.

"Eggs and bacon. To expect anything more than that would be to tempt fate."

"Sounds good."

~

She was asleep by the time he finished, and he walked over to the sofa to look at her. He'd seen her sleep before; sometimes she dozed off while he held her after sex. But that was always a restless nap. Nothing this deep or peaceful. She looked young and vulnerable asleep, with her pretty mouth slightly open and her hair obscuring half of her face. Sam absently massaged the center of his chest as he watched her. God, she was so beautiful. He ran the tip of his finger down the smooth curve of her cheek, edging her silky hair behind one pretty ear.

"Lia," he called softly, going down onto his haunches in front of her so that he wasn't hulking above her when she woke up. Her brow furrowed, and she sighed. "Come on, sunshine, time for breakfast."

Her eyes opened without warning and immediately found his. For a split second, in that vulnerable, naked space between sleep and wakefulness, he could see her every emotion. Trust, hope, helplessness, and something that looked uncomfortably close to love. He didn't know how he recognized these emotions, he just knew with absolute certainty what they were. And it terrified him. If she felt these things for him, she would get hurt, and that was the last thing he wanted.

She blinked and the moment of vulnerability passed, her eyes now only revealing pain and confusion.

"I don't feel well, Sam," she whispered, and he felt a flare of panic. She was pale, but an unnatural flush was beginning to form on her cheeks. He dropped a hand to her forehead and the flare developed into a full-blown explosion of absolute terror.

"Jesus, Lia, you're burning up!" he said, his voice shaking. "How long have you been feeling ill?"

"Felt funny this morning," she said. "But it's worse now. I feel . . ." She sat up and clutched a hand to her mouth. She pushed him out of the way and leapt to her feet to run to the guest bathroom downstairs. She barely made it before he heard retching sounds.

Sam shoved his hands through his hair, his fingers digging into his scalp as he tried to calm his anxiety. He followed her into the bathroom and dampened a towel. She wasn't throwing up anymore but was still hunched over the commode, her slender body trembling violently. Sam gently swept her hair to one side and stroked the cool towel down the nape of her neck.

He helped her to her feet and wiped her face before urging her to rinse her mouth. She complied weakly and leaned heavily on him as he led her back into the living room and to the sofa. She felt like a furnace, and her high temperature scared him. How could she get this sick so quickly?

He left her sitting on the sofa and rushed to the kitchen and grabbed his cell phone to call Daff. He didn't have her number programmed on his phone and had to consult the list on the fridge. He was shaking so much he misdialed twice.

"Hello?" she answered on the third ring, and Sam swallowed as he tried to find his voice.

"Daff. It's Sam. We have to get Lia to a doctor. Something's wrong. She seemed fine when she got here, just said she had a headache. But she's been here about an hour. She napped on the sofa while I was cooking. She's fucking burning up. She threw up." He heard his voice rising in increments and wondered if he sounded as completely terrified to Daff as he did to himself. "Please. I-I'm not sure what to do."

He couldn't remember the last time he'd admitted to not knowing how to resolve a situation. Sam always knew how to fix things. How to make it better. How to save lives. And maybe—if it had been anyone other than Lia—he would have known what to do this time as well. But all he had to do was look at her curled up on the sofa, so small and vulnerable, and all rational thought fled.

"You're at the cabin?" Daff asked in her no-nonsense voice.

"Yeah."

"We'll be right there."

"Hurry."

They took her to the emergency room, and as Sam sat waiting with her family, he vaguely registered that he was wearing track pants without a top and socks but no shoes. He didn't care—all he could think about was the paramedics putting a respiratory mask on Lia's face as they transported her into the back of the ambulance. Daff had climbed into the back with her, Sam had gone with Spencer and Charlie, and they had all met Dr. and Mrs. McGregor at the hospital.

Daff had joined them about an hour after their arrival, saying that the doctor was with Lia. Sam had wanted to drill her about Lia's condition, but everybody else was already asking all the questions he wanted to, so he sat quietly and listened. She was fine, no worse, doctor seemed relaxed, with no sense of urgency about him, which Daff seemed to think was a good thing. But the information only made Sam want to hunt the doctor down and shake some urgency into him.

"Brand?" Sam stared dazedly up at Spencer, not sure how long the man had been standing in front of him or what he had asked.

"Do you want some coffee?"

Sam nervously rubbed his hands together and shook his head. "No." He paused before belatedly tacking on, "Thank you." He averted his eyes as he comprehended just how much Lia's sweet, polite manners were starting to affect his own behavior. He wasn't sure how he felt about that and right now he didn't care. All he wanted was to see Lia and to know that she was safe.

As if in answer to his desperate thought, the waiting room doors opened and an older man in a white coat looked around the room.

"McGregor?" Everybody surged to their feet and surrounded him, and the man held up his palms in surrender. He was grinning, which made Sam breathe a bit easier.

"Your girl has a touch of the flu. A particularly nasty strain of H1N1. It's been going around and she tells me she works at a preschool, so that's probably where she caught it. I've had a few little ones in here over the last week. She had some difficulty breathing, but nothing to be alarmed about. We'll keep her for a couple of hours before discharging her, just to monitor her. But with proper care, medication, and a *lot* of rest, I have no doubt she'll make a full recovery. I take it you've all been exposed to it? She would probably have become contagious yesterday."

"We haven't seen her in a couple of days," Mrs. McGregor said.

"Same here," Daff said. "Well, I suppose the ride in the ambulance with her counts, but I've had my flu shot."

"It's transmitted through sneezing or coughing. But if you've had the shot, you're probably okay. If you don't show any symptoms over the next two or three days you should be fine."

All heads turned to Sam, and he stared back at them awkwardly, trying very hard to avoid Lia's parents' eyes.

"Suffice it to say I've been pretty thoroughly exposed," he said, his voice ironic as he comprehended the unintentional double meaning to his words.

"Well, *that* answers a couple of questions," Dr. McGregor muttered beneath his breath, leveling a steely-eyed look at Sam.

"Bus-ted," Daff singsonged softly, then yelped and glared at Spencer when he tugged a lock of her hair.

"Well, there are ways to avoid getting it if you've already been exposed," the doctor said. "I suggest you pick up a pamphlet at the nurses' station before you leave. I wouldn't recommend visitation, unless you've already been exposed or have had the shot. She's going to be pretty miserable for the next few days, and it will be best for her to have someone around to keep an eye on her, at least for the first day or two. It will run its course between three and seven days. Scary morning, I know, but she'll be fine."

He went on his merry way, actually whistling as he left the waiting room. Sam sat down heavily and once again listened to Lia's family talk around him. Discussing what the best course of action would be.

"We'll have to postpone the weekend, of course," Daff was saying. "I'll see if we can get a refund on the airfare. I'll stay with her, since I've had the shot. The rest of you should get yours, too, by the way. Seriously, people, am I the only sensible person in this family?"

"Why postpone the weekend?" Sam was shocked to hear himself say. "I've already been exposed, I'll stay with her over the weekend and you can still go on your trip."

Daff planted her hands on her hips, tilted her head, and gave him a long, assessing look.

"I'll be looking for a wedding dress, Brand. I'd like my maid of honor to be present."

"We could set up a Skype connection or something so that she can see everything and give her opinion on the dresses."

"It won't be the same," she dismissed curtly, and he shrugged, letting it go, but at the same time wondering why he felt so fucking disappointed by her refusal to consider his suggestion.

All he knew was that he probably wouldn't be seeing Lia for a week—and he found the prospect completely abhorrent.

"Daff," Mrs. McGregor said softly, "don't dismiss his idea out of hand. Planning another weekend like this with everybody's busy schedules will be quite difficult, especially if you definitely want that October wedding. You want to get the dresses organized sooner rather than later."

Daff looked torn and hesitated before shaking her head.

"Let's discuss this later. I want to talk to Lia about it first. Since I'm the only one who can, I'll go and check on her now."

Sam pushed himself up and moved to stand beside her, and she looked at him in surprise, her eyebrows shooting to her hairline.

"What are you doing, Brand?"

"I'm going with you."

"I don't fu—fricking think so! I don't want—"

"Daff." Spencer's deep voice interrupted whatever she'd been about to say, and she stopped abruptly, glaring first at her fiancé and then at Sam before she turned and flounced toward the door. Sam nodded gratefully at Spencer, met Lia's father's eyes for an uncomfortable moment, and followed Daff out of the room.

"Hi, sissy." Lia smiled when she saw Daff enter the room; she felt shockingly weak and extremely hot one moment, then ice-cold the next. "I feel so stupid. All this drama for nothing."

"Don't be silly, Lia," Daff admonished in that no-nonsense way of hers and came farther into the room. She was followed by Sam, and Lia's eyes widened at the sight of him.

"Sam, where are your shoes?" she asked, finding it hard to talk when her throat was on fire. "And your shirt? You should have put on a shirt."

"And deprive you of the sight of all this manly magnificence?" he teased. It was a half-hearted attempt at humor, but Lia smiled for him. Because he looked like he needed it.

"I'm sorry," she said. "I was so looking forward to your breakfast."

"Nah, it would have disappointed you, and I, for one, am happy you upchucked before you ate, because my ego would never have recovered if it was after breakfast."

She laughed and then coughed.

"Ugh. I feel so gross," she complained. "When can I go home?"

"This afternoon, they're just making sure you have no respiratory issues before discharging you," Daff said.

"I can leave now. I want to sleep. I can't sleep here. The nurses are always buzzing around me."

"Soon," Daff promised, stroking Lia's damp hair back from her forehead.

"You guys are going to get sick."

"I had the flu shot, and Brand will probably get it anyway on account of all the spit you guys have been exchanging."

"Jesus," Sam muttered, sending Daff a glare before going around the other side of the bed to take one of Lia's limp hands in his. "I'm glad you're okay, Lia."

"I'm so not okay," she complained. "Everything hurts, I'm tired, I hate coughing, and I hate being here."

"Jeez, she's so rarely sick, I forgot what a pain in the butt she is when she's not feeling well. I may take you up on your offer after all, Brand. Let you deal with her miserable ass."

"What offer?" Lia asked curiously, her eyes going from one to the other.

"That's not important right now. Just rest and don't worry, you'll be home before you know it."

"I don't think I'm going to be better before Friday," Lia said morosely. She had been thinking about the shopping trip to Cape Town. They were supposed to fly out on Friday evening, which was just two days away. And Lia was definitely not going to make it.

Daff winced and met Sam's gaze.

"What? Why are you guys sharing secret looks? I'm *sick*, not dead," she said irritably. Being sick was bad enough, but having people keep secrets from you just because you happened to have a touch of flu was insufferable.

"I was thinking of postponing," Daff said. Lia sat up and the wonderful, uninterrupted flow of oxygen cut off as she unintentionally pulled out her nasal cannula.

Sam growled and she met his glare with her glower but allowed him to tug the cannula back into place. She was irritated, not stupid. She was enjoying the oxygen too much to willingly sacrifice it at the altar of righteous indignation.

"What do you mean, you're thinking of postponing?" Lia gasped and then coughed, thanks to the scrape of air over her vocal cords.

Crumbs! This was the absolute worst.

Daff grabbed a glass of water and handed it to her, and she took a thankful sip.

"Daff, you can't postpone," she said, her voice raspy after the bout of coughing. "There's no time. Send me selfies and stuff, keep me involved . . . there are ways I can be there without really being there."

"There's always Skype," Sam suggested with a hint of *smugness*—why smugness?—in his voice. Lia nodded and pointed at Sam, too tired and her throat too sore to actually verbalize her approval.

"You're knackered, aren't you?" Sam asked, while tugging free some hair that was trapped between the cannula and her cheek. She nodded again, feeling like a limp noodle. And her head felt *huge* and like it was floating somewhere above the bed, staring down at everybody.

"Tell nurses . . . ," she managed, her voice sounding wheezy. "Sleep."

"I don't know what you're doing, Brand," Daff said, her voice low and urgent as they both watched Lia drift into unconsciousness.

"That makes two of us, Daff," he admitted tiredly. "Look, just think about going ahead with this dress-shopping business. Lia took care of me, I'd like to return the favor."

"Is that all this is? Repaying a debt?" Sam considered her question thoughtfully, then glanced down at the way he was dressed—or undressed, as it were—and grinned wryly.

"You know it's not," he said quietly.

"Do you know what it is?"

"No. It just is, okay? Can we leave it at that for now?"

"I worry about her. After Clayton, she shut down emotionally. It took her months to actually start behaving normally again. It made all of us a little overprotective. We don't want to see that happen to her again. I'm not sure she could recover a second time. She's . . . she feels things deeply."

"Was she in love with that prick?" Sam asked, not sure he wanted to know the answer. He looked down at Lia, at her pale, exhausted face, and knew with absolute certainty that she would not agree to marry someone unless she had strong feelings for him. The thought of her in love and having her heart broken was absolutely maddening. How could anyone crush something so precious?

"You know I can't answer that. It's something you should ask her." Sam sighed. Daff turned to leave the room and paused at the door when she noticed that Sam hadn't moved to follow her.

"Are you coming?"

"I'll stay awhile longer," he said. "Can you call the retirement home? They'll be expecting her for their Wednesday social mixer."

Daff looked somewhat startled by the request, and her eyes narrowed as she gave him another penetrating look before she nodded.

"Yeah, I'll call them. Since you're so familiar with her weekly routine, are there any other cancellations I have to make?" Sam thought about it for a moment.

"Maybe give the animal shelter a heads-up. And I think she was going to do that Books Are Fun thing at the library today. Not sure, but it won't hurt to call them anyway."

"Right," Daff said, her eyes still calculating. "Anyway, after I do that, I have some stuff to discuss with the family. I'll let you know when we're ready to leave."

"Thanks," Sam muttered, his eyes glued to Lia's face. He wasn't going anywhere until Lia was discharged, and if that meant sitting here shirtless for the rest of the day, being ogled by curious nurses, then so be it.

~

"Lia, have some of this soup, come on," Sam coaxed, and Lia peered at him through one swollen eyelid.

"No." Her voice was embarrassingly croaky and completely unappealing at the moment. "Can't taste it. Don't want it."

"God, I think you're a fucking worse patient than I *ever* was," he complained, exasperation peppering his voice.

"Can't eat. It's like swallowing razor blades," she said, and he winced in sympathy and set the soup bowl aside. It was the third day of her illness. Her mother, Daff, and Charlie had left for Cape Town earlier that day, and the knowledge just made Lia crankier. Spencer had dropped Sam off on her doorstep after four that evening. And Sam had brought a bag, because he claimed to be staying with her for the weekend.

Lia hadn't agreed to him staying over. He had some nerve to just move in for two days. She was angry about it—nobody had informed her that she would be getting a new minder after Daff left. After two days of Daff's not-so-tender care, Lia had been looking forward to mooching around her house alone. But Daff had been replaced by Drill Sergeant Brand, who had only been there for four hours but kept ordering Lia to do things.

Eat this! Drink that! Sleep there! Take these!

Ugh.

But there were other perks to having him here. He gave great back rubs and foot massages, and even when she was being unreasonable, he remained infinitely patient and tried to fulfill her every need. She would never have taken him for a nurturer, but Sam Brand just kept on surprising her.

She curled up on her side on the sofa, and he covered her with a blanket. He lifted her feet and sat down, dropping them into his lap and absently rubbing them through her socks. He reached for the remote control and put on the TV, and Lia fell asleep to the comforting drone of some sci-fi movie or other playing in the background.

Sam kept one eye on the movie and the other on Lia. She seemed fine. In discomfort, cranky as hell, but leagues better than she had been on Wednesday. Still, he couldn't stop looking at her, touching her, reassuring himself that she was fine, that she was breathing easily, that she was just sleeping and not unconscious.

She was such a quiet sleeper—she barely moved and her breathing was so faint he often paused the movie and leaned closer just to hear that reassuring rasp of her breath.

By the time the movie had ended, he was ready for bed as well. Much earlier than he was used to, but it had been an exhausting day. He carefully, so as not to disturb her, lifted Lia's feet from his lap and went into the bedroom to change the bed linens. It wasn't anything he'd ever found himself doing before and it probably took him a lot longer than it should have, but in the end, he was proud of the result. He turned down the covers and went back for Lia.

He was a little annoyed with himself for not being strong enough to lift her yet, because he really didn't want to disturb her. But in the end, he had no other recourse than to gently shake her shoulder.

"Lia, time for bed," he coaxed, and she sighed.

"I'm sleeping," she said, her voice cranky while her eyes remained closed.

"I know, but you'll be more comfortable in bed. Come on." It took some doing, especially with her being irritable and reluctant to move, but he managed to get her to the bedroom. She was wearing thick, fleecy pajamas that he couldn't imagine being very comfortable to sleep in, so he eased her out of them. He couldn't find anything really appropriate-looking for her to sleep in. Just endless amounts of long, bridal-looking lacy nightgowns.

"Jesus, Lia," he muttered beneath his breath. While he would *love* to see her in some of these overly feminine, almost Victorian nighties—just so that he could have the pleasure of peeling them off her—they didn't look very practical. Surprising, considering what a practical soul Lia was. He shook his head and rummaged through his own bag before finding a well-worn, much-loved vintage X-Men T-shirt. He dragged it over her drooping head and fed her arms through the short sleeves before tucking her beneath the covers.

He did a quick security check around the house before brushing his teeth, stripping to his boxer briefs, and climbing into bed beside her. She was already asleep, which he was grateful for, since it curbed any pointless arguments about him sleeping with her.

He draped an arm around her waist and tugged her back until he was spooning behind her. Of course, they'd cuddled this way before, but this was different—she was asleep and it kicked his every protective instinct into hyperdrive. She was asleep and vulnerable, and it was his duty to keep her safe. He couldn't imagine never doing this again, of leaving her to sleep on her own on Monday when he now knew how small and defenseless she was in her unconscious state.

He sighed and buried his face in her hair; it smelled hot and sweaty, with lingering traces of her shampoo still present. As he felt himself start to drift toward sleep, he found himself acknowledging that Lia was right—sleeping with someone was different. It was intimate.

It meant more.

The urgent buzzing of his phone jarred him awake just an hour later. Sam turned his head and glared at the lit-up phone as it vibrated on the nightstand. He reluctantly lifted his arm from around Lia's waist to reach for it. Colby's name was on the screen, and he swore beneath his breath.

"Brand!" he snapped.

"Boss, we have a problem," Colby said in greeting, without any of the usual pleasantries. Brand only half heard her, because Lia stirred and then coughed. The sound was harsh and grating and made him wince.

Fuck! That didn't sound good at all.

"Colby, as you so succinctly informed me the other day, I pay you to solve problems. So fucking *deal with it*! I have more important things to worry about at the moment," he whispered.

"But—" Lia's coughing was getting worse, and he disconnected the call before Colby could complete her sentence. He switched off the phone and tossed it aside before easing his arm under Lia's back and helping her to sit up.

"Deep breaths, sunshine," he instructed, keeping his voice calm. "I'll get you some water and some of that cough syrup, okay?"

She groaned in response, the coughing relentless. He rushed to get her water and her medication. Anxiously watching while she swallowed everything down and then curled up into a miserable ball as the violent paroxysm of coughing continued. He wrapped himself around her, gently stroking her back and murmuring comforting little words that made no sense into her hair. Eventually the coughing fit subsided, and he reached for a tissue to dab the tears from her face and then gave her another one for her streaming nose.

"Not a pretty sight, I'm sure," she croaked. Her throat sounded absolutely lacerated, and he gave her another sip of water. Her eyes were red rimmed and the tip of her runny nose was pink in her pale face, her full lips dry and chapped. Not her finest hour, to be sure, but all Sam saw was his adorable Miss Priss.

"You're always gorgeous and you know it," he responded, and she half coughed, half laughed in response.

"You're such a liar. You're finally getting your way, aren't you?"

"How so?" he asked.

"Sleeping over. Is it everything you dreamed it would be?"

"Well, there's more wheezing and snoring than I anticipated, but it's right up there with my first kiss"—*with you*—"and the first time I had sex"—*with you.*

Because, while he hadn't known it at the time, both of those moments had irrevocably changed his life. He wasn't entirely sure *how* yet, but he definitely wasn't the same man he had been a mere seven months ago.

"I don't snore," she protested weakly, and he grinned.

"Sure you don't. Now get back under the covers and try to get back to sleep." She curled up on her side without protest, and he slid in behind her to spoon her again.

"What am I wearing?" she asked drowsily.

"My favorite T-shirt. You're welcome. And no, you can't have it."

"I have nightgowns," she pointed out.

"You have nightgowns straight out of *Downton Abbey*. They don't look comfortable at all."

"You watched *Downton Abbey*?"

"It was inescapable. Stop talking, your voice is making my eyes water."

"Not sexy?"

"Sure it is, if you find frogs sexy." Her breath hitched in her throat, and a tiny, delightful sneeze escaped on the exhale. It was followed by two more.

"What the fuck was that?" he asked, and she reached for another tissue to noisily blow her nose.

"I sneezed. It's polite to say 'gesundheit' or 'bless you,'" she informed him, sounding like her old self, despite the exhausted slur in her hoarse voice.

"It sounded like fairy farts, I wasn't sure what I was hearing," he teased.

"Shut up," she said grumpily.

"How rude, Miss Priss, your manners are slipping," he goaded, dropping a kiss on her temple.

"Sam?"

"Yes?"

"Thank you. For being here."

"No place I'd rather be, sunshine."

And wasn't that the absolute truth?

Lia felt marginally better the following morning when Sam set her laptop up on the coffee table. He placed a box of tissues on the easily accessible side table and a bottle of water and a roll of throat lozenges on the table beside the laptop.

After that he retreated to the kitchen to do some tidying up, and Lia settled in to watch Daff try on dresses.

The video image was thankfully clear, and Lia grinned when she saw the four faces pop up on her screen.

"Hi, Lia!" they all squealed in unison, and she grinned, waving excitedly in reply. Her voice wasn't great after her constant coughing the night before. She had woken up coughing at least three times during the night, and Sam had patiently helped and comforted her through each horrible convulsive attack.

"How are you feeling, sweetheart?" her mother asked.

"Better," Lia whisper-croaked in response, and everybody winced at the sound of her voice.

"Ugh, don't talk, okay? You sound like an old man who's been smoking a pack a day for the last eighty years."

Ah, Daff. Ferociously descriptive as always.

Sam, who could hear everything, snorted in amusement, and Lia shot him a glare. He widened his eyes and lifted his shoulders, obviously battling a grin.

"So what's the plan?" Lia asked, ignoring her sister's previous comment.

"Daff has to tell us what kind of dress she has in mind. I'm thinking something princessy and poofy." Daisy grinned.

"Over my dead body!" Daff dismissed.

"I want to see you in a poofy dress, Daff," Charlie piped up. "It's always been my dream to get married in a poofy dress."

"*Your* dream, kid," Daff said pointedly. "Not mine. And you'd better not let your brothers know you're dreaming about wedding dresses already. Spencer will shit a brick and then badger me for information about any secret boyfriends you may have."

"Well, what's *your* dream wedding dress?" Daisy prodded, and Daff rolled her eyes.

"A bikini . . . in Thailand!"

"You wouldn't *dare*," her mother gasped, sounding genuinely terrified that Daff would follow through on her words.

"Nope. We're doing this thing," Daff said grudgingly. "So I suppose I'm looking for something simple and elegant. A bit vintage."

"And *boring*," Charlie pouted. A shop attendant, who had been listening to the exchange, directed them to a rack of stunning crystal-encrusted designer gowns, all gorgeous and elegant. They picked out a few to try on, and Daff disappeared into the dressing room to get changed. Another attendant brought a bowl of fresh strawberries and champagne for the ladies—sparkling grape juice for Charlie. Sam, who was remaining discreetly in the background, but also seemed to be following the flow of conversation, brought Lia some sparkling water in a champagne flute. She giggled appreciatively when he presented the glass with a flourish.

Daisy was holding the phone and all Lia could see were feet and floor as the other ladies looked through the dresses while waiting for Daff.

The attendant announced that Daff was ready to show the first dress, and everybody scrambled to sit down. Lia made a frustrated sound when Daisy's camera skills left a lot to be desired. Her hand kept moving, her finger partially obscured the view, and she kept muffling the speaker with her hand. Sam peeked over her shoulder to see what the problem was and swore.

"Hey, Daisy! Hand the phone over to Charlie—her camerawork is bound to be better, she spends so much time taking selfies."

"Hey!" they heard Charlie protest, and Daisy's hand wobbled.

"Is that Brand? Why is Brand with Lia . . . What's going on?"

"We'll explain later, now hand the phone over, Daisy. Daff will be right out. I don't want Lia to miss it," their mother urged impatiently.

"Fine," Daisy muttered, sounding disgruntled, and there was a moment of confusion as the phone exchanged hands. Sam was right—the girl was a *much* better camerawoman than Daisy.

"Thanks," she murmured, then shooed him away. This was a girls-only affair. He winked at her and retreated again, just in time.

Everybody inhaled collectively when Daff entered the room. Or rather, she *trudged* into the room. She looked far from happy.

"This looks like a frickin' nightgown, doesn't it?" she complained. "The collar is also way too high, and all this lace is really scratchy."

Womp, Womp, Womp, Womp!

Lia stared at her glass of water and really wished it was alcohol, because she sensed this was going to be a *long* day.

It was on the sixth dress that the nascent bridezilla stepped out of the dressing room, looked at her reflection, and promptly burst into tears.

Everybody else was sighing and sniffling, too, because Daff looked absolutely beautiful.

It was a slinky silver-white 1920s-style dress, with intricate, scalloped beadwork, a modest V-neck, and sheer, beaded butterfly sleeves. It had a dramatically low scoop back and a slight chapel train, also with that intricate embroidery and beadwork to give it that extra wow factor.

"Oh my God, you look amazing," Daisy breathed reverently, breaking the hush that had descended over the group.

"Isn't it too much? It's too much, right?" Daff lamented, unable to take her eyes off her reflection. "Spencer won't recognize me in this. It's . . . it's . . . Oh my God, I love it. How can I love it? It's just a dress."

"It's so pretty," Charlie said. "You look like a movie star or something."

"Mom?" Daff's voice was questioning, and Charlie swiveled the phone to focus on their mother, who was fanning her face with one hand and dabbing at the tears on her cheek with the other.

"You look beautiful and you *know* it's the right dress. We all know it."

"It's so expensive. We could use the money for our honeymoon or something, it seems a waste to—"

"Your fiancé is rich AF," Daisy reminded her, and Daff frowned.

"I don't want him to pay for my wedding dress, it's—"

"Your father and I are paying for it, Daff," their mother interrupted her in a no-nonsense voice.

"But . . ."

"No buts. Now, do you want that dress?" Charlie turned the phone back to Daff, who was running her hands over the beadwork. She turned to look at her back.

"My butt looks amazing in this," she joked and then giggled like a schoolgirl. "Oh my God, I can't believe I'm actually getting married. To my gorgeous Spencer." She squealed and covered her face. "Of *course* I want the dress!"

Everybody cheered and Lia, who couldn't stop smiling, swallowed past the lump of emotion in her throat. She so wished she could be there with them in this moment, but she was grateful she got to share it even if the circumstances were less than ideal.

She looked up at Sam and discovered him staring at her. She couldn't quite read his expression, but he smiled when their eyes met.

You okay? he mouthed, and she nodded. And she *was* fine. She felt only elation for her sister. None of that envy and no residual "it should have been me" sense of entitlement.

It was wonderful to finally be free of those destructive emotions. But staring at Sam, it soon dawned on her that those feelings had just been replaced by something much stronger and potentially a lot more destructive.

She had broken the number one cardinal rule of a successful short-term fling. She had stupidly gone and fallen head over heels in love with Sam Brand.

CHAPTER FOURTEEN

"Were you in love with him?" Sam asked unexpectedly the following afternoon, while they were cuddling in front of the TV again. "Your fiancé. Were you in love with him?"

"With Clayton?"

"If that's his name," he muttered. "Unless you've had more than one fiancé."

"At the time, I thought I was. Now I know I wasn't."

"How do you know that?"

Because I now know what real love feels like. And it was *nothing* at all like what she'd felt for Clayton—it was deeper, more painful, and more frightening. She also knew Sam better than she'd ever known Clayton. Taking care of someone during the worst period of their life was pretty revealing. Then there was his passion when they had sex, his tenderness when he was cuddling her, the genuine sweetness he displayed at the retirement home, his compassion and patience with Trevor, his sense of humor, his irreverence . . .

The list was long, it was filled with both strengths and flaws, and she loved every single one of them.

"Lia?" he prompted. "How do you know you weren't in love with him?"

"Because I'm not married to him. If I loved him, I would have overlooked his flaws and married him anyway, wouldn't I?"

"What you said he did to Daisy wasn't just a little flaw that could be overlooked," Sam pointed out.

"And then there was that, his behavior proved that I didn't really know him. How could I be in love with someone I didn't really know?"

He took her hand in his, his thumb absently stroking her palm as he contemplated their joined hands.

"I've never been in love," he admitted, and she laughed.

"Of course you haven't. You don't do commitment. You've been pretty clear on that, and falling in love is a huge emotional commitment."

"I always thought of commitment as something that requires foresight and planning. Falling in love is something that just happens, isn't it? Nobody plans on it. You're just fucking about, minding your own business when, *boom*, you look up at someone, lightning strikes, and you realize that you're in love with them. Isn't that how it works?"

Considering that that was pretty much exactly what had happened to her yesterday, Lia couldn't argue against that.

"Perhaps," she acknowledged uncomfortably. "Although it could be a gradual slide into love, too, I suppose. I think that's how it happened with Daisy and Mason. They were friends and they spent a lot of time together, getting to know each other, getting to like each other . . . Falling in love was like an awakening for them, I think."

He seemed to mull over her words.

"That makes sense, too, I guess, a gentle slide. It sounds less painful, or potentially lethal, than a lightning strike."

"Why are we talking about this?" she asked, and he shrugged.

"I was just interested."

"It's a weirdly specific thing to be interested in," she pointed out, and his thumb made little circles in her palm.

"I was curious about the guy," he said with a shrug. "The prick who hurt you."

"It could have been worse," she said, and his eyebrows slammed together.

"How?" he asked blankly.

She snorted and rolled her eyes. "I could have married him."

Spencer took Sam back to the cabin the following morning. Lia was feeling a lot better and didn't need anybody else to come and stay with her. Fortunately, Sam showed no signs of getting sick, so it looked like Lia was the only one unfortunate enough to get the flu. One of the hazards of working with children.

Lia would be returning to work and her charities in two days' time and found herself at loose ends after Sam left.

She should have known Daisy would call her as soon as she was able, and sure enough, late Monday afternoon, her phone trilled. She sighed when she saw Daisy's name on the screen but lifted the phone to her ear anyway. Better to get it over sooner rather than later.

"I can't believe you're sleeping with Sam Brand," her sister started without preamble. "I told you he's an ass with women, didn't I? Because if I haven't, allow me to tell you now . . . he's an *ass* with women, Lia. Erased numbers, pictures, contact details, remember? Harassment charges, *remember*?"

"I'm not about to harass the man, Deedee," she said with a little chuckle. But her youngest sister was not amused.

"Lia, he's going to hurt you."

"Oh, I know that, but it's my own fault. I stupidly went and fell in love with him. It was against the rules, but I had to go and break them, didn't I?" Lia heard the bitterness in her own voice and shut her eyes tightly.

"Oh, Lia," Daisy whispered.

"Look, it's okay, Deedee. Honestly. I knew the risks going in, and it's not Sam's fault I went and broke the number one rule of our fling. He did nothing to *make* me fall in love with him. I mean, have you heard him speak? It's enough to turn the air blue . . . and I fell in love with him despite that. He told me he doesn't do love and commitment, and I still went and fell in love with him. It's like I'm a sucker for punishment or something. That said, I don't regret a single moment and wouldn't change a thing about the last few weeks with him."

"What are you going to do now?" Daisy asked softly.

"I'm going to do what I must. I'm going to protect myself."

When Sam switched his phone back on, it was filled with missed calls and messages. Most of them were from Colby, a few were from Tyler Chambers, three or four were from Lally, and two were from his mother.

He wasn't in the mood to deal with work-related issues right now. He hadn't felt a single pang of regret for hanging up on Colby the other night and wasn't in a particular hurry to find out what the crisis was this time. Based on the people who had tried to reach him, it was definitely Lally related. He shook his head, not even bothering to check the texts, and called his mother instead.

"Hello, darling. I've missed you," she greeted warmly, and he smiled.

"Hi, Mum, how're you?" They'd exchanged only text messages since his arrival in Riversend, so it was great to hear her voice.

"Quite fine. I've made a new friend, Malcolm. Lovely man. He's a ski instructor." Sam's lips tilted. *Of course he is.*

"What happened to Craig?"

"He's been too demanding and possessive lately. It's becoming tedious. I'm going to have to cut him loose." She sighed. "But never mind that, tell me about you. Are you quite bored in your little rural African town?"

He laughed.

"It's hardly rural, Mother. It's a quaint little beachside town inhabited by friendly people."

"And how have you been coping? Have you hired a nurse?"

"I've started rehab. My arm is still a bit weak, but it's getting better, my dexterity is improving daily. Mason's in-laws have been very helpful."

"Do you miss your life and your work terribly?" she asked sympathetically, and Sam frowned as he considered the question. His instinctive response would have been *yes*, but that wouldn't be true. At all.

He was worried about his business—he had worked hard to build it, and it was important to him that it continued to do well and grow. But he didn't miss it at all. And he didn't miss his huge, sterile, upmarket apartment in Chiswick, either. And he didn't miss his friends, because he had none outside of work. Even Mason, one of his best friends, was a former colleague. Spencer Carlisle was the first friend he had made as an adult who was completely removed from his work life.

"I haven't been bored," he replied. "I've kept busy. Mason's sister-in-law Lia has been allowing me to tag along with her during the day. You'll be happy to know that I've been putting my dancing skills to work at the retirement home. I promised to teach some of the ladies the Viennese waltz this week. Lia's been ill, so we've had to postpone the first lesson." He went on to animatedly describe his progress with Trevor, his visits with the McGregors, his movie nights with Spencer. He described the magnificent scenery, how he wanted to try out the surf and do some paddleboarding here. Told her how Bertie and his mates were blatantly fleecing Sam on their poker nights, and when he finally ran out of steam, he comprehended that she hadn't said a single word while he was talking.

"Mum? You there?"

"Are you thinking of adopting the dog?" she asked, her voice casual.

"Uh, no. My lifestyle doesn't lend itself to having a pet, you know that."

"I know you've always wanted a dog."

"I haven't. I never once said that I wanted one," he protested indignantly.

"You were always such an accommodating child. You didn't want a dog because you thought *I* didn't want a dog."

"But you didn't want one. Did you?" He frowned—this conversation was becoming confusing.

"Of course I didn't, we were always moving. Imagine the inconvenience. But I never said as much—in fact, I once offered to get you one because I thought you were lonely. You didn't have any friends."

"Hard to make friends when you're never in one place for long," he muttered. Then immediately felt terrible about the words. "I'm sorry, Mum. You always made things fun. I didn't need friends."

"See? Accommodating child, even now. Trying to make your Mimsy feel better. You did need friends, but you never complained, you never acted out, you were always an absolute sweetheart. And we *did* have fun. It was the least I could do, considering how abjectly I failed you in other aspects."

"Mum . . ." He was absolutely shocked by her words, not entirely sure where this was coming from.

"A boy needs a dog, Sam. Maybe you could make room for Trevor in your life."

"I'm hardly a boy anymore, Mum."

"Tell me about this Lia."

"What?"

"You mentioned her quite often during your narrative of adoption fairs, old-man poker tournaments, and family cookouts."

"She's . . ." His mind blanked and he swallowed before shrugging helplessly, despite the fact that his mother couldn't see the gesture. "There's nothing to tell."

"Sam, I'm your mother. I carried you in my womb, watched your nannies change your nappies and burp you, supervised your first bicycle ride, endured the horrid braces and pimple stage of adolescence along with you . . . I've known you for thirty-four years, and not *once* have you referred to a woman you were interested in by name."

"I'm *not* interested in her. Not in that way." His mother laughed at that. "And I also mentioned her sisters. Why would you make that assumption about her and not about them?"

"Your voice changes when you say her name."

"That's such a cliché." He snorted. "Are you turning into one of those old women who try to hook their sons up with any random single woman? You trying to marry me off? Looking forward to becoming a grandmimsy, are you?"

"You bite your tongue. I'm not old, I'm mature. And my grandchildren will call me Catherine."

"Mum, not sure how to break this to you, but unless you have some other kid stashed away to give you these imaginary grandchildren, you won't be getting any." The words lacked conviction, even to his own ears. He kept thinking about Lia, teasing him with the possibility of an accidental pregnancy while knowing full well there had been little to no chance of it happening. He hadn't been as resistant to the idea as he would have expected.

His mother laughed again.

"Is she pretty?"

"She's lovely," he answered without thinking, and then winced. His mother remained absolutely silent in response to his words, and that in itself spoke volumes.

"I see," she said eventually, her voice uncharacteristically solemn. "I think I'd like to meet her."

"Mum, I'm coming home in a couple of weeks' time. Alone. I don't know what you're reading into my words, but I assure you, it's erroneous."

"You always were a stubborn boy." She sighed. "Sweet and accommodating, but *so* stubborn when it came to accepting good things. I had hoped you would outgrow that tedious air of martyrdom you sometimes liked to adopt."

"Got to go," he lied. "Love you, Mimsy."

"Calling me Mimsy doesn't count when you use it sarcastically, Sam," she protested, and he grinned despite himself.

"'Bye, Mum." He chuckled.

"Take care of yourself, Samuel."

After the call ended, he sat for a long while and thought about it. *Did* his voice change when he spoke about Lia? It made sense that it would, considering what happened to him when he thought about her. Not just physically, but mentally and emotionally. He got, well, the only word he could think of to describe it was *excited.* Every part of him—including the most obvious one—got *excited.* His breathing increased along with his heart rate; he had the ridiculous urge to grin like an idiot all the fucking time. And lately he found himself on a knife edge of anticipation whenever he knew he would see her. What would she say? What would she do? What would she be wearing? Would her hair be tied back or left to fall around her shoulders? How many times would she correct his behavior? What ridiculous breakfast art would he find himself eating next? When would she say something unintentionally funny? How long before he could make her smile? Before he could make her sigh his name?

Logically speaking, he knew it would be best to call this thing with Lia to a halt. Because she was so different from the usual types of women he associated with, his mind hadn't dumped her in the "casual sexual partner" category. Instead it had given her a corner all to herself. A corner neatly labeled "Lia." And because his brain had made that distinction, he was fooling himself into thinking she was special. He was losing sight of their initial arrangement. Just a fling. Casual fun. He'd smashed all her carefully considered rules and had failed to acknowledge that they made complete sense. He'd cuddled, talked to her, gotten to know her, slept with her . . .

She *was* different. Because Sam had made her different. But he was fooling himself. They were existing in a bubble right now. As soon as the real world intruded, his fascination with her would end. Continuing to make love with her would only serve to make that inevitable reality check all the more jarring.

"Ah, *fuck*," Sam breathed a few hours later after finally contacting Colby. He squeezed the nape of his neck, hoping to ease the tension building there. "Repeat that, please. I want to be sure I heard you right before fucking firing your ass."

Colby sighed.

"Lally's done a runner. Friday was a nightmare of a day. The police confirmed that one of the prison guards was smuggling the notes out and sending them to Lally on Weathers's behalf. The guy was arrested, but press got wind of the story and falsely reported that Weathers had escaped. Naturally Lally panicked, she stormed in here and demanded to speak with you and then had a meltdown when we wouldn't tell her where you were. We tried to tell her that Weathers was still safely behind bars, but she was completely freaked out."

"Damn it, Colby! I *should* fucking fire you," Sam said wearily, his words lacking heat. Both he and Colby knew he wouldn't make good on his threat. She was good at her job. Lally was a difficult client. Sometimes, despite the company's best efforts, the client was their own worst enemy. "And you've tried pinging Lally's phone?"

"Of course. We know she went incognito and bought a couple of tickets on Eurostar. So I'm guessing she's trying to put as much distance between herself and Weathers as possible. When she calms down and realizes that he's really still in prison, she'll surface again. The press doesn't know that she's gone, and she doesn't have any concerts or appearances scheduled over the next couple of weeks. Look, it's not all bad. While she ditched the rest of her team, I think Tyler is still with her. But he hasn't checked in since last night. His phone is out of order or switched off. We can't ping the GPS and locate him through it. My theory is Lally did something to it or even chucked it. It's exactly the kind of shit she would pull. But maybe her being under the radar for a while is a good thing? Tyler will keep her in line."

"I don't like not knowing where she is," Sam muttered, still squeezing his nape. It definitely wasn't helping with the tension.

"Tyler will check in as soon as he can, I'm sure of that. I'm so sorry about this, Brand."

"Lally can be hard to curb and unpredictable when she has her mind set on something," Sam said. "Just keep me in the loop, okay?"

"What happened with those 'important things' you had to deal with?" Colby asked, her tongue firmly in her cheek.

"Don't push it, Campbell, you're already on thin ice."

"Yes, boss. Sorry, boss." Sam shook his head at the impertinence and disconnected the call.

Fucking Lally. He got that she was frightened, but she had never truly trusted his team, and that made her hard to work with. He wouldn't have been able to remain her CPO indefinitely, even if the attack hadn't happened—eventually he would have had to entrust her to one of his other officers. But in typical spoiled Lally fashion, she had been resistant to the idea, and he had pandered to her longer than he should have.

After this he'd make it clear to her that if she continued to make her security team's job difficult, then she'd have to find another agency to handle her protection.

"Hey, sunshine," Sam greeted when Lia answered her phone later that evening. He had tried not to call, but an entire day without hearing her voice was proving to be too long. "I missed you today. Trevor did really well in his first socialization class. I wish you could have seen him."

"He did?" she asked. Her voice was still hoarse, but it was improving.

"I'm not going to lie, I was nervous. But our boy was the star of the show. Best-behaved pup in the class. He seemed a little uneasy around the other dogs, but they were all pretty even tempered. He didn't engage with any of them, but he was more relaxed by the end of the class."

"It'll get better," she said. "That's really good for a first class, considering his history."

"I went to Sunset Manor. They all send their well wishes."

"You *did*?"

"Why do you sound so surprised?" he asked, not sure how he felt about her incredulity.

"I just didn't think you'd go without me."

"You jealous, sunshine?" he asked with a smile. "Afraid you're going to lose me to one of those cougars if you're not around to keep an eye on things?"

"You can't lose something you don't have, Sam," she said, her voice quiet, and the rejoinder wiped the smile from Sam's face. Her words bothered him more than they should have. And the knowledge that he was bothered irritated him.

Long after their phone conversation had ended, he found himself still mulling over his reaction to her words.

Was he losing focus on what was important in his life? He knew that he should be more concerned about finding Lally, but, despite the threat to his company's reputation, he had no interest in getting personally involved with the situation. He was content to let Colby and Chambers solve the problem. He didn't recognize himself anymore. After his disturbing conversation with Colby, he'd put on his running gear and headed straight for the animal shelter to see Trevor. And then he'd spent the remainder of the morning faffing around with the seniors.

His negligence had been amplified by the fact that he'd come directly back to the cabin and called Lia. And now he was more bothered about some throwaway remark she had made than he had been about Lally's disappearance.

What the hell was happening to him? He had to end his fling with Lia. It was fucking with his mind. The next time he saw her, he would tell her it was over. It would be best for both of them.

Lia quietly let herself into Mason's cabin the following morning. A quick glance around confirmed that Sam wasn't there, and she knew he was probably out on his morning run. She got the coffee going and then sat down at the kitchen table with her palms wrapped round a steaming mug of coffee.

She had done a lot of thinking since her phone call with Daisy the previous morning and knew exactly what she had to do. It would take more bravery than Lia thought she possessed, but it had to be done.

The back door swung inward, and a sweaty, panting Sam stumbled into the kitchen. His face lit up for a second when he spotted her before it uncharacteristically went blank. It was so unusual for him to switch off like that around her that Lia was taken aback for an instant.

"Hey," he greeted, lifting the hem of his loose T-shirt to wipe his dripping forehead. Lia tried not to react to the sight of his flat, ridged abdomen. Best not to let desire get in the way of what she had to say.

"Hey."

"Shouldn't you be in bed?" he asked, his voice carefully neutral.

"I feel much better. Just the occasional coughing fit and this voice." She expected him to come back with something racy about her newly husky voice, but he said nothing, going to the fridge and grabbing a bottle of water instead. He twisted the cap off and drank thirstily before refocusing his attention on her.

"You don't have to cook my breakfast or anything, I'll grab an energy bar."

Why was he being so . . . *awkward*? Lia knew why she was here, he didn't. She had expected to find the teasing, friendly, incorrigible Sam Brand that she knew. Instead there was this cold, unapproachable, slightly intimidating man in his place. And she wasn't sure how to react to the change.

It doesn't change what you've come here to say, she told her herself sternly, strengthening her resolve.

"Sam, we have to talk," she said, and he nodded. He didn't look surprised. He didn't look *anything*. It was unnerving. "Uh, there's fresh coffee in the pot if you want some."

"I'm good," he said. He dragged a chair out from beneath the table and turned it around to straddle it. He put his water on the table and folded his hands over the top of the chair and focused all his attention on her. "What did you want to talk about?"

"Well, I . . ." She sucked in a breath.

Be brave, Dahlia.

"I've messed up," she confessed. His eyes remained steady on hers, and she swallowed. "Sam, I've fallen in love with you."

No reaction.

"I'm not telling you this because I want anything from you. I'm telling you because I wanted you to know the reason I'm ending our fling. I've complicated things. And this thing between us can't continue. It would . . . it would hurt. M-more. It would hurt more. So it's over, and I'm sorry."

Still no reaction. Lia wasn't sure *what* she'd expected from him, but this absolute lack of emotion wasn't it at all. She bit the inside of her cheek hard enough to taste blood and felt the sting of tears at the back of her eyes. She blinked rapidly, not wanting to add to her humiliation by crying.

She cleared her throat.

"Well, then . . ." The words were a space filler. Why didn't he speak? "I should probably—"

"Knock, knock!" a light female voice called from the front door. Sam's head shot up and his eyes widened in horror when the door swung open to reveal . . .

Laura Prentiss? Lia blinked as her world immediately took a turn for the surreal. The woman looked exhausted and—without makeup—much younger than her twenty-eight years, but she was unmistakably Laura Prentiss.

"Brandy Snap," she squealed when she saw Sam, who was kind of hovering between standing and sitting. He looked completely astonished to see the woman here. Laura Prentiss crossed the short distance from front door to living room to kitchen and launched herself at Sam. He managed to get upright in time to catch her, his arms instinctively closing around her slender waist.

"Did you miss me?" the woman asked, wrapping her legs around his waist as she planted kisses all over his face. She had an English accent with a slight American drawl to it and sounded vaguely exotic. "I've missed you. I don't know how I managed without you. Why did you sic this unfriendly, horrible monster on me?"

She gestured toward the front door, and Lia's dazed eyes drifted over to see a huge, hulking man in jeans and a T-shirt standing in the doorway. He was an intimidating specimen, with hair cut close to his scalp and tattoos snaking from his shirt collar up over his neck and down over his very impressive biceps. His face was harsh and unsmiling.

"Sorry, boss. She stole my fucking phone—apologies, ma'am—out of my jacket pocket while I was in the john and tossed it. It was either find a phone, call you and lose her, or follow her onto the plane." The man, the only one of the three who had thus far taken the time to acknowledge Lia's presence, had a southern American drawl.

Sam, who had his hands on the woman's waist to keep her steady, glared at the man.

"We'll discuss this later, Chambers." His voice promised dire consequences, and Lia didn't envy the man. Her eyes went back to Sam, who was tugging at the pop star's arms.

"Lally, get down, for fuck's sake! Have you forgotten that I was stabbed?" The reminder proved effective, and she unwound herself from him and slid down his body until her feet hit the floor. The woman finally noticed Lia, who was still sitting at the kitchen table.

"Oh, hey, are you Brand's nurse? Brandy Snap, introduce us."

"No," he denied, his voice harsh. "She's nobody. Lia, go home."

His words eviscerated her, and Lia felt the blood draining from her face as she stumbled to her feet. She'd always known she was just a bit of fun for him, but to be relegated to a nobody in front of this woman, who was clearly somebody to him, was absolutely gut-wrenching. Especially after she had so stupidly lain herself bare to him just moments before.

"Sam," she whispered, not sure what she wanted to say. Not sure if she even had anything to say—she just couldn't believe the man she was in *love* with would treat her so shabbily. Not the Sam Brand she'd grown to know, to love . . .

"Lia, I'm serious. Get the *fuck* out of here!" His voice was taut with anger and something else, something intense and frightening. He met her eyes for a split second, and she saw absolute, burning fury in them. *"Now!"*

She lifted her chin and kept her eyes on his.

"Goodbye, Brand," she said, her voice strong and emerging on a satisfying note of finality. She took one last look at him before turning around and walking away.

~

"Christ," Sam swore shakily beneath his breath after the door closed behind Lia. He would fix it later, he would apologize, he would fucking grovel on his hands and knees if he had to, but at least she was gone.

She was safe.

To be sure he threw Chambers a look and tilted his chin toward the back door through which Lia had exited. The man nodded, understanding, before following Lia.

After he was sure that Lia was safe and taken care of, he focused his attention on Lally, who was blatantly snooping around the cabin. He had taken one look at the pop princess and completely lost all rationality.

Lia had just told him she was in love with him. How the fuck was she in love with *him*? A woman like Lia. Who could have anybody. It took some processing. She told him she was in love with him and then she fucking broke up with him.

And then Lally came waltzing in and all Sam could think about was that Hurricane Lally courted disaster wherever she went. She had stalkers and dangerous, crazed fans, and innocent people got caught up in her trail of destruction, got hurt when she was around . . .

Sam didn't want Lia in the same room with Lally.

Ever.

He kept recalling Marshall Weathers slashing at him with that knife and had the bizarre, irrational fear that someone like Weathers was lurking close by, that they would attack and Lia would get caught up in the turmoil.

No. He needed her safe.

"Lally, why the fuck are you here?" he asked irritably. And she pouted. "No, scratch that, *how* the fuck are you here? Who told you where to find me?"

"Craig."

"What?" Sam asked blankly. *Who?*

"Craig. Your mom's boyfriend. I called her to ask for your address, but Craig answered. He's such a sweetie. We had a lovely chat. He told me he was a huge fan."

Sam groaned. Of course it was Craig. The idiot.

"Look, you need to go home. You're intruding in my private life, and that's uncalled for. You're my client, *not* my fucking girlfriend. Tyler is my best CPO, he had the situation under control and you made his job incredibly difficult with your childish and inappropriate behavior."

"You can't speak to me like this. I pay your bills."

"But you don't fucking *own* me. If you cannot comply with our rules—rules, I might add, that have been put in place to keep you safe—then I'm afraid I will have no option but to sever the agency's relationship with you."

"I was scared. The news said Marshall Weathers escaped." She sniffled, looking contrite, and Sam rolled his eyes. He knew all her tricks, and the wounded-little-girl thing was something he'd indulged in the past when he gave an actual fuck about keeping her business, but right now his single major priority was to get her the hell out of Riversend and away from Lia and her family.

"You and Chambers can stay here tonight. But I want you out of here by tomorrow. Meanwhile, keep a low profile. Do not leave this cabin for any reason."

"Where will you stay?"

"That's none of your concern. I want you to think long and hard about whether you still want to retain our services. If not, I'll instruct Colby to commence with contract severance procedures."

Lia barely remembered the short drive home, and after she parked her car in her driveway, a rented sedan slid to a smooth stop in front of the house. Lia glanced at it and then froze. She felt her face settle into a glower and marched up to the car and rapped on the window. The big, muscled man in the driver's seat opened the window and removed his sunglasses. He had really lovely violet eyes. Quite striking on a man. She was momentarily distracted by his pretty eyes before glowering again and folding her arms over her chest.

"Why did you follow me?" she demanded, and he shrugged easily.

"Boss wanted me to."

"Well, you can tell your boss that I don't need random strangers following me for no reason."

"He probably felt there was reason to keep an eye on you."

"No, there isn't. Go keep an eye on his girlfriend—that's your job, isn't it?"

"Lally's not the boss's girlfriend." He reached into the glove compartment and withdrew a pack of gum. He lifted it inquiringly toward her, and she shook her head. He unwrapped a stick for himself and popped it into his mouth. Chewing lazily while he squinted up at her.

"I would like you to leave."

"Can't do that, ma'am. I'm in deep shit as it is, I won't make it worse by telling the boss that I left his lady unprotected."

"I'm not his lady. You heard him, I'm *nobody*." She choked on the word and felt that stupid sting again, this time accompanied by the familiar burn in her nose. She would not *cry* in front of this amiable thug.

"Don't rightly know why he lied about that, but I think it's because he was pissed off with Lally." He popped his gum. "Ma'am, I don't mean to be a bother, but I'm just coming off a seventeen-hour-long journey with someone who is not the easiest of travel companions, and I wonder if I could trouble you for a glass of water and an aspirin, please?"

Focusing on the man's discomfort gave her something to think about other than her own heartache, and Lia immediately went into fussing mode.

~

Sam was packing an overnight bag and listening to Lally talk to her agent, then to her parents, then to her secret backup-dancer boyfriend. Finally, she lapsed into silence for two seconds before finding the TV remote and starting to flip through the channels.

Somebody needed to keep an eye on her after he left, and that meant taking Chambers off Lia duty until Sam could replace him. Which left him in a bit of a quandary—leave Lia alone or leave Lally alone. It was like one of those fox, hen, grain crossing-the-river-type conundrums that he'd so enjoyed when he was a kid. Except now there was no logic in his decision making.

He made the only call he could.

"Hey, Spencer, it's Brand."

"What's up?" Spencer asked, sounding distracted, and Brand grimaced—it was the middle of the day and the guy was launching the new store soon. It wasn't an ideal solution, but it was the only one available to him.

"I'm in a bit of a bind, mate. I was wondering if you could keep an eye on someone for, like, twenty minutes?"

"That sounds a bit ominous. Like a prisoner?"

Sam snorted. "Seriously? No, not like a fucking *prisoner*. It's Laura Prentiss. She just showed up this morning. I'm going to stay with Lia while Lally and her CPO stay at the cabin overnight."

"Where's her CPO now?"

"With Lia."

"Why? Is Lia in some kind of danger?" Spencer asked, his voice sharp.

"No, but Lally is a magnet for trouble, and I . . ." He broke off, not knowing how to explain rationally.

"Hmm. I see," Spencer rumbled. "Yeah. I'd do the same for Daff."

"Right. Uh . . . so . . ."

"Yeah, I'll be there in ten minutes."

"Thanks, mate. I really appreciate it. Oh, and while I'm asking for favors, would you mind if I borrowed your truck?"

CHAPTER FIFTEEN

When Sam drove up to Lia's little house half an hour later, the rental car was parked outside her house, but there was no sign of Chambers. Where the fuck was he? Like he wasn't in enough fucking trouble already.

Sam grabbed his bag and strode through the front door without knocking. He stepped into the living room and froze.

"What in the name of *fuck* is going on here?" Lia was standing behind the sofa, where Chambers sat with his head tilted back and his eyes closed. She had her hands on his temples and seemed to be giving him a massage.

"Get your fucking hands *off* her!" he roared, and Chambers leapt to his feet, his eyes huge and his hands held palms up in the classic pose of surrender.

"Technically speaking, *I* didn't have my hands on *her*," Chambers pointed out calmly, and Sam heard himself growl. Lia was scowling at him. She looked seriously pissed off, actually, and it made him pause a moment before refocusing his attention on Tyler.

"Get out of here, Tyler! Keep an eye on that demon woman."

"Seriously, Sam," Tyler said, his deep voice losing its usual amiable tone and his eyes narrowing. They were longtime friends, but the man rarely used Sam's first name. "If you don't take me off Lally duty when we get back to London, I'm quitting."

Sam sighed, shoved his hands into his jeans pockets, and nodded curtly.

"Noted."

"Thank you kindly for the massage, ma'am," he said, laying on the drawl for Lia, who blushed in response while Sam contemplated punching his friend. "I feel much better."

"Piss off, Tyler," Sam commanded through clenched teeth, and the guy grinned at him and flipped him the bird while Lia's head was turned.

Lia wasn't sure why Sam was here. Or why he had a bag. All she knew was that she was angry with him. Very, very angry. And *so* hurt by what he had said that morning.

"It was lovely meeting you, Miss Lia," she heard Tyler say, and she smiled at him through the sheen of hot tears that was starting to obscure her vision.

"You too, Tyler. Have a safe journey home."

"Thank you, ma'am."

A heavy silence descended on the house after he left, and Lia wasn't about to break it. He'd invited himself into her home, he could darned well talk first. The silence extended into minutes, and, finally, he sighed heavily and swore. It felt like a victory of sorts and bolstered Lia's courage.

"Lia, look . . . I know how that must have looked back there. But I swear to God, I wasn't lying about Lally and me. We aren't involved, we never have been. That's just the way she is."

"Oh, I know there's nothing between you," she said. Her voice sounded worse because of the lurking tears. "And at this moment, I *really* don't care. I don't know why you came here or why you brought that bag, but I want you to leave."

"I can't stay in that cabin with Lally and Tyler. I thought I would stay with you."

"No."

"Are we doing this again?"

"Why should I let you stay here? You have no respect for me. You don't think anything of me. You're . . . you're so despicable!"

"Come on, Lia, is this about what you told me before Lally showed up? I know my reaction wasn't ideal, but . . . to be honest, I was going to end our fling as well. And then when you did, I felt kind of deflated."

"Why? Couldn't your ego handle being the dumpee instead of the dumper for a change?"

"What? No, that's not it. I was going to end the fling. I don't want to fling anymore—for the first time in my miserable fucking life, I want *more* than that."

"I told you I love you and you said I was *nobody*," Lia said, not really hearing him, not *wanting* to hear him. Not when it would only lead to more pain.

"Lia, I didn't say that," he whispered.

"You did. Right in front of that woman, you said I was nobody and you told me to leave. I knew it was just a fling and I know I broke the rules, but you didn't have to say that. You didn't have to hurt me and humiliate me."

Sam watched her fold in on herself and melt into tears, and it just about killed him. It had been a throwaway comment meant to dissuade Lally and to get Lia out of harm's way as soon as possible. But what he'd essentially done was tell this beautiful woman, who mere moments earlier had confessed to being in love with him, that she meant nothing and that she didn't merit so much as an introduction.

He had fucked things up quite royally, and while it would be easy to blame Lally's horrendous timing, he should have picked his words more carefully.

"Lia, don't cry," he muttered helplessly. He wanted to hold her but knew that she would reject any overture of affection from him right now. "Please. *Please* let me explain."

"I want you to leave," she insisted through her tears.

"No." He could play that game, too.

"Sam . . ."

"No, Lia. I'm not leaving. In fact, I think I'll be moving in here, and I'll be in your face every fucking day until you listen to me."

She wiped the heels of her hands over her cheeks, tilted her chin, and folded her arms tightly over her chest. Her body language was completely closed off, and he could tell that she wasn't ready to listen to him at all.

"Fine! I'll listen, then you have to go."

"You're angry with me. You're hurt. And it's my fault. I told you I'd fucking hurt you, didn't I?" he couldn't help reminding her defensively. "I warned you."

"Gold star to you for being a man of your word, Sam Brand."

"It wasn't intentional, Lia."

"That makes it worse."

"For God's sake, I'm trying to apologize."

"Don't bother. There's no point. There's nothing between us anymore."

"For such a mellow, sweet person, you're a huge drama queen at times, you know?" He couldn't keep the exasperation out of his voice and sighed hugely. "I'm sorry," he said, quieting his voice. "I'm sorry for saying what I did. You're not a nobody to me, Lia. You're . . . pretty much the opposite of nobody to me."

Lia read and reread the note. Not sure if she was reading the words right, she blinked and dislodged a tear she hadn't even known was there. It trailed down her cheek and landed on the paper, just missing the last rule.

"Lia?" he prompted, his voice shaking.

"Sam, you don't have to do this," she whispered, her own voice less than steady. "Not now. I'm happy. I want you. I have you. That's enough for me."

"Yes, but back when you were pretending to go all gaga over the thought of being pregnant," he began, and she remembered the night in question with a smile. He'd looked totally freaked out. "I was thinking about medical plans, kids' names, schools, and how our little girl would look. And then I really freaked out when I realized that I was disappointed when you took me from 'Ha-ha, maybe I'm pregnant' to 'Ha! No, on the pill, sucker!'" He affected a high-pitched voice to imitate her, and she grinned at his falsetto before his words sank in.

"Are you serious? You were disappointed?"

"Imagine how weird it was for me," he said. "I think that's when I first had an inkling about my feelings for you."

"I love you," she said, swiping at another tear, and he cupped his palm around her nape and tugged her closer for a kiss.

"Will you marry me?"

"Yes. Eventually."

"Eventually?" he asked, lifting his head and glaring at her. "What the fuck does that mean?"

"I'm not upstaging my sister. I want her wedding to be the only focus right now. Let's tentatively schedule our marriage discussion for . . ." She squealed and then laughed when he yanked her onto his lap and kissed her again.

"You're so full of shit," he muttered against her mouth. "You said yes, so we're engaged. It can be a long engagement or a short one. But

I want at least an engagement ring on your finger before arseholes like Gregory think they still have a chance with you. We clear?"

"As crystal."

"Lia, I'm going to say it now, okay? Out loud," he warned, and Lia couldn't stop herself from grinning ear to ear. For someone who had already told her he loved her more than once, he was certainly turning this into a production.

"Aaanytime now," she singsonged when he swallowed nervously. He glared at her.

"I love you." The words were curt and not very romantic, but she'd take them, because they were completely sincere.

"I know, Sam. And I love you, too."

EPILOGUE

Five years later

Mason Carlisle slammed into the hospital waiting room. He was wearing green scrubs and a huge grin on his handsome face. Lia entwined her fingers through her husband's and they both surged to their feet along with the rest of the room. Heavily pregnant Daff had to be assisted by Spencer. She was expecting their second child, a girl, to go with their beautiful three-year-old son, Connor.

"It's a girl," Mason announced proudly, his eyes gleaming with tears. He and Daisy had chosen to wait until after he completed his degree and they moved back to Riversend before starting their family, and this was their first addition. Neither had wanted to know the sex of their baby, but Lia had known it would be a girl. She'd always known their first child would be a girl. She squeezed Sam's hand smugly, and he laughed quietly beneath his breath.

"Daisy's fine. God, she was so amazing," Mason continued, self-consciously scrubbing a hand over his wet cheeks. "We're naming the baby Primrose."

"Ha, told you it wouldn't be Delphinium!" Sam muttered triumphantly. "You owe me breakfast in bed tomorrow morning. Along with my *other* B of choice for dessert." She shot him a scandalized look before wildly scanning the room to be sure nobody else had heard his words. Thankfully they were all too focused on congratulating Mason.

"Primrose?" Lia repeated, a little disgusted. "Oh gosh, oh no . . . this means Pansy's next, followed by Poppy," she continued in dismay, and Sam laughed out loud this time.

"You're fucking crazy, but I love you," he said, dragging her close for a kiss. He led her to Mason, and they both hugged and congratulated him before asking if they could see Daisy. Mason nodded, he had his phone to his ear and was telling Charlie the good news. The twenty-year-old was currently in her second year at college in Cape Town. She was studying marine biology, and her brothers could not stop bragging about her to anyone who would listen.

"Come on, let's go check out this kid," Sam said, tugging Lia toward the door, and she sighed in exasperation.

"Sam," she said, then repeated it more loudly when he continued forward. *"Sam!"*

"What?"

"Forgetting something, are we?" she asked pointedly, and he stared at her blankly before his face cleared and he grinned sheepishly.

"God, sorry!" he apologized and picked up one of the little baby seats from the plastic hospital chairs, while Lia got the other one.

"Forget the babies again, Sam?" her father asked. It was becoming a standing joke in the family. Sam was an amazing father, he loved the twins to bits, but after six weeks, it was still hard for him to remember that it wasn't just him and Lia anymore. They'd only been married for three and a half years—Lia had insisted on a long engagement while they figured out their careers and living arrangements.

They had spent a fair amount of time between his place in London and Daisy's little house in Riversend during that first year. Aisha had been happy for their preschool arrangement to continue more sporadically until Lia and Sam finally settled into a regular routine. Sam had spent the year setting up the South African division of Brand Executive

Protection Services, which he now ran from his office at their home in Riversend. Sam had people and systems in place on the ground to ensure he still delivered top-notch service, but he was happy to only travel a few times a year.

The rest of the time he spent on or in the water. He and Mason had collaborated on a house, not too far from the Carlisles' houses, for Sam and Lia. And while helping with the build, Sam had discovered a talent for carpentry, a hobby that was becoming a side business as more people took interest in his dramatic, beautiful pieces of bespoke furniture.

Lia, in the meantime, had continued slogging toward her degree and was now a qualified full-time teacher at the preschool, where she had been teaching for the last three years. It was the happiest and most rewarding work of her life.

Life had been wonderful, but a year ago, while they were making love, Sam had told Lia he wanted to make a baby. She smiled at the memory. They'd discussed it afterward and decided the time was right. The twins were conceived less than two months later.

Trevor, the gentlest dog in the world, was an awesome big brother to little Sophie and Noah. The dog was still Sam's constant shadow, but he loved the entire family, canines, kids, and all. They couldn't have asked for a better dog. Even Sam's mother—whom Lia happily called Mimsy, despite his protests—adored Trevor, and suffice it to say, she was a tough lady to please. The woman had been an irregular visitor over the last five years when she wasn't happily partying all over Europe. But she was usually content to visit for weeks at a time, just long enough to drive everybody mad. She had been present for the twins' birth and had stayed for a week afterward before leaving again, content to adore them from afar.

"Daddy's going to handcuff himself to your seat from now on, okay?" Sam cooed to Noah, who was watching him through narrowed eyes, the infant on the verge of falling asleep. "I promise I won't forget you again."

Lia laughed. He always felt so guilty after one of his little lapses.

"You'll get used to them," she comforted, wrapping her free arm around his waist as they followed the crowd to the viewing room, with Mason proudly leading the way. Sam dropped a kiss on top of her head and stopped, allowing the rest of the family to pass them until they were the only ones in the hospital corridor. Lia looked up at him questioningly.

"What's wrong?"

"Nothing at all. Everything is perfect. I just love you, Dahlia Brand," he said, his heart in his eyes. His gaze dropped to the babies before drifting back up to hers. "I love *all* of you. You make me so fucking happy."

ACKNOWLEDGMENTS

Elsje, thank you so much for the invaluable information on the ins and outs of foundation phase education.

Mark, thanks to you I now know that a euro sign is the absolute best cap for a sexting penis. And the vagina—using round parentheses instead of the more flabby-looking back and forward slashes I originally wanted? Inspired.

Lorinda . . . coitus carousel? This is why we've remained friends for so long.

Melody, I'm truly grateful that every single one of my books so far bears your awesome editing touch. It's always fabulous working with you.

ABOUT THE AUTHOR

Natasha Anders was born in Cape Town, South Africa. She spent the last nine years working as an assistant English teacher in Niigata, Japan, where she became a legendary karaoke diva. Natasha is currently living in Cape Town with her temperamental and opinionated budgie, Sir Oliver Spencer, who has kindly deigned to share his apartment with her. Please feel free to contact her (or Oliver) on Twitter @satyne1.